COLD BLOODED

Jessica McClain:
Book Three

AMANDA CARLSON

orbit

www.orbitbooks.net

Carlson

Orbit
Hachette Book Group
237 Park Avenue, New York, NY 10017
HachetteBookGroup.com

First Edition: October 2013

Orbit is an imprint of Hachette Book Group, Inc. The Orbit name
and logo are trademarks of Little, Brown Book Group Limited.

The Hachette Speakers Bureau provides a wide range of
authors for speaking events. To find out more, go to
www.hachettespeakersbureau.com or call (866) 376-6591.

The publisher is not responsible for websites (or their content) that
are not owned by the publisher.

The characters and events in this book are fictitious. Any similarity
to real persons, living or dead, is coincidental and not intended by
the author.

Library of Congress Control Number: 2013939681
ISBN: 978-0-316-20522-1

10 9 8 7 6 5 4 3 2 1

RRD-C

Printed in the United States of America

For Bill.
My partner in all things.

1

"Get down!" Tallulah Talbot, the most powerful witch in the country, grabbed on to my arm and hurled us both into the bushes. Seconds later an explosion hit with the force of a meteor. I shielded my face and body as rocks peppered down around us. Once it stopped, I rolled over and opened my eyes, coughing and spitting out dirt as I rose to my knees.

I squinted through the brush. "Do you see what I'm seeing?" I pointed to a crater the size of a city bus in the middle of my office parking lot. The noise had rocked my eardrums, but other than that I was fine. I stood, dusting off my clothes. Tally was already up next to me. "What kind of an explosion was that?"

It had come out of the blue.

Before she could respond, Rourke was in front of me. He had several holes in his shirt, but the small wounds had already closed. He hauled me out of the bushes, his big hands encircling my waist. "Jessica, are you all right?" His gave me a long once-over.

"I'm fine." I placed a palm on his warm chest. Touching

him calmed me and I needed it. After the ordeal we'd just gone through battling Selene, I was still on edge. The Lunar Goddess had put up quite a fight, but in the end I had managed to defeat her immortality long enough to send her to the Underworld. The low growl in Rourke's chest made my fingers tremble. He was as agitated as I was. Five minutes without someone trying to kill me would've gone an extremely long way.

"That wasn't a normal bomb." Rourke turned toward the parking lot. "Look at the damage. That hole has to be fifteen feet deep and just as wide."

"It was a Mask Orb." Tally emerged out of the brush behind us, readjusting her skullcap. She was dressed in all black, her white hair neatly tucked away, and at five feet tall with zero chest, she channeled a twelve-year-old boy, not an all-powerful spell caster. "It searches out a target and explodes once it finds its mark. It's an old sorcerer standby. Those guys only have a few tricks up their sleeves, so they tend to use them tirelessly." She smirked. "The Mask Orbs are impossible to detect until two seconds before they detonate, when they give off a tiny *pfft* of air. It's a flaw in their spell. You just became the luckiest people alive, because I have a built-in detector on me at all times." She patted her backside.

Tyler ran up, followed by Danny and Nick. They were all in one piece. Thank goodness supernaturals had preternatural speed, because most supes couldn't regenerate from the damage of an explosion.

When Tally had yelled, everyone had moved.

"We need to get out of here," Tyler said as he started to herd us forward. "The Humvee is armored. We can take it back to the Safe House and figure out our next move. I'm not waiting for another one of those things to explode."

"If there was another one, it would've gone off already," Tally said. "A Mask Orb is left as a calling card. It was meant to go off right when you arrived." She nodded toward me, because we all knew it had my name all over it. "But the chunderheads must have activated it by the front entrance, so it took time to find you. Which, considering everything, was a very lucky break." She bent over and dusted debris off her jeans. "But now that it's been detonated, they know you're here, so lingering isn't advisable."

I glanced around at the group. We were all assembled behind my office building. We'd just learned that James Graham, my father's second-in-command, whom we'd thought had gone rogue, had taken off after Marcy Talbot, my secretary and Tally's niece. According to Tally, Marcy had been recently abducted by sorcerers, the ones behind the new gaping crater in my parking lot. There was no reason to argue with Tally's logic about who was behind the kidnapping. She clearly knew what she was talking about, especially if she had a Mask Orb detector embedded in her ass.

"Well, we're certainly not sticking around to see if they show up," Tyler said. "So like I said, let's get out of here."

"Agreed," Nick added. "It's best if we leave quickly."

There were no arguments. We started moving toward our vehicle, passing by the huge hole as we went. It was a very specific area of damage, and other than things being pelted by falling debris, nothing else was touched. Cars were still parked in their spaces, riding on the edge of the crater. Humans were going to scratch their heads when they saw this. I'd never had a run-in with any sorcerers, so I wasn't sure how they operated, but it appeared to be along the lines of blow something up and ask questions later.

We walked toward the yellow Humvee, which illuminated the night like an awful phosphorus specter. It hadn't been damaged by the blast at all, which was a total shame. Dents and bruises could only improve it. "Once we arrive at the Safe House, we can lay out a plan to get Marcy back," I said as I turned to make my way around the vehicle. But before I could take a step, Tally snatched me by the shoulder, yanking me backward.

I stumbled but recovered quickly.

"You and I are not going to your *Safe House*."

She was incredibly strong for five feet of skinny witch.

Rourke, Danny, and Tyler all moved forward to intercede.

"Stop." I held up my hand, keeping my eyes pinned on Tally. "I refuse to handle this with violence." I was tired. We'd driven all night. I'd just been in an epic battle with a deranged Goddess, followed by an encounter with a Demon Lord, who had informed me I had a court date in the Underworld to face crimes I'd inadvertently committed. Fighting with the witches would be counterproductive to both my health and to our case, which was to get Marcy back unharmed.

She was my best friend and I was willing to do whatever it took, including keeping the peace with an angry witch.

Rourke eased up reluctantly, sensing my mood. He was a strong alpha, and I knew it was going to be tough for him to follow my lead, especially after so many years on his own. But for now, his willingness to try was appreciated. My wolf barked her approval in my mind. Tyler and Danny were still poised and ready to spring, their blood and anxiety jumping in my veins as we all glared at each other. Danny had recently sworn a pledge to me, making me his Alpha, and his duty to protect me at all costs blinded him to good judgment, especially in this high-stress environment. I tried to send out a calming vibe, but I had no idea how to do anything remotely Alpha-like or if it would even work.

Tally stood completely unfazed by our show of aggression.

Instead, her stony gaze bored a hole straight into my soul. She crossed her arms, waiting. "Three minutes ago we all could've been blown to smithereens." I obliged her by continuing, trying to defuse the situation. "As far as I can tell, we all want the same goal. We want Marcy back. So let's start acting like we're on the same side." Tally's power pecked at my skin. My wolf growled and clacked her jaws, resenting the feel of it as it pressed against us. I turned and gave Tally my full attention. "How would you like this to run? You have our cooperation." I didn't need to specify "up to a point" because that went without saying.

Supernaturals tolerated each other for brief interludes when it was mutually beneficial. Tally blamed me for Marcy's disappearance and I owned that. I should've been more diligent. I couldn't keep running around pretending the Prophecy wasn't real and the supernatural race wasn't going to notice me. My negligence had put people I loved in danger and I owed it to Marcy to cooperate with her aunt.

"I don't care where they go"—Tally flicked her head toward the group—"but you're coming with me. We head back to my Coven and gather information, including from the wolf who you say is tracking her. Regardless of what we find, we move in two hours. I'm not leaving my niece in the hands of the Baldies any longer than necessary."

Nick stepped forward, composed as always. "Ms. Talbot, I'm sure there's a way we can find neutral ground—somewhere we can all gather that's not within your direct boundary or ours." I could always count on Nick to stay levelheaded. Tally's home base would be a giant disadvantage if we had a disagreement about how things should run. I smiled at Nick to show my appreciation. I'd missed his brown curls, golden eyes, and sweet smile. There wasn't a nicer guy on earth.

Tally shook her head. "It's too dangerous. The sorcerers will pick up our trail as soon as they arrive. Our signatures are all over this parking lot. We can't linger at any unwarded location or we'll be vulnerable to attack, and I don't have time to put up the necessary spells to keep us safe somewhere else. We head to my Coven, where I have full protection in place. No compromises."

Rourke took a single step forward. "You guarantee our safety first, or nobody goes with you, witch."

"Of course," Tally snipped. "What do you think I'm going to do—harvest your body parts for my bubbling cauldron? You'll be safe as long as the priority remains to get my niece back."

Tally had a point.

Because the sorcerers knew we'd arrived, protection was the most logical option. But the best thing for my team would be to keep some people on the outside in case things went wrong in the Coven. "Fine, the three of us will go with you." I motioned between Rourke, Nick, and me. "Tyler and Danny will head to the Safe House." I nodded to them both. "Find out anything you can on James's whereabouts. I want a phone call in less than two hours, whether you find something or not. Contact Dad," I told Tyler, "and let him know what's going on. After that, we rendezvous at an agreed-upon spot outside the Coven and head out."

"Jess—" Tyler started.

I cut him off in my mind.

Tyler, we don't have a choice. If I refuse to go with Tally, it'll bring more trouble than we need right now. And the priority is Marcy.

I don't like it. That witch could do a thousand things to you inside that house, not to mention she wanted to use you as ransom an hour ago.

Tally's original plan was to ransom me to the sorcerers, which was still a viable option if we couldn't track them. I'd trade myself for Marcy in a heartbeat, but not without a solid plan. Tyler didn't have to know that, and in order to move forward, we needed to pick Tally's brain about the sorcerers anyway. *I hear you, but you're going to have to trust me on this. We'll take the necessary precautions, and I have an angry cat with me who's not about to let anything go wrong.*

He grumbled but looked resigned.

"Give me the keys," I asked him out loud. Tyler reluctantly reached into his pocket and pulled them out. The Safe House was only a few miles away. They could make it on foot in a few minutes. *Remember, we still have this.* I tapped my finger to my temple, trying my best to reassure him. Then I glanced over at Rourke, who stood frowning at Tally.

She glared back, her arms still crossed.

"Before we leave, I want you to swear an oath, witch," Rourke said. "Or the deal is off. Covens are notorious for holding prisoners, and breaking layered wards by multiple witches is next to impossible."

"I swear not to hold you against your will," Tally stated evenly. "But I want a vow in return that you will do whatever we deem necessary to get my niece back, including a ransom if your wolf has failed to track her." She narrowed her eyes. "Without doing so, you risk a war with us."

Before Rourke could protest, I said, "I swear we will do everything we can to find your niece. Whatever it takes."

Tally nodded once, accepting me at my word.

"Keep your wits about you, then, Jessica," Danny quipped as he gently prodded an unhappy Tyler backward. "We'll plan on seeing you shortly." He winked as they took off into the night.

As they ran, their combined uncertainty jumped through my blood. Being an Alpha, even for this short time, wasn't an easy job. The responsibility for their well-being pressed down on me. We needed to find my father soon so he could take back their Troths and fix this.

I directed my attention to Tally. "I'll drive, because there's no way we're fitting in your car."

She didn't argue. Her silver two-door Camaro was still parked at a haphazard angle by the back door where she'd clearly spun it to a stop. The car had missed the mayhem of the Orb, but just barely. It had to have been warded against damage, because there wasn't a scratch on it.

I walked around to the driver's side of the Humvee with Nick following closely.

"I haven't had a chance to tell you," he said, reaching out to give me a quick hug, "but I'm incredibly glad to see you back so soon. It's been quiet around here with you gone. And as much as I knew you'd make it home, seeing you *not* dead, broken, or battered is the best gift I could've asked for."

"It's really good to see you too," I told him honestly, hugging him back. Nick had been my best—and only—friend growing up on the Compound, where physical strength had meant status, and we'd both had none. During our childhood we'd forged a solid, unbreakable bond and I was extremely happy to see him. "I'll fill you in on all the details as soon as I can, but Selene is going to be gone for a very long time, in a place where she can't touch us."

In the Underworld, specifically.

"I knew you'd beat her." Nick chuckled as he opened the back passenger door. "I never doubted you for a second." He cocked his head slightly as he got in. "Well, maybe I had a few errant thoughts, but they passed quickly enough."

I grinned as I climbed into the driver's seat. "The battle was intense and it wasn't very pretty." Rourke growled his agreement as he settled in next to Nick. Selene had eviscerated him, intent on doing the greatest possible damage to us both. Images started to invade my psyche and my wolf huffed. Time to change the scenery. "Nick, after we find Marcy, the next priority will be to prepare for New Orleans." We were due at the Vampire Queen's to provide guard duty services in three weeks and we couldn't go in unprepared. "I refuse to let Eudoxia gain the upper hand."

Tally slid into the front seat and slammed the door. She raised her eyebrow at me but stayed silent. Our business wasn't hers, and with a small nod, she acknowledged it.

The Vamp Queen's request for us to guard her was ridiculous at best, but I had sworn a binding oath, meaning that if I didn't deliver, bad things would happen. There was no doubt she had ulterior motives for wanting me on her home turf, so we had to prepare. I needed to know everything about vampires and how they worked. Having Naomi on my team was my ace in the hole, and between her and Nick, I hoped we could gather enough information to stay at least one step ahead.

I'd been a wolf for only a short time, but my on-the-job training had brought my skill level up exponentially in the last few weeks. I was fairly confident I could get Marcy back *and* survive my time with the Vamp Queen.

If not, life was about to become extremely interesting.

I turned the diesel engine over and the beast roared to life.

"By the way, where's Ray?" Nick asked, leaning forward. Raymond Hart, the detective who'd been the bane of my existence for a very long time, had accompanied us on the journey to find Rourke. As I'd fought Selene, he'd been brutally attacked by a vampire and, right this minute, I had no idea if he was dead or alive.

"Ray is in…transition," I said, settling on an ambiguous word. I glanced sideways at Tally. "It requires some explaining."

I'd left Ray in the capable hands of Naomi, our vamp guide, who through an unexpected blood exchange, had not only become bonded to me, but also had become my friend and ally. Ray's wounds may have been too severe for any kind of transformation, but I'd given her the okay to try. I'd felt I owed Ray that much. In my opinion he had the right to choose his own death. Eamon, Naomi's brother, had ravaged him cruelly and it had been an awful way to die.

Nick nodded once without question. He knew me well enough to catch on; whether he liked the idea or not was hard to tell. He sat back in his seat, his face pensive. Ray was a tough human being, not necessarily someone you'd choose to become a supe. It's true Ray was rough around the edges and cranky, but Nick hadn't witnessed what he'd been capable of on the journey, as I had. In the end Ray had defended me and there had been a grudging respect growing between us. I desperately hoped, as a supe, he would come around to seeing our side of things.

If not, it was going to be a tough road. But there was no going back now.

I pulled away from the curb. "Where to?"

2

Tally directed me around a chain of lakes inside the city. Halfway around Lake of the Isles, she pointed to a huge mansion perched on the tip of a peninsula. One I'd seen a thousand times. "Pull around back," she ordered. "The gate knows it's me."

I wasn't going to question the gate's prowess.

The long driveway disappeared as it wrapped behind the house. Once the vehicle crossed the boundary line from the street, a current of energy pulsed through my body. Strong wards were up, and if they hadn't liked us, they would've slapped us back, like a flyswatter eliminating a pesky problem.

Once we were through the main gate, the backyard opened up. I followed the driveway as it curved to the left. Tall shrubs ran around the perimeter of the yard. It was completely private from any curious onlookers. Up ahead was a huge garage with three stalls. Tally snapped her wrist at the windshield, and feathery lines, almost undetectable, shot out from her fingertips.

The third garage door on the right opened.

"Drive in there."

I maneuvered the beast into the stall with only inches to spare on either side. The moment I tugged it into park, the ground beneath us jerked and rattled and the vehicle began to sink. "I'm assuming we're on a lift." I angled my head at Tally, laying it on the headrest. "Either that or earthquakes have finally found the upper Midwest."

Nick tried to roll his window down, but it was locked into place. "It's an underground lair." There was a hint of awe in his voice and I knew he was refraining from making a Batman joke. We didn't have anything cool like this up in the north woods where I grew up. No need for underground lairs when you had a thousand acres separating you from the world.

"Of course the entrance is underground," Tally said. "This is a Coven, one of the largest in the country. We protect ourselves well."

The hydraulic lift squeaked as it came to a stop and the Humvee bounced on its gigantic tires as it settled.

The room was well lit and, unsurprisingly, held a dozen witches.

Shifters and witches were not friendly, but they weren't exactly enemies either. Tally had already indicated she'd known who my father was before she allowed her niece to work for me, so it was not out of the question to think these witches also knew who I was. It irritated me, because for the past seven years I'd been under the assumption I'd created the perfect cover. No one had seemed to lift an eyebrow or question me at all. I'd believed my alias had been foolproof. But I'd been mistaken.

The supernatural community had indeed been onto me, possibly from the beginning. I knew this for certain, because the day after I'd become the first female wolf on the planet, I'd been brutally attacked. The rogue attack had been planned, and if that wasn't enough, I'd found out my building super had been a supe himself. We were still trying to figure out who he was and who he'd worked for, but it had been no accident he'd been chosen for the job.

"We're not getting out to a roomful of hostiles," Rourke said, his voice low, broaching no arguments.

"Cool your jets." Tally opened her door. "They're harmless unless I tell them otherwise."

"I can taste their power from here," he said. "And it's far from harmless. They're primed and ready to go. Tell them to stand down or we don't move."

I glanced back at Rourke and raised a brow. I wasn't going to argue with him, but I wasn't detecting the same threat. I inhaled, pulling air lightly over my tongue. Their combined power prodded against my senses, but it didn't raise any internal alarms. Not like Selene or the Demon Lord had. My wolf hadn't even bothered to get up to investigate once the lift had stopped. *Am I missing something?* I asked my wolf. She lifted her muzzle and gave a gratuitous sniff. Alrighty, then. *You know, we can't afford to keep barreling into trouble because you think we're above the threat. I need to be aware of everything, and once we have the data, we can make an informed decision together.* She was my internal radar, my supernatural sensor, and she hadn't triggered a warning when Tally had broken into my office, and Tally was a definite threat. My wolf was clearly taking a more relaxed stance than she should. *You know, just because we're strong doesn't mean—*

A witch with long golden hair burst through a door on the other side of the room and hustled toward us. "Magdalene just had a vision," she called, addressing Tally directly. "She wants you." Then she grimaced. "And she said to bring along the... female wolf."

Tally nodded and took a step forward, sliding off her black

skullcap as she slammed the car door. White hair cascaded down to the middle of her back. It was a lot longer than I would've guessed, and actually kind of pretty. It made her appear decades younger.

I hadn't expected that.

"Keep your fingers at the ready, ladies," she ordered. "As of right now, we are on a yellow alert. The sorcerers are on the hunt. These are my guests"—she jabbed her thumb behind her—"and they are not to be harmed...unless, of course, they draw first blood." She glanced back into the car. "Good enough for you?"

Rourke scowled but opened his door.

Nick and I followed.

I made my way around the vehicle, my internal feelers open despite my unaffected wolf. This Coven hadn't accepted Marcy, and even though her aunt was the most powerful witch in the country—and presided over the Coven—Marcy hadn't been voted in. Witches were expected to perform precisely every time. Their rituals and coming-of-age tasks were legendary. Marcy was extremely powerful but had a habit of misfiring under pressure. Tally may have been able to overrule to let her niece in, if Marcy's last task hadn't been such a spectacular blunder. Over the years, on those rare occasions we drank together, she'd given me snippets of a disjointed tale—something to do with a local donut shop, naked coeds, and a dead rooster.

Needless to say, these witches were no friends of mine.

We followed Tally through the curious spectators, who had stepped back to give us some space. Rourke had waited for me and ushered me in front. Nick had taken up the rear.

"Nice assets, cat," one witch cackled. "Those tattoos are rockin'."

"She doesn't feel strong to me. I could take her."

"She smells like a garbage dump."

I had on a road-worn pair of leggings and a wrinkled T-shirt. I'd showered only once in the past few days. My wolf growled. *Now you're upset?*

"That cat is hawt."

Rourke ignored them like a champ, his hands firmly planted around my waist, his power sparking me through my shirt.

"I like the brown-haired one. What is he?"

"Smells like a total fox to me."

All these comments were for my benefit. These witches weren't challenging me for Pack status, but they were challenging me nonetheless. My wolf was ramping herself up, getting more agitated by the second.

"She does travel with some delicious men. I don't care if he smells like a mangy feline—I'd still do him." Several witches snickered.

"I would totally fuc—"

In the time it took to blink, I was an inch away from the speaker's startled face.

I clacked my teeth in front of her nose and smiled widely, showing her all my pearly whites. My growl was low and harsh and she backed up quickly. Her shocked reaction was immensely gratifying. My wolf let out a shallow huff of laughter. "In order to *do* my man, you'll have to go through me first," I said through a clenched jaw. "And after defeating Selene, kicking your ass would be like punching a kindergartener. Not exactly a fair fight."

Murmurs started in earnest, as I knew they would.

Selene, the Lunar Goddess I'd just sent to Hell, was legendary among witches. She'd been a witch herself before ascending to her godhood. The spell caster in front of me gathered her composure with effort. She was young and not very powerful, according to her low signature. But she was gorgeous with sleek black hair and almond-shaped eyes. And I'd just called her bluff in a roomful of her peers. Her expression raged as she seethed, "You don't scare me with all your big talk, mutt. There's no way you took on Selene and won. You're a *liar*."

Calling me mutt was standard fare, but calling me a liar was a hefty insult. Questioning someone's honor provoked a challenge on the spot. I had to respond, but fighting her here would start something bigger than I intended. "I'd be very careful if I were you. Calling me a liar makes me itchy." I made a fist. "My wolf is begging me to show you some of our new skills."

"Go right ahead." Her eyes narrowed.

Tally turned from the door, her authoritative voice rang out. "Enough, Angie," she ordered. "What she says is true. Selene's presence on this plane has blinked off permanently. According to Lani, it happened more than a day ago. I don't have time to referee a pissing match right now, so I'm ordering you to step down."

The beauty's eyes widened just enough and I unclenched my fist.

I knew without a doubt Marcy hated this witch with a fiery passion. Her inflated ego, likely due to her beauty because she had no power, was nauseating. And if I had to guess, Angie had led the vote to keep Marcy out of the Coven. I wanted to take a bite out of her in solidarity for my friend.

Instead, I settled for snapping the air in front of her nose again with a decisive bite.

She flinched, hitting her head against the wall.

I grinned, ignoring her murderous glare, and whispered, "I win."

"You have no idea what I can do!" she yelled at my retreating back. "You better watch yourself!"

"Quiet, Angie," one of the other witches muttered. "Just let it go."

"Yes, Angie," I said without turning around. "Let it go. If we fight, you lose."

"I won't lose," she called. "I can promise you that. And when I'm done, I'll—"

Rourke physically picked me up and carried me out the door.

Nick slammed it firmly shut behind him, muffling the rest of Angie's threats, which included a hearty description of her talents in the bedroom. "Easy, Jess," Nick said when he saw my face. "Just ignore it. She got in over her head and she couldn't back down."

"I don't care," I said. "She brought it on herself. A challenge is a challenge. You can't expect me to ignore it." Wolves didn't back down from a fight. Ever.

Tally stood at the bottom of a staircase, her hands on her hips. "Angie is no threat to you, but her sister is. Leave it alone. If Magdalene had a vision, we need to see her now before it's gone. You're wasting valuable time."

Rourke covered my lips in a quick kiss. He broke with a low growl and leaned in close, whispering, "I like you jealous." He licked my earlobe and chills raced up my spine. "It's sexy as hell."

Tally tapped her foot.

I broke away, grinning. I wasn't going to tell him it wasn't jealousy that had motivated my reaction, because being sexy as hell worked for me. Not being able to have any alone time with my mate was testing my willpower on every level. The car ride home had been a torture of emotions and feelings, none of which we could act on, so right now I was willing to take what I could get. Sexy, jealous lover. Check. I turned, reluctantly tearing my gaze away from his clear green eyes, warm body, and delicious blond stubble, and headed down the long hallway. "Out of curiosity, who is Angie's sister?" I asked Tally.

"Ceres."

My brain filtered through the small information I had on her. "The Goddess of Crops?" I asked. Crops weren't so scary.

"Fertility. And if you want to keep your mate, stay away from her. Her specialty is stripping libido. She's a cranky goddess and Angie is her only blood-kin. She's not like Selene. She doesn't *play* with her prey. She leaves them crying and eternally deadened with one flick of her wrist."

Jesus. "Good to know."

We wound our way through the mansion, passing by room after room filled with plush carpets and ornate furniture. The house was a strange mix of Mediterranean meets Tudor with lots of gables and dark woodwork, with the addition of huge, airy windows. It had a pleasant feel. Two sets of staircases later, we entered a small room in the attic. I ducked my head as I passed through the low doorway. The boys had to physically bend over.

There, sitting on a bed covered in white chenille, was a toddler no older than three.

"Maggie," Tally crooned. "Mommy's here."

3

"That's a child." The tot in question extended her pudgy arms out to her mother. Tally plucked her out of bed and skillfully perched her on her hip. The toddler was flushed, appearing to have just awoken from her nap. Her fine blonde hair stuck to her rosy cheeks. It was clear she'd been crying.

"Indeed," Tally said. "She's two." Tally lovingly wiped her hair away from her face and planted a kiss on her forehead.

A baby soothsayer? I assumed this child was the oracle, since Tally had just addressed her as Maggie.

"Is she yours?" I asked. I wasn't trying to be rude, but Tally was old by anyone's standards—whether her face looked thirty or forty meant nothing. She had to be centuries old, gauging by her power alone. It radiated off her in currents that came only with age. I didn't know the average life span of a witch, but I knew, like us, they aged slowly. No supe was truly immortal, and unless we obtained a godhood we could be killed a number of ways, such as by severing our heads or burning us alive. But the average mortality of a supernatural was thousands of years. "I mean"—I cleared my throat when she didn't readily respond to my question—"not that she couldn't be yours biologically, but I know witches adopt often." Many Sects brought in children through legal adoptions.

"She's mine," she answered. "A witch is fertile once every year for her entire life. We are born of the earth and renew each year. Our problem is finding a compatible partner, like most Sects. It has been...difficult. This is only my second child and she is a gift. And if we don't hurry, the information she has will be lost." She turned and crooned, "Maggie, we're going to play the Tell Mommy game, okay?" The child nodded and brought a chubby finger to her mom's hair and started twirling. "Let's get the crayons. This time we'll color pictures. How does that sound?"

Marcy had never mentioned a cousin her own age, so it was a good assumption Tally's other child was no longer living. Children of leaders were vulnerable for many reasons, but I wasn't about to ask. We followed them into an adjoining room, which was clearly the playroom. Tally set the child down at a little white table decorated with pale pink flowers and grabbed a box of art supplies from a nearby shelf. Two other witches were already in the room.

"Maggie, did you see Aunt Marcy in your dreams today?" Tally coaxed, setting down an array of crayons and several sheets of white paper as she knelt by her side.

The child nodded as she picked a brown crayon and started scribbling circles on one of the blank pieces of paper.

"How did she look?"

"Boy," the child murmured quietly.

"She was with a boy?"

The crayon stopped moving as the child's eyes fluttered and her head tilted up toward the ceiling. When she brought it back down, her eyes were completely white—like when you pulled your eyelids up and rolled your eyes back to freak out your friend kind of white.

And they stayed like that.

I covered my mouth to stifle a yell, but not very well. My wolf bared her teeth in my mind and we took a step back, knocking into Rourke's chest.

Tally glared up at us.

"*Sorry*," I squeaked.

Nick was pale across the room. Shifters were concrete creatures. Witchiness of any kind made us uncomfortable. Rourke stood behind me, a low rumbling in his chest. We were all a little freaked out. Not because the child could harm us but because what she was doing was so creepy and unnatural.

"You must be quiet," Tally snapped. "She only has visions when something pivotal in our world happens. This means something. And it's no coincidence she asked for the female wolf. She could have the answers to where my niece is, which would mean—"

"Boy, he help her. They get away," Maggie interrupted in her little voice.

That was great news. "They get away" had to mean James had successfully tracked Marcy and they were out of danger. I blew out a big breath. "Ask her where they are so we can go pick them up," I urged.

Tally shot me a death glare and I shut up.

We all watched as the child started drawing circles again, which quickly bled onto the tabletop. I leaned forward as she discarded one crayon and picked up another. A crude drawing started of what appeared to be a wolf. It had pointy ears, so it was as good a guess as any. Then she drew a stick figure holding hands with the wolf. It had long hair and was smiling. It must be James and Marcy.

The child's eyes snapped shut and her head bobbed down like she'd suddenly fallen asleep.

"So are you telling us that Aunt Marcy is okay, Magdalene?" Tally prodded in a voice full of love and patience.

"They running." Maggie's head came up and I was relieved to see her eyes were back to normal.

"Is someone following them?"

"Bad men."

"Is Marcy going to come home?" Tally coaxed.

Brief pause.

We all held our breath.

The child nodded. "Auntie Marcy. Home again."

Whew. "Ask her when?" I pressed. I couldn't help it. A toddler having visions was a crazy thing to witness, but when she delivered good news, it made it less so.

The child's small face turned toward me, her gaze locking on mine like a clamp.

I shivered.

Her eyes rolled back to white as I watched. I cringed, but didn't yell. I didn't have time to congratulate myself, because I was crossing my fingers too fiercely, hoping like a madwoman her eyeballs were receiving the story from her brain so she could fill us in on Marcy's location. I flinched back as she continued to stare at me with that milky stare. Rourke drew me to him, comforting me once again by wrapping his warm arms around my middle.

Maggie pointed at me, eyes still frightening. "Finds you."

"Marcy finds me?" I asked hopefully. "When?"

"Oracles don't do time." Tally shook her head like I was a moron. "Things shift. People make choices. They affect outcomes. There is never a time frame involved."

That sounded somewhat logical.

Abruptly, Maggie turned her head back to her table, her pudgy little fingers grabbing another crayon. This time she drew right on the tabletop.

A simple picture of a face emerged, this one with pointy teeth.

She dropped the crayon and reached for a red one.

"Is that supposed to be blood?" I whispered as Maggie started scribbling like mad. She added more pointy teeth and more red. "A vamp, Maggie? Are you drawing vampires?"

Tally hovered over her daughter protectively. "She doesn't know what a vampire is yet. That would be highly unlikely—"

"Yes," Maggie said simply. "Vampires." It sounded like *van-pirates* in her little rasp. So much to know when you're only two years old.

My heart broke a little.

Surprise laced Tally's expression. She was wary watching her daughter go through this ordeal. This was her baby, and knowing she would never escape these visions, this life, had to be incredibly tough.

"Is Marcy with the vampires?" I asked. That wasn't ideal, but my insides relaxed knowing James was with her.

"They're *coming*." This time her soft voice sounded ominous. She glanced up at me as her eyes slid back to normal. For the first time I noticed they were the brightest blue.

We weren't talking about Marcy any longer.

All the hairs on my arms and neck shot to attention. Nick coughed and Rourke ground his teeth.

Maggie picked up another crayon, this time in her left hand, and started to draw like something had possessed her. Her eyes fluttered and she rocked back and forth in her chair, chanting, "*Run, run, run, run.*"

All of us moved closer, craning our necks over the table, including her two witch nannies. This little child was going to run out of steam in about two seconds.

"What is she drawing?" I whispered. "Hurry, we have to figure it out before she stops."

The drawing was a jumble of stick figures, all layered on top of each other. There were more wolves with pointy ears; some looked like they were ejecting something from their mouths. There were a lot of them.

"I think that's the Vamp Queen," Rourke murmured in my ear as he pointed to a stick figure with fangs and a long dress. It was a decent guess.

"What's she doing?"

"Biting," Rourke said.

Indeed, the Vamp Queen looked as if she was trying to bite someone. A wild guess said it was me. The victim had long hair like my own and she was screaming.

Perfect.

Maggie's focus shifted slightly to the right and she started scribbling a single circle over and over again. It got bigger and bigger as she went. Then she uttered one last word.

"Demon."

It sounded like *denim*, but we all knew she wasn't talking about a pair of jeans.

Tally reached down and plucked her daughter out of her chair. Maggie sagged in relief, dropping the crayon and resting her head on her mom's shoulder. "It's okay, lovey." Tally kissed the crook of her sweaty neck. "You did great. It's time for us to take a break. Auntie Meryl is going to take you downstairs for some cookies and milk." One of the witches strode forward, her arms outstretched.

Maggie's head rose with effort. She was exhausted. "Okay, Mommy." Her face was even more flushed now. As Tally shifted her toward the waiting Meryl, the child turned.

"Bad men coming"—she pointed her little finger directly at me—"for you."

Tally paced over a well-worn Oriental rug to stand in front of a huge picture window that faced the lake. Rourke and I sat close together on an antique chaise, which almost wasn't big enough to hold the both of us. We were in a well-stocked library that appeared to double as Tally's office. It was lined with thousands of books, and from their crumbling leather bindings, many of them appeared to be ancient. Nick sat across the room in a high-backed chair, his hands clasped in his lap, his short brown curls falling around his worried face. This day wasn't starting off very well and it wasn't even dawn.

"You can't stay here. Not with a Demon Lord after you," Tally said.

Since Maggie had signaled out the demons, there had been little use to hide it, so I'd just finished telling her what had happened in Selene's cave once the Demon Lord had showed up. "I understand your concern, but you're the only one who can help us figure out how to defeat them. We know very little about demons, or their laws," I countered. "It said I had a court date in the Underworld. There has to be some way to stop it, some information to help my case."

"I'm sorry, but helping you is out of the question. Witches and demons are sworn enemies. Our magics have battled each other since the dawn of time. Our power is of the earth and theirs is of the blood." She turned from the window and walked toward the large desk situated in the center of the room and sat. "If I involve myself in your mess, I bring the entire House of Witches, and potentially every Coven in the world, into your fight. I will not do it, so don't ask me again."

I scooted to the edge of the settee. "What about a simple swap of information? Nobody has to know you gave me anything, and to be clear, I'm not asking you to join my fight. I'm only seeking data, anything that can aid me, something to bolster my odds of winning a court battle or of finding a way out of it entirely. And we both know the only way to do that is by obtaining intelligence about the demons and their habits, of which I currently know nothing."

She rested her hands on the desk and leaned over. "What kind of information do you have that I could possibly want enough to risk putting my Coven in jeopardy?"

She had a point. I was short on supernatural info. "Okay," I said, thinking quickly, "what if the witches made a formal alliance with the wolves? Then you'd be privy to any information the Pack had, within reason." It wasn't unheard of for some supernatural Sects to join together during times of strife when it was advantageous. In those rare cases, there were formal agreements to sign, but certainly my father had something of value to give to the witches. I knew he would be agreeable if it kept me out of the Underworld. "The witches could also benefit from more protection, and in return you agree to give me something on the demons. Tally, you know it's the only real chance I have. Knowledge is the only way I'll be able to talk myself out of this sentence."

On our long ride home, Rourke had filled me in on what little he knew about demons and their thing with language. We agreed if my defense was worded perfectly, and if I sighted enough overarching supernatural laws in my favor, I had a slim chance of wiggling my way out—and talking my way out would be infinitely easier than trying to fight my way out of the Underworld, which was our solid plan B.

Tally gazed at me so intently that a line of energy zipped between us. "I'm sorry, but I cannot align with you. If I do, the demons will consider us accomplices to your crimes."

I rested my head in my hands. Suddenly I was very tired. "But there were no real crimes committed, so they have no actual case." I glanced up, closing my eyes for a moment. "Everything I did was within my rights. I defended myself—yes, at the cost of their imps and pets, but I have undisputable proof they attacked first. The first imp had abducted a human teenager in a public place. That has to be against supernatural High Law. The second put a knife to my throat." All supes had to follow High Laws, which were very strict about exposing ourselves to humans. Each Sect also had its own internal laws that had to be obeyed.

Tally rose out of her chair and started to pace. It was a move much like my father's, and my heart constricted. I hadn't heard from him in too long. "It doesn't matter. The demons have you in their sights, for whatever reason. I can't risk it."

I nodded once, accepting her decision.

Rourke shifted in the small space next to me. His voice came out deep and rich. "We have an idea why the demons want Jessica," he said, changing the topic. "The imp who attacked her in the parking lot alluded to her taking control of their crown. But what doesn't make sense right now is why the sorcerers would involve themselves. By abducting your niece they've started a war with both the wolves and the witches." He moved and I adjusted. "That seems like a very hasty decision on their part. They are run by a council, not an entity. From what I know, they are almost monklike in their rituals and are known to be weaker than most Sects. Why start a war they have no chance of winning?"

"They want what they always want." Tally shrugged as she came to a standstill behind her desk.

"And what's that exactly?" I asked, leaning forward.

"Power." She crossed her arms. "Their magic is born of the earth, like ours, but they have a much weaker gene pool. You have power, so they want it." She inclined her head toward me. "They are always after some trinket or other that's supposed to unleash 'ultimate power,' and they are willing to risk anything to get it, regardless of their chances of success. It makes them predictable."

"But I don't have a *trinket* to steal. In order to steal my power, they'd have to siphon off what's living inside my body," I said. "Is that even possible?" Did I even want to know?

"There are ways," she said. "But none of them are very effective in the long-term. They are a bunch of fools." She waved her hand dismissively in the air and pulled out her chair to sit. "You don't have to worry. They won't succeed."

That didn't sound comforting. Extracting raw power from someone had to hurt. But as much as the sorcerers were an irritant, the demons were still the biggest threat to me at the moment. "The demons still pose the greatest—"

An explosion ripped through the front yard, shaking the house on its foundation.

We all hit the ground.

Books toppled off the shelves and lamps crashed to the floor. The blast felt like an earthquake. I covered my head, expecting the plate-glass window to explode inward, but it held.

Tally was up first. "That was an Orb. The sorcerers have tracked you here. That was quicker than I thought they'd be able to amass themselves."

I jumped to my feet. Rourke and Nick were already up. "Can they get in?"

"Of course not." Tally sniffed. "But they're going to try."

Out in the hallway, there was a flurry of activity, but instead of panic I heard glee. There were several decisive "Bring it, Baldies!" All sorcerers shaved their heads. Rumors were it was some sort of magic-enhancing tradition—which I now knew wasn't a rumor. Magic boosting must be their main focus.

"Sorcerers are cowards by nature," Tally said, moving toward the window. "That Orb came from more than ten miles away or we would've sensed them. Close proximity would've triggered our alarms. But there's no doubt they will be here shortly. This is your chance to get out of the Coven." She turned and met my eyes. "I'm prepared to wait them out, but we could be locked in a standoff for weeks if you stay. They don't give up easily, tenacious bastards, even if they only attack from afar. If you leave now, you have a chance to outrun them." When I didn't move immediately, she pointed toward the door. "Your window of opportunity is *now*. I suggest you take it."

I turned, not needing any more incentive. We couldn't afford to be locked in here for weeks, and now that we knew Marcy was safe, our agenda with Tally had changed. My staying here would risk unneeded damage to her Coven. Rourke was in front of me, and Nick's hand rested on my shoulder. I glanced back before I went through the doorway.

She met my gaze and nodded once. "Marcy doesn't trust many people, but she's chosen to trust you," Tally said. "I'll consider your request to exchange information. That's all I can do."

"Thank you," I said as we left.

Tally called behind us, "Head down to the carport. Take a vehicle, and once you're out, get somewhere far from here. The sorcerers' network is fairly small. If you get out of town quickly, you should be able to stay ahead of them."

We didn't look back as we raced through the house.

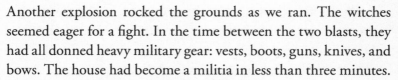

Another explosion rocked the grounds as we ran. The witches seemed eager for a fight. In the time between the two blasts, they had all donned heavy military gear: vests, boots, guns, knives, and bows. The house had become a militia in less than three minutes.

Note to self: Don't fuck with the witches.

We followed our scent trail and Rourke skidded to a stop in front of the basement door. He yanked it open and we ran down the steps to the underground garage. We barreled into the room that held the hydraulic lift only to find it was completely empty.

Save one person.

Angie's lips curled with distaste. The feeling was more than mutual.

I fisted my hands, forcing myself to ignore her with everything I had. I turned in a full circle, but the room was bare. No Humvee and no other vehicles in sight.

"Looking for something?" she sneered as she angled her body back against the concrete wall, clearly enjoying what she thought was her moment.

I turned to Rourke and he nodded once, needing no other prompts. He took a menacing step toward Angie, his shoulders back, his growl low. Her eyes widened, but she stayed put.

"Listen, you—" I said as Rourke continued to pace toward her.

Before I could get the words out, Nick's hands went up, interrupting me. My eyebrows arched. Nick addressed the witch, "I know it doesn't appear that way, but we'd much rather handle this without violence." Angie was looking more alarmed by the second, which worked in our favor. "But only if you cooperate. Tallulah, your Coven mistress, ordered us to find a car. If we stay here, the sorcerers will keep attacking. We leave and they…eventually leave. She wants us out, and it seems you're the only one who can help us."

Nick was right to try and avoid catastrophe, but I was too mad to put things into perspective. It wasn't going to be a fair fight, since Angie didn't stand a chance against us, and if we did her harm, we could count Tally and Ceres as enemies. He had the right idea, and I was going to have to control my wolf, who was laser focused on inflicting some payback.

Rourke stopped moving, awaiting her decision to cooperate on her own.

A nasty smile lingered on her lips once she realized we weren't going to tear her to pieces. "Yes, well, we've taken your vehicle as payment for your entrance, which is why you don't see it here."

"You…you can't do that," I snarled. "It was packed with all our supplies. You can't just take what you want—" I stomped forward as Nick whipped his arm out to keep me back.

Angie moved forward as well, her irises sparking with a low scarlet light. "You just had your future foretold. Do you think that comes without a cost? Ignorance must be one of your best qualities. I'm sure your mother is very proud." She knew shifters were raised by their fathers. My mother had died in childbirth.

I clamped my teeth together, and a fierce growl, fueled by my pissed-off wolf, echoed around the room. I wanted nothing more than to wring her beautiful neck. "I'm willing to pay the price for meeting with Maggie," I managed with as much calm as I could muster. "But taking our vehicle and supplies without our consent is not in good faith." Witches were notorious for charging exorbitant fees. "You are free to bill us for services rendered, but we want our vehicle back *now*."

She cackled. "Well, it's *gone*. Do you see it in here?" She mocked looking around the room.

Nick cleared his throat, but before he could speak, Rourke cut in, his voice laced with danger. "The truck doesn't matter. We need a vehicle. Any will do. And I suggest you deliver one in the next three seconds or I will tear your throat out."

Angie's face changed for the merest second, but it was enough. "Well, I guess it's your lucky day then, because I have *one* vehicle left." She pushed off the wall and shouldered past me, her glossy hair swinging behind her.

By the smallest margin imaginable I resisted the urge to yank it completely out of her head, my hands curling inward.

She lifted her fingers at a far wall. A door, seamlessly hidden, lifted, making no sound. Behind it stood a lone vehicle.

An ancient-looking Vespa.

My voice sounded savage in my ears. "You expect us to escape on a *scooter*? You must be out of your mind. We need something with four doors and a roof. And there are three of us, not two, in case you haven't noticed."

Hands on her hips, she declared, "This is what I have available. Everyone left after the first explosion. It's actually the best-concealed transportation we have. Spells go by weight—the bigger the object, the harder to spell. Your precious Humvee will only stay spelled for a few hours at most. This one"—she gestured at the aged moped—"will stay spelled for a week." Her eyes glittered with laughter. She was playing us, but another explosion hit and there was no more time to argue. "Take it or leave it. That's all I have."

I took a step forward and Nick wrapped his hands around my shoulders, steering me away from her and toward the battered Vespa. "Jess, listen to me," he whispered in my ear. "Just get on it and go. You're running out of time, and arguing with her is not doing us any good. The sorcerers will arrive soon. Head out while you still have time, and once they stop the assault, I'll head back to the Safe House. Everything will work out."

Rourke walked over and grabbed the scooter by the handlebars and lifted it out of its parking space with the effort it took an accountant to lift his phone. He strode over to the platform and set it down with a clang, snarling, "If this thing breaks down once we're outside, I'm coming back in here to kill you. Do you understand me?"

Angie had the nerve to grin. "It won't. It's spelled in more ways than one, big fella. It doesn't need gas and it can carry two people no problem."

"There are *three* of us here," I muttered.

She shrugged. "Like I said, this is all I have. I couldn't care less if you use it or not. Stay in here if you want." She spun around and headed for the door right as another explosion rocked the foundation. Light fixtures swayed and concrete cracked, sprinkling dust from the walls. We were several floors underneath the mansion, so that one had been closer. Angie angled her head back before making her dramatic exit. "If you don't leave now, however, you're going to miss your golden opportunity. The sorcerers will be here in moments, and we wouldn't want you to *die* out there or anything." She turned, slamming the door with a clap.

Rourke's movements were hostile. He was one step away from kicking the stupid moped across the room. "Jessica, if we didn't need to move quickly, I'd bash down these walls and try to find something else. But that will take longer than we have right now. It's either this or we stay."

I eyed the hydraulic lift. "Fine. I say we go. Once we're out of range of the sorcerers, we can figure out another ride. If this thing is spelled like she said, it should be undetectable. We ditch it the first chance we can and find something with doors."

Resigned, Rourke slid onto the seat. The bottom bowed dangerously close to the ground, groaning against his weight. He swore as he turned the key. The thing puttered to life reluctantly like an old motorboat as he shifted it to neutral and directed it to the middle of the platform with his feet.

I spotted a green button on the wall across the room as I walked toward him. "Gods," I said. "Nick, punch the green button on the wall and stay down here until it's over. There's no reason to stick your neck out and join the fight." I swung my leg over and straddled what was left of the seat, which was about four inches. There was more creaking as the moped took my weight, but surprisingly it held.

"I'm not planning on getting in the middle of it," Nick answered as he headed for the activation switch. "But once this is over, I want a drink and some more explanations."

"I know." I smiled. "I owe you a full recap."

"Just stay alive."

"That's the plan." He punched the button and the platform jumped once, rising quickly. When the bottom of the lift met the garage floor, it clicked seamlessly into place and Rourke revved the scooter. It coughed and sputtered, threatening to die.

"I am going to wring her scrawny neck," Rourke growled. Without a trigger from us, the garage door began to move up on its own.

I slid my arms firmly around Rourke's waist, intertwining my fingers, pulling him tight. He was warm and smelled delicious. "Okay, let's do this," I whispered in his ear.

Rourke gunned the Vespa to full throttle, which was roughly human jogging speed, and we began to buzz toward the gate.

Almost at once, I heard something in the sky and glanced over my shoulder. "Something's coming right at us," I yelled as the ball of light began to gain speed, like it suddenly recognized us. It had come out of nowhere, but there was no question it knew we were its target now.

At the last minute, Rourke angled the scooter, swerving hard to the right. The light exploded behind us, rocking us in our seats and bouncing the moped off the pavement.

"Hold on!" Rourke yelled. "I'm going to have to take this corner hard."

I locked my arms against his chest, turning my head in time to see another light arcing toward us in the sky. I watched as it changed course to follow us as we bounded onto the street.

"She lied!" I screamed. "This thing isn't spelled! It's probably Maggie's toy scooter." Fury radiated through me and fur erupted along my arms. "The sorcerers have my signature, they know where I am!" We would've had a chance to outrun them if we'd been on Rourke's motorcycle, but on this thing we were sitting ducks.

"Not for long," Rourke roared. We took the curb, Rourke wrenching the wheel as we went.

One jump and we cleared the boulevard.

One more and we hit the lake.

4

Rourke and I both leapt off the Vespa right as another explosion rocked the embankment we'd just crossed. The impact flung us far into the lake.

"Stay under—" Rourke managed before we splashed down, both of us plunging feetfirst into the water.

The force of my landing shook my equilibrium and I whirled around in the cold, discombobulated for a few beats. I steadied myself, throwing my arms out to get my bearings, and opened my eyes. It was dark as night and the water was murky, full of algae and weeds. My wolf had fed me a constant stream of adrenaline since we'd left the garage, but another shot hit my system with warm, delicious heat. My muscles coalesced under my skin and my nails sharpened. I glanced around and spotted Rourke just ahead of me. I took off after him, kicking my feet powerfully as I swam. Taking a swim was becoming a new norm for me. I just hoped there were no Naiads in Lake of the Isles.

If there were, it was going to be a long-ass swim.

Two more strokes and the water behind me exploded, pushing both of us forward in a rush. But the Orb wasn't on mark. The water had masked me, however slightly. Rourke had been right to dump us into the lake. It was the only chance we had.

But we couldn't stay under indefinitely.

As I swam farther, the need to take air into my lungs pressed painfully against my diaphragm. Rourke motioned me with his hand. I came up beside him. He pointed to the surface and then to himself. We needed direction.

I nodded and he shot to the surface.

He was back under in a moment. Rather than try to explain, he grabbed my arm. We took no more than ten strokes and the water became shallower. He gestured to some concrete pilings and indicated up. We both bobbed to the surface under a small bridge. I gulped air into my lungs.

"I want you to swim to the far side of the lake." He pointed toward the east. "See those islands? Swim between them. I'm going to find us a ride. The bombs aren't looking for me. When you get across, I'll be waiting." He pulled me close and kissed me roughly. His mouth was hot on mine after the cold water had chilled my lips, but it ended too quickly as he pressed me back under just as the sky above us lighted with several more Orbs.

I kicked hard, using the bridge footings to jettison me into the lake. The bombs exploded behind me. *Okay, we need more speed.* On a thought, I switched control to my wolf. She was ready, and my full Lycan form was almost instantaneous. It took us only a few minutes to reach the islands with her in control. We veered close to the shore of the southernmost island and I had to risk taking a quick gasp of air. Light started streaking toward us immediately. Her reaction time was much quicker than mine and we dove fast, going as deep as we could, but it was still incredibly shallow between the islands.

Water exploded directly above us.

That was too close. She swam hard, guiding us to the bottom. We touched both feet on the ground, half walking, half swimming. My lungs started to ache as more explosions peppered the lake.

Fairly quickly the depth leveled out, and as we neared the main shoreline, the bottom began to incline steeply. We were close. *No matter what, we run once we clear the water. If we don't see Rourke, we follow the road.* The street ran one way around the lake. We would follow it until we saw him. He would be there.

I shot out of the lake at a dead run.

The shoreline merged into a small hill, and I covered the expanse of the grassy slope in a blur, bounding over a park bench in one leap, morphing back to my human form in an instant. I gulped in deep breaths as I sprinted toward the road, hitting the asphalt right as a car screeched around a corner. It was coming toward me fast, going the wrong way on the one-way street. Several arcs of light hit the sky from the east at the same time. This was going to be close. The car raced up to me and did a 180, tires spinning. The passenger door popped open and Rourke shouted, "Get in!"

Out of the corner of my eye, I spotted several petite figures running up the street behind the car. Tally's white hair flowed out behind her. She was in the lead and yelled, "Go! They've put a containment bubble over the lake. We'll get you out." Several spells shot up from the witch's fingers and the Orbs around us exploded into nothingness. "Take the car due south at full speed. Don't stop. We'll break a hole in the barrier right as you hit."

I threw myself into what appeared to be a black Porsche and slammed the door.

Rourke wrenched the wheel to the right. "Here we go."

I grabbed on to the handhold above my head as the car flew

forward. I was sopping wet. Lake water leaked off of me all over the interior of what smelled like an extremely expensive car. "Where'd you get this?" I asked as Rourke took a curve at seventy.

"Tally had it waiting. Seems little Maggie had another vision."

"Bless that possessed child." I glanced in my side-view mirror. I could barely see the witches on the road behind us.

"Brace yourself. We're going to hit this thing hard." Rourke gunned the car forward. A shimmering mass loomed in front of us. The air wavered like a mirage on a hot day, but other than that there was no indication anything was there. A human wouldn't be able to detect it.

We hit it at 120 miles per hour.

A huge sound, like a sledgehammer crashing down on a mountain of glass, echoed around us. I instinctively covered my face with both forearms, expecting the windshield to spray us, but it held. There was a blast of red light, which must have come from the witches, and electricity shot through me like a bolt of white-hot lightning.

As we broke through to the other side, the force of it pinned me back in my seat, taking my breath.

The car had absorbed the brunt of the impact, or we would've fried in our seats. "Thank goodness this car is spelled," I called over the ebbing noise of crunching glass and metal as we sped away.

"We should be less detectable now that we're out of their enclosure," Rourke said. He took the next curve at a hundred and the car slid sideways. "Tally guaranteed on her life this car was spelled. Your signature will be cloaked as long as you stay inside." He turned to glance at me briefly, his eyes blazing. "Angie dies if I ever see her again."

As nice as that was to hear, I pointed ahead. "We've got company." Roughly three blocks ahead, a wall of sorcerers blocked the road. There was no doubt they were sorcerers because they were all bald and were decked out in flowing robes. Plus they all held wicked-looking staffs pointed directly at us. "My signature may be cloaked, but this car is not invisible," I said. "These guys can see us just fine."

"These cowards were positioned here to keep the shield up, nothing more." Rourke stamped on the accelerator and the Porsche sprang forward. The speedometer jumped to 140 as we closed in.

We were on them in seconds. They scattered, springing out of the way, swinging their staffs in unison. Blue light shot out of the tips, consuming the car as we sped past.

The force of the combined hit brought the tires temporarily off the ground.

"Is the car going to hold?" I yelled, grabbing on to the door.

"We're about to find out." Rourke gnashed his teeth.

Magic vibrated all around us, sounding like cymbal crashes in my eardrums. I wasn't sure if the witches' spell on the car would hold against this many sorcerers firing at the same time. I fumbled for the handle, pushing power out of me in a rush, channeling it into the frame of the car. *Help me fortify this. It may not work, but we have to give it a try.* My wolf was one step ahead of me, fueling energy through us so quickly I felt light-headed as a mountain of gold strands erupted in my mind. My power signature was the color of sunlight. *Aim it outward.*

It was a simple transfer of power.

The car took it greedily.

I think it's working. The car, which had glowed blue with the sorcerers' magic for a moment, now turned a hazy golden yellow. There was a sizzling sound as the spell disintegrated completely and the car returned to its normal color, thank goodness, because driving around in a glowing car would be a problem.

Rourke's foot hadn't moved off the accelerator. It was too early in the morning for anyone to be up, so the streets were fairly clear, which was a lucky break. I glanced out the back window, but the sorcerers were long gone and no one appeared to be following us.

I eased back in my seat, relaxing my death grip on the door handle. "What's the plan?" I asked as Rourke made several quick turns.

"We head out of town. I don't know how far the sorcerers' magic network stretches, but I know they need physical bodies to amplify their power. Without it they're weak. That's why there were so many of them maintaining the barrier. Once we're out of the city limits, if you stay in the car, it will be almost impossible for them to track us." Rourke's gaze was locked on the rearview mirror. "We're heading south now." He finally turned to me. "I say we continue until we hit the Ozarks."

My hands tingled with leftover adrenaline and I wrung them absentmindedly. We'd already planned to rendezvous in the Ozarks with Naomi and Ray, if he survived, in a few weeks. Rourke's cabin in the woods had been the only mutual out-of-the-way meeting spot we all knew about and could come up with in a hurry. Plus it was on our way to New Orleans. But the plan had not been to stay there. Both the vamps and the rogue wolf pack knew the location. "Do you think that's a wise idea to go there and stay for a while? Is it safe?"

"I've been turning it over in my mind and it's highly unlikely the sorcerers know about it. The vamps aren't interested in you, since you'll be on their doorstep shortly," he replied. My agreement to provide services to the vamps had not been an easy thing to tell him after we'd left Selene's lair. To his credit, he'd taken it fairly well. If crushing boulders with his fists equaled taking it well. "Your father is busy dealing with the Southern wolves, so they're occupied. If any of the fracture wolves had the balls to stick around after the fight, we can pick them off easily enough. They're young and inexperienced." The fracture pack had formed because of me, their prime objective being to eradicate me and form a new ruling power among the wolves. We'd fought them outside Rourke's cabin. "And think about it, nobody would believe we'd be stupid enough to return. The Ozarks may be the best under-the-radar place we have."

He had a point. "There's only one complication I can think of, and his name is Hank Lauder," I said. Hank had been an enemy of mine since birth and I'd recently killed his son in the same battle with the fracture pack. His last known location was in the Ozarks. According to my father, he'd never left the fight. And he was not young and inexperienced.

"So you're saying there's a chance a pissed-off werewolf out for revenge is hanging around on my mountain?" Rourke asked.

"It's definitely a possibility. My father sent two wolves to track him before I left, but I don't know if they were successful. We should talk to Tyler before we head out. He may have additional information and I want to let him know what we're doing any-way. With any luck, he's been in touch with our father by now. It's been too long since we've heard from him. Drive by the Safe House on our way out of town—we're not far from it." I gestured to the right. "Take that street."

He made the turn, but shook his head. "The Safe House is too risky. I'll buy you a disposable phone and you can call him on the road."

I turned in my seat, eyeing him. "Rourke, I understand your concern and I'm a reasonable girl. I promise to stay in the car. But I need to see my brother before we head out of town for good. If something's up with my father, we can't circle back here if we're halfway to the Ozarks. Now's the time or I don't get a chance. I'm their Alpha now. I owe them a visit before I leave town."

Rourke's knuckles flexed on the steering wheel. "Fine," he said. "But we can't linger very long." He ended on a teensy snarl.

I couldn't really blame him. It was risky to stay in town when we didn't have to, and making the adjustment to having me in his life after all those years alone with no one to question him had to be hard, but he had yet to really complain. I inhaled slowly, taking in his sweet scent. Molasses and cloves. My hand wound its way to the back of his neck, my fingertips brushing his nape softly. The man was gorgeous, so fierce and strong, and he had an innate protective nature that was not so different from the members of my own family. "I agree with you," I said quietly. "I'll talk to him quickly. In fact, you can pull over a block or two away if you want, and I'll see if I can reach him internally first, and if we sense any trouble, we can skip it altogether."

Rourke turned toward me, surprise lining his features. "That's it?"

"What?" I chuckled. "Did you expect a tantrum? I told you I was a reasonable gal."

"Well," he said, giving me a sideways grin, "it's been my experience with most women that once you—"

"Ah," I interrupted, cutting him off cleanly. I angled my body to face him. "Rule number one to building a nice, healthy relationship with me is you never, ever start sentences with 'in my experience with other women.' Ever. In fact, that phrase should be stripped from your vocabulary starting right now. I know you've lived a long life, and I don't begrudge any of your dalliances, but I don't want to know about them. And if you haven't already noticed, I'm not like 'most' women, so I don't give a rat's ass how they conduct themselves."

A low sound came out of his chest, a mixture of need and want. "Believe me, I've noticed. You're not like any female I've ever come across before." His eyes found mine. "I've waited a long time for you."

Chills raced up my spine as my wolf howled in pleasure. My lover, my protector, my mate. "I'll be sure to remind you of that often, especially when you're cursing me for making another rash decision that plunges us headfirst into trouble. Life with me isn't going to be easy, Rourke. I hope you understand what you're getting yourself into."

He gave me a smoldering stare that raked the entire length of my body and sucked all the thoughts right out of my head. "My eyes are wide open."

The need to consummate our bond rushed up in a fierce swirl of emotion, taking me by surprise. All my brain synapses fired at once. "That's...that's good to hear," I stammered. Heat flushed my face. I knew bonding with him would cement us together in a new way and I was ready—my wolf was *more* than ready. She howled again. I wasn't sure if the sudden reaction I was having to him was from all the adrenaline still racing through my veins or not.

But I didn't care.

I wanted him.

Before I could put my need into words, Rourke nodded toward my passenger window, pulling the car over slowly. "Looks like our chat about stopping at the Safe House was a little premature after all."

I turned and followed his gaze.

Outside, standing on the street corner in front of us, were my brother and Danny.

Wearing only their underwear.

5

Rourke eased the Porsche to the curb, and Tyler and Danny strode up to the window.

"Tyler, I can't get out of the car," I told him through the glass. "It's keeping me cloaked. The sorcerers tracked us back to the Coven.... But more importantly, why are the two of you standing on a street corner in your underwear?" I stifled a giggle. It was just so unexpected.

"Someone spelled the outside of the Safe House," he answered, hearing me perfectly. "The moment we set foot into the parking lot, we were covered in a slimy gel. We had to strip down to fight off the spell. Everything but our boxers came in contact with the toxic mess, and when we changed back to human, our clothes had disintegrated."

I bit my lip. "Well, I'm happy you're both still in one piece."

"Don't worry, my important bits weren't affected, in case you were wondering. If they had been, it would've been quite a different story." Danny grinned. "Where are you off to, then?" He bobbed his head toward our new ride. "It's not safe to linger here any longer. We'll meet up with you soon, but you should get out of town immediately." Danny was in charge of Pack security for a reason. He was always on alert and he was good at his job.

"We found out Marcy is safe for now. Rourke thinks we should head to the Ozarks," I answered. "He's got supplies there and knows the mountains. The sorcerers need a network, and they won't have one outside the city limits. You two can meet us there in a few weeks, once things cool down." I directed my next question at Tyler and tried not to sound too hopeful. "Did you get ahold of Dad?"

"Yes, but it was disjointed," he replied. I sat up straighter. That was good news. "He was too far away to get a clear signal—I think he said they were still somewhere in the Everglades. They're tracking the fracture group, and Redman and the rest of the Southern wolves are with him." Redman Martin was the Alpha of the U.S. Southern Territories, and my father was not a fan. It was unprecedented that he had gone down there to try and work as a team to eradicate the fracture pack. "He was glad to hear we were all safe and was a little frustrated he couldn't get through to you on his own."

I shook my head. I internally blocked my father's natural communication as Alpha, but I had no idea how I was doing it. Or how to fix it. "Did he say anything about James?" My father thought his second had gone rogue. "Did you tell him we figured out he went after Marcy?"

Tyler cleared his throat. "I did, but it didn't make him happy. I told him we'd fill him in when we knew more."

Going rogue meant a wolf willfully defied his Alpha's command. It wasn't a small thing. No matter James's reasons, my father could choose not to forgive him, which meant James would be exiled from Pack. And if James didn't assimilate into a new Pack quickly, he'd have a bounty on his head.

Rourke put his hand on mine and I turned to him. He and James had fought together long ago, and I knew they had a grudging respect for each other. "If James went after your secretary, and left his Pack willingly in a time of war, that can mean only one thing," he said, his voice firm. "Irish found his mate."

The same thought had crossed my mind the moment we'd found out he'd gone after Marcy, but there hadn't been any time to put the pieces together in a way that made sense. "If they were mated, it would certainly explain a lot." I thought about it for a moment. "And it would definitely explain his reaction to her at the Pack meeting. He pretty much carried her out of the room when she'd tried to bring me water. I think that was the first time they'd ever met face-to-face." I shook my head in wonderment. "That's big news. I don't know much about bonding, but finding your mate outside your Sect is rare, correct?" I looked to Danny, who was older than Tyler and I. He was also English. Maybe Europeans had a bunch of interspecies relationships we knew nothing about?

"I've never heard of it before," Danny answered. "But the two of you are quite an unlikely pairing as well, even though you're both shifters. Something must be tainting the well we've been drinking from, eh? Or a major tide is shifting for supernaturals everywhere, but either way it's unprecedented as far as I know."

Cats and dogs were definitely not the norm. Shifters mated with human women, since there were no females born. It had always been that way. If a Sect had males and females, they found their mates among their own kind. A pairing of two supernaturals of different gene pools had the potential to be explosive, their offspring being a rare mix of powers. Danny was right. It felt like a tectonic shift was happening in the supernatural world—and the only one who had any answers was fate. "But the two of them together is good," I said, nodding once as I made up my mind. "It means Marcy will remain safe. James will protect her ferociously.

My father will have to find a way to understand, and if he doesn't, we'll have to make him understand."

Tyler turned away from the window as he glanced down the street. "Something smells different all of a sudden." He had an uncanny knack for scenting, so it meant it was farther away than the rest of us could detect. Tyler was talented enough to smell an aura, picking up on the subtle layers of someone's personal magic. Smells still overwhelmed me. Parceling them away took skill and practice, and I hadn't had enough time to figure it out since I'd made my first change.

Danny's head went up, too, but he shook his head. "I don't smell anything, mate."

"Time to go." Rourke revved the engine, his eyes scanning the road behind us.

"One last thing before we leave," I said through the glass. "You guys need to pick up Nick. He's still at the Coven with the witches and the baby oracle. It's a long story, but it's how we found out Marcy was okay. We had to leave him there, but the sorcerers have likely bailed now that I've left, so it shouldn't be an issue. I'll be in touch as soon as I can. But if you don't hear from me before then, meet us in the Ozarks in two weeks."

Tyler's mouth opened and closed. "You lost me at 'baby oracle.'"

"Too much to go into, but he's in the huge stone mansion on the northern peninsula of Lake of the Isles. You will know which one once you arrive. My scent will be all over the yard." Rourke put the car in gear. It was time to move. "Oh, and you might want to think about finding some pants before you head over. If the witches get a gander at the two of you in your Calvin's, they may never let you leave." I grinned.

"That's hilarious, Jess." He bent over the window. His face changed to pensive in the next beat and his emotions ran through me, a mixture of worry and love. "Just make sure you stay safe.

That's the only thing that matters. Stay alive. And, cat, make sure she doesn't hurt herself. We'll see you in a few weeks."

Rourke responded, "That's my prime objective."

A few blocks up a grumbling noise shook the street.

Tyler slapped his hand on the top of the car. "Go! Get out of here. We'll take care of this."

Rourke took off from the curb, tires squealing. I glanced back to see Tyler and Danny running toward the disturbance. *You can't fight the threat in your underwear!* I yelled at my brother.

I'm not planning on staying in my underwear for long.

They dropped to the ground to shift right as Rourke turned the corner.

We drove all day, stopping only for sustenance, which Rourke went in and bought. This car was truly spelled. It didn't need any gas and there was a never-ending supply of loose twenties in the glove box, which replenished as soon as we used them. There were also insurance papers and driver's licenses with our names and pictures on them.

Witches were freaky.

I'd slept some, but most of the hours had been spent staring at Rourke with naked longing.

His delicious scent was driving me out of my mind. The small sports car was crawling with pheromones, and because we couldn't risk opening the windows, we couldn't escape them. No matter how many times I'd tried to convince him to pull over, he wouldn't, and it was clearly taking its toll on both of us. Nothing had convinced him to stop—save hunger, and that had required threatening to eat the dashboard.

I hadn't allowed myself to physically touch him in any way.

Because once it started, it wasn't going to end without a powerful climax. The adrenaline raging through my system from escaping the sorcerers had no place to go, which made his scent all the more intoxicating.

And of course we'd gotten a car without a backseat.

Tally probably had an arsenal of vehicles, and we were lucky enough to get the one with no room to do anything fun. My wolf continued to pace back and forth in my mind like a caged animal, as she had for the past fourteen hours. "So," I asked, affecting another causal conversation, "when we finally reach the Ozarks, do you think it will finally be safe enough to ditch the car?" The sun had set a few hours ago and we were close to our destination.

"Nothing has followed us thus far, so it should be okay. If not, there's no real choice but to keep moving forward," he replied. "I've taken all the back roads I can, and when we're on my turf, we have a chance to fight or outrun anyone. I have supplies all over the area. I'm not risking anything less than full armament at this point." His voice was strained as he caught me up in a look. His eyes were filled with a deep craving. "You know, this is not easy for me either. You sitting so close to me, within my reach. It's making my head pound in agony and my beast is beyond reasoning with."

My wolf howled in frustration. "Once we finally step outside this car, I'm ripping your clothes off. Enough is enough."

The steering wheel cracked and Rourke shot a glance at me, his irises radiating a beautiful emerald fire. Through clenched teeth he managed, "We're not doing anything until we get to the cabin."

I chuckled. "Yeah, like that's happening."

"Jessica—"

I sprang forward in my seat. No more reasoning. It had left the building thirteen hours ago. "Listen," I said, barely resisting shaking my finger in his face. "Our mate bond is all but choking us to death in this godforsaken car. I'm a newborn wolf in every sense, and my rationale left a long time ago. I need to finally be connected to you, and it's overpowering any good judgment I've ever had." I ran my hands through my hair and leaned over and plucked a bag of pretzels off the floor. Dry convenience-store food was a sorry substitute for sex, but it's all I had. I grumbled as I popped a handful in my mouth. "Honestly," I said around a mouthful, "I'm surprised I haven't straddled you while you're driving."

The car swerved as Rourke made a strangled sound. "You have to stop saying things like that!" His voice dropped to barely above a whisper. "Like you, my control is hanging on by a single thread. Do you know how much I want that? Want you? But our first time isn't going to be hurried like a couple of teenagers in the front seat of a car." He snarled his frustration. "I will take my time with you. Our first bonding means something."

"Fine," I grumbled like a petulant child, tossing the bag by my feet. "But I'm hiking to the cabin naked." I crossed my arms in front of me.

"Jessica!" The car bumped wildly off the road.

He straightened it with effort as I craned my neck behind us, recognizing the area. "Isn't this near the place you stored your motorcycle last time?" It was dark as night outside, but the area looked familiar. My arms prickled in anticipation—not only at the thought of being with Rourke, but I was excited because I'd fallen in love with this place once before and I thought I'd never see it again.

"Yes," Rourke said grimly. "And it couldn't have come at a better moment." He ran a slightly shaky hand over his face as he took his foot off the accelerator.

"Where are you going to park?" He'd stowed his bike behind the brush in a shallow indent of rock. "The car won't fit with your bike."

"There's a place up ahead, closer to the sulfur stream, which means less walking in the water."

"Do we have to douse ourselves again? It didn't really work out for us last time."

"The pool is mandatory."

I turned, resting my head against the seat, my eyes blazing. "You don't say?"

He gave a strangled cough. "We need to do it because it will give us an advantage if we have any unwanted visitors. They won't scent us as easily, and I want to know who's on my mountain before we hit the cabin."

"Hmm, yes, that sounds like a perfectly good explanation to get all wet."

"Jessica"—he turned to me, his face set—"if we do anything in that pool, we're never getting out."

"And I don't see anything wrong with that scenario." He shouldn't be surprised at my reaction. I'd told him five seconds ago there was nothing rational left rolling around in my brain. He shook his head and I sighed. "Okay. Fine," I conceded. "I get it. We swim, we splash, we hike, we investigate, and then we—"

He slammed on the brakes so hard the car skidded to a stop, gravel from the shoulder fanning in an arc around us, alarm all over his face. "I just saw a flash of something in the trees." His arm went up, pointing directly into the forest next to the passenger side of the car.

"Where?" I asked, immediately at attention, scanning the trees. The moon was out, but it was cloudy, which made it harder to see.

"It looked like two people, but then they were gone before I could see what they were doing."

I squinted. "I don't see anything."

"The only reason I haven't sped off in the other direction is because they weren't focused on us, and it could've been two humans."

"If they were humans, we'd still see them bumbling around." I leaned forward in my seat, still searching.

"Maybe they were apparitions."

I raised my eyebrows, turning to him. "Are you talking about ghosts? I've never seen one, but that seems highly unlikely. You know, all we need to do is open a window and scent the area." I was sick of this hermetically sealed car. It was time to make a break. "We're getting out anyway. Let's see who's here and then we can decide what to do."

"Let me straighten the wheels out first," Rourke answered, resigned.

The hairs on my arms started to rise to attention. "Hurry," I said. "I'm starting to feel something." Otherness was seeping through the witch's spell on the car. Every supernatural had the ability to detect the other. I had no idea how it worked, I was just happy it did.

"I can feel it, too, but it's muddled in here."

"I'm cracking the window," I said as Rourke put the car into park. "You ready?"

He'd angled us into a semisheltered place on the side of the road. "Fine, but I'm keeping my foot on the gas pedal, so don't get any ideas about leaving until we find out what's going—"

My window went down less than a centimeter and I knew who was out there and so did Rourke.

I flung my door open before anything else could register.

"Naomi! We're here!" I yelled as I ran headlong into the forest.

6

I slowed to a jog, turning my head from side to side trying to search for Naomi's scent trail.

"*Jesus Christ*, you can't keep doing that," Rourke growled, running up alongside me. "In the future, I'm going to have to shackle you to my wrist with some spelled handcuffs."

My wolf barked at the word "handcuffs," but I was too preoccupied. I stopped and inhaled as I spun in a slow circle. "Why isn't she here?" Then I picked up a new scent. It was familiar, yet changed. I grabbed on to Rourke's sleeve. "Do you smell that?" I started running again. "Naomi!" I called. "Where are you?"

Rourke moved behind me, keeping pace with me easily. "He smells pissed off."

"I know." Ray's signature had changed, but he still smelled like his usual malice. But I guess that was to be expected. At least we knew he had survived the transformation. Ray was going to be angry whether he lived or died. He always smelled pissed off. Now he just smelled like a pissed-off vampire.

We both jogged farther into the forest, into thicker tree cover, our noses finally leading us in the right direction. We covered a mile in a few minutes, running parallel to the river, heading toward the sulfur. Their scents were stronger here, even though the sulfur was doing its best to interfere.

"There's a break in the trees." Rourke pointed. "Let me go first."

"Let's go together." I slowed next to him. "I'm not breakable china."

Rourke snorted as his hand shot around my wrist, bringing us to a stop. "Just be prepared for the worst. He smells lethal."

I tried to steel myself. *Get ready*, I told my wolf. *This is going to be ugly.* "If Naomi was forced to bring him here early, there must have been major complications. It's lucky we arrived when we did."

"There's a possibility something went wrong with the transformation process," Rourke said.

I didn't want to think about that.

I was ultimately responsible. I'd made a split-second decision to let Naomi try to save Ray's life. My logic had been if Ray didn't want to be a vampire, we could end his life again. But this way he had a choice. In the end, I felt I owed him something. For all his orneriness, he had begun to accept us, to understand there was something different in the world. He had tried to help me and had his throat torn out for his efforts.

I hoped I'd made the right choice.

Rourke and I crept through a natural parting in the trees and entered a small clearing right by the stream's edge.

"*Ma Reine*, it's good to see you again," Naomi said as she moved forward. "I'm sorry I could not come out to meet you. I could not leave him alone, even for a minute."

I was shocked by her appearance.

But I was even more shocked by the scene in front of me.

Chains rattled as an angry voice ripped through the air. "Nice of you to join the party, *Hannon*. Glad you could finally pencil us in. Do you like what you see?" His irises shot silver one beat before a blanket of cruel black cascaded over them completely, leaving no white. He looked feral. "This is your fault," he accused. "You did this to me."

"Ray," I whispered.

"No, not Ray anymore." He hissed, his fangs snapping down sharply, distorting his sneer. "Was this your plan all along? To make me into a freak? You wanted me to sign up for your cult from the very beginning. But then on the road you made me start to trust you. Hell, I even *helped* you. And this is my reward? I'm going to eat your intestines once I'm free. Do you hear me?" He raged against his chains, which were wrapped tightly around his chest. They held, but just barely. "I've got nothing better to do than hunt you down, Hannon. For a goddamn eternity!"

"I am sorry," Naomi said, her head bowed, her hands crossed in front of her. "He has been . . . difficult to control."

"I thought newborn vamps were fledglings? Shouldn't he be concerned about where his next meal is coming from instead of exacting his vengeance on me?" Rourke paced over to the tree where Ray was chained. "I was under the impression new vampires were incoherent in the beginning."

"He did not go through any of the normal stages." Naomi shook her head, her soft French lilt barely above a whisper. "I do not understand it. He awoke in a rage. I was able to find these chains, but he breaks them often. He is weak, because he has refused to feed, and he cannot fly, so I am able to catch him when he . . . flees. But it has taken its toll. I had no choice but to come here. I had hoped you would come early, because I could not risk bringing him into a populated city to find you."

I wrenched my gaze from a furious Ray to take in Naomi's appearance again. Her clothes were tattered and full of blood. Fresh claw marks stood out along her neck and arms, healing as I watched. Her normal chestnut locks hung in dirty strands. "Naomi, I'm the one who's sorry. I should've known this could've been a possibility. Ray was a volatile human, and he died a horrendous death at the hands of your brother. I should've stayed with you to make sure there were no issues. This is all my fault."

"*Non*," she said. "We could not have known. I have changed two others before him and this is…unnatural. He is too strong. His thoughts should not be so well…formed. He should be eager to gain my approval, to learn the new ways. I am his Master, but he does not seem to feel any connection to me at all."

Ray started raging again, and surprisingly I felt a tiny flare of his emotions in my blood. My brows furrowed as I peered at him more closely. I'd given Naomi my blood to heal from an attack she would've died from when we'd been on the road, and she, in turn, had given her blood to Ray. It made some sense that he would have a bit of my signature inside him now, except I'd never felt a spark of anything from Naomi before. I'd attributed that to her being a vamp, and the emotions and feeling that were tied to my blood with the wolves didn't apply to her—that it was a species thing. That wouldn't be the case if I were connected to Ray.

"It's a conundrum," I finished.

"What did you expect, huh?" Ray snarled. "Why would you think I would ever want this? You should've let me die in peace, Hannon." Ray still referred to me by my alter ego, Molly Hannon. It was a habit I'd given up trying to break. I'll always be Hannon to him.

Rourke met my gaze. "How do you want to work this?" he asked.

I turned to Naomi. "We'll knock him out, and you fly him up to Rourke's cabin. We'll deal with him up there. I'll give him twenty-four hours to see reason. If that doesn't work—"

"What?" Ray sneered. "If I don't cooperate, you're finally going to kill me? Put me out of my misery? But guess what? I refuse to die without payback. Do you hear me? I will kill—"

Rourke's fist shot out, straight into his face, crushing the left side and knocking him out completely. Ray's head crashed down, leaning at an odd angle. If his neck had stayed intact, he should live, but healing was going to hurt like a bitch. "Nobody threatens us," Rourke growled, leaning into his unconscious body. "Especially *you*."

I had no idea how quickly Ray could regenerate from that kind of an injury, but if he was as strong as Naomi said, it would be a few hours; if not, it might take a full day. "Naomi, once you get him up the mountain, you'll have to secure him again. There's a clearing behind the cabin—a natural ring of pine trees. Put him there and chain him to the biggest tree you can find." I glanced at Rourke. "Do you have extra rope or anything that will work to bind him before we get there? Those are about to go." It looked as though Naomi had repaired the chains with her bare hands each time he'd broken through, but Ray had stressed the links to their maximum.

Rourke nodded. "There's a cave three miles east of the cabin. Look for a tall white pine growing out of the base of the mountain and you'll find it. Supplies are in there."

"Rourke and I will shift," I told her. "We can make it in less time in our true forms, and once we get up there, we'll decide what to do."

Naomi bowed her head. "I will see it done."

I grabbed on to her arm before she could leave. As I touched her, a light current of power ran through my fingertips. I'd inadvertently broken her bond with her Queen by giving her my blood, and she'd sworn her fealty to me in return. It was my duty to protect her, and I was doing an extremely shitty job.

"Naomi," I said, her eyes flicked to mine, "once Ray is secured, I want you to go. Leave here and take some time for yourself. Get cleaned up. Feed. Whatever you need. I will take care of this. It was my decision to turn him, not yours. This is my problem now. Go back to my city, north of here, and find Tyler and Danny. We had a problem with the sorcerers, but so far they haven't tracked me here. Stay there, make contact with the boys; they will help you find a place to stay and you can all come here together in a few weeks."

"I can't leave you like this. You will need my help. A new vampire is—"

"*No.*" I said the word with as much power as I could. "You've done enough. And I appreciate it more than you'll ever know. Ray will either be dead or ready to go with us when you return. I'm hoping it's the latter, but I'm not going to hold my breath. We're heading to New Orleans once you return, and I need you focused and refreshed. I've been trying to come up with the best way to tackle your bonding—or lack of bonding—with your former Queen and I have some ideas, but I need you *ready*. If you're not, there's no chance of us finding an edge. And we need an edge when we face her. That's an order."

"*Oui, Ma Reine.* I will go, then."

"And, please, for the love of everything good in the world, you have to stop calling me that. We've already covered this. I'm not your queen. This is a partnership, not a monarchy. You came into this of your own free will. You're not my subject."

The first glint of a smile spread across her lips, revealing some of the old, strong Naomi I knew was still in there. It was nice to see her again. Losing her brother Eamon and having to deal with Ray had taken its toll. It was time for me to make it right.

"It is a term of endearment only, as I have told you," she mused. "But it fits you. It truly does."

"There is nothing remotely queenly about me," I scoffed. "It's the worst title you could possibly give me."

Naomi shook her head. "That's where you are wrong. You are very queenly." Before I could argue, she walked over to Ray with purpose. Rourke had unchained him. She lifted Ray under one arm and draped the heavy metal links across her other shoulder like she'd slung on a purse. "Until then, *Ma Reine.*"

She shot into the air.

Watching vamps take flight was amazing. I'd have to ask her how it worked. My guess was their bones must be light and hollow, because they didn't need any marrow, like a bird's, and they could somehow siphon air through them or something cool like that. I shook my head and turned to Rourke. "We have to break her of calling me her queen and come up with something with less of a sovereign ring to it."

"I think it's fitting." Rourke grinned. "You're my *Reine* too." He strode over and grabbed my hips, bringing us together.

I glanced around, realizing we were suddenly alone and out of the godforsaken car. And there was no imminent threat bearing down on us. He lowered his head slowly and I let his scent wash over me for the gazillionth time. I would never grow tired of it.

When he was this close, I couldn't focus on anything else.

All my neurons fired at once and my brain became hazy. It didn't help that my wolf started running in circles yipping, contributing to the chaos.

His tongue entered my mouth, hot against mine.

I opened myself up to him easily, taking him in, my lips parting with a long sigh. *Finally.* He was soft and hard and perfect. All his strength pushed tightly up against mine, the way it should be.

He growled and pressed us together, deepening the kiss.

Our heads tilted farther and my hands shot to his chest, landing on the ridiculously tight T-shirt he'd borrowed from Tyler, now dirty and torn from the explosion. "We need to get this off of you," I murmured as I started to pull, immediately hearing a satisfying rip.

At the sound, he broke our embrace, appearing as dazed as I felt. "Jessica." His irises radiated a beautiful deep green. "Not yet. We can't do this yet." He took a small step back and ran the back of his hand over his mouth. "Your taste is like an addiction. It's so damn hard to quit once I start, but we have to go up to the cabin. Staying here is a mistake."

He was right.

I pounded my fist against his chest in frustration and then rested my forehead against it. I was one millimeter away from kicking someone's puppy. I leaned back so I could glance up at him, knowing my irises flashed the same emotion as his. "I hear you. My brain just doesn't work properly when you're around, as we learned from our happy fun time in the car. All my wolf wants to do is rip your clothes off in a mindless frenzy. It's hard not to be resentful of our obligations when all I want is to be with you."

A snarl ripped from his diaphragm and he tugged me against him, flattening his strong hands against my back, his arms locking around me tightly. He lowered his mouth against my ear and rasped, "I haven't denied myself *anything* in a thousand years. Resisting you is taking every ounce of everything I've got. My beast is clawing me from the inside out, fighting me to make this official. All I can think about is throwing you down on the grass and taking you from every angle I possibly can. Repeatedly." A small moan escaped my lips. "But if we do that, we will be lost to it for *hours* and we can't afford it right now. Your safety is more important to me." A low sound from the center of his chest spread outward and made my toes curl. "And you better believe that when I take you, I take you on *my* terms"—he ended on a whisper—"*repeatedly.*"

Goose bumps covered my flesh.

I pressed my face into his chest and tried to recover. My brain was mush. I had to take a step back to regroup. Rourke had been around a lot longer and his control was impeccable. I was a newborn and mine was not. "Rourke, how old are you?" I tilted my head up at him.

His expression held a glint of surprise. "I haven't answered a question like that in a very long time."

I shrugged. "We're a couple now, and it's time for us to be on the level about everything or this won't work. I don't know what you are—only that you're a cat of some kind. I think the basics are in order here. Don't you agree?"

"Instead of answering, I'd rather show you. Reaching the top of the mountain will be quicker and easier in our animal forms. Once we change back, we can talk." His voice held an intensity I couldn't place. Was he really worried what I'd think?

"Listen," I said, placing my palms on his pecs. "I don't care what you are, or even how old you are. We're way past that. None of it matters. You could be a two-thousand-year-old Griffin and it wouldn't matter to me."

He laughed. It was a rough, rich sound. "I'm no Griffin, but it's better if I show you."

I hesitated, reading his gaze.

He was anxious.

"Okay." I turned toward the river. "Where do you want to shift? And I hope you have spare clothes at the cabin, because mine aren't going to magically morph there."

He took my hand and led me toward the water. "I have extra clothes, but you'll have to make do with mine until everything is settled up top. I'll come back down and get yours when we're done dealing with Ray. Let's cross the river before we shift. We're fairly close to the sulfur stream, and it's straight up from there. Since we're shifting, it doesn't make sense to douse ourselves—sulfur won't mask our animal scents. They are way too strong."

I followed him into the river. The water wasn't that deep and we managed to cross to the other side without getting totally soaked. It was dark as night in the forest. He guided me to a small grassy patch. "You change here and I'll shift over there." He pointed to bushes twenty paces away. "I haven't been in front of anyone in my true form in longer than I can remember. I don't want to scare you, so let's take it slow."

I rubbed my arms absentmindedly. "You're kind of freaking me out," I admitted. "Should I be scared? And why don't you have to change very often? I thought shifters needed the release—their bodies *had* to shift."

He leaned down and planted a kiss on my forehead. "I don't ever need to shift. Once you're old enough, you gather power to yourself automatically and I've perfected it without shifting. I can't do what you can do—and achieve a full suspended form—but I can reach my beast without a full change. It gives me more power than the average shifter, but it's not like yours." I'd seen him channel his beast when we'd fought the wolves, and then again with Selene. He was incredibly controlled. The only thing that had given him away both times had been the golden fur that had sprouted along his arms.

"How old is old enough?" I pressed, curiously.

He chuckled. "Old."

Naomi's words filtered through my mind. When we'd been on the road, she'd informed me there had been rumors Rourke was close to acquiring a godhood, which was the ultimate mix of power and immortality for a supernatural. You had to be old enough, powerful enough, and have a god or goddess as your patron. But it wasn't something I felt comfortable asking yet. We hadn't even consummated our relationship. Chatting about possible god-*ness* sounded too over the top, especially since he was shy about telling me what kind of cat he was.

I pushed it out of my mind for now. "Okay"—I looked around—"this is as good a spot as any. I'll change here." Without waiting, I reached down and grabbed the end of my shirt and pulled it over my head. Rourke stood watching me, and I grinned as I tossed it away. "You better get a move on, Big Boy. You don't want to risk jumping me once I'm naked. Or I might just jump you, so you better leave while you still can."

Reluctantly he turned and left. I shimmied out of my leggings and lay down completely naked in the cool grass. Summer was moving on and the nights were getting chilly, especially in the mountains. My nipples budded painfully and I forced myself to ignore how much they ached.

"Are you ready?" Rourke called from his spot. His voice sounded strained and I knew without a doubt he could see me and it was killing him.

I felt a little better. At least I wasn't the only letch in town.

"Ready." I switched control to my wolf on a thought.

The shift was smooth and effortless.

My body had become more accustomed to shifting with each change. The first time had been a train wreck. I'd fought it with everything I had, and it had been the worst thing I could've done. Now it felt natural and fluid. My back arched as my legs extended. Fur sprouted along my skin like a soft blanket.

The change took less than a minute.

Once I was finished, I blinked and glanced around. The night was clear. Everything was more detailed and easier to see in this form. We called our animal form our "true form" because it was our body's most natural form. We hailed from humans, spent most of our time in a human form, but animals were our true nature. It felt unbelievably free to be in this body. This is what all shifters craved.

I lifted my muzzle to the sky, resisting the urge to howl. The darkness wasn't absolute. Instead objects glowed around me in an amber haze, my eyes gathering light from everywhere so I could detect the smallest details. As I stood, I inhaled, raking air in over my sensitive tongue, tasting all the flavors of the night.

Then his scent hit me.

My wolf barked and our voice carried into the night sky. We were linked so closely in this form that control hung on a blink. My heart began to race as his musk engulfed us. I was in control now, but my wolf was agitated and a low growl escaped.

His scent was a thousand times stronger in his true form.

Cloves and rich molasses were intertwined with a kind of power that I didn't understand. It didn't feel godlike, like Selene's had, but it was still incredibly strong. His smell calmed us, but his power frightened us. It sent currents of pressure into our body, warning us, urging us to flee. My wolf wanted to run. *No, hold still. This is right.* She whined and pushed herself into me, making us stagger. *I know. I smell it, too, but he's not going to hurt us. Focus on the signature, not on the power.*

Rustling came from the bushes.

Rourke had finished his change even before we had, but he was letting us get used to him.

That may take longer than we had.

I opened my mouth and huffed into the air, telling him we were ready.

After a second, he stepped into view. One paw at a time until he stood only a few paces from us.

Oh, dear gods. What is he?

He lifted his tawny head to the sky and roared.

7

He took another step closer and stopped. Power surged off him in crisp waves and it was all I could do not to turn tail and run.

He was massive.

And one of the most beautiful creatures I'd ever seen. *Is he a lion or a tiger?* His fur was a rich gold, like a lion's, but intricate dark stripes flowed over him, like a tiger. He didn't have a mane. His fur was short, not shaggy—more like a puma's. But he was clearly a Big Cat. His front incisors were curved and long, indicating his age. Nothing like him existed today. No lions and tigers had curved canines anymore. His weren't massive like a saber-toothed tiger, but they were long enough.

Whatever he was, I'd never seen anything like it.

I took a tentative step forward and he whined at me, urging me to come closer. Cats and dogs were naturally leery of each other and this was strange in the extreme. For a moment it felt like fate had played a trick on me. And instead of being mated, Rourke would gobble me up the moment I stepped closer.

Sensing my trepidation, he sat down.

When I didn't move, he sprawled on his stomach and lowered his head so I stood clearly above him.

It was enough to make me take another few steps closer.

My muzzle stretched out to him, scenting. He smelled like heaven, which was in direct odds with this scenario. When I got close enough, he reached up and licked my chin, his giant tongue covering all of it. I eased considerably, as did my wolf. She yipped, and the sound carried out of our shared vocal cords. I had to be careful, because all these heady emotions made our control bounce back and forth, and she would love nothing more than to take the reins.

He snuffed at us.

I moved back as he stood. He was a shoulder taller than I was, his beautiful eyes radiating outward. He was glorious.

He paced by my flank, rubbing up against me, scenting me and marking me to others. Then he started forward into the woods, and when I didn't immediately follow, he huffed once over his shoulder before taking off into the night.

I took off after him, barking joyfully into the darkness.

We ran quickly, hitting the base of the mountain within moments. A cat was better tailored to pick its way over rocks as we climbed, but I kept up just fine, even though he kept circling back to make sure we were okay.

After the third time, I snarled a warning.

He can't keep babying us. We may not be as seasoned as he is, but we're strong too. My wolf growled at the thought of us being weak. *I didn't say we were weak, but on a scale of power, Rourke has us beat.* She flashed an image of us tearing a similar lion to shreds. *Come on, you felt his power. It's off the charts. It almost hurts it's so strong, and a minute ago you wanted to turn tail and run.* She snarled, flashing a box in my mind. The very same one she'd shown me when we'd gotten into trouble with the Mahrac. I'd thought that once she opened it, it would contain more power than I could handle. But I'd absorbed it fully because it had been mine all along. At the time, I hadn't known how to tap into it. *I get it. I can sense the power inside us, but stronger than Rourke? That seems unlikely. He radiates it. Power leaks out of him like he can't possibly contain it. Ours is not like that.*

At once my body quivered and adrenaline raced out before I could stop it.

My wolf was teaching me a lesson.

Hey, no need to go crazy—Before I could say any more, my muscles coalesced under my skin, harder and bigger than they'd been a second ago. My fur started to prick as currents of energy raced along my spine, like fireworks bursting outward from all the nerve endings in my body.

Rourke snarled, turning toward us, sensing the power fluctuation.

He raised his head, trying to scent danger, wondering what I was reacting to. Not seeing anything around us, he charged into the trees roaring. A giant buck leapt out of the undergrowth and bounded off. Rourke paced back out, his body lithe and primal. He was so lethal; currents of his power whipped up and down my hide, reaching me easily where I stood.

There was no way to tell him I was only reacting to my stubborn wolf.

Power was still seeping out of me at an alarming rate, from every cell of my being, where it seemed to have been patiently waiting all along. I felt light-headed but invincible at the same time. It was a dangerous feeling. *Why are you doing this now?* She growled at me, frustrated. *I can't help that it's going to take me longer to figure out the stuff you already know, just like it's going to take you time to be patient with our human obligations. Manipulating power is no small task.* She clacked her jaws at me. My wolf was an old soul, that much was certain. She was sure of herself in ways that came only with age. It made reasoning with her incredibly difficult when she was intent on proving her point. I had no idea how the Prophecy worked, and what it entailed, but this was the card I'd been dealt. She and I had to learn to work together for the long term. We were two sides of the same coin and we had to start acting like it.

Rourke paced around me, a low growl emanating from him in a constant thrum. Instead of trying to deal with the situation, since I had no words to give him, I took off, leaping ahead of him in one giant bound. I flew over the surfaces, making my way up the mountain quickly.

Rourke followed at my heels, quiet but alert.

We crested the top and I raced across the expanse, bounding into the clearing where the small cabin stood before I realized I was even there. I skidded to a stop in front of the quaint structure. Moonlight cascaded down on the grounds and it looked as picturesque as I remembered. I moved forward and stuck my nose near the doorjamb and inhaled.

I could detect traces of vamps, wolves, and Selene, as well as residual smells from the battle we'd fought, but no humans had been here. It was a difficult place for them to access easily, but I wanted to be sure. I was tall enough to see inside the glass partition in the door, and it was just as homey as the image in my mind. A growl escaped, knowing there was food and a bed for us in the loft.

I turned slowly.

Rourke stood a safe distance away, his head up, nostrils flared. A low, menacing sound issued from the back of his throat, but it wasn't because of any danger.

He was reacting to me.

I paced out from the cabin as he came forward.

One step at a time.

He notices we've changed. I wonder what our power feels like? As soon as we shifted back, I'd ask him, but it still made me wonder. *Okay, I confess, you were right—we have more power than I realize on a daily basis—but I don't necessarily think we'd win a battle against Rourke just yet.* My wolf snarled. *Please, we are so inexperienced. Someone like Rourke, who's been fighting and honing his skills for centuries, would beat us. Power or no power.* She bit the air in front of her. *It's nothing to be ashamed of. It just means we need some polishing. And guess what? I know just the cat to help us. And that's a lucky break if you ask me. The top fighter in the supernatural world is our mate. Score one for us.*

Rourke sensed something.

His ears perked, and he took off into the trees. I followed, catching up as he slowed just outside of the cathedral of pine trees. This was the very same place where I'd made my second shift into a wolf and discovered he was my mate. This area had a special aura, heightened to me in this form. It vibrated with a quiet intensity. Natural circles, such as this one, were very powerful. This one was no exception.

I'd bet my life that Rourke finding this place had been no accident.

Ray's new vamp signature was all over.

By the smell of it, Naomi had left less than five minutes ago, her scent just beginning to fade. She'd waited until she heard us, covering my ass like a champ. But I was glad she'd taken my order to leave seriously. Dealing with the Vamp Queen was going to take skill. She needed to be rested and ready before we took on that challenge.

Ray was inside the circle.

I followed Rourke through the trees, ducking my head to dodge the low-hanging branches. We both padded into the middle. The grass was neatly trimmed, which added to the uniqueness of the surroundings. It shouldn't be this groomed, yet it was.

Ray was secured to a massive pine tree on the other side. Naomi had doubled his bonds with chains she'd found from Rourke's stash. I yipped at Rourke and he huffed, unmoving, nodding once. I stepped closer, inhaling.

There was blood in the air.

I scented only Ray's, but we had to make sure. His face was still caved in, but from my vantage point, it appeared to be healing. He was still out cold, thank goodness. I lifted my head to the starry sky, gauging it was about ten or eleven at night. There was still time, but we would need to get him out of the direct threat of sunlight before dawn.

Power vibrated around me.

I glanced over to see Rourke had begun to shift back into his human form. I dropped down to follow his lead but stopped when I heard his voice. "Jessica, don't shift yet. Stay here. Keep your senses focused outward while I move Ray to a safer place. We can't leave him here overnight. There's another cave less than a mile away where I can hold him securely." He stretched as he stood. "He's not my first guest."

I barked my objection. I wanted to go with them.

"It's better for you to stay here." He walked over to Ray. "I don't smell anything brand-new, but there is a lingering scent of wolf that could be trouble." He bent over and grabbed on to the massive padlock Naomi had used to secure Ray and crushed it with his fist.

He was completely naked.

Even though I thought he looked glorious nude, perfectly chiseled with hard lines and firm muscle, I hoped to the high heavens Ray didn't wake up. *If he does, he's in for the first ever vampire cardiac arrest.* I chuckled to myself and the sound came out in short snuffs.

Rourke wrapped the layers of chains around his chest and hoisted a still-unconscious Ray over his right shoulder. *Well, at least the chains are separating all his parts from Ray.* It afforded Rourke a little modesty. He disappeared into the forest and I trotted to the other side of the tree line closest to the cabin. There were a lot of smells, but none of them seemed particularly fresh.

Picking up a strange smell of mustiness, I followed the circle, weaving my way in and out of the trees. I walked outside to investigate and was just about to head back to the center to wait for Rourke when a low growl rent the air.

No more than thirty paces from me.

It sounded like a wolf, but I couldn't see what it was.

I lowered myself into a fighting stance and cocked my head, lifting my nose. *I still don't smell anything clearly. Do you?* My wolf was at attention, already standing sentinel against the threat. *Can you detect any movement?* We took a step closer. The growling increased and something rustled to my left. It rose off the ground slowly and shook itself off, and right as it began to move, its scent hit me.

An old, decayed smell almost fully masked its signature, but there was no mistaking who it was.

Hank.

How come we didn't scent him before? As he shook his coat and paced forward, I realized why.

Hank had lain down to die.

He'd dug himself into the earth and had been covered in mud, pine needles, wet leaves, and moldy dirt.

There was no indication any other wolves were here. My father had told me before I'd left town that he'd dispatched two wolves to track and find Hank. As I inhaled once again, I opened my mouth, tasting the air. There was a very faint scent of death, but it wasn't in the immediate area. Hank had likely killed them and taken their bodies somewhere days ago. *We attack first and catch him off guard. It looks like he hasn't eaten in a long time.* I hoped that meant he was weaker than usual, because Hank was a fighter.

He growled at me, his eyes beginning to spark a deep amber.

My wolf pitched her muzzle in the air and we let out a deafening howl into the night sky, letting Rourke know there was trouble.

Then we sprang.

My claws hit Hank's flank hard, tumbling us both down to the ground. He snarled, rolling away quickly, adrenaline aiding his fight-or-flight instincts. Hank was a mean wolf, which had always given him an edge, and he was getting his gumption back more quickly than I'd hoped.

He turned and lunged, snarling furiously, saliva leaking from his jaws. I'd just given him the only reason to ever emerge from his grave. To exact revenge. I'd killed his only son and this was his chance—his *last* chance, and likely one he didn't think was possible until a few minutes ago—to avenge his son's death.

I sidestepped him as he came at me, sinking my teeth into his hind leg and biting hard.

He yipped and stumbled forward and I rounded on him quickly. *We are not losing this advantage. I want to be done with this … and him.* I aimed for his neck, but he surprised me by lashing out and connecting with my head. His jaws were around me before I could blink.

A mew escaped my throat as a ferocious snarl erupted right behind me.

Hank heard it too. He unlatched his hold on me reluctantly and peered around my body. I followed his gaze. Rourke stood behind us. He had shifted again. *He's not taking any chances,* I told my wolf. *He can kill Hank in seven seconds in that form.* The snarl coming out of him was full of menace.

But this was my fight.

It was mine and I wanted it. Hank had made my life a living hell since the day I'd been born. I'd dispatched his son with no regret, and I needed this saga to end on my terms. Wolves fought for status constantly; it's what we craved. It was our hierarchy. If I beat Hank, it meant I was superior to him in all ways. I wanted that. I *deserved* it.

I snarled back at my mate, warning him to back off.

His ears shot up. The surprise lacing his features almost made me laugh.

He took a tentative step forward and I snapped my jaws decisively, letting him know I'd keep him posted if I needed him. He cocked his head and sat down with a thump, a small questioning huff escaping his lips. *I'm sorry you don't like it, honey. But that's the way it's going to be.*

Hank growled. All my wounds had already healed from our little altercation. I took a step back and allowed Hank to regroup. I wanted a fair fight. He glanced from me to Rourke, trying to figure out the dynamic. I barked until Hank brought his attention back to me.

If wolves could sneer, Hank achieved it.

Then, surprising me, he turned tail and ran.

I took off after him. *That coward!* He'd always been gutless, riling up the younger wolves to threaten and abuse me and do his dirty work for him. I'd had enough. I flew through the air, landing on top of his back, sending us both somersaulting. We separated as we hit the ground. He smashed into the trunk of a massive tree, shaking it to its roots.

Rourke had followed and paced to my right, agitated.

As Hank stood and shook himself off, I yipped and barked, telling him exactly what I thought of him. *I can't believe he ran! No wolf with any self-respect runs from a fight.* My wolf agreed and the sounds of our yips echoed around the forest. *Can he just give up?* He'd chosen to lie down and die instead of coming after me. He was a proud wolf, and finding out his son was a traitor to Pack must have crushed something in him greater than his need to kill me. My father had always trusted him, even though I'd felt he never deserved it. There must've been more to their bond as Alpha and wolf than I knew. *If I don't kill him now, my father will have to. His son was a traitor to Pack and there's no way he didn't know. He faces a sentence of death either way.*

I paced back and forth, trying to figure out how to handle this. I was learning I wasn't a cold-blooded killer. Hank deserved to die, in more ways than I could adequately count, but if he wasn't going to fight me, it would be hard for me to finish him off.

Hank seemed to sense my change of heart, as did Rourke, who snarled his objections loudly. Hank's eyes flared as he opened his mouth in what could only be another grin. He yipped at me once and it held one word: *pussy*.

I snarled and splayed my paws on the ground, lowering my head, barking, and urging him to fight.

Instead of lunging, Hank turned parallel to me and lifted his back leg. The pungent smell of his urine hit the air.

He did not just do that. It was a clear challenge. And it was enough for me. I took the bait without regret. *This is all you*, I told my wolf as I handed the task over to her with relief. She, unlike me, had no qualms about killing him. We dove for his neck in a blur, taking hold and biting deeply. Hank fought back, snarling and lashing out with his hind legs. I was happy he decided to fight; it made it easier. He wiggled at just the right angle and my wolf lost her grip. He had me in the next breath, his jaws embedded deeply in my back.

Rourke sprang forward, bellowing.

My wolf twisted our body and we slipped out of Hank's grasp. I snapped my teeth at Rourke before he could intervene, a snarl ripping from my throat. He slid to a stop midstride and yowled at me angrily, but I ignored him.

Hank was fighting. And he was mine.

I moved to face him and we circled each other. Hank's neck was torn, and because he hadn't eaten in days, he wasn't regenerating quickly. He sprang without warning and his teeth caught my leg, hard.

It's time to be done. My wolf barked her agreement.

She leapt, tearing free of his grasp, our body twisting, claws slashing down deeply into his body. He howled in pain as we landed on him, crushing him to the ground with our weight. She brought our jaws down on his neck and didn't let up. He struggled beneath us, spitting and growling. No need to drag this out.

In one motion, she twisted his neck and gave it one final, powerful snap.

There was one loud crack and Hank went still beneath us.

She dropped her hold on him and control switched back to me. I took a few steps backward.

Relief flooded through me to see the deed done, but it was far from the satisfaction I knew a normal wolf should feel. Instead I just felt tired. This was a man who hated me. He deserved to die. I shouldn't feel sorry for him.

But I did.

Rourke brushed up against my body, comforting me.

He sat close to me as we watched Hank shift. His final death would make him human for the last time.

In his human form he was gaunt and dirty. I hoped he'd finally found some peace. Even if Hank hadn't known exactly what his son had been doing, he had willingly ignored it and in the process became an accomplice.

Rourke nudged me once it was over and I turned to follow him.

He led me back into the circle, checking over his shoulder to make sure I stayed with him every step of the way.

Once we were inside, we lay down side by side and shifted back.

The moonlight highlighted our naked forms as he reached for me.

8

His lips sought mine as my arms wrapped around his neck. He gently rolled me on my side in the grass, our bodies pressed closely together. He felt wonderful.

He pulled back and stroked my hair and face as his irises blazed a beautiful green. "Are you okay?"

"I'm fine," I murmured. "Much better now. It had to be done and I don't regret doing it. Hank would've died at the hands of my father and he knew it. But I don't think killing will ever be my thing."

He brought our faces closer, his stubble stroking my cheek in a delicious way. "I could've helped, you know. When I'm around, you don't have to kill. I am happy to do that for you." He kissed me.

Finally.

I raked my fingers through his hair, twisting it in my hands. It was soft and thick. He pulled back slightly, studying me, making sure I was really okay before we started something that couldn't be undone.

"I'm good, really," I said, answering his gaze. "It was our first status fight and my wolf is happy with the outcome." I leaned up and bit his bottom lip before he could reply.

He responded in kind by plunging his tongue deeply into my mouth while his lips locked around mine, and I took it, pulling greedily, finally fully tasting him.

I moaned, the pleasure of it overwhelming and maddening at the same time.

Power swirled around the circle as our kisses became fast and frenzied.

This was the perfect place for us to bond. Energy pushed and prodded against our skin, urging us along. The grass felt like velvet beneath my back and the cool air brushed deliciously against my naked skin.

I knew we were safe and protected, even if it was just for the moment.

Rourke broke the kiss and hovered over me anxiously, his eyes filled with the same longing as mine. "I haven't cared about another living soul in longer than I can remember. I want this to be exactly right."

"It will be." I smiled.

Rourke arched one perfect eyebrow down at me and grinned. "It better be, or my manhood will be in serious question."

"I don't think your manhood will ever be in question." I laughed, feeling his hard, and very adequate, length against me. "You've got that department all shored up."

"When we finish this bonding, it will mark us both." His chest pressed tightly to mine, and as he spoke the vibrations sent delicious currents dancing through my body. "Once it's over we will be connected. Forever."

"That sounds like heaven to me." I ran a hand behind his neck and pulled him down, murmuring into his lips, "And just so you know, I think we should do this bonding thing over and over again, just to make sure it sticks." I wiggled beneath him to show him my body was more than ready.

His breath hitched, and he grabbed on to my hips, rocking them forward in his grasp as he tilted his head up to the sky and roared. His fierce call echoed through the trees, and I was certain every animal in the forest turned tail and ran.

Mine.

He took my mouth again with a savage snarl. His kiss held so much intent, my libido skyrocketed, flushing my body with liquid heat. His intensity made me insane with need, and I plunged my tongue against his, lapping and tasting and biting. He broke the kiss with a moan and ran his hot tongue over my jaw, down my neck, nipping and nibbling as he went.

My back arched and I groaned.

He took one of my hard peaks into his mouth, sucking hard.

I yelled as my hands shot to his hair again, grabbing thick handfuls, pressing him down against me as far as he could go. He snarled with pleasure and took more of me in his mouth, his fingers seeking the other tip, rubbing and pulling deliciously.

"*Oh.*" My spine bowed backward until it felt like it would break in half. But I didn't let go. I wanted him closer—*needed* to feel him everywhere.

He obliged by pressing us together as he devoured me, his mouth greedy, his hands just as skilled.

Sensations I'd never felt swept over me, threatening to overload me. Nothing in my life had prepared me for something like this. As we moved together, our energy mingled, combining and weaving itself into one. The intensity mounted, climbing quickly.

Mine.

His hand slid down my stomach, lingering for a moment before he teased open the inside of my thigh. Once there, a single fingertip feathered its way in, circling slowly. I thrashed, barely stifling a scream. At my reaction, Rourke slid his hand back up my thigh.

"*No...please, you can't stop,*" I moaned. "Rourke, I know you want to take it slow, but maybe that can be round two... or three?" My eyes sought his, my pupils struggling to focus. "There's no way I can do this slowly. I need you, and my body isn't going to play nice." I panted, shifting my legs toward his hand. "If you don't want me to be early to the party, we need to move *now.*"

Without hesitation, Rourke reared up, grabbing on to my waist and rolling us both in one motion. He swung me into a sitting position on top of his rock-hard abs as his back hit the grass. His eyes locked onto mine the entire time.

I couldn't break my gaze from his even as his hardness pressed against my backside. Anticipation raced along every nerve ending in my body and I panted. "I'm sorry." My breath hitched. "I'd love to take this slow, but I'm a newborn and it's too—"

"*Shhh.*" His palms ran over me, caressing my stomach, my breasts, and finally my lips. His thumbs traced over my jawline; his fingertips spread along the back of my neck. "I wasn't going to be able to wait either. If you had touched me in any way, I would've exploded. I just wanted to make sure you were happy."

"I'm so incredibly happy." To prove it, I took his thumb in my mouth, surprising us both. I sucked, pulling hard, and we both growled in pleasure. I turned my head to taste the other one before he slid them both down and ran the wet tips back and forth across my aching nipples. My head fell backward and I moaned, arching my head up, lost.

"Gods, you feel so good," he murmured. He ran his hands up and down my sides, each of his fingertips sending tingles of energy pinging into my skin.

His touch was threatening to overload me on every level.

My eyes were fully dilated. Rourke was talking to me, but I couldn't decipher his words. Instead of trying to understand, I rocked my hips, rubbing myself over the tip of his hardness.

He gave a strangled yell as our heat met.

I bent forward and angled my hips up, readjusting myself, bracing my knees along the length of his body. I splayed my palms across his hard chest and broke contact with his skin for the first time. His hands shot to my waist. "Yes, Jessica, just like that." He guided me upward, the rumblings of his voice making me shudder.

In the moment before we connected, I lowered a hand between us and caressed his length softly all the way to the base.

"Jessica! My gods, do it now!"

"Glad to see I'm not the only harlot around here." I arched up and guided him into me, stroking my hand down his length as my body took him fully.

The moment his tip broke through my barrier, everything changed.

Energy and power swirled around us, engulfing us in a fog of magic. Every touch we exchanged was electrified, every connection point heightened. I seated myself on him, rocking forward, absorbing the moment, my head tilted up toward the sky, my hair streaming down my back.

"Jessica," Rourke whispered. "Look at me. Please." He moved beneath me and I cried out.

I brought my head down slowly, arching over him, my hair falling onto his chest. I ran my hands across his shoulders, my fingers stopping to cup the back of his neck, the cool grass contrasting my searing heat.

He growled, eyes pinned on mine. At once he shifted his weight and eased himself up into a sitting position. I wrapped my legs around his waist as he moved, my arms winding tightly around his neck, and in one swift motion we were connected completely, every one of our body parts aligned.

He leaned up, his mouth covering mine, his tongue thrusting deep.

I moaned into his lips as we started to move together. His hands slid around my thighs, his muscles deftly angling me up and down in a rhythm that made me cry out. My hands sought his shoulders tightly, my nails sinking into his flesh, every inch of me on fire.

Intensity mounted with each stroke, making me frenzied. I rocked my hips harder against him with each thrust. I couldn't believe I hadn't climaxed yet, but the passion and energy kept building, needing to reach its absolute peak before the final crescendo.

"We come together," he said through gritted teeth.

"I'm so close," I panted. "But it feels so good . . . I don't want it to stop."

Rourke's grip tightened; his chest strained against my stomach as the strokes came harder and harder. My hands fisted into his hair. It was almost there. I lowered my gaze to meet his, my eyes blazing violet. His emerald stare consumed me, his features crushing me with their need. I leaned down, connecting our lips right as I reached my release. I latched on to his mouth as I came, my body contracting hard.

"*Jessica*," he shouted, right behind me.

As the shudders came, one after another, a blast of energy raced through our bodies, connecting us, binding us together.

My eyes shot open as the last of the currents of pleasure claimed me, my arms encircling Rourke's neck, my cheek to his. "Did you see that?" I murmured. "Was it my imagination or did we both just light up like Christmas trees?"

"You definitely had an inner glow going on for a beat or two," he said. "That was intense."

"Crazy good." I traced the tip of my nose along his stubble. He smelled rich and potent. I wanted to bathe in his scent.

He chuckled. "*Good* doesn't come close. That was the best sex I've ever had in my entire life, and believe me—"

I rapped a knuckle down on the top of his head, which he responded to with a laugh as he rolled me carefully onto my back.

To my surprise, he was still hard enough to stay inside, and as he braced his hands on the ground next to my shoulders, he drew himself in and out languorously, his face full of mischief. My fingers curled around his forearms as delicious aftershocks rippled through me. "Oh," I said. "You are extremely... *talented.*" My toes curled as my body pulsed for a third time.

He leaned down to nip at my neck. "Did you doubt it?"

Cocky bastard. No, I didn't doubt it. This is the best sex I've ever had.

That's good to know, because this is how I'm doing it each and every time. Nice and thorough.

"*Ohmygod,*" I sputtered out loud. "You heard my thoughts!"

He chuckled. "Yes, I did..." *But just so you know, I'm the last cocky bastard who ever gets to do this to you.* He rocked into me hard to prove his point, putting the perfect pressure right where it belonged, and my body spasmed again.

I grabbed handfuls of earth to steady myself. He felt so damn good.

When my body finally quieted, Rourke lay down on top of me, covering me with his warmth, grinning like a cat. I obliged by locking my thighs around his ass. "We needed that," I said. "I finally feel settled. Well, other than all the tingling and zinging, I'm totally and completely content."

"We are a bonded pair now. I can feel your essence inside me, and you can do things for me no one else can, including calm my beast, as I can quiet yours. It's a good thing, too, because you're going to need it."

I tried to swat at him, but he batted my arm away, chuckling.

"Speaking of your beast—you are magnificent." My voice was full of awe and respect, and I wanted him to hear it. "I know your species is extinct. I've only seen pictures of Big Cats in books, but nothing exact. What are you? Some kind of saber-toothed tiger?"

"There's actually no 'tiger' in saber-toothed tiger. We're just big cats, but yes, I'm from a similar gene pool. I'm what humans classify as a *Barbour's Cat*. Those big saber-toothed cats were my ancestors. A small pack of Barbour's evolved and remained alive until roughly a thousand years ago."

"Barbour's are certainly fierce," I said. "You radiate strength."

"We were always the fiercest," he said, a little sadness tingeing his voice.

"How long have you been alone, away from your Pride?"

"A long time."

I lifted my head and gave him a long kiss. "Well, you're not alone anymore."

His eyes flared as he rolled off of me, disconnecting us and making me feel an instant loss. Before I could protest, he bent down and scooped me up, cradling me closely in his strong arms.

"I could get used to this." I laughed as I wrapped my hands around his neck.

He walked us out of the circle of pines, and as we passed through their protective branches, the foggy night air opened around us. I shivered and glanced over his shoulder as he made his way toward the cabin. The air inside the circle seemed to shimmer.

Rourke carried me to the door of the cabin. Our cabin. It was unlocked, and I reached down and turned the knob so we could enter together. He carried me over the threshold and I smiled like a fiend. It was bar none the most romantic thing anyone had ever done for me.

"My first priority is to feed you," he said as he slid my body slowly along his and set me on the counter. "Which I'm going to thoroughly enjoy watching."

We'd both been politely ignoring my stomach grumbles for a while.

I had learned to master my hunger, which meant I ignored it. There was no possible way I could ever feed myself enough to feel fully satiated, so I continued to parcel it away so it didn't drive me insane.

But he was right; I was starved.

"Then I'm going to take you again right on this counter." He bent down and cupped my bottom, nipping my lips as he read-justed me on the smooth surface.

"When you look at it like that," I said, "all I want for dinner is *you*." I ran a single finger from his chin to his sternum, a sly smile playing on my lips. "Unless, of course, you need time to recuperate before... what is it? Round three?"

"I've never had to recuperate a day in my life."

I barely had time to grab on to the cupboards.

9

"We broke the countertop." My voice was full of sleep as I peered down at the carnage from the loft. Sunlight had begun to filter out of the small western window. It was going to be full dark soon. We'd slept all day—well, *almost* all day. "And that adorable antique table is in pieces."

"It can all be fixed," Rourke murmured as he wrapped his warm arms around me and nuzzled my back. "I'll make sure I bring stronger building material next time. Something tough enough to withstand an insatiable female werewolf."

"Very funny." I ran my hands over his warm forearms, my fingertips tracing his beautiful tattoos. "You're the one who should talk. You threw me around the room like your own personal puppet. This place is breakable. We need to watch ourselves. I love this cabin. I don't want to destroy it."

He growled, low and raspy, his breath hitting my neck and smelling like sweet cinnamon. "If we have sex like that, I don't care if there's one piece of furniture left standing when we're done. Whatever damage we do is totally worth it."

It *was* damn good sex.

I continued tracing the lines of the dark tattoos running up both his forearms, loving the feel of his skin against the pads of my fingers. "Rourke, these tattoos are unique and amazing, but this is not ink. They follow the pattern of your fur exactly, but they're only on your arms. How did you get them?"

"They appeared the day I became Alpha."

Of course he'd been Alpha. "I should've guessed you were the leader of your Pride." It must've been hard losing everyone over the years. "Is that what happens to all Alpha cats? I've never seen another shifter with distinct markings like this." But that didn't count for much, since I didn't know many other species personally.

"I honestly don't know," he said, adjusting his body to lie on his back. "I was the first in my line to get them and I've never seen any other shifter with markings that weren't man-made. But they might have them and just keep them concealed. It's hard to know."

I turned and propped myself up on my elbow. "What do you think they mean?"

He grinned. "I've had a long time to ponder that very question, and my best guess is they're linked to why I can channel my beast so well without shifting. But in recent years, I've been leaning toward the theory they're pure eye candy. Meet Chick Magnet One and Two." He pulled his arms up and flexed. The tattoos wrapping around his biceps jumped tantalizingly.

I shoved his chest, laughing. "I already told you, there's no need to talk about—" I sat up abruptly, my head turning toward the door.

"What is it?" He was alert next to me.

"My blood just jumped with something. I think it's Tyler, but it's too muddled to tell," I replied. "We need to get out of bed—"

Shouts hit the yard, and ten seconds later the front door of the cabin burst open and Tyler tumbled into the room, followed four seconds later by Danny.

They were both out of breath.

I was relieved to see they were all right but couldn't help being irritated. "Jeez, you two. Doesn't anyone knock anymore?" I leaned down and grabbed the old patchwork comforter bunched at the bottom of the mattress. I snagged it too quickly and it ripped. I put a scrap no bigger than a throw pillow in front of me as Rourke wrapped his arms around my more delicate parts while I tried to organize myself.

"What's happened in here, then?" Danny asked, glancing around at the damage. "I see someone with a violent nature has ransacked the place." He bent over and picked up a piece of the countertop, examining it. Then he looked up at us and winked.

I pointedly ignored his toothy grin. "It's time to explain why you're here." Now that they were standing in front of me, I felt their anxiety bubbling in my blood. Something was seriously wrong. Their arrival on the mountain must have been what had finally woken me up; I'd just been too sleepy to read the signs. "Tell me nothing has happened to Dad." I scooted to the edge of the loft as Rourke handed me the rest of the covers.

"It's not that something's happened to Dad yet," Tyler answered, moving forward into the tiny room, kicking debris out of his way. "But something *may* happen and I can't reach him to find out if he's okay or warn him."

I mumbled behind me, "Rourke, I'm going to need some clothes."

"I'm on it." Rourke deftly maneuvered himself out of the loft, which was no small task given how large he was and how tiny the headroom was. I don't even remember how we got up here last night. I must have been half asleep. Or more like drowning in ecstasy. I shivered, remembering.

He jumped, landing easily, and walked over to a cedar chest tucked under the window and lifted the lid. One of the few things that hadn't been damaged. He had no qualms about being naked and the boys didn't even glance at him.

I addressed my brother. "Why didn't you try to talk to me internally if you thought something was up with Dad?" I asked.

"I've been trying all night." He guffawed. "But it seems you were a little *busy*. I thought something was wrong because you didn't answer. But I can see from the carnage around me that everything is going along swimmingly."

My face flushed.

"Don't worry, sis," Tyler joked. "I didn't hear anything. It was like your mind just sort of checked out. But this warranted a trip here to find you, because we need to adapt our plans quickly."

"What are you talking about? What's wrong?" Rourke tossed me up an old T-shirt of his and a huge pair of sweatpants, thankfully with a drawstring. They both smelled like dusty old cedar mixed with cloves. I pulled them on quickly, both boys averting their eyes politely.

Once I was done dressing, I looked around for the ladder and saw why Rourke hadn't used it. It was broken in three pieces on the floor. *Jesus.* I leapt, landing easily on the balls of my feet.

Tyler started to pace, which was never a good sign. "I tried to connect with Dad a few times after you left town. At first I got this strange humming sound. Then it turned to this funny static. After that, I was worried, so I shifted again and tried for an hour to get through with no results. It was like a void."

"That doesn't sound good," I said, rubbing the back of my neck. "But he can't be dead or we'd know it." An Alpha was bound to his Pack. Upon his death, it reverberated through our bodies, because without a leader, wolves were lost. A replacement had to be found quickly.

"I don't think he's dead...yet," Tyler said, meeting my eyes, anguish lying just behind them. "But, Jess, this isn't good. He's either on his way or under a spell—neither of them are good options."

Shivers ran up my spine. "Okay, we have to think. We can travel from here to Florida in a day, at the latest. We'll just have to go down, find him, and fix whatever it is that's wrong."

"There's one more thing, the real reason we're here," Tyler added, his voice strained. "We went to get Nick, like you asked. But the witches wouldn't open the door—that is, until this little kid finally ordered them to. An army of witches decked out for battle, dressed in fatigues and carrying weapons—some of which I've never seen before—and they did what a toddler told them to do like a bunch of robots. It was one of the strangest things I've ever seen."

I took in a sharp breath. "Isn't she freaky?"

Danny nodded his head. "Yes, and she came running up to Tyler like he was a long-lost relation. She wrapped herself around his leg with her little arms and wouldn't bloody let go."

"Then she started to cry." Tyler shook his head. "It was awful. How am I supposed to defend myself with a little kid wrapped around my leg? Those witches could've killed me where I stood and I wouldn't have done anything to stop them."

"What did she say?" I urged. "It must have been big if you ran straight up here to find me."

"She said if I didn't find you and take you to New Orleans now, Dad would die." His face was grim, all the playfulness gone. "At least that was her mother's translation. The kid was sobbing a lot."

I dropped into the only chair in the room that was not demolished. This was huge news and I needed to process it. I put my head in my hands. "How did she say it? I need her exact words. Tally said there were no timelines in the future, that things change depending on the choices we make. How would Maggie know Dad dies if I don't go to New Orleans?" Something must have changed drastically from the time Rourke and I had been at the Coven until now. "Tell me what she said, in her own words."

"She was hard to understand." Tyler scratched his head. "She kept crying about something over and over. It sounded like 'vamp bay,' until I finally figured out she was talking about vampire Ray."

I stood quickly, knocking the chair over. "What did she say about him?" Tyler had no idea Ray was here.

"She was crying, something like 'can't die, can't die.'"

"Why can't Ray die?"

"She only said one word after that. It was the clearest one she uttered."

"What was it?"

"Salvation."

I ran through the trees so fast everything flew by me in a blur. Branches and switches slapped me in the face, but I didn't slow. I had no idea where this cave was, but I had no problem following the scent Rourke had laid last night. Everyone was right behind me.

But it didn't matter how fast I ran.

If Rourke had accidentally killed Ray last night, or Ray couldn't repair the damage to his head, I knew my father was lost. Once my brother had said the word "salvation," I knew it was true. Something had triggered in my mind. I don't know where it had come from, but I knew we needed Ray. Alive. *He's going to be okay... he has to be okay*, I told my wolf. She barked, urging us on faster.

"Jessica," Rourke called. "Veer to your left. The opening is against the mountainside. It's covered with brush."

I saw it. Ten more paces and I whipped the branches away with one hand and dove headfirst into the cave, somersaulting and landing crouched, senses alert.

"It's about time, Hannon." A surly voice hit my eardrum without missing a beat. "The sun set twenty minutes ago. What were you going to do, starve me to death? I'm hungry as hell and I need a fucking shower. There's blood and gunk plastered all over me and my veins feel hollow."

The relief he was still alive threatened to consume me. I inhaled and exhaled deeply, trying to control my emotions as I stood, clapping the dirt off my hands.

His reaction to me hadn't been what I expected, which made me wary. He should be much more pissed off.

Where was the savage fledgling vampire? "Ray, I thought you wanted to chop my head off and eat my insides for dinner? Did you manage to grow a whole new heart while you were fixing your head?"

"Why would I bother to grow a new heart when I don't even need the one I have now? It hasn't beat in days. But chopping your head off still sounds fairly appealing," he grunted. "At least then I could get a drink."

"Okay, what gives?" I asked. "Why are you so . . . *normal*—for lack of a better word." He'd never been normal, but this was as close to his "normal self" as he got. It was a complete 180 from last night.

Rourke, Tyler, and Danny had gathered in the small opening behind me, making the cave overcrowded.

Ray leaned his blood-caked head against the cave wall. "I don't have an answer for you, Hannon. I get confused a lot, and then I get angry. But when I woke up in the middle of healing from that painful-as-hell injury, I realized I'm never going to die. I had my face bashed in and my skull crushed and now I'm good as new. It

doesn't make any sense. But I'm not sure I hate it. But I don't...
like it either."

"So...what you are saying is I might have made the right
choice trying to keep you alive?" I hedged.

Everyone was quiet, waiting for his response.

Ray grumbled for a few seconds. "When I woke up with fangs
and this dreadful thirst, I wanted to kill you every minute of the
day. I won't lie. I don't think I slept, and I know I didn't eat. But
I feel different today and I don't know why." He peered up at me
as he brought a chained hand to his head and pressed his temple
like he had a headache. As he did, a flutter of his internal struggle
tugged along my senses. "The madness may come back at any
moment. Most of the time my mind feels like an amusement park
ride from hell."

I squatted in front of him, peering into his face, trying to figure
out what all this meant when I heard light footsteps behind me.

"I believe the reason for his clarity is he is reacting to you, *Ma
Reine*," a small voice echoed in the cave. "You are able to calm
him, as I could not. I have been puzzling over the pieces ever since
I left, but I think I understand now."

Tyler and Danny moved apart as Naomi stepped into the cave.
"Naomi," I said as I stood. "What are you doing here?"

Danny cleared his throat. "We forgot to mention we ran into
Naomi. She was outside the Safe House when we arrived back
from picking up Nick. We encouraged her to follow us, as we figured we would be on the move shortly."

"Good thinking." I nodded at Danny and then turned to
Naomi. "I'm sorry you didn't get the break you deserved, Naomi,
but I'm glad to see you here." She was dressed in new clothing and
flushed so she had made at least one pit stop. "What pieces were
you talking about puzzling out?"

She walked forward. "Once I left and fed"—she gave me a

small smile—"I tried to reason out why Ray was different from any other fledgling I have ever seen and I think I have come up with the only possible answer."

"It's because of my blood, right?" I said before she could say it out loud.

"*Oui.*" Her voice held a hint of surprise. "I do believe your blood is the cause. It is like none I have ever tasted. It was able to break my bond with my Queen, which should have been an impossible task. I think it must have interfered with Ray's transition and has somehow made him different. I believe he is partially bonded to you already, which is why he has calmed just now in your presence. You must give him more of your blood to complete the transition, and once you do, I believe he will become fully bonded to you. A young vampire needs guidance and attaches himself to his Master without thought. The bond will grow into love and loyalty over time. That is our way."

I gaped. "Wait a minute. Did you just say you want *me* to become his Master?" I did not want Ray as my responsibility. Not to mention I knew nothing about baby vampires—or fully adult ones for that matter. "Naomi, you made him. He wouldn't be alive without you. This is clearly your role, not mine. I have no idea what to do with a vampire. And Ray is hard on a good day. A newborn wolf raising a fledgling vampire is wrong on so many levels I can't even count them."

"Hey, this is not what I want either," Ray complained, his new fangs snapping down in protest. He shook his chains to accentuate his point. "How can she help me with anything? She's not a bloodsucker."

"I will be here to aid in his teachings," Naomi replied, her demeanor calm and reasonable. "I will not desert either of you. But it must be this way, or I believe he will continue to go mad. His instincts are muddled and his thought processes are off. He is too powerful from just drinking a mere dilution of your blood. I will not be able to make another after him. It is too unpredictable."

"So you're saying my blood botched the job of making him into a fully functioning vampire, and only I can fix it?" I asked. "By giving him more blood?"

"*Oui*." She shrugged. "There is nothing more I can do now. He must feed from you, or you must end his life. He cannot go on like this."

I glanced down at Ray. Killing him was no longer an option if I wanted my father to stay alive. I sighed. "Looks like this is your lucky day, Ray. You get to cause me some pain and in return I finally set your mind straight. I guess we should've done this from the very beginning all those years ago. It would've saved us a lot of trouble."

"Yeah, we'll see about that, Hannon," he said. "My mind is full of some crazy shit right now. I don't think even your blood can erase it completely." He eyed me as I knelt in front of him, my knees sinking into the dirt floor. This cave was rudimentary to say the least.

"Well, we have no choice but to give it a try."

"What if I don't agree and I don't want you as my new *Master*?"

"If you can come up with another alternative, I'm all ears. But I don't see any other powerful vamps waiting in line to give you their blood. Like it or not, this is the only option we have in front of us." I gestured at Naomi. "Ask her if she had a choice in picking her Master." I turned to address her. "Naomi, did anyone ever ask you if you wanted to become a vampire before they turned you?"

"*Non*," she said. "Of course not. Vampires hunt their prey and their prodigies with precision and care. There is no free will involved. If you are chosen, and given the gift, you are eternally grateful."

I arched an eye at Ray. "See? If you want to stay a vampire, you bite me. There's no other way."

Rourke strode toward us, his face set. "Jessica, I don't like it," he said. "I've never heard of a shifter making a vamp. There could be unforeseen problems we don't know about."

"I know it's not ideal." I switched to internal because Ray didn't need to know what we were discussing. *But saving Ray has become a top priority in the last half hour. There's no way I'm letting my father die if Ray is his salvation. And I'm not technically* making him—*Naomi did the making—but he already has my blood in his veins so there's no choice. Rourke, I have to finish this or he dies and with him, my father. I can't let that happen.*

I still don't like it. What if something goes wrong?

My best guess is this will work. I'm already getting hazy internal signals that he's bonded to me. I think once he has my blood, he might actually be forced to listen to me.

Rourke crossed his arms and gave me a hard look. *I understand you feel the need to do this, and I will support you if you choose to do it, but, Jessica, if something goes wrong, we have to agree to end his life.*

I will agree—I paused, meeting Rourke's gaze—*but only after he fulfills his role in all this.*

Jessica, the sacrifice may be too big. What if he goes crazy and we can't control him? What if he kills you instead?

I have to do whatever it takes to save my father. We can't go into all the what-ifs or we'd drive ourselves crazy. If this were your father, you'd be doing the same thing. We are having this conversation prematurely. Let's go ahead with the transition and see what happens. If it's anarchy, we can regroup after.

"Are you two finished?" Ray asked, glancing from me to Rourke. "Because I'm hungry as hell. And if I don't have a choice about you being my *Master*, I can still choose to eat. And there's one more stipulation. When you're done *making* me, I want these chains gone." He rattled them to accentuate his point. "Or the deal is off."

"One thing at a time, Ray," I said. "Let's see if this works first and then we can negotiate your freedom next." I leaned closer to him as Rourke's worry thumped against my chest, along with Tyler's and Danny's. I extended one arm and met my mate's eyes. *Pull him off of me if I lose consciousness, but don't kill him. Promise me you won't kill him if he hurts me. He needs to stay alive.*

I won't kill him, but I'm not going to promise I won't make it hurt.

I glanced at my brother. "Tyler, you know I need to do this."

"I know." Tyler nodded. "At this point, I'd feed the bastard too."

"Come on, let's go," Ray said impatiently, his eyes oscillating between silver and full black as he eyed my arm like a meal. "I'm starving here."

"Take it easy—I'm going as fast as I can," I said as I maneuvered myself into a better position. I slowly moved my arm in front of him and braced the other one against the wall. His fangs elongated even farther as my flesh came closer, and then his face started to do the horrid vamp slide, his cheekbones extending, his chin lengthening.

He lunged once I was within reach, his fangs penetrating my skin deeply.

Followed by a loud crack.

"Dammit, Ray! You broke my arm."

10

"Okay, that's enough," I told him after a few minutes. I was dizzy. Ray drank faster than I could replenish.

No response except for slurping noises. *Ew.* That was something I would never get used to.

"Let go of her now, vampire," Rourke ordered. He stood over us, his voice threatening. "Or I'll bash your head against the rocks and we'll see how long it takes you to regenerate from that."

Naomi stepped forward. "He is not in control. His instincts have taken over. It's very hard for a fledgling to disengage on his own from any feeding, much less the blood of a supernatural."

"That figures," I muttered. "So how do we get him off?"

"You must rip your arm away. We will brace his shoulders." She nodded at Rourke, who already had Ray by the back of the neck.

"Let's go on three," I said. *This is going to hurt like a bitch*, I told my wolf. A shot of adrenaline hit my system in the next beat, fortifying me.

"As much as I'd love to stick around and witness Ray tearing your arm to pieces, I'm going to head out if that's all right with you," Danny said. He inclined his head at me. "I'm assuming it's not necessary to stay. Seeing you harmed is ghastly on any level, but this is particularly gruesome."

Tyler grumbled, "I'm going too."

I felt their need to somehow fix the situation, but there was nothing they could do. Giving them a task would help. "Yes, go. Hank is out there. Find him. We need to figure out what to do with his body."

Tyler's eyebrows shot into his hairline. "I scented him here, but it smelled off, too old to be recent." His nose immediately went into the air and he turned toward the tunnel entrance.

"It seems he never left," I said. "We fought last night. I'll explain it all later."

"We're on it." They both trotted out of the cave, and I turned back to a concerned Rourke and a poised Naomi.

They both nodded to me.

"Are you sure this is our only option?" I asked. "How about we try and coax him off with sweet talk? He's such a sucker for niceties. It just might work."

Naomi stifled a smile. "We must do this; I know it is not ideal, but he has already taken too much."

"On three," Rourke said. "Let's get this over with. And if this bastard goes crazy, he's in for the shock of his sorry life."

"One . . . two"—I clenched my teeth—"*three*." They held him as I tore my arm from his grasp. His fangs shredded my skin in a horrifying way, making my eyes water. "*Gahhh*," I screamed through a locked jaw. I cupped my good hand over the wicked wound. It was healing quickly, but *damn*. I took a deep breath and blew it out. "Remind me not to do that ever again. If that wasn't enough blood for a lifetime of normal for Ray, I don't want to hear about it."

In one motion, Rourke ripped the shirt clean off his body and wrapped it around my arm before I had time to stop him. "If I have to witness you feeding a vamp again," he growled, "we're going to have a serious problem."

I grinned, holding the bloody T-shirt as I stood. "Ripping your shirt off was totally unnecessary, but the view is spectacular." I nodded down at my wound. "My arm is already healed."

I unwrapped it and tossed it back to him. He growled, "There's no control when I'm around you. I just react." His voice got throaty and I shivered. "But next time I'll be sure to sacrifice my bottoms instead."

Naomi interrupted us politely. "It seems the fledgling is unconscious."

My gaze shot to Ray. His head was indeed lolled at a funny angle.

"Ray," I said, bending next to him. "Are you okay?" I reached an arm out to shake him, but the moment it came close enough, he lunged forward snarling, his fangs lashing out, his eyes flickering like a movie reel. "Easy there." I braced my palms firmly against his shoulders. We were lucky he was still in chains.

He seemed stunned by the sound of my voice, and calmed considerably.

I peered at him closely. "Is my blood hurting you?"

"No," he half gasped, half coughed. "It's energizing and… making shit change. I feel…different already."

"What kind of shit is changing, Ray?" I asked patiently. "You need to be more specific." I turned toward Naomi. "Is this normal?"

She made a sound close to a snort. "No. But nothing is normal when it comes to your blood, *Ma Reine*." Touché. She edged in closer to examine him. "Does your mind have more clarity, fledgling? Do you see the way now?"

"What is he supposed to see?" I asked curiously, immediately envisioning a vampire headmistress with a high collar and a pointy stick tapping a blackboard to inform him about the basics of flight and impaling your fangs into unsuspecting humans.

"His inner mind should open and he should 'see' the way of the vampire. His body should give him cues. A normal fledgling vampire would be in awe of this and look for immediate guidance." She narrowed her eyes at Ray. "However, I suspect he will remain himself, but now with a second sight."

"I see it," he grumbled again. "It feels like I'm remembering myself from a long time ago, but the visions can't be real. I've never been afraid of sunlight or had an aversion to eating any food."

"I get a cranky she-wolf in my head fighting me for control and you get nice, peaceful daydreams. It so figures." I stood and took a step back. "Ray, pay attention to what you're seeing. This is how you get your survival information. Make sure the pieces fit together so you don't lose your mind again. Once you finish catching up, and my blood does what it needs to, all the information should seem like a nice, coherent package."

"When does it stop?" he complained. "I don't need my brain filled up with a bunch of useless crap. I get that I'm a vampire. I suck blood and sleep during the day. What more do I need?"

Naomi shook her head. "He is unlike any I've ever witnessed. There are no explanations."

Raymond Hart was the most stubborn soul I'd ever come across, and as a human, he'd never been susceptible to Nick's persuasion. It seemed logical to assume Ray's mind had been resistant to change as a human so as a supe it would be twice as bad. That, coupled with my powerful blood, meant there would be no dealing with him now.

I waited for a minute and watched as his eyes continued to flicker. "How's it going now?" I asked, glancing at Naomi. "How long do you think he needs? Didn't you tell me new vampires lose their humanity for a time? He's obviously gone through the major part of the transition already, because he *is* a vampire, but what happens now?"

Naomi shook her head. "I do not know. He might need another night or two to adjust fully, it's not easy to see. I believe he will continue to be unpredictable."

"I'm fine," Ray grumbled. "And I want out of these chains. I need clean clothes and a shower."

I sighed. "Ray, you just heard Naomi. You're unpredictable, and I can't let you out of here until we know for sure you won't run amok. You wanted to eat my intestines only a short time ago," I reminded him. "If we let you loose on humanity, and you're not back to yourself, you could kill innocent people before we could stop you."

As a former police officer, this should still be important to him. I knew Ray would hate the thought of being a harbinger of death to innocent people—if he was still Ray on the inside.

He eyed me, his eyes finally settling into their normal hazel color. "My head is clearing. I get what happened to me. I'm a vampire now. I see the dreams and I can guarantee I'm not going crazy. But if I *were* to go crazy again . . . you can tie me up. Is that good enough for you, Hannon? Now let me out of this place."

I bit my lip.

If he learned to fly, he could disappear. Naomi could barely control him before, and he'd been weak. "I think the best thing to do is establish the Master-fledgling thing before I set you free," I answered. Ray didn't know he had to accompany us to New Orleans in the next few hours or that he'd be a key piece in saving my father's life—whatever that meant. So I couldn't risk him taking off and not returning, and I wasn't exactly sure how much to share with him until I understood our new relationship. I turned to Naomi. "How much control does a Master usually have over the fledgling?"

"They have considerable control, but normally it is unnecessary to wield any power, because the fledgling would willingly do anything for their Master. They seek approval and love, much like a puppy to its new owner."

I arched a skeptical brow at Ray. That so wasn't happening. The day Ray was my puppy the Earth would cease to turn. I was going to have to barter with him and we both knew it. I turned to Rourke, who stood next to me, his expression severe. "What do you think about letting him go?"

"I've never come in contact with a fledgling before, but I think threatening him within an inch of his life to do what we say is the first step. I've heard young vamps can be unwieldy, and I have zero problem killing him if he doesn't follow your program."

"I don't want Rourke to kill you," I told Ray, "so it would be nice if you followed the program. Does that mean anything coming from me as your new Master?" Crossing my fingers would be childish, but that's exactly what I felt like doing. Any extra nugget of help I could get, I'd take right now.

Ray's irises flicked silver. "Yes."

His response had come through gritted teeth, but it was a start.

I'd also felt something jump in his blood at my question. Like he hadn't wanted to answer but had been compelled to do so. Naomi had knelt next to me. She'd had my blood, too, but nothing like that had ever happened to us. "Naomi, I have to ask you something. I gave you just as much blood to heal your wounds as I did to Ray, but Ray and I seem to have an internal connection. I can feel Ray's emotions, almost like I can with the wolves, but I don't get much of anything from you. Do you know why that is?"

She shook her head. "I do not. But I'm very old and have drunk from many, including some very powerful supernaturals. My blood is a thousand times more potent than any human's. I would likely need to drink much more from you for us to forge the same kind of connection. But, again, your blood is an anomaly, so it's hard to know."

"Hannon," Ray said. "I don't care about all this other bullshit. I want out of here." He rattled his chains. "I promise to follow your program, but I'm done with the prisoner routine. I deserve time to myself to process this like a grown-up. I've been on your leash for weeks now and I want my life back, starting right now."

"How do I know you won't get into trouble and that you'll come back?" I asked.

"Where the hell else would I go?"

"It's not that easy," I replied.

"Of course it is. You let me go and I come back. End of story."

"When?" I asked.

"When I'm good and goddamn ready."

"I don't think so." I put up a hand to quiet his protests. "And before you go off on another tangent, consider what we just talked about. You're too unpredictable. We need one more day to see how things settle, see how this is going to work."

He leaned forward, his eyes narrowing. "If you don't let me go now, you will regret it. I can feel the bond between us, and it's not like it was with her"—he nodded toward Naomi—"but I want to be *free*. I'm not going to compromise. You can't keep me locked up here like an animal." He strained against his chains, some of the links bending. "You want me to follow your program, but you're not willing to give me a chance to prove I can. Looks like the shoe's on the other foot and you're the one who needs to *trust* me. It's either that or we keep fighting." His fangs snapped down and he hissed. "And I get out of here on my own and don't come back."

I threw my hands up in the air. "Gods, Ray, why do you have to be so damn bullheaded? This would've been so much easier if Nelson were here instead," I complained. Chris Nelson had been Ray's partner when I'd been on the force. He was a mild-mannered cop who'd transferred willingly to traffic violations after two years with Ray.

"Nelson was a putz. He had no gumption," Ray retorted. "Consider yourself lucky I'm strong and capable and not going to be some ninny vampire."

"Why can't you be like all the other fledglings?" I said. "I want a puppy, not a hound from hell. Is there any part of you that feels the need to *obey* me?" I pushed power into the last words and I watched Ray react as the echo of my voice bounced around the cave.

He'd tried to cover it, but he hadn't been fast enough.

"Raymond Hart, if I let you go, will you come back here in a few hours?" I shoved as much emotion as I could into the words.

His eyes went full black. "I already told you I would. What else do you *want*?" He gritted his teeth as he fought against my question, his features shifting slowly, but I knew he was answering truthfully.

"If I let you go, you can't go near humans." I continued the onslaught of power, until he was cringing back into the cave wall. "You can't get into any trouble and you can't feed from anyone."

"I'm not fucking hungry. I just ate," he snarled.

This was working, but I needed him cooperative in the end, not hostile.

I glanced at Naomi and she shrugged. "I'm obviously getting through to him, but he's still as pigheaded as ever," I said. "I don't think the Master shtick is going to work. If I continue to use it, we'll be at each other's throats when this is all over. Literally. We're going to have to think of something else."

"*Oui*," she replied. "It is quite shocking."

In the meantime, Rourke had leaned over and hauled Ray up by his dirty shirt. The chains cinched tightly around Ray's middle, causing him to gasp. I guess that counted as *something else*. He brought Ray close to his face and snarled, "If we let you go, you return in two hours. Don't go anywhere near humans. If you're not back on time, we hunt you down and kill you. Understand, vamp?" He shook him hard. "And I will make it personal. You will hurt like you've never experienced, and I will start by removing your feet at the ankles and move my way up." Rourke's power pinged around the cave. Ray felt it too. But this may work, because it was pure strength and not a Master's order. "This is your test. The only one you will get. You pass it and you're free. You don't, you die. This is it, so don't fuck it up."

"Fine," Ray bit out. "I'll be back in two hours."

With his other hand, Rourke pulled the chains from the wall in one tug, demonstrating in a single instance what he could do that Ray could not.

The chains dropped to the cave floor, unraveling at once, and Ray shot out of the tunnel before I could take my next breath. He disappeared into the night without looking back, no doubt testing to see if we would go after him.

Naomi made a move to follow.

"No." I held her arm. "He goes alone. Rourke's right. This is his test. If he's not back in a few hours, we'll decide what to do then. I can't be in a constant head battle with him. I'll kill him myself before that happens. Let's go back to the cabin and figure out the plans. We leave for New Orleans at dawn. You and Ray can meet up with us after nightfall tomorrow."

Naomi cleared her throat. "It will not be necessary for us to wait. We will accompany you when you leave."

"What are you talking about? Don't you have to sleep during the day?"

"Not anymore," she replied.

Everyone was gathered in the cabin except for Ray. "Run that last part by me again," I said to Naomi. My hips were pressed against what was left of the counter, my arms folded. "I don't quite understand what you're telling me."

"As vampires age, our abilities strengthen, like most supernaturals. One of those abilities is our tolerance of sunlight. We mainly feed on human blood, which is weak, but as our own body ages, we eventually strengthen ourselves: bones, skin, everything."

"But sunlight is your 'vice,' right?"

"We cannot die from sunlight exposure," she said. "Or explode as some myths like to portray. Our skin simply gets severely burned, a reaction to the sun's strength. Our skin is very thin and it's painful. It takes time to heal, but nothing more. We are also very sleepy during the day; it's our natural time of rest. We are nocturnal by nature, but we are not comatose when the sun rises. But your blood has strengthened me. I do not feel pain when sunlight hits my skin." She smiled shyly. "It is quite wonderful to feel it again. It has been a very long time."

"I understand why this may have happened to you. You're hundreds of years old and have had time to strengthen your body before you drank from me. But how do you know Ray will have the same reaction? He's only had my blood for a few hours."

She shrugged. "I do not. It is purely an assumption. But if your blood worked that way on me, it will likely do the same for him."

Ray hadn't returned, but he had a half hour left before his imposed deadline. "Okay, things my blood can do is ramping up to fantastical levels, but more importantly, we have to keep it all a secret," I cautioned. "Does everyone understand?" I glanced around the group. "We're heading deep into vampire territory, and if word gets out that I can break bonds and allow them to walk outside during the day, there could be an uprising. The Queen won't tolerate a single vampire defecting." If they found out, I imagined it would be like a gaggle of vampires running after me with their fangs out, screaming for sunlight.

A chorus of voices agreed.

I turned to my brother. "After you found Hank, did you find any trace of the wolves who were sent here by Dad to find him?"

Tyler had dealt with Hank. He and Danny had just come in a few minutes ago. "Yes," he said grimly. "He'd broken their necks and tossed them over a cliff."

"Did you know either of them?"

"We couldn't get down close enough to them to get a facial ID, but going by scent I only knew one," Danny answered. "He'd been a nice enough fellow, but too young to know any better."

"Dad should've known." Tyler shook his head.

"Those were likely the only wolves he could spare at the moment," I replied. It was very unfortunate. I pushed away from the counter. "I want you to try and get in touch with Dad one last time before we move out. Go shift while we start to hammer out the details. We need to figure out how to handle the Vamp Queen and get us all safely to New Orleans. We can't waste any time if Dad's in trouble—"

Something thudded loudly on the roof. The ceiling beams cracked, but held. Dust and dirt rained down on us as someone walked across them.

"Ray's back," I announced. I shouldn't be surprised that he would make an extreme entrance. This was so typical of him.

Tyler opened the door and we all filed outside.

Ray stood on the roof looking quite proud of himself. I rested my hands on my hips. "I see you've learned to fly," I called. "That's fairly impressive, but it seems your landing skills need a bit of work. The front door is down here."

"Yeah, I wasn't watching," Ray called down. "But I have a good reason. I was heading back fast, because something's coming."

"What do you mean *something's coming*?" I asked, alarmed, dropping my arms and moving forward.

Naomi didn't wait for him to answer. She shot into the air to investigate.

"I mean, there's some strange shit flaring off in the distance. It's miles from here, but they're starting to crop up all over. The power feels strange, like something is pushing against my chest. And it stinks."

"It stinks?" I strode closer to the roofline.

"I flew over to one, but once I got there, there was nothing left but the smell of rancid eggs and some leftover energy. On my way back, two more popped up east and another one southwest. It seems like something is searching, and since you're always stuck in thigh-high crap without waders, whatever it is... I figured it's probably looking for *you*."

Rotten eggs was bad.

That meant sulfur, and sulfur meant demons.

Rourke was next to me in the next moment. "I don't feel a strong power signature close," he said. "But I'm not willing to doubt him. We need to get on the road. I want you back in that car. If whoever's searching has your signature, I'm not sure how many miles it will take to get you in its sights."

Naomi landed right in front of us. "He's right. The disturbances are off in the distance, but the power is strong and stinks of sulfur."

"Are they demon circles?" I asked.

"*Oui*," Naomi said. "I believe so. None but a Demon Lord can summon itself to this plane, so these must have been made by another."

"You mean like the sorcerers?" I asked. "Who else would team up with the demons?" Of all the supernatural Sects in existence, the demons stood alone in all ways. Demons and fey were the only two I knew about who lived on a different physical plane, but there hadn't been a fey sighting in hundreds of years. Demons were their own creepy race and they kept to themselves for a reason.

"The lesser demons have to be cooperating with spell casters to get on this plane," Rourke said. "So the sorcerers would be the most logical choice, since they're gunning for you already."

I turned around, frustrated. "This is crazy. Sects don't team up with each other like that. Especially demons. They don't make allegiances with others."

Rourke grinned. "You might want to take a look around at your current allies. Cats, wolves, vamps, and witches all working together. Things are changing in our world very quickly."

I glanced at the two vampires in front of me. Ray had jumped off the roof and stood next to Naomi. "Yes, but we didn't team up on purpose. It just . . . sort of happened," I ended lamely. I'd been the first Pack wolf to swear an oath to the Vampire Queen, which is how Naomi and I met. And I'd done it in a matter of days after my first change.

"You just became a vamp Master *willingly*." Rourke chuckled. "Your secretary, and best friend, is a witch. Her aunt, the most powerful witch in the country, just helped us escape, and her daughter is giving us information to help save your father. Jessica, there's no doubt in my mind you were put on this earth to change things up in a big way. The moment I met you my world turned upside down, and so did each of ours."

"He's right," Ray said. "My life couldn't be any different than it was just a few weeks ago. When I saw you that day at your apartment, I knew you were different. Something had changed, but I didn't know what. Now look where I am."

"It could all be just a big coincidence," I said, even though I knew that wasn't true.

"Jessica," Rourke said. "I wouldn't change any of this. It's time to shake things up. This feels right. The supernatural world has been stagnant for my entire life. It's time for all of us to evolve and change."

"I agree," Danny piped in. "A world with too much repetition is a drag. We have been the same for far too long. Plus, I like having a female Alpha. Makes me feel daring."

Ray walked up to me with a swagger in his step, his new power hitting my skin in small pressure points. "Your detective pal, Nick, is on the road, just so you know. He's not too far. You should probably go get him before he drives through one of those circles and gets himself hurt."

My head snapped to Tyler and Danny. "Did you tell Nick to come here?"

Tyler shrugged, moving forward. "Yes and no. We all left the Coven together and he was with us when we went back to the Safe House and saw Naomi. He knew roughly where we were heading. He's one of your best friends, Jessica. You can't keep him out of danger forever. He'll survive. He's smart. We need all the help we can get and he knows that."

It was selfish of me to want to keep him out of harm's way. He was worried about us and had a right to be here. "What's he driving?" I asked.

"A big black Suburban," Ray answered.

"Sweet," Tyler hooted. "That means he has the Safe House truck, which is stocked to the hilt with supplies. That's why I love Nick; he's always thinking."

"Even sweeter"—I glanced around the group—"we all have a ride to New Orleans."

11

I was dressed in my own clothes, waving my arms like an air-traffic controller on the side of the road. We'd just come down the mountain and I was trying to flag Nick down without giving him a heart attack. The Porsche purred quietly next to me. Rourke was waiting not so patiently inside. Danny, Tyler, Naomi, and Ray were back at the stream waiting for us to return with Nick.

The Suburban's headlights finally flashed into view and I jumped up and down. When Nick saw me, he slammed on his brakes and bumped onto the shoulder. By the look on his face, I'd surprised the hell out of him. I could've done a supernatural maneuver, but why make things more complicated? My arms worked just fine.

Naomi had spotted him from the sky a half hour ago. But rather than her stopping him, because they didn't know each other, we agreed it should be me. He hadn't been on the right road, but we'd cut across a few back roads to reach him.

The moment his tires came to a halt, he was out the door. "Jess, what's going on? Are you okay?" He ran toward me and grabbed me up into a big bear hug.

"I'm fine." I hugged him back. "I just didn't want to give you heart failure, so we thought this was the easiest way. Nobody's phone works out here, so we couldn't warn you we were coming."

"Well, it worked," he said. "Seeing you on the side of the road was completely unexpected. But I was coming to find *you*, not the other way around."

"We had to make some quick changes to the schedule. We're leaving early for New Orleans, as in—we're leaving right now. Strange power blips are popping up all over. We think it may be the demons working with sorcerers, so we've got to skedaddle out of here. Circles are popping up all over. Jump back into the Suburban and follow the car. Tyler, Danny, Naomi, and Ray are a few miles away."

"I'm sorry, but did you just say the demons and sorcerers are working *together*?" he asked, already heading back to the SUV without question. "I've never heard of that happening."

"Neither had any of us, but that's the best guess we have at the moment," I said. "Ray, of all people, picked up on the magic when he was flying around." Rourke tapped the horn. "We have to get moving. I'll explain it all later. I promise. I know I owe you so much, but I can't explain it all now. I'm going to be sequestered in this car, because it's spelled, until we hit New Orleans. Once we're there we'll work out a decent plan." I walked over and slid into the waiting Porsche.

"Ray," Nick muttered as he slammed the door of the Suburban. "Who would've guessed?"

That's fine, Tyler, but you can't risk anyone seeing you. He, Nick, and Danny were in the SUV behind us and we were having an internal conversation. It was four in the morning and we were a few hours outside of New Orleans.

It was more than time to try and connect with our father again, so we were deciding on the best course of action. I was getting more and more anxious by the moment. Maggie hadn't given Tyler any specific details, only that we needed to arrive in New Orleans *soon*. Now that we were closer to the city limits, it was time to try again.

I can't get out of this car yet, I told him. The car had done its job well so far. *We'll pull over and park while you shift. Up ahead looks pretty dense with good cover.*

Nobody is going to see me. I've been doing this wolf thing for a long time. If I make contact with Dad, I'll let you know. We were both worried. It had been too long since we'd heard from him. This wasn't normal. We were always in touch with him.

Wait, I'm having second thoughts. Have Danny shift with you, I told him. We'd just decided Tyler was going to shift alone. *It's better if you stay together. I want you to have backup if anything goes wrong.*

The circles had continued to pop up all night, but they were almost always near a populated town. So we had simply steered clear of towns. If the demons really were working with the sorcerers, it was a massive collaboration. They must have gathered sorcerers from all around the country to act together, which was no small undertaking. Naomi and Ray had taken turns keeping an eye on the magic and directing us away from any activity.

The Porsche had kept me cloaked, which was a very good thing. Every supe had their own signature, kind of like a magical DNA, and the Demon Lord who'd come to pick up Selene and tried to trick me into accompanying it to the Underworld had told me they'd gotten a sample of my signature off an imp I'd fought. So if the car wasn't spelled, they would be able to find me eventually.

Jess, it's easier if I go alone, Tyler said. *I can catch up with you faster once I'm done.* Tyler's special gift was the ability to run faster than any other wolf.

No, take Danny, and don't argue with me on this. There's a town nearby. It makes the most sense to have full backup.

Fine. Pull over up ahead. I see a bunch of trees after that road sign.

"Rourke, pull over right there." I pointed to the break in the trees. As we cruised up to it, I could see it was an old logging road. "Follow it in. Tyler and Danny are going to shift. Tyler's going to try and connect with our father one more time before we reach New Orleans."

Rourke turned down the road, the Suburban right behind us. He drove fifty yards along the bumpy dirt road and parked. Tyler and Danny jumped out of their vehicle immediately.

Before they could get to my car, Naomi and Ray landed in front of us.

"Tyler and Danny are shifting," I told the vamps through the window. "They're going to try and communicate with my dad. Any more issues from the sky?"

Since Ray had arrived back, he'd been civil and fairly cooperative. Our connection felt stronger each time we interacted. I knew he felt it, too, but he wasn't acknowledging it, in true Ray fashion. I wasn't going to push because I had no idea if having us tied together was a good thing yet or not. "There was one a few minutes ago about fifty miles from here," Ray answered. "We shouldn't hang around any longer than necessary. Every time one flares close by, I feel like gagging." Ray carried himself like a police officer even as a vampire. Maybe it wasn't such a bad combination. I doubted Ray would ever stop being a cop, so maybe that would make him an extra diligent vampire.

Naomi nodded. "Yes. The magic tastes very bitter. We must not linger."

"How can they possibly keep coming so often?" I said. "They

haven't let up all night, and I'm guessing they're doing this all around the country trying to find me."

"I do not understand it myself," Naomi confessed. "I had not thought it possible for them to come so often. There must be an army of demons, each paired with a sorcerer or witch of some kind. A spell caster must be present to do the summoning, which is why they cannot pop up in the middle of the forest, because no one lives here."

"Jess," Tyler called over his shoulder as he and Danny headed into the trees. "You should take off. No sense lingering. We'll follow you on foot. I'll let you know when you need to stop and pick us up." Nick followed them in, likely to pick up their clothes.

Before I could answer, a rumble came from inside the Porsche.

"Something's vibrating," Ray said from his position against the car. "Do you feel that?" He placed an open palm on the hood of the car.

"It has to be the spell," Rourke said. "This is not good."

Inside, the car began to buzz and shake. It was like old-time TV interference, and we just happened to be inside the TV.

"Damn," I said as a quiver of energy blinked through me. "Didn't Angie tell us the smaller the vehicle, the more it held the spell? The bigger the vehicle the quicker it dissipated?"

"This car wasn't meant to hold a spell for very long," Rourke finished.

"Tally never thought we'd take it to New Orleans." *Damn, damn, damn.* "How long has it been since we left the Coven?"

"It's coming up on the third day."

Naomi stepped back from the car. "Go now, while you can. Get to the city. You can find cover there," she urged. "We will follow you closely. If there's trouble—"

A loud popping noise rent the air, like a giant piece of bubble wrap, and the car shuddered for the last time.

Then everything stilled.

I yanked open the glove box.

It was empty. No money, no passports. The spell was gone.

Ray turned in a slow circle outside, his eyes flashing sliver. His concern and anger zinged through our blood connection, much stronger this time. Seconds later, a pulse of energy shot through the entire area, ending with an eardrum-sucking *pop*.

Either the sorcerers were incredibly lucky, or they had the best tracking system in the world. They'd managed to find me. And it had taken only seven seconds.

Rourke jammed the car in reverse. "Hold on!"

"Go to the Vampire Queen's immediately!" I shouted to Naomi and Ray as we peeled out. "It's the only place I can think of with enough protection. Naomi, act like you just arrived back from our journey, but don't tell her anything else. I will find you."

Eudoxia may be only one of a handful of supes who might be strong enough to ward off an attack from the Underworld. It didn't matter in the end, because I didn't know any other supes in New Orleans anyway.

We had only one choice.

Naomi appeared horrified. "She will know our bond is broken. I will be punished!"

I grabbed on to Rourke's arm to stop him as he wrenched the car around. I rolled down the window and craned my neck out. "No, she wants me too badly to risk harming you. Naomi, you have to go. I promise, we will be right behind you. It's the only safe place that can shelter all of us. Ray will be the perfect distraction. Introduce him as your—"

A huge burst of energy broke through the twilight, roaring through the predawn like a fog of malice-laced power.

"Time's up!" Rourke shouted.

As the car sped off, I spotted Tyler and Danny running along-side us in their true forms.

Naomi and Ray took to the sky. Nick was behind us in the SUV, but as I watched in the rearview mirror, he spun the Sub-urban 180 degrees in the opposite direction once we hit the pave-ment. "What's he *doing*?" I yelled, turning my head around to look out the small back window.

Rourke glanced behind us. "He's buying us time."

"He can't take on a demon alone!"

"He won't. Once they figure out he's not who they want, they'll move on."

"What if they kill him first because they can? We have to go back."

"Jessica, we are not going back. Nick is an adult supernatural who makes his own decisions. He is giving us a chance and we're taking it. He knows the risks."

Go back and help Nick, I yelled at Tyler. *He's trying to block whatever is coming. If you stand together, you have a better chance. Naomi and Ray have already taken off.*

Got it, Tyler said. *But get the hell out of here as fast as you can. Once we get to New Orleans, we'll track you. We won't be too far behind.*

Another shock of power rocked the car.

The force of energy brought all four wheels off the road. On the way down, the car bounced, bucking us in our seats. Rourke yelled, "Put your head down!" right as all the windows in the car exploded simultaneously.

I ducked fast, covering my head with my arms as tempered glass rained down all around us. Adrenaline shot through my sys-tem and my muscles coalesced in an instant. Once the barrage was over, I unlaced my arms and tilted my head up. Rourke had the Porsche at 150. The wind was incredible. "Can you outrun power like this?" I shouted as we flew down a back road.

"We just broke through the end of that demon circle. That was the power burst." He wrenched his head to look behind us, not slowing the car. "There are two things working in our favor right now. Demons have to stay within the circle they were summoned in. And daylight is breaking. It's my understanding demons hate sunlight. If we stay rural and change our direction every fifteen minutes, we have a shot. The spell on the car is gone, but we still have GPS. It'll have to do. We'll use it to stay on the back roads until sunrise."

I punched on the GPS and reached out to my brother.

What's going on? I asked. *Tyler, talk to me!*

As soon as you made it through the circle, they left. Nick is on the road already. We aren't far behind him.

Any luck with Dad?

Not yet.

Okay, keep trying. Rourke thinks we can make it to New Orleans if we stick to the back roads. Once the sun crests, we are hoping they back off.

Don't worry about us. We'll find you.

I sat back in my seat and reached up to secure my hair, which was flying around like a cyclone in the wind. I bound it with a twist tie I'd found in the ashtray. No windows at this speed was going to make it an interesting ride.

I leaned over and opened the glove box, moving the car insurance papers around, searching for anything that might help us. I half hoped I'd find a big red witchy help button to push for backup.

No such luck.

I closed my eyes and tilted my head back, mouthing a few simple phrases.

"What are you doing?" Rourke asked, his voice loud to compensate for the wind.

"Hoping that if I focus hard enough, a bag of beef jerky will appear in the glove box."

12

"*Dammit*," I muttered. "I never should have told them to come here before we had a concrete plan in place." We were parked outside of what Rourke had just informed me was the Vampire Coterie, which literally meant "clique" in French. It so figured the vamps would be cliquey. I was second-guessing my decision to order Naomi and Ray here ahead of us. "I just wanted them to be safe, but it's not going to come without some serious consequences."

"There was no way we could've known," Rourke assured me. "You did what you thought was best in the moment, and I agreed with you. Demons aren't something anyone takes lightly. They are feared for a reason. We were lucky to escape the circle before it had a chance to stop us. Naomi and Ray would've tried to protect you at all costs. It was much better they had gone."

It was seven in the morning. The disturbances had stopped at daybreak, but that hadn't meant we were clear of danger.

The sorcerers wouldn't stop hunting us during the day.

Now that we were in the city, it was only a matter of time until they found us. We were waiting for Tyler, Danny, and Nick before we made our next move. "I don't think we'll be able to knock on the door until dark," I said, nodding toward the imposing mansion with its turrets and high walls. "I'm assuming the Queen has to be awake in order to have a conversation, and we don't know if she receives guests during the day. She is going to be less than thrilled to see us, to say the very least."

Rourke's tension filled the car. "Entering a Coterie full of vampires uninvited will be tricky no matter what—day or night—but with demons on the prowl, it's our only real choice," he said grudgingly. "As much as I hate the idea of going in there, I can't come up with a better plan. The vamps are the only game in town powerful enough to keep the demons out. Once we connect with your father, and your Pack arrives to back us up, it will be a different story. Once we have strength in numbers to fortify us, we can move to a better location." He gestured to the stone fortress the Queen called home. "This will only be temporary. Your father is one of the strongest supernaturals on the planet. You have to remember, the demons aren't going to mess with him easily and they won't want to tangle with Eudoxia either. It's the best plan we've got."

Tyler hadn't been able to get in contact with our father after repeated tries. I was beyond worried and had crept into full-blown panic. Something was very wrong. "We have to believe what Maggie predicted to be true, or I'll lose my mind with worry." I undid the twist tie from my hair and tried to brush it out with my fingers. It was like trying to comb through straw. "We have to stay in New Orleans no matter what happens. Ray is already here, and because of that I have to believe my father will live. He has to."

"Jessica, your father is an extremely strong supernatural," he said. "It would take something immeasurable to defeat him. You have to remember that. He can take care of himself."

"I know he is," I said. "But the uncertainty is killing me." I needed to focus on something I could fix. "Do you think Eudoxia has hurt Naomi and Ray? I mean, do you think she listened to them at all or just threw them in the dungeon?" I leaned out the open window to peer at the Coterie again.

Rourke gripped the steering wheel. "I think the Queen will use caution at first. She's diplomatic if anything. She hasn't stayed in power this long without learning a few tactical moves. But when she finds the bond is missing from her underling, there's no doubt she will be agitated. Naomi will have a big job of smoothing things over."

"Naomi is the embodiment of calculated intelligence, which is what I love the most about her. On the other hand, Ray is an impetuous hothead who has no idea what's at stake." I turned my head toward Rourke. "I should've told him what was going on. It may have bought them some needed time. If he's his normal cocky self, they are likely in big trouble already."

"There's a definite chance the detective will hose things up," Rourke replied. "But if he listens to what I'm certain Naomi told him repeatedly, I believe they have a chance. The Queen will know something happened, but she won't know exactly what, and she may choose to believe Naomi. After all, she thinks her faithful servant is returning home after her mission, not coming back with an agenda."

Jess! Where the hell are you? Tyler's voice barreled into my brain.

I jolted upright in my seat, mouthing *Tyler* to Rourke.

I'm here, Tyler. Where are you?

We're just getting into the city. We ran into an issue.

Demons? I asked. "They ran into a problem," I told Rourke. He turned over the engine in the next breath.

But where would we go? We were stuck.

No, the sorcerers, Tyler said. *We saw one of their vans just inside the city limits and we investigated. We managed to capture one of the assholes before the reinforcements came. I think he was a scout, too young to know any better, and we got him to spill some information. They're working with the demons in a technical capacity. The sorcerers are summoning demons all over, but the deal is whoever gets to you first wins the prize. He didn't know why the demons wanted you, but the sorcerers want something big. After we convinced him his life depended on giving us an answer, he said they were trying to steal your life force.*

My life force? I turned to Rourke. His brow was furrowed. "The sorcerers are trying to steal my life force. Is that even possible?" That sounded way worse than trying to siphon my power.

"Hell no," he snarled. "How would they even do that? I'd like to see them try."

How can they steal what's inside of me? I've never heard of that. It can't be possible. And how bad would that hurt?

I have no idea, but according to their scout they're going to try. They are rushing around and seemed fairly unorganized. The demons have gone home for the day, so they're hoping to snag you first. Whatever the parameters of their agreement, I'm pretty sure the demons are in charge at night. Jess, you need to get out of the city as fast as you can.

And go where? There's no safe place to get to before dark. I eyed the vamp stronghold. *There's nowhere left for us to run.*

Well, you have about three minutes to decide. Five vans full of sorcerers are behind us on this road alone. It's taken them time to regroup, but even if we don't lead them to you, your signature is all over. We've been able to track you with the windows down. Once they stop and get a plan, they'll be all over you.

Damn. *Then we only have one choice left. We barter with Eudoxia for refuge until we can reach Dad.*

The vamps are not going to protect us, he argued. *We'll be walking straight into enemy territory. I've told you all along this is not a good idea.*

I don't agree and neither does Rourke. The Queen wants my life force too—let's not kid ourselves. If stealing my power is on everyone's list, there's nowhere I can go. As long as I'm still tantalizing to Eudoxia, we have something to bargain with. The goal will be to stay in control at all times. If she denies us, we get Naomi and Ray and fight our way out. But taking refuge in the vamp stronghold is the best we've got.

Tires squealed down the street.

I turned to Rourke. "Tyler has five carloads of sorcerers on his tail. We have to move now."

The Suburban, with Nick at the wheel, rounded the corner, going up on two wheels. There was a loud explosion and an Orb flew over the trees, coming at us like a heat-seeking missile.

Rourke leaned over and threw open my door, yelling, "Go! I'm right behind you."

I sprang from the car and took off at a dead run. The Orb exploded behind me, taking out the Porsche.

Car doors slammed and Tyler, Danny, and Nick joined us as we ran for the huge stone wall surrounding the mansion.

"Let me go first. If I get through, follow me," I called over my shoulder, clearing the massive height in one leap. Nothing kicked me back, but a strange pulse of energy whipped through my body as I crossed the boundary line. Thank goodness it wasn't warded.

I landed easily and kept running. I was up the steps to the front door, happy that nothing exploded behind me, before I took my next breath. I slid to a stop just short of kicking in the door, which would be considered bad manners for a visiting guest. I turned and glanced back for the first time and realized no one was behind me.

I watched as each of them tried to clear the wall again and was repelled backward.

Damn.

It was warded. I just hadn't been affected by it.

I ran back to help and Rourke called, "Jessica, stay inside the boundary. We'll find another way in." Another explosion rocked the wall from the outside, but none of the Orbs were breaching the ward.

Before I could decide what to do, huge French doors directly above the portico of the mansion shot open and the Vamp Queen strode out into the morning light, a single finger pointed directly at an Orb hovering in the sky.

The thing froze in place.

Half a beat later, with one flick of her wrist, it evaporated into nothingness.

"You dare declare war on me?" her chilly voice rang out.

It seemed the Queen had no problem with sunlight and she was wide-awake.

That was a bonus.

I stayed inside the yard and moved to the top of the stairs so I could get a better vantage point. The sorcerers who had jumped out of their vans were now tumbling all over themselves trying to get back in them. So much for badass.

"Yes, scurry away like rats in a sewer," the Queen's voice raged. She shook an extremely pale fist toward the errant sorcerers. "Tell your High Priest he owes me restitution for this attack or he will pay the price in blood." To punctuate her statement, the tires on one of the vehicles blew and the thing did a triple spin in the air. Her magic had manifested physically in a shock of white. The same shock of white that had hit me in the chest just a short time ago. I knew how powerful she was and now so did they.

The vans carrying the sorcerers peeled out, tires screeching as they went. I turned discreetly, trying to stay out of the Queen's line of vision, and edged my way back toward the wall. I needed my team in here with me.

"You," the Queen called. "Little Wolf Girl. You play with fire coming to my door unannounced, trailing trouble right behind you."

I turned to face her, moving into her sight line. No use pretending I wasn't here. "I apologize," I replied. I had to play this right. Even if the sorcerers had temporarily left, the demons would be here soon and I still needed to bargain for shelter for the night. "Our Pack became separated on the road and it was either come here or risk death. I figured you were interested in keeping me alive, at least for a while. My duties to you don't start for a few weeks, but as you can see, I'm ready and willing to meet with you now."

She cocked her head at me, calculating. "You may enter, but know that I am not bound by our oath until three weeks from this date. You come into my Coterie at your own risk."

"Hmm, as tempting as that sounds," I responded, "how about we make a deal instead? I'm not entering without my companions, and we enter as your guests for the duration of twenty-four hours and are free to leave alive and unharmed at this same time tomorrow."

"And what would interest me enough to welcome you into my home and keep all your lives intact?" she asked.

"If I die, you don't get what you want. It's pretty simple." She moved to the edge of the railing that ran around the portico. I had chosen to call her bluff right from the get-go and I had her attention. "The sorcerers want my power and so do you. You want it through my blood and they want to somehow pull it out of me, but it's the same thing. So if you keep me alive, you keep the power alive. Next, if you don't offer us shelter, you risk war with the wolves. By denying us, you act against us." That wasn't technically true since we weren't formal allies, but if she denied us and I was harmed as a result, it would be a valid enough reason for my father to declare war. "You already know my father is itching for a fight after the last time we met." I tried my final tactic. "He would do almost anything to keep me away from you, including fight you before I'm due to honor my deal. But I'm here right now. This might be your last chance, Eudoxia. I wouldn't let it slip through your fingers."

She didn't try to deny any of it, which earned her a few points. "What are your terms?" she asked coolly.

"I will agree to follow your rules once inside and you agree no harm comes to me or my team. I think that's fair enough for now."

"Ah, but you seek protection, do you not? Protection comes with a fee."

I exhaled slowly. Of course she was going to make me work for it. "Then I guess the bigger question is, what do you want from me, Eudoxia? If protection comes at a cost, what is it going to cost me?"

Her face showed a hint of surprise. She hadn't expected me to turn the tables so quickly. "The sunlight is burning my retinas. I will meet you all inside the foyer." She flicked her wrist once toward the perimeter and left her perch without glancing back.

I turned to see the boys coming into the yard, Rourke in the lead.

"Jess," Tyler called as he ran forward. "You can't do this. You can't make another deal with her. We don't need protection that badly. The sorcerers are gone for now. We can hit the road and take off. Anything you agree to once we're inside will put us at too great a disadvantage."

"I believe he's right," Danny added. "We'll be sitting ducks if we take up with these biters without a prior agreement. Anything you offer the Vampire Queen to keep us safe will be too high a price in my estimation. I say we cut and run."

"Cut and run *where*?" I asked them both as they came to a stop, lowering my voice to barely above a whisper. "Right now she thinks the threat is sorcerers. We don't have to mention we are having *another* issue. And don't forget Naomi and Ray are inside. I'm not leaving here without them. It's not ideal, but I agree to her terms and we stay. For one night. Enough to get in touch with my father, get the rest of our team, and come up with another plan."

"We can't forget the child oracle said we had to be in New Orleans," Rourke added, directing his words at Tyler. "The sorcerers know we're here. As soon as we leave the grounds, they'll hunt us down. Even if we get out of town, there's not another sanctuary near enough. I support Jessica. We stay here overnight, and if things improve, there's a possibility we can head out tomorrow. If not, we renegotiate with the Queen. Jessica's in more danger out there"—he pointed over the wall—"than she is in here at the moment."

Tyler's anxiety pinged through my system. He knew Rourke was right, but we all hated being in this predicament. This was a little more dire than being stuck between a rock and a hard place—it was more like being stuck between fangs and death. "Fine, but I'm not putting up with any of their shit. If they try to bite us, it's going to be anarchy," he growled. "I will kill any vamp who comes near me, no matter what we agree to."

"They won't risk biting us if their Queen doesn't want a war," I said. "And maybe it's no accident we're here." I pondered that. "It makes the most sense. This is the first place Dad would look for us." I glanced around the group. "I have to trust my instincts, and this feels right—"

Like a cue from a B movie, the massive front doors of the Coterie slowly creaked open on their own, signaling us to enter.

"Well, that was a bit creepy," Danny said. "Let's go on, then. We've reached our decision. And I don't like the idea of leaving our mates in there any longer than necessary, so I guess it's time to have a little fun fraternizing with the enemy."

"That was a quick turnaround, Daniel Walker. From against to for in less than two minutes." I chuckled as we all moved forward.

"What can I say?" he responded. "You've convinced me. And this choice happens to be a tad better than getting charred by an angry demon. As long as the vampires keep their distance, we should be able to cope. Plus, I wouldn't mind learning a thing or two about their habitat. A bloke can learn a lot if he pays close attention." He winked.

Rourke splayed a warm hand on the small of my back as we walked. *Eudoxia is shrewd, but this is your game to win*, he said in my mind. *She's not going to let this opportunity pass her by. Whatever she wants, she wants it badly enough to give you refuge, so use it to your advantage.*

We ascended the massive marble steps and went through the open door.

That's my plan, I replied. *Once we have Naomi and Ray we can—*

13

As soon as we stepped into the ornate mansion, with its dark mahogany interior, our mind-connection abilities snapped off. I wasn't surprised, since that's exactly what had happened to my father and me last time. Eudoxia had some sort of interference spell that kept mind communication closed. It made sense that she'd want to protect herself. If her minions could talk, they could plot.

The gigantic foyer was draped with gold fixtures and deep red carpets, all the furniture polished and well kept.

The Vampire Queen was nowhere to be seen.

A moment later a voice chirped from the top of the staircase. We all glanced up to see Valdov leaning over the banister. He brought his long white fingers together in his standard steeple pose as he cackled, "So the rutting was a success, I gather?" At our last unfortunate meeting, he'd guessed correctly that Rourke and I were a mated pair.

I took a step forward. "It was actually mind-blowing, but we're not here to discuss private affairs. Where is your Queen? She said she'd meet us here."

"Eudoxia is lying down, mending her eyes. Sunlight is so very powerful and nasty on us, you know." He made a clicking sound with his tongue. "She handled the threat against us perfectly, however, and with great authority. You have been ordered to deal with me. When she wakes at sunset, she will meet with you then, if you ... *er* ... decide to accept our demands."

"I'm not swearing anything to you, Valdov," I said, clearing things up from the start. "You have no honor and I wouldn't loan a guy like you five cents. I'm certainly not going to bind myself to you. So you and your Queen are going to have to rethink your tactics. Go see what else she has in mind and we'll wait here admiring her Ming vases."

Before any of us could blink, he launched himself down the stairs in a rage.

As he came at us, his face slid and his fangs elongated. We all took a few steps back because it was so unexpected. "You will not question my honor!" he slurred through his pointy incisors. He huffed to a stop a few feet in front of me, his eyes fully black, no white showing. "You are below me in every sense, you rotten mongrel. Do you hear me? You will swear whatever I ask in return for the Queen's favor. There is no other compromise! You should count your blessings you are even allowed to stand here in our home."

I didn't flinch.

His power was strong, but nothing like his Queen's, and I'd learned a thing—or several—since we'd last met. "If there's no compromise, we're leaving," I said. "I don't need anything badly enough to swear to you, Valdov. You can tell your Queen you let her prize slip right between your bony white fingers. I'm sure she'll be extremely happy when she wakes up and finds out I'm gone."

As one, we turned and headed toward the door. It was a power play, but we had no other choice. I would leave if I had to. I couldn't trust Valdov to keep his word. It was too risky. Once we were outside, we'd regroup.

"Aren't you forgetting something, mongrel?" Valdov snickered behind me. "A certain vampire or two you've become... acquainted with... perhaps a bit too *deeply*?"

I stopped midstride.

Motherfuckeronacracker.

"Did you honestly think we would not notice she had changed? You cannot possibly be so naïve." He strolled toward a big open room to our right like he hadn't just gone bat-shit crazy on us. I refused to acknowledge him or look his way. "She reeked of your blood, you know. And the abomination she brought with her? He shan't be allowed to survive the night." He tut-tutted as he picked up a knickknack and pretended to examine it. "We choose our humans extremely carefully, and with the utmost discretion. His making was nothing less than a... travesty. An utterly uncouth individual cannot become a *Nosferatu*. Do you know, when we hauled them away, he had the nerve to try to *bite* me, all the while ranting and raving about the 'ass kicking' he was going to mete out once he became free? Can you imagine? A fledgling that stunk of *werewolf* was going to give *me* retribution?" He threw his head back and cackled.

It was an ugly sound.

I clenched my teeth. Unable to contain myself, I glanced up and said, "They came here for *protection*. They are part of my group and will not be harmed."

A slow, evil smile slid across his ivory features. "*Ah, ah, ah.*" He wagged his cruelly sharp nail at me. "You have chosen not to swear anything to us, remember? They came of their own free will into our *home*. Naughty, naughty Naomi, with a broken bond to her beloved Queen, and that…abomination. They are ours now to do with as we please—"

Rage covered my eyes in a film of red, churning my irises a deep, menacing violet. I reacted before I knew what I was doing, my wolf fueling me, my Lycan form morphing instantly, faster than it ever had before.

I had Valdov by the throat.

We were on the stairs.

Someone had me by the shoulders, but I didn't move. Not even an inch. "Listen to me, Valdov," I said, my voice gravelly, my vocal cords strained, "you will let *all* my friends go and we will all leave peacefully, or you die here. Do you understand me? No compromises."

Genuine surprise lit his features so completely, I almost laughed. He had never guessed my true strength and now he paid the price. As much as he had tasted my power, he had chosen to categorize me as a nonthreat. I squeezed a little harder to prove to him how big a mistake he had made.

"Let him go, Little Wolf Girl, or you will not enjoy my wrath." A commanding voice full of power shook the walls of the house. Picture frames bounced and delicate artifacts tinkled on tables.

Eudoxia stood at the top of the stairway.

Her eyes apparently healed enough for her to witness the scene of me taking out her favorite henchman.

I didn't let go. Instead I glanced up at her and snarled, "You had your chance to keep me here fair and square. I came willingly. I'm certain you had an elaborate scheme to drink me dry, or siphon off my power, during your gala in a few weeks. But I'm here *now*. And once I leave, you're going to be too busy to chase me down. You'll have you hands full trying to keep the sorcerers from blowing your Coterie to pieces."

"The sorcerers are fools," she snarled, gliding down the grand stairway like she wasn't using her feet. "They believe you have the power to rule the race of supernaturals. But I know better. You are not here to *rule*, as the other Sects may believe. You are here to *cause* a war between us." When my features flashed my surprise, she continued. "Yes, that's right, Little Wolf Girl, it's because of you that we will fight, and not because you will rule us, but because you are the *determinate*. When one like you surfaces, magic changes and morphs, cross-couplings occur, Sects that would never speak will unite as one. Our world is changing again, as it has once a millennia since time began. And there will be an outcome, but it will only emerge after you rain chaos down upon our heads as you bumble through this life." Her fangs flicked down as she hissed. "But you see, I am smarter than the rest. Because I will *pick* no side!" She finished with a grim smile, obviously satisfied with her tirade.

It grated that she knew so much about me, and even more so because I was still very much in the dark about everything. The Prophecy of the True Lycan had surfaced right before I'd gone to find Rourke. My father was only five hundred years old and our history had been tampered with, our sacred book burned, whole entries unaccounted for. It was clear the vampires knew much more and likely had since I'd been born, along with many of the other Sects. It put me, and the wolves, at a huge disadvantage.

Eudoxia had stopped a few steps above, gloating over me as I growled my displeasure.

We stood on uneven ground, her magic swirling around me, pushing and prodding at my skin. I made a split-second decision about how to move forward in this game, aided by my furious wolf. I had to make her choose a side. "The vampires don't get to be Switzerland, Eudoxia," I snarled. "You're already involved. You jumped in willingly when you kidnapped me weeks ago, and now you hold my friends hostage. The damage is already done. The sorcerers will be back and they will bring their High Priests and their powerful allies, seeking retribution for your counterattack." No need to mention their allies were, in fact, demons. "You will be forced to pick a side, and I suggest you pick the winning side. *Mine.*"

Valdov had used my conversation with the Queen to wiggle loose from my grip and I let him go. It would achieve nothing to kill him now. I stepped back. Rourke stood right behind me; his warmth calmed me as I slid back into my human form, his strength fortifying me.

Tyler stood to my left, ready to react, Danny slightly behind, his face set.

Their anger and need for retribution pounded in my veins. It made us strong.

"You cannot force me to choose anything, you fool, and I took no one *hostage.*" Eudoxia's voice shook, her face twitching. She was dangerously close to losing it, but managed to keep it in check as her power thrummed inside my chest like an amp at a rock concert. "My servant tried to pretend nothing was amiss when she arrived. She didn't even try to *deny* our bond had been broken when confronted or that she had murdered her blood-kin. And it will do you well to remember that she is *mine*, not yours. I care not about the human fledgling. He is of no use to me. But you will not take my tracker. She will pay for her indiscretions and the death of her brother dearly." The Queen wore a deep red satin gown, her lipstick a matching blood red. Her hair was once again piled high on her head to give the effect of maturity, but none of it masked her youthful appearance.

"She killed her brother because he was Selene's spy," I grated. "Did she inform you of that? Did she tell you he delivered her to Selene's door to be tortured? Eamon was never in your control. It was only an illusion. He couldn't wait to get back to his true *Master*. The one he'd never left."

Valdov shifted impatiently next to me.

"Impossible." The Queen sniffed. "Eamon was a faithful servant. Naomi was the conniving one. It was she who beheaded Selene all those years ago, snatching the sacred cross and fleeing like a thief in the night. It was she who deserved the punishment from the goddess herself. She should've taken heed, as I told her before she left. She was not to cross the river into Selene's territory. And now she will pay the price for ignoring her Queen's order."

"Eamon was deeply in love with Selene," I countered. "He betrayed you and his sister willingly, and if he'd stayed alive, he would have done it again. *Willingly*. He was hers to wield."

"You are mistaken once again, mongrel," Valdov spat. "You know nothing of what you speak. All the Queen's servants are faithful beyond reproach. If they are not, they are dispatched quickly and efficiently. We do not tolerate traitorous actions at court. The penalty for such a thing is death."

I turned to examine Valdov, taking in his hands, which were clasped in front of him, and his practiced demeanor. Underneath he was seething. "Is that your job?" I asked him. "To weed out the threats? To dispatch those unwilling to follow their Master blindly?"

His chest puffed with pride. "Of course! I've kept this court functioning in its purest form for hundreds of years, and I will continue to do so until there is no blood left in my veins."

It'd been clear to me from the start that he and his Queen had been together since the very beginning; both of their accents still held traces of their Russian roots. But one discrepancy kept Valdov apart from all others, which jumped to the forefront now as I eyed him. All vampires appeared to have been converted in their early twenties or thirties. They were usually exceptionally beautiful and vibrant, each chosen, as Valdov had said, with the utmost discretion.

Except for Valdov.

He appeared more like the former chancellor of a boarding school, curved nose, sharp features, late forties. He held an air of superiority, like the kind of teacher who would've enjoyed rapping a metal ruler over your knuckles just to see you squirm.

I narrowed my eyes. "I don't believe Eamon worked alone. He wasn't smart or powerful enough to keep a secret relationship with Selene going by himself. Not one where they shared information on a regular basis. He had to have help."

"What you say is false," Valdov replied briskly. "Eamon was faithful to this court. If he was a spy, I would've known in an instant. His sister is the wily one. If there is something amiss, a leak in our ranks, it is she who is responsible and I will see she *dies* a wretched death for it."

Before he could mask it—at the very center of his eye—a tiny flare of silver ignited. It was almost undetectable. If I hadn't been staring right at him, I would've missed it.

The Queen waved her arm before I could respond. "It doesn't matter what you think, Little Wolf Girl. We will not deal any longer." The Queen huffed. "I offer you nothing and I pick no sides. But you may be thankful I am allowing you to walk out of my door unscathed. I do not care if the sorcerers harvest your body parts on their altar and wash themselves in your blood. I want you out of my sight. Your chaos will not touch us any longer."

Valdov's lips formed a cruel grin. He clearly enjoyed his Queen's order to kick us out.

But I wasn't leaving.

I'd just figured out something vital. "You might want to hear what I have to say before you send us away," I said, and without waiting for her consent, I asked, "Was Valdov your schoolroom teacher?" It was clear Eudoxia had been turned into a vampire at a very young age, and her real father had been mad. It made sense she would've turned the only father figure she'd ever had into a vampire. At her confused expression I added, "You know, did you change him because you were scared and sought his guidance?"

"*What?*" she responded, obviously taken off guard.

"You heard me," I persisted, taking a bold step forward, ignoring her building wrath. "Your father was Ivan the Terrible. You were born in Russia. I catch your accent, even though it's clear you've spoken French for a very long time. I've heard the rumors of your lineage. You come from royalty, and with peerage comes private tutors." She peered at me, her gaze becoming steely. "I'll ask it again. Was Valdov your schoolroom teacher?"

"I owe you no answers, and you will get none from me." She crossed her arms, folds of red material cascading down the front of her body in silky waves. Her impatience had reached its peak with me, and I was running out of time. Her eyes flickered between gray and jet black. She was unsettled. Just enough for me to know the truth. "My heritage is of no concern of yours. I want you out of my—"

I turned like a shot, switching control to my wolf as my fist smashed into Valdov's face as he stood sneering next to me. His body rocketed into the wall because it was so light, exploding the plaster, sending pictures flying in every direction.

I growled, turning my focus back to a livid Queen, her irises a kaleidoscope of silver. "I think it's time you hired some new advisors," I said. "It seems this one isn't working out so well for you after all."

14

The Queen's shriek rocked the foundation and vamps came running from every direction. They filled the stairway and hallways, most appearing to be fresh from sleep.

Eudoxia flew forward, coming to a halt inches from me. Her eyes were fully black, her fangs as sharp as I'd ever seen them. Her power struck me hard, but I was ready. My wolf had infused us with adrenaline, fortifying us in a cloak of our own power. The golden strands, my magic signature, coated me, providing a solid barrier against Eudoxia's magic as it tried to needle its way in.

We kept her out for now.

I ran the back of my hand over my mouth, anchoring myself.

"You will answer for that." The Queen hissed. "I will happily skewer you to the wall and lap up your blood as it drains from your body." White light shot out of her hands, hitting me fully in the chest, as it had once before.

The impact launched me backward, right into Rourke's body. His hands steadied me and a fierce growl erupted from his chest.

"I've had enough," he snarled. "No one strikes us and lives. We came in here to offer you a deal, which could've been beneficial to you, but I see you've lost your touch when it comes to negotiations, Eudoxia." Power radiated off of him, his muscles tightening under his skin. "But you're not the one doing the killing here. I am. I will tear your head from your shoulders so fast your body won't have time to react."

Eudoxia's hands were fisted, and she vibrated with anger, more livid than I'd ever seen her. She was beside herself that her magic had not worked against us. By all rights I should be a babbling puddle on the floor. And as much as I wouldn't mind seeing Rourke tear her to pieces, I still needed her.

I wrapped my hand around his arm lightly, tugging him back. "Nobody is killing anyone," I said. "At least for the moment. Because the bigger problem here is the man you've trusted for years has turned against you. Valdov's a spy. You can't ignore that."

"How dare you make such accusations. You know nothing!" the Queen spat. "He has been my loyal servant for centuries and I will not listen to nonsense spouted by a lowly dog like your-self." Her power continued its assault against me, my wolf work-ing diligently to keep her out. At this pace, she was going to break down our barriers shortly.

Valdov had risen from the ground already healed. He moved for-ward, spitting his malice, but his Queen put her arm out to stop him.

She wanted me for herself.

Tyler and Danny both stepped toward Valdov and they all eyed each other critically. Nick slid to the right, ready to come up from behind if necessary. Valdov was outnumbered.

"Eamon couldn't have been a traitor on his own. You and I both know that," I pressed. "Even if you don't want to admit it, it's clear Valdov has been with you from the very beginning, and how very tired he must be of taking orders from his lowly pupil. He betrayed himself to me a moment ago, but if you need more proof, ask yourself this: Whose idea was it to bring in the goddess when you cornered me? Yours or his? You don't seem like the type to hire an archrival to do your dirty work." It was a hunch Selene and the Queen were rivals based on what Naomi had confided to me on the road. When the Queen's eyes flicked quickly to Valdov, I knew I'd guessed correctly. "Once you ordered Eamon and Naomi to accompany me, it must have played perfectly into his hands. Get Selene to kill me, finally get the cross from Naomi for himself—something you had failed to do—and finish you off so he could finally rule. Over five hundred years of taking orders from a nineteen-year-old girl. I bet he didn't even like you that much when you were human."

"You speak filthy lies," Valdov snarled as he came forward, ignoring his Queen's objections. "And I will enjoy ripping your neck out for speaking them." His face morphed further, and energy ricocheted around the room, bouncing off everything.

Before he could reach me, Rourke stepped deftly in front of us.

The vamps around the room went crazy, hissing and chomping their fangs. Rourke's snarl was enough to stop Valdov in his tracks, but Valdov was so worked up it wouldn't last long. There was going to be a serious throw-down in less than one minute unless I could end this and make some kind of deal to benefit me, as well as free Naomi and Ray. I wasn't going to leave here without them, especially now that I knew they were in trouble.

The Queen's eyes darted to Valdov.

I smiled inwardly. "You know what I'm saying is true." I addressed only the Queen, dropping my voice. "I bet he leaves sometimes and you don't know where he's been. You don't torture him like the others because of his loyalty and servitude. You have given him incredible freedom. The kind most vamps don't get. You thought in exchange for your leniency there would be unconditional—"

"*Stop!*" she commanded. My mouth snapped shut and so did every vamp's in the room. Mine shut because she surprised me, everyone else because she was the boss. She turned toward Valdov. "You will join me in my chambers *now*. The rest of you go back to sleep." She gnashed her teeth once and all the vamps slid out of the area as quickly as they'd come, including a reluctant Valdov. She hissed, her fangs still down, "I will make you suffer for playing me the fool, starting with your cherished *friends*, who are being tortured as we speak. Leave this house now before I rip your heart from your chest. Your chaos will not be tolerated here any longer."

"If I leave now, I leave with everyone," I said. There was no way I could go without them now. "In my world, exposing a traitor wins the recipient a favor. You have honor, Eudoxia. I can smell it on you."

She lashed at me, her curved nails coming within a hairsbreadth of my chest. I didn't flinch as she screeched, "I owe you nothing!"

"I just aided you," I said calmly. "If you choose to ignore me, you bring the riot down on your own head. How long before Valdov escapes from here, worried you will change your mind and believe me after all? Who does he take with him? Does your Coterie become fractured? If there's truth to my words, my reward should be a favor and we both know it. All I want is to take Naomi and Ray with me and I will leave peacefully."

She took a step backward. A slow smile crept across her features. Her demeanor changed in an instant, the grin making her fangs appear more exposed and her face skeletal. Her power continued to press against me, seeking to injure. She was still frustrated it was having little affect and it showed. "You chose that word correctly—if. *If* I uncover an untruth. And if I do not? If I find my dearest Valdov innocent? What then? Are you willing to wager on that, Little Wolf Girl? How much are your poor friends worth to you? Enough to pay the price—your life for theirs? Swear to me and you have a deal."

"The hell she will," Rourke snarled. "She already owes you one oath, vampire. She will not give a second."

The Queen gave her hand an errant wave. "I am willing to

amend the guidelines of our prior agreement to allow for her stupidity." Her eyes flickered. "And standing in our way will not help your lover's quest, cat. You should know such things by now." Her eyes went to mine. "So what will it be? Your life or theirs?"

This was an abrupt change. I had to think fast. She obviously thought she'd found a way to gain the upper hand in this situation, but if it meant I could stick around without a fight, I had to play along. "It depends on your conditions," I answered as Rourke's displeasure jumped between us. He kept quiet, but I knew it took everything he had. The Queen smiled, almost giddy in the hopes of snaring me. "What do you want in exchange for setting them free?"

"You, and you alone, will stay inside these walls." Her face dared me to object. "You will be held in a cell until I decide whether my trusted second is a traitor. You will have no contact with the outside while you are here as my prisoner. In the end you must abide by my decision whatever it may be. If he is found guilty, you and your *friends* go free. If he is innocent, I release the vampires, but you will remain until I choose your fate."

A bevy of snarls erupted behind me. I put my hand up. "If I agree to this, there has to be a timeline. I don't stay your prisoner forever. That would be—"

"There is no timeline," she snapped. "Do not forget, by harboring you I am giving you my protection and you will pay for it dearly. I will negotiate nothing more with you." Her hand made a decisive gesture downward to punctuate her point.

I met her stare, power zinging between us. "Eudoxia, if you keep me prisoner, the wolves will tear this place down and you know it. My father will not allow you to hold me indefinitely. I agree to give myself over to you to protect my friends, but I will not agree to an open-ended deal. Three days. I'll give you three days."

"You will give her *no* days," Rourke boomed, his voice stony. He turned to the Queen. "She will not be your prisoner. Amassing wolves to free you isn't necessary, because I will take this place apart before that happens, Eudoxia." He paced closer to her, snarling deeply. "There is no way you are taking my mate hostage."

Eudoxia put her hands on her waist, a smug look settling into her face. "Is that so?" Her eyes bled slowly to black. "Then you can kiss your precious allies goodbye. They are as good as dead once she sets foot outside this house. I will see to it myself."

I placed my hand on Rourke's shoulder as he made a move forward, restraining him as best I could. One hand was not enough. I encircled my other hand on his arm and tugged him back with effort.

My touch seemed to wake him up.

He was so angry he'd almost given himself over to his beast. Fur sprouted along his forearms as he turned and gazed at me, his face incredulous. "You can't be serious, Jessica! I can't stand here and let you agree to this. I've spent a lot of time in the company of vamps, and this is…madness. They drink their prisoners dry. Eudoxia has a plan and I can't let you—"

"Rourke," I said quietly, trying to reassure him by channeling my power into him through my touch as fast as I could. After a second it seemed to work. His eyes dimmed as his gaze locked on mine. I needed to convey the urgency in my words because we couldn't talk internally, so I picked them with care. "Eudoxia is a businesswoman. I am certain she will see reason in the end. Valdov is a traitor. There's no doubt. We have no reason *not* to negotiate and I can't let Naomi and Ray die at her hands, so we have no other option at the moment."

His tension was palpable. "Jessica, my beast won't allow it. I'm a fraction of a second away from taking this house down."

"Jess," Tyler added quickly, his trepidation running through me. "He's right. We can't let you do it. It's our job to protect you, and giving you over to the vamps as a hostage is not happening. We can bring an army back here later. There are too many risks and unknowns."

Gathering up an army would take too long. Ray and Naomi didn't have that kind of time. Instead of trying to convince them, which wasn't going to happen, I did what I had to do. I turned to face Eudoxia. "Three days. I leave with my life. My previous oath to you will be null and void, or I will not acquiesce. My friends go free after your judgment no matter what. After my sentence is complete, I owe you nothing."

"Done," she said loudly over the howls and outrage from my family.

"You have a deal, Eudoxia. But I want a word with my team privately before they go."

"Five minutes," she said. "The library is here." She walked with purpose to a room on the left. We followed, Rourke's rage barely contained as Eudoxia grabbed the double doors and pulled them open. We entered, and I turned to meet her gaze as she tugged them closed behind her. Haughtiness and superiority was written all over her face. "You will find one of my servants when you emerge. He will escort you to your new home. I hope you enjoy your stay." Her lips cracked into a crafty grin. "I'm certain you will find the accommodations... *inviting*."

Once the doors were closed a furious eruption of protests flooded the room.

Rourke was the only one who stayed quiet, awaiting my explanation. His expression was hooded, and a moment of regret took hold of my heart. Being mated to me was going to be a constant trial for him, because none of these decisions—decisions I had to make to save the lives of people I loved—was ever going to be easy. He knew what had to be done, but his beast wasn't rational, and he had clearly been fighting with him, and his instincts, to let me choose the right course of action to take. A decision that would land me in peril.

"Jessica," Nick's patient voice cut through my thoughts first. "This doesn't seem like the most logical choice. We could've done more to negotiate. Or come back with reinforcements as Tyler pointed out. Being the Queen's prisoner will put you at a grave disadvantage, one that will be hard to overcome."

"I agree," Danny said, shaking his head. "Inviting yourself into the Queen's dungeons isn't going to end well."

"That's exactly why I did it, Danny." I spread my hands in front of me. "None of this was going to end well. They weren't going to give Naomi and Ray up without a fight and they weren't willing to give us protection. I just bought us some much needed time and ensured us protection." I lowered my voice. "You can't forget the real reason why we're here. My father has to survive. I would sacrifice myself a thousand times over to keep him safe and so would each of you." I challenged the boys with my stare and they all nodded. "He has to live, and to ensure his life, I have to keep Ray safe. That's my *only* priority. Eudoxia would have killed Ray—there was no question. You are all going to have to trust me on this, especially you." I gazed for the first time at Rourke. "I know this is exceptionally hard for you, and your beast, but I had to do this. Eudoxia was about to kick us out. It was the only choice I had left, other than start a war where we were outnumbered fifty to one."

"Jess," Tyler pleaded. "I hear what you're saying, but three days is too long. Maybe we could've worked a day, but we can't let you stay in there for three."

"I'll be down there for a few hours at the most."

Danny cocked his head at me. "Did I hear you correctly just then?" he asked. "Did the word 'hours' come out of your mouth?"

All four of them looked at me incredulously.

"How could you possibly know that?" Tyler asked. "You just made a deal to stay for three days!"

"Because when the sun goes down, the Queen is going to have her hands full and there will be no more room to think about me."

Nick's expression opened up. "And you're stronger than she expects, so she's underestimating your abilities."

Rourke unfolded his arms, his expression still guarded. "I hear what you're saying," he said. "But Eudoxia has a plan. You can't forget that. She wasn't fooling anyone by making this agreement. Even if that asshole is a traitor, she'll never admit it. Something else is going on here."

"Of course she's not going to admit it," I said. "But she never stipulated I couldn't fight back." I gave him a slow smile. "Or that I had to stay in my cell."

Rourke raised a single eyebrow.

I inclined my head to him. "My plan is to get free as soon as possible, find Naomi and Ray, and get someplace safe." My voice was barely above the smallest whisper. "And if you don't hear from me just before sunset, you have my permission to tear the house apart."

After a moment he finally nodded.

"While you're outside, scope out the grounds and keep an eye out for James and Marcy," I told them. "Nick, I want you to make your way back over the wall and see what you can find. If you're successful in locating James, he can help coordinate the wolves. If my father is badly injured, we need him. We can't afford status fights in the middle of all this. Maggie said they would turn up here and Marcy has to stay safe."

"Will do," Nick said. "I have all the emergency Pack numbers in the SUV. If James and Marcy are free, he has likely put a call in to the Safe House. I can let them know where we are and make sure the rest of the Pack members are alerted."

I turned to Tyler and Danny. "Don't worry about me in here. Contacting Dad is your top priority. Go somewhere to shift. Keep trying. If you don't hear from me once the sun sets, find Ray and keep him safe."

The library door clicked open by itself.

Our five minutes were up.

"Are we all good?" I asked, glancing around the group.

Everyone nodded. I walked out into the foyer, Rourke behind me, followed by the boys.

There was a lone vampire waiting for me, as the Queen had promised.

He was the exact opposite of Valdov in every way: young, blond, and built like a Mack truck. I had no idea vampires could have that many muscles. He must've been changed in his absolute prime as a bodybuilder. It was weird to see, because most vamps were lean with sinewy muscle.

His incisors snapped down as he took a step toward me.

"No need to touch me," I told Conan the Vampire Barbarian, blocking Rourke with my back. If given a chance, my mate would go for his throat if this vamp mistreated me in any way, especially with a buildup of adrenaline bouncing around his system. "I will go with you willingly, as agreed. I won't put up a fight. Just let me say goodbye to them."

"You will not dictate what I can and can't do," he sneered as he reached a beefy arm toward me.

One second before Rourke took a step forward to snap him in half, I snarled, "If you touch me, I will kill you. How about that instead?" To accentuate my point, I lashed my power outward. This vamp was a baby, and even though he tried to keep up his macho façade, he shrank back against my power. "Like I said, I will follow you. Your Queen left you in charge because she knew I would not resist. I gave her my word and I will honor it. If you don't fight me on this, nobody has to get hurt."

I turned back to Rourke without waiting for Conan's approval and wrapped my arms around his neck.

He leaned down and brushed his lips against mine, whispering, "I will find you."

15

The underground maze Conan led me through was easily twice as big as the mansion above it. There were no windows and the walls were made of thick, porous limestone. Lit torches hung every ten feet, giving it an ominous feel, perfectly fit for a dank dungeon.

"The Queen couldn't spring for electricity down here? This is a little on the Addams Family side if you ask me. If anyone were watching us now, we'd be in black and white and you'd look exactly like Lurch."

"This place is off the grid and we keep it that way on purpose," Conan grumped. "And keep your mouth shut, or I'll shut it for you."

"I'd like to see that," I snickered under my breath. I could easily incapacitate him and make a break for it, but it would lead to immediate complications I didn't need. This was probably a test anyway. Send me with a baby guard and see what I'd do. She probably had fifty guards waiting around the corner. If I pushed too hard from the beginning, she would be justified in torturing me next, which I'm sure she was hoping for.

We'd passed a few closed doors, but I hadn't heard any heart-beats or movement behind them. I hadn't scented anything familiar either. I was fairly certain Naomi and Ray weren't down here, but that wasn't an absolute. Things were likely spelled.

The real question was: How was I going to break my way out of limestone and dirt?

Once I sprang myself from the cell, I would find Naomi first. She would know her way around this place. Then we could free Ray and meet up with the boys, hopefully before the demons arrived. There was no question they were coming. I just hoped my father would turn up before then. I gave a little silent prayer to Maggie. *I hope you're right, little one.*

The muscled vamp stopped in front of a huge iron door with a tiny barred window. He took his brawny arm and unlocked it with a key from his belt. He strained as he tugged it open, so I knew it was ridiculously heavy. Once it was open, he gestured for me to enter.

I walked into the cell.

And stopped. "You have got to be *kidding* me. I'm not staying in here with them."

Two vamps occupied the cramped quarters.

I turned to sucker punch Conan in the throat, but he was already slamming the door shut. Much more quickly than he'd opened it. Creep. I knew the door was spelled, but I put my fist against it just to be sure. A strong current pulsed beneath my skin. The spell had a strange signature. I'd felt something similar to it on the walk down here. It didn't feel like witch magic. Witch magic was organic; this felt concrete.

"Put the chains around your wrists," Conan ordered through the tiny window. "The ones hanging on the far wall." A single, thick finger came through the bars to point me in the right direction. I growled. I wanted to tear the digit off his hand.

"I'm not staying in here with . . . *them*, so go tell your Queen the deal is off," I snarled, bringing my face close to the window as he hastily withdrew his finger.

"If you don't do what I say, I will kill the male vamp who they say is yours," Conan sneered. The guy had one look. "I hope you refuse, because I need to feed and he looks like he'd put up quite a nice fight."

Ray could likely hold his own, but if Conan drank my blood, it would be disastrous.

I turned and glanced around the dirty cell.

The two emaciated vamps hissed at me from their respective corners. It seemed they hadn't fed in . . . years.

I was fresh meat.

The only light in the cell came from one lone torch hanging precariously from the seeping stone wall. It appeared in jeopardy of going out. "I didn't realize your Queen was so sadistic. This is hard-core imprisonment. How long have they been in here?"

"That's no concern of yours. Now put on the chains. The cuffs are spelled so you won't be able to get free."

We'd see about that.

I walked over to the chains dangling from the far wall.

The good thing was they weren't silver, so they wouldn't burn my skin. The bad thing was they were several inches thick and likely made from reinforced wolfram, one of the strongest rare metals on earth and extremely hard for a supe to break out of, hence the name.

Anything with pure natural qualities was tough for us to defeat.

I picked up a single shackle and glanced behind me at the two vamps. Defeating them and freeing myself at the same time was going to take some skill. I tried not to be too regretful of my decision to acquiesce to the Queen's wishes. *We have to be on our best game here*, I told my wolf. *We break the chains as soon as possible and keep the vamps from drinking us at all costs.* She growled her agreement. She was laser focused on the two bloodsuckers. They were so gaunt their faces appeared permanently skeletal.

"I said put on the chains," Conan snarled from the kiddy window. "But then again, I am getting pretty thirsty."

"I'm going, I'm going," I said. "And you better stay away from Naomi and Ray if you know what's good for you. If I find out you've hurt them, or partake in a single drop of their blood, I'm coming after you."

He laughed ominously. "You aren't getting out, wolf. Meet Yuri and his wife, Alana. Our resident cave dwellers. They will rip you to shreds and leave you wishing you were dead, most likely before I can walk back to my office. This is the end of the line for you. Only the worst offenders are put here. Welcome to hell."

My eyes darted to the vamps as I clicked both shackles around my wrists. I needed Conan to leave quickly. The vamps seemed to be waiting for him to leave, too, because they hadn't moved. But it was hard to tell by their vacant stares. They were each slumped in a corner opposite me. I lifted my arms and wiggled the chains at him to prove it. "I'm in. You can leave now. I'm sure you have pressing business to attend to."

"I might just stay and enjoy the show," he said.

As the weight of the wrist cuffs settled on me, I felt the spell. It had the same weird signature as the door, but this spell had a taste, which was even more bizarre.

The two vamps perked up once they saw I was secure, rising to their knees on the dirty ground and starting to gyrate like a couple of snakes in the grass. *Jesus, they're completely deranged. It looks like they've been down here for centuries and get to drink only when they have naughty visitors. We need Musclehead to vacate the area. I'm going to throw some power into my words and see if I can send him away. If not, we'll have company before we're ready. You focus on breaking the spell or we're going to be vamp dinner.*

As she sent power into the spell, it manifested strangely in my mind. It was honey colored and tasted sour. It wasn't nearly as powerful as what we'd tackled with Selene. The cuffs rang with it, but it hadn't penetrated farther into my body, which was a bonus.

"I think your Queen is calling you, Lurch," I said, throwing strength into my words, aiming it right where his face sat pinched in the window. "You better scurry away and see what she wants."

His head tipped back, glancing down the hallway.

"Yup, I just heard her again." I pushed outward, filling my mind with bright golden light, making each word count. "You better go and see what your Queen wants. Could be important. We don't want a repeat of last time, do we?" This guy had "inept" written all over him. Once I successfully got him to leave, the power I'd used to urge him would evaporate, but I hoped he'd be gone long enough for me to do what I needed to do, which was escape. And just maybe he would forget to check on me again, because he was that stupid.

He turned and grumbled, easing away from the window. His footsteps finally echoed down the tunnel, and I joined my wolf in trying to break the spelled cuffs.

As soon as he'd gone, the male vampire, whom he addressed as Yuri, scuttled up the wall *Exorcist* style. Without stopping, he clawed his way along the ceiling, making his way to me from above. *Jesus! That's the creepiest thing I've ever seen. We need to break these chains quickly.* My wolf threw all our power into the spell. It was a more technical spell than we'd encountered before, kind of like picking a lock. She yipped at me anxiously as she went. I took that as a *Please try to stall the creepers if you can while I focus on the hard stuff.*

"Listen, buddy," I told the specter, who clung upside down eyeing me, his dirty hair dangling from his head in greasy hanks, his eyes a dead, listless black. "You don't want to mess with me. If you come at me, I'll have to kill you. Do you understand what I'm saying? You've managed to survive down here for, what, a hundred years? You don't want to die now at the hands of a wolf." I knew I could put these two out of their misery fairly easily. "Or maybe you do?"

Before I could say any more, the female, Alana, lunged at me from the corner.

Without thought, I extended my arms fully, flexing my wrists hard on the chains while I arched my back against the cold stone and swung both legs up like a gymnast balancing on the rings. My feet connected with her squarely in the chest, right as my body morphed into its Lycan form. It all happened in less than a heartbeat. She flew with a screech into the wall across from me, hitting it hard, and tumbled to the ground. *Dammit, she's not down.* She rose immediately, albeit on wobbly legs, and shook herself off while Yuri hissed at me, enraged I would dare hurt his female. He primed himself to spring, bending his arms and snarling.

My wolf continued to work feverishly on the lock spell, unable to aid me with the vamps. *You have to speed it up. I can't fight them both in chains.* She gave me an irritated bark. I couldn't use my feet against Yuri, because he was coming at me from the wrong angle. Instead I primed my right fist, bringing it up to my ear, and waited. He'd have to be almost a foot from my face before I could act. And once I did, I would only have so much room before the chain expired, culling my punching radius down to two feet at the most.

He dove.

My wrists were coated in fur, the unforgiving metal gouging into my new larger frame. Once Yuri was within a foot of me, I smashed my fist into his cheek with so much force the entire chain snapped out of the limestone—bolt plate and all. Yuri flew into the stone wall across from me and crashed to the ground in a jumble of arms and legs. He lay there unmoving. *Thank goodness.*

He wouldn't stay down forever, but he'd hit the wall harder than his bride and since he was so starved, it would likely take him some time to heal his injuries.

I turned to inspect the holes where the chain and bolt plate had pulled out. *I don't get it. How could we pull the entire thing out of the wall? It should be spelled. Or maybe it was and we're just stronger?* No time to contemplate because Alana gurgled from behind me. *Let's pull the other plate out and use the chains to our advantage.* I lifted my left arm and jammed it downward in one quick motion. The second bolt plate snapped cleanly from the wall and sailed in the air. I turned, flicking my wrist at the last moment and directed the chain toward Alana.

The corner of the plate took her in the forehead.

It landed there and stuck with an ugly *thunk*. She wheeled backward, clearly not used to this much resistance from a prisoner. Right as she spun from the impact, my wolf broke the spell and the shackles on both wrists snapped open. Alana crumpled in a heap, taking the rest of the chain with her, the plate still lodged in her head.

Well, that was horribly gruesome.

I glanced from Yuri to Alana, both looking like nothing but bags of bones piled on the floor. *I kind of feel sorry for these two.* I turned back to the wall and scratched my head. *Breaking out of those chains was too easy. Eudoxia would never allow her restraints to be broken so readily. Something's up.* My wolf perked her ears in agreement. *I don't hear anyone coming. Let's see what we can find.*

I gathered power to myself and sent it outward, trying to sense if there were any other spells or signatures around me. The two vamps had surprisingly strong magic pulses when my energy cascaded over them. *They must be very old. Almost as old as Eudoxia, but not nearly as strong. Conan had said the male's name was Yuri. That sounds Russian to me. Maybe we should shackle him up and try to wake him? If he's been around that long, he must know something.*

My wolf growled, undecided. *What else are we going to do? I don't feel any other power signatures nearby. I want to know why she put me in here with these two, because I don't think this was a mistake. She knew they would be easy for us to defeat.* Something was definitely up and that was puzzling. I was missing something big. *I'm beginning to think there was trouble brewing all along between her and Valdov and I've somehow propelled us right into the middle of it.* I glanced at the still-unmoving Yuri. *Let's find out what he knows. We don't have a better option.*

I didn't wait for my wolf to agree. I walked over to the crumpled Yuri and crouched next to him, not wanting to touch him yet. I peered closely at his face. It was beginning to heal, but it was going to take a while. I stood and paced over to the free chain that had dropped off my arm—the one that wasn't currently tethered to Alana's forehead.

I couldn't look at her without cringing.

We'll have to deal with her next. I'll have to secure her before I pull the plate out so she can heal. Gross. *When I do it, we pray she doesn't wake up. Of the two, she seems the most deranged. Yuri may be our only chance of getting any good information.*

I grabbed the chain and went back to Yuri. I bent over and gingerly picked up one of his dirty feet and tugged him by the ankle toward the wall where the chains had hung before. *I'm going to try and twist the bolts back in. He's not that strong, so they may hold. I don't want him to come after me once I wake him up.* I stopped in front of the wall, resting my hand on the stone and running my fingers over the holes. They were completely torn open. *There's no way the bolts are staying in there. Let's look for something else.* I eyed the room critically and spotted a piece of rebar sticking out of the far wall. Bending the rebar over the chain might work. I made my way over, toting Yuri behind me. I reached up and hooked the end of the link on the rebar.

Now we just have to bend it.

This was going to be straight out of a superhero movie.

I knew I was strong enough, but actually doing it was another matter. I went on my tiptoes and palmed the end of the steel and pushed upward. *We can't break it off, so watch the angle and go slow.* My wolf channeled power into my hand and the muscles hardened to aid me. The metal began to move. I slid my hand down and wrapped my entire palm around it so I could mold it like clay. It totally worked.

It was kind of badass bending metal with my bare hands.

Once I secured the rebar over the chain link, I slid Yuri in front and hooked his ankle with the shackle, snapping it shut. He hadn't woken, but his face had improved. The chain didn't quite reach the ground, so his leg hung in the air a few feet above the floor. It was an awkward position, but it would help him stay put.

Now we just have to wake him up.

I went to the opposite wall and sat down, wanting to be clear of him just in case he awoke in a rage. I laid my back against the cool stone and called, "Yuri, can you hear me?"

No response.

"Yuri, it's time to wake up." I tried to infuse power into my voice.

Nothing.

He's too badly damaged and malnourished. He needs more power. But in order to transfer power directly, as Tyler had done to me when I was in Stasis, it meant I had to touch him.

I really didn't want to touch him.

Resigning myself, I crawled forward. Transferring power was coming more easily to me, especially after I'd done it on Selene, and most recently on the Porsche. As I moved, I gathered gold strands in my mind, concentrating them as I settled next to Yuri. *We give him one burst and move out of the way.* I rested my palm on his forehead and released the accumulated power. It shot straight into Yuri with a jolt, making my hands tingle. I retreated backward quickly.

The old vamp jumped like he'd been defibrillated.

His eyes blinked open.

"Hello," I said once I settled back against the wall. "My name is Jessica McClain, and I'm sorry I had to smash your face in, but I think you're going to heal. You may want to rethink your attack modes in the future, however, to avoid another massive head injury."

He hissed at me, shaking his leg, struggling to right himself.

"I don't think you can get free, but if you do, I'll just knock you out again and try something else. So instead of trying to get free, how about we just make some kind of a deal? I need information and you want out of this cell. Right? If you tell me what I need to know, I'll release you and...your bride. Does that sound fair?"

"Waaast do you want?...I"—his voice was broken with a strong Russian accent—"need..."

It was clear Yuri hadn't spoken or dealt with anyone in a very long time.

"You need what? To escape this place?" I prodded.

"More...power..." He hissed. It was paining him to speak. He had healed more, but it was still going too slowly. *What we won't do for information.* My wolf yipped in agreement. I crawled back over to him, mostly because it was easier to stay on his level.

"I'm here to help you," I cautioned as I moved closer. "But if you lash out, I won't hesitate to defend myself. After I give you power and you heal a little more, we are going to make a deal. Nod if you agree." I looked down at him, wondering if I'd receive anything coherent back. "And once you make that deal, I'm going to hold you to your word."

He nodded once.

I placed my hand over his forehead and pushed more power into him. His head arched under my grip, his eyes fluttering. They went from dead black to a hint of normal flecked with silver. "*Ahhhh...*" he moaned. "Haven't...felt...in too long..."

After a moment he went still and I brought my hand off his head and moved back on my heels, but stayed where I was. He blinked a few times and then glanced up at me.

"How long have you been down here?" I asked curiously. "Did Valdov put you here? Or was it the Queen?" I had so many questions, but being in the shape he was, he may not be able to answer all of them.

"Valdov," he managed, "has doomed us...the Queen can do...nothing."

I sat up a little straighter. "Valdov is in charge?"

"He wields...much power...over her." His eyes flickered in earnest now, mostly staying free of black, his face almost fully healed. What he really needed was blood, but he wasn't getting mine. That was not an option. "My niece...will not rule...much longer...have to...stop him."

Niece? "You're Ivan the Terrible's *brother*?" I gasped, jumping to my feet. "How did you get locked in here? If you're Eudoxia's blood-kin, this is even worse than I first imagined."

He shook his head, his eyes rolling back in his head for a moment. I understood. It was too much to tell me right now and we needed to move on.

"Listen"—I crouched onto the balls of my feet—"what I really need to find is a way out of this dungeon without raising attention. I'm beginning to think I've been put in this cell for a reason. All this can't be a coincidence." His eyes were focused back on me. "I'm searching for a vampire named Naomi. Do you know where they might keep her? She has something valuable in her possession, and if Valdov has already gotten ahold of it, it may be too late for your Queen."

"You are not...in a dungeon..." He gasped. "It is trickery. We are in a crypt...behind the mansion. Below us...is only one way out. There are...tunnels below."

"*What?*" I exclaimed as I stood. I had not expected that to come out of his mouth. "The muscle vamp took me down steps and we never came back up. We have to be underground. That can't be right."

"It is an ancient ward...few can sense..."

The strange signature I'd felt was a ward? It had all been an elaborate illusion. Damn. "You said the only way out was tunnels beneath us. How do I find them?"

He lifted his hand and pointed to the corner.

Right where Alana was lying like a corpse.

"It is below..."

I peered at the corner skeptically. "So we're actually in a crypt aboveground? And below us are underground tunnels. Is that what you're saying?"

He nodded. "There is a vast...graveyard on the grounds. Each crypt is connected...by a network...of tunnels."

It was hard to wrap my mind around it, but I had no reason to doubt him. There was an easy way to find out if he was telling the truth. If there was no access to a tunnel in the corner, he was lying. "If I free you now, will you stay away from me?" I asked. "I need you to tend to your bride so I can uncover the tunnel. I knocked her out, but she should heal—I have to warn you it's a little gory."

"I will not attack," he managed. "But you will...promise to... honor your part..."

"Of course I will honor it," I said. "Once I find my friends, I will come back and break you out of this horrid prison." I had no idea what freeing him would do, or why the two of them were kept here, but I didn't care.

"It's been too long..." He sighed. "We will finally...have our retribution."

"I'm going to unchain you now, and then I need to move Alana." I reached above his head to the rebar. It was easier than trying to pry the cuff off his leg.

Right as my palm touched the metal, a cold, bony hand wrapped around my ankle.

I had to resist a very strong urge to kick him off and quiet the growling wolf in my head. Instead of reacting, I angled my head down to meet his gaze, my eyes holding a question.

"We have waited...for you." His eyes were now a clear muted blue.

I pried the rebar open just enough to unhook the chain. Then I stepped back, breaking his grip on me. He let go without a fight. "What exactly do you know about me?" It was hard to believe this emaciated vamp, left in a crypt to rot for centuries, would know anything about me.

"It was foretold..." he whispered.

"But you attacked me when I first arrived. You didn't think I was anything special then," I pointed out. "Why the sudden change of heart?"

He said one word in Russian. "*Sila.*" When my expression didn't change, he said another. "Strength."

16

I waited for Yuri to elaborate on his comment. "Okay..." I said when he remained silent. "I guess we can choose to continue this discussion at a later date." I glanced around the cell. "I need to get out of here," I muttered.

I strode over to Alana.

Dragging her along the ground would just be wrong, so I bent down to pick her up. It was the only decent thing to do. She weighed next to nothing and thankfully did not stir. As I carried her to Yuri, the end of the chain still attached to her forehead clattered along the ground. Nice.

I lowered her carefully into his open arms.

His face said it all. This was his bride. "I'm sorry, you know"— I pointed to her head once I deposited her in his lap—"about her wound. She wasn't very reasonable and I had to stop her." And a metal plate to the forehead did the trick. "I'm sure you'll be able to work it out, but you may want to act fast and do it while she's still unconscious."

"She will…heal…" he said quietly. "Go now. They will be back soon…"

I headed over to the corner.

The entire cell was full of dirt. I knelt, plunging my hands into the ground. About a foot down I hit wood. It was some kind of trapdoor. "Do you use this often?" I asked, glancing over at him. "It doesn't seem like a super-duper idea to have a permanent escape hatch in the floor of a prison cell."

"It is not nice…below," he answered. "You must…beware."

That sounded ominous.

My wolf snarled. After the creatures we'd encountered fighting Selene, I wasn't looking forward to meeting any new surprises. "Care to shed a little more light on that before I head down into the depths of despair?"

"Trows," he answered.

"Trolls?"

Gads! I didn't want to fight a troll.

He shook his head. "No, Trows. The Queen employs them… to keep intruders out and…us in."

"You mean like fairies?" I replied, flipping quickly through my mind for my limited knowledge of a Trow. If I was right, I had a vague recollection of them from old books I used to page through in my father's library when I was a kid.

"Much worse than fairies…evil…small…mixed with troll… lives in water."

Water. That's right. New Orleans was at sea level. I'd been so stupid. I felt like slapping myself between the eyes. Of course we weren't in a basement. Down meant water.

I ran my hand around the wooden trapdoor, searching for a way to pry it open. I found it in the form of an old iron ring and pulled. The old wood hatch creaked as it bowed, caught by matted earth around the edges. I yanked harder, careful not to rip the iron ring off completely.

It finally swung fully open.

The smell was horrific.

I gagged, covering my mouth. "You have to be kidding me!" I coughed through my closed fingers. "It smells like death lives down there." Eudoxia was going to get an extra sock in the jaw for making me go through this. "Maybe I should just tear the main door off its hinges and we can all go free right now? That sounds like a much better option." I let go of the trapdoor and made a motion to stand.

"No!" Yuri's voice held a strong note. The first I'd heard from him. I looked over at him. He was totally healed, still cradling his bride. "If you do that, the vampires will swarm. An alarm will sound and we will all be punished. Down is the only way."

Damn. He was right. Swarming vampires would not be ideal at the moment. I couldn't free anyone with a horde of vampires after me. I reluctantly knelt by the hole and pulled the hatch up again and glanced down into the putrid darkness.

This time I heard movement. "What's the trick to defeating a Trow? And once I do, how do I know where to go?"

Alana stirred, moaning. Yuri petted her hair as he spoke. "There is only one way. Once you reach the end, there will be a gate." His voice cracked, but it was almost back to normal. He cleared his throat, his heavy Russian accent still pronounced. "You will need to break the ward. Once you do, you will have only seconds to pass through or you will be trapped inside the gate forever." His eyes danced with adventure. Yuri was definitely on the mend. "Remember . . . it must be done quickly."

"How come you've never broken out?" I asked from my position crouched over the opening, studying the darkness below. "You obviously know what's down there." Being trapped here for that many years would teach you a thing or two. I was surprised he hadn't been driven to escape, if anything for the sake of his bride's sanity.

"Breaking the ward will take everything you have, and much more power than I have ever possessed," he confessed. "Though I have tried to disastrous results. Mending the ravages of the Trows is no small thing. Keep them from biting you if you can."

I raised an eyebrow. "Are they poisonous?"

"No," he answered. "But their teeth are jagged and honed to tear the meat off your bones. Move swiftly. And once you breach the gate, you will not have time to tarry. The ward will try to hold you if it can."

"Anything else?" I asked. "Run faster than the Trows and make sure I bolt through the ward."

He nodded, satisfied.

His improved demeanor was nice to witness, but he still looked like a ghoul. If he really was Ivan the Terrible's brother, he was the true blood tsar to the Russian throne. If Russia still had one.

I eyed the hole again.

My wolf had not stopped growling since I'd opened the trap-door and exposed the hideous smell. *We have no choice. We have to get through whatever is down there in order to find Naomi. Once we break through the ward, I hope to locate her quickly, and when we do, let's hope she hasn't been hurt too badly. There's no more time left to discuss this.* My wolf paced in my mind. She was as agitated as I'd ever seen her. Knowingly jumping into danger wasn't on the list of things that made her the happiest. *Time to go.*

"Wish me luck." I saluted Yuri once before leaping through the trapdoor, falling about twenty feet and landing with a huge splash in three feet of rancid water.

The smell threatened to overtake me.

My calves were buried in thick sludge. *Good grief. I can see why Yuri doesn't venture down here very often.* My wolf snarled, keeping her nose in the air, scenting for danger. *How can you smell through this muck? We have to try to do what Tyler does. Once we categorize a scent, we have to parcel it away in our minds. I'm categorizing this as "putrescence from the vamp crypt."* I focused on the essence of the smell and tried to fit it into an empty space in my mind. It finally slid into place, but only after I opened myself up to the myriad other smells lingering in this hole. *Did you see that? I concentrated on the dirt smell, not the water smell, and it went away. Let's keep doing that. Is there anything nice down here? Like a bed of roses?* Of course there weren't any flowers, but a girl could dream.

I wrapped my hands around one of my thighs and yanked my foot out of the muck. It made a huge slurping noise as it came loose. My shoe managed to stay on, but just barely. *Well, if the Trows didn't know we were here before, they do now. Can you see anything?* It was pitch-black. My eyes began to take in grainy shapes, pulling in a fraction of light from someplace.

There were scurrying sounds behind me.

I took off, moving as quickly as I could, and considering the wretched, sloppy terrain it was impressive I could actually maneuver through it so fast. As I ran, my splashes echoed loudly in the tunnel. The Trows would be on us soon.

From the pictures I remembered as a girl, Trows were hideous little creatures with trollish features, wicked nails, and long jagged teeth. They were always depicted emerging out of a murky stream next to an English cottage, presumably to terrorize small English children. Many of the creepiest animal-like creatures were native to Europe. America had birthed a few nasty ones, like the windigos—the Native American flesh-eating bogeyman—but Europe had a run on the creepy-crawlies. They had gremlins, goblins, drakes, ogres, and brownies to name a few. Eudoxia likely had the Trows brought over from Europe. She apparently preferred to import her terror.

More than one splash echoed behind us.

Can you get a sense of how many are coming? Soon the splashes became too numerous to count. *Dammit.* My wolf was so focused on the path ahead of us, all she had time to do was to snap her jaws. *We have to try and outrun them, give us more juice.* A rush of adrenaline hit me and I started to sprint faster. A few strides later a loud keening sound rent the air to my left. I wrenched my head just in time to see something jump on my back. It was much smaller than I'd anticipated, about the size of a large house cat, but its claws were sharp. They cut deeply into my back. *I'm going to smash it against the wall, but we can't stop moving. It's not very big—*

Its teeth sank into the base of my shoulder.

"*Motherfuc—*" I collided with the side of the tunnel as hard as I could at a dead run. The tunnel walls were only hollowed-out earth, but I'd hit it with enough strength to knock it off me. *I think I squashed it.* There was no time to look back. Yuri had said their bites weren't poisonous. I didn't feel anything suspicious. I was just pissed off it had bitten me before I could shake it off. *I guess their only real tactic is to tear you to pieces one bite at a time.* This was exactly what I'd been cautioning Danny and Tyler about on our last journey. An army of *anything* could bring even the most powerful supernatural to their knees. *If there are too many, it's going to be a huge problem. They're going to swarm us if they get the chance.*

We just couldn't give them the opportunity.

I kept running, increasing my pace as much as I could, using every available body part to aid me.

My legs went higher with each stride, which allowed me to move through the water quicker. I was in my Lycan form, but I needed more power. *Hit us with more adrenaline.* As my wolf fortified us, a flicker came from my peripheral vision. Another Trow leapt at me from the shallow embankment. As it flew through the air, I got a good glimpse of its face. It was mean-looking with deep-set eyes, scaly skin, rows of uneven pointy teeth, and an accentuated piglike snout.

I swung my fist around in a blur and knocked it cleanly out of the air.

It bounced out of my field of vision and I heard it plunk in the water. *We're moving too fast for most of them to mob us, but when we reach the gate, we'll have to work fast. I don't know how we're going to keep them from attacking us.* My wolf barked and showed us glowing, our power pushed out like a shield. *Do you think we can do that? Like Stasis?* She yipped. I'd gone into a cocoonlike state the last time I'd been bitten by a poisonous insect. All my power had been channeled outward like a protective bubble to keep me alive. *We can try, but if we go into full Stasis, we'll be trapped down here for a long time. We have to try for half-Stasis. Is that even possible?*

I had no idea, and judging by my wolf's reaction, neither did she. But we needed to do something or we weren't going to make it out alive. These little beasts were going to eat me alive until there was nothing left but a skeleton.

Twenty more paces and I spotted a large glowing area. *I see something.* My wolf funneled more power to my muscles. Together we were siphoning everything we had. Another Trow ran into my line of vision, but I dodged it easily as it lunged haphazardly. *It sounds like there's a horde of them behind us. Let's start transferring our energy outward.* Gold strands of power manifested in my mind. *We need to weave it together.* I concentrated on the golden light pushing it together to form an opaque mass. The glowing up ahead became clearer. *That doesn't look like any gate I've ever seen. What is it?*

It was a monstrous brick wall.

The only thing adorning it, or making it appear remotely like any kind of passageway, was a gigantic curved knocker with the head of a vampire bolted to the middle.

I knew instinctively if I touched the vampire bad things would happen. *We don't go near the knocker.* My wolf barked in agreement, still focusing on managing our magic. We were steadily moving it outward. *How are we going to get past that brick wall? It will take too long to tear a hole through it, if that's even possible. Once we stop, we aim the magic out like Stasis and pray it's enough to keep the Trows off us until we can figure out how to break through.* I'd been unconscious the last time I'd gone into Stasis, but when I'd woken up, I'd felt the power. I had to make it feel almost like that. We couldn't force it too far outward and risk losing consciousness. That would be a very bad thing. *I'm counting on the fact the Trows don't have much magic. If they do, we'll need a plan B or they'll rip through our barrier with their greedy pointy teeth.*

I ran straight up to the wall without stopping, jamming my claws into the bricks. *Now!* My wolf shot the concentrated power outward like a balloon. My golden power flexed tightly around us, right as the first one launched itself forward. *Can you feel them? Are they bouncing off?* I craned my head around. *Ohmygods.* We were already knee-deep in nasty Trows. But they couldn't get to my body. The power block had worked and they were furious, jumping and spitting, that they couldn't get to the prize.

It's working and I don't feel much magic coming from them. Now we just have to break the ward. I closed my eyes and ran my hands along the wall, trying to sense the magic. As I did, my bubble of protection flexed. *Shit. I don't think we can keep the Trows out and break the ward at the same time. It's going to take too much of our resources to do both. Once we grasp the ward, we'll need to shift the power from our shield into the spell. It's going to leave us open to bites for a few moments, but it can't be helped.*

Double damn.

I continued to run my hands over the coarse brick. The ward tasted tart and old, like biting into an unripe crab apple. It had the same underlay as the cell chains. *What kind of magic is this?* I'd never come across it before. *It doesn't have a witchy signature like Tally's or Marcy's, or even Selene's.* My knowledge of spell casters was limited, so it wasn't saying much. *Do you taste that?* The spell had manifested in the back of my throat in a physical way, settling on my tongue like a coat of pollen. *Whatever it is it's ancient, and I have no idea how to break it.*

The Trows continued to snarl and leap around my feet.

This was becoming a funhouse. *We need to split our power and start filtering half of it into the spell.* With effort, I grabbed on to some of the power, and as I funneled it forward, as predicted, the barrier between us and the Trows shrank. *We have to keep no less than a foot between us and them.*

Suddenly their behavior changed and they quieted.

Do you hear that? What are they doing? The Trows had stopped jumping and were now emitting weird clicking noises. *They're pissed they can't get to us and I think they're discussing their options.*

Thinking these little beasts had intelligence was almost too much for me. *Yuck.*

I had no choice but to ignore them and turn back to the task of breaking the ward. I searched for a weakness. *Yuri said it would take everything I had, but I can't even find what to focus on. The spell feels like a cloud. How do I break apart cloud? When I try to touch it, it moves.* She flashed me a picture of us pouring air into a balloon. *You mean fill it up?* Yuri had stated emphatically I needed to close the gate when I was done. *Then once we're through, we suck our power back out?* That must be it. I had to inflate it and then take it back out so the ward stayed intact and nothing else could get free and come after me. *We can't fill this sucker up slowly; it's too big. It will drain us dry and leave us to the Trows. We have to go all in and jam it full in a few seconds. Hopefully it will work. If not, I got nothing and the Trows are going to eat us.*

My wolf growled uneasily, but I took it as a yes.

We really had no other option.

Ready? The Trows had backed off for the moment and were having a full-on clicking discussion likely on how to get around my barrier and end me. I hoped like crazy that whatever I did to the wall would be so shocking that they wouldn't have enough time to react for the few precious moments while we stood unguarded.

My wolf went into a fighting stance in my mind, ears back, low snarl.

This was it.

In the time it took to blink, I grabbed on to the power outside of my body and threw it all into the bricks. The wall took it greedily. I closed my eyes and focused on filling the rest of it up. I grit my teeth hard as the energy yanked us forward, crushing me into the barrier. I held my ground, shoving my power to the far recesses of the gate as fast as I could.

Almost there, I panted.

Without warning there was a massive tearing sound and both my arms slid through the bricks.

Keep pushing outward. Along with the ward cracking, there was a ridiculous shriek behind me and a beat later multiple sharp teeth tore in to my legs. Pain zinged up my spine. The Trows had figured out I was fair game. I kicked my legs out in a desperate attempt to fling them off me.

Just a little more and we're there.

My waist and shoulders began to inch through the opening. The bricks hadn't moved. My body was literally seeping through the barrier. The entire thing must be an illusion. I pressed my face into the ward and found it was black like a void.

We're almost inside. I gave one more internal shove, throwing the last of my power into the final nooks and crannies, and passed completely through the bricks with a loud pop. Absolute darkness consumed me. The Trows shrieked their displeasure on the other side. They sounded muted from in here. I was relieved they hadn't been able to pass through. Surprisingly, it didn't feel claustrophobic inside the ward, but I knew if I stayed much longer, a possible phobia might develop.

I extended my arms outward, testing.

My power was still all around me, keeping the space open, but the ward pressed down against us, trying to beat my power back. *We're in a no-man's-land. We need to blast through to the other side and we have to do it before the ward chokes our power out.*

I closed my eyes, even though it was dark, and concentrated on the energy around me. *The only thing we can do is gather our power and try to force it back out in a blast and hope it's enough.* I exhaled, and in one motion, sucked all the power that I'd encased in the ward back into my body. It plunged back in like a shot, making me stumble. The ward compressed as I took my magic back, stealing the air out of my lungs.

I braced my hands in front of me.

As quickly as I could, before the ward crushed the life out of me, I shot a concentrated blast of power out in front of me. A big boom of thunder hit my ears and the next thing I knew, I was sprawled on a dirt ground panting.

I blinked and looked around.

I think we're out.

I sat up slowly, dusting off my hands. I twisted my legs around and examined them for Trow damage. I'd been so amped up on adrenaline and power, I hadn't felt the continued assault. My spandex was full of holes, but it was still intact. *Everything is healed already. Thank goodness those little shits didn't have any venom.* I was in my Lycan form, and apparently my muscles were harder to ravage.

Brushing off my legs, I stood and tried to figure out where I was.

It was dark, and I took a step forward, right as something rammed into the back of my legs. I crashed to the ground, rolling once before I shot to my feet, crouching low, arms out to the sides in my fighting stance.

"It's wonderful you could join us," a voice whispered in my ear. "We've been waiting."

17

There was no one in front of me. The tunnel was empty. It was not as dark as where I'd just been. My eyesight adjusted and I saw there was a slight incline leading uphill, which I assumed would eventually lead me out of this underground hell to freedom.

The breathy voice hit my ear again as soft prods, like invisible fingers, landed all over my body. "We need you, *Jessica*. Come help us."

Another voice, this one childlike, cried, "You took too long. I want to see my mommy."

My fur sprang on end as my skin erupted in millions of goose bumps.

Ghosts.

Yuri had said the tunnels ran under a cemetery. *No, no, no. Please don't tell me we're trapped underground with a healthy number of ghosts.* My wolf's ears were pinned back. *Don't panic*, I told her—but really, I needed those words myself. I cringed at the thought of ghosts. How do you fight against something you can't see? My wolf was equally freaked out. Her canines were exposed, her lips curled. It would be hard to defeat beings who had such little power and no magic.

I had no idea how to make them go away.

"What do you want?" I asked, taking a few steps forward. Currents of air continued to brush against my face and arms. There was no way to know how many were here with me.

"We want to be *free*," a voice whispered right next to my ear.

"*Outside*. I want to go outside."

"My mommy is calling. Can't you hear?" Something shook my pant leg.

Baby ghosts?

Did I really need to be assaulted by infant specters? I tried to rack my brain for a reason why I deserved to have tiny invisible children haunting me, but I came up with nothing.

Vicious Trows were worse than being trapped in a tunnel with a few ghosts, right?

I needed some perspective. These ghosts obviously wanted something from me and I needed to find Naomi. Maybe they would make a trade and leave me alone. "I don't know if I can help you," I called around me, cautiously moving forward. "But if you help me, I will try and help you. That's all I have to offer."

"Power." Something glided by my face, shifting the air currents around me. "So much...*power*."

"Come with *us*." The voices sounded far away yet close, like an invisible hand was toggling a huge volume control knob.

"We will show you the way."

"You will take care of us."

Invisible fingers prodded me forward and I let them guide me. I addressed the crowd at once. "I'm looking for a vampire named Naomi. Do you know where she is? Medium height, chestnut hair, pretty features, smart as a tack?"

"Yes."

"We know her."

"They brought her here."

Hope pricked along my senses. "Is she being held somewhere close? Do you know if she's safe?" I asked.

"Awful."

"Sad." A ghost started to cry.

Jesus, when ghosts cried, you knew the news was going to be as shitty as possible. "How badly is she hurt?" My voice rose several octaves, and even though I had no idea where I was going, I started to trot down the tunnel. It leveled off after the first small hill and started to twist and turn. "What is this place? Where are we?"

"The House of Death." Voices clamored around me, echoing the word "death."

Well, that was nice.

I tried to project my inner voice out to Rourke and my brother. If we were all out of the mansion, it may work. *Can you hear me, Rourke?* I switched channels. *Tyler, are you out there? What's going on?*

"They cannot hear you."

"The Queen prevents it."

"Hey," I yelled. "Stay out of my brain!" I couldn't feel them floating around in there, which is what I guessed they were doing, but I wanted my thoughts to stay my own. "Why can't my Pack hear me?"

"The same reason we cannot get out."

"And?" I asked. "What reason would that be?"

"The barrier."

"Is stifles us."

"It holds us tightly."

This wasn't getting me anywhere. I had no idea what barrier

they were talking about, but Naomi was my first priority. "Is Naomi in the...House of Death with us?" I asked. "Can you lead me to her?"

"Crypts...crypts...crypts."

"Are all the crypts connected?" I asked.

"Yes."

"Just underground."

"Beneath the soil."

They continued to usher me forward, their ghost fingers tickling my skin. Grainy outlines made maneuvering possible, but having the invisible guides made it much easier. "Are we moving toward Naomi?"

"Yes."

"We will take you."

"For a price."

That wasn't surprising. Everything had a price.

The tunnel changed course while I ran. They prodded me in the right direction each time I hit a roadblock—I hoped. I really had no idea. They could be leading me to someplace terrible and I'd be none the wiser. "Are we almost there?" Before they could answer, I spotted a wooden door up ahead. It was old and corroded, set into the earth on an iron frame, anchored by ancient timbers. It must be a way up to one of the crypts aboveground.

I slid to a stop.

"No, no," a breathy voice said so close to my face I flinched. "That is not the one."

"Mustn't go up there."

"He should not wake."

"Danger to us all."

"I take it this is the wrong door?" I said sarcastically. "You guys need to pick up the pace. My team is looking for me. I need to find my friends. Can't we just head through here"—I gestured to the old door—"and take a more direct route through the cemetery?" Being underground was beginning to take its toll. It was so dark and dank it was messing with my state of mind.

"No. Can't go."

"Bad man." A child's voice began to whimper.

"He will harm us."

My sarcasm was clearly lost on the incorporeal. "If this is not the right door, you need to show me where the right one is, and after I free my friend, I will try to...break the barrier you keep chattering about." Maybe if the barrier went down, I could finally talk to my Pack.

"Yes. The barrier must come down."

"Freedom."

"We will show you the way."

I started to run once again. Two more turns and several doors later the hands guided me to a stop. This door was the most detailed one I'd seen. It also appeared to be well used. It was decorated with ghoulish pictures of graveyard bandits, with masks and shovels, digging up graves. If I had to guess, this must be one of the main torture chambers. "If she's not okay, I am going to seriously hurt someone," I murmured to myself.

"Asleep."

"Sleep of the dead."

"Not much time left."

A concentrated shove sent me tumbling closer to the door.

"No need to push," I growled. "I'm going." I grabbed on to the black doorknob and was immediately flung back by a strong jolt of power. "*Cripes.*" I recovered, shaking my hand until the sting abated. This door was spelled, and it was decidedly witchy. I had to be more careful in this madhouse. "Why didn't you tell me it was warded?" I grumbled to my ghost posse. "That would've been extremely helpful."

"Magic is weak."

"Cannot keep us out."

"We will help you."

At once the door popped open, creaking on its old hinges. That was an unexpected surprise. "I could've used you guys in the Trow tunnel."

"Cannot pass there."

"Magic keeps us out."

"Old wards are strong."

"Okay, okay," I said. "I'm going to try and dial my sarcasm down to a minimum from now on." I ducked my head through the opening and tread carefully up steps made of packed earth. They were terribly corroded and barely counted as steps. They were more like lumps of dirt. Once I reached the top, a trapdoor made of thick, white marble loomed above me.

The bottom entrance to the crypt above.

"Is this warded?" I asked.

"It is free."

"Vampires leave it so."

"You may enter."

Let's make sure, I told my wolf. I tentatively pressed a single fingernail on the marble. A soft hum of magic met my touch, but nothing threatened me directly. It was probably residual magic. The main door to the outside of the crypt was likely heavily spelled, but whoever was in charge of the torturing must think warding the trapdoor was unnecessary.

"Here we go," I said as I braced my palms against the cool surface and pushed upward. I had to use a considerable amount of strength because the marble was crazy heavy. "This must be two feet thick," I grunted. "But it's working." There was no resistance, so I kept sliding.

Once it was fully open, the smell of blood hit me.

I caught Naomi's scent immediately following.

I leaned up and peered into the room. There were faint Gothic shapes decorating the ceiling of the chamber. It was dark inside the crypt. Just like the tunnels, and I could tell from my position and the sloping beams of the roof it was big inside, more like a mausoleum than a crypt. "Is it safe to go inside?" I asked. "No other nasties waiting to attack?" Why not ask my ghost pals if I had the chance? I didn't detect anything, but that didn't mean something wasn't lurking.

"You can enter," a whisper floated by my ear.

"No one is here."

"Can I see my mommy now?"

Good grief.

I eased myself through the opening, my body back to my human form. My change was automatic now, not even triggering much thought. I didn't know if that was good or bad.

The first thing I noticed was a long, rectangle slab of stone perched in the middle of the room.

Normally it would've held a coffin with a dead person inside. Instead there was a single shrouded figure lying on top. This wasn't like Selene's lair with torture devices hanging all over the walls. This was obviously a place where they took vamps to make sure they didn't wake. Naomi had once told me she knew how to incapacitate a vamp. I should've asked for details while I'd had the chance. Now I was left to my own devices. *I hope she's not badly hurt. That mummy wrap doesn't look too promising. It could be hiding a lot of damage.*

I paced toward her slowly, scenting everything I could.

There were traces of Valdov's signature, but he hadn't been here recently. I couldn't identify anyone else, because I'd never smelled them before. I scented lots of blood—mostly Naomi's, which smelled oddly like me. But the white sheet wasn't swathed in red. *How do you think they're keeping her unconscious? I smell blood but I don't see any.*

"You must hurry."

"It takes too much."

"Cannot regenerate the bloodletting."

"Bloodletting?" I asked, alarmed. I rushed to the fabric containing her and tore it apart. It ripped easily, falling onto the cold mausoleum floor with only a whisper of a sound. She was swathed in a few layers so it took me some time to get through it all. "Come on," I urged as I tore. "Please be alive." The first thing I uncovered was her chest. It was unmoving, but that was to be expected. She was still dressed. I took both my hands and split the last layer of cloth straight up to her neck. There was a loud *zzzzzzip* as the fabric fell apart in my grasp.

A still, bone-white face stared back.

Her eyes were closed and there were heavy dark spots sunken just above her cheekbones. She was so still she appeared to be dead. I had to remind myself that was still normal.

"The arm."

"Must take it out."

"It's hungry."

"Blood fills the walls too quickly."

What walls? I didn't hesitate. Her arms were each wrapped separately. I tore the cloth completely away. One of her arms was hooked to what looked to be a tiny silver funnel. Where it touched her skin, a patch had burned away completely. It was oozing thick red blood. Anger bubbled up inside me so fiercely it took all I had not to bellow my rage and alert everyone within a twenty-mile radius. I reached over her body and tore the funnel from her arm. It burned my fingers, but it didn't register. As I did, a plastic tube I hadn't noticed flew with it, breaking from wherever it had been secured, spraying blood all over the room.

"What the hell was that?" I yelled, jumping out of the way, wiping blood off my face with my forearm. "Why was she hooked to a tube?" I leaned over and picked up some of the discarded fabric and blotted the blood off Naomi's pale skin, hovering over her hoping she'd wake.

"You must feed her quickly."

"She yearns for blood."

"The walls are almost full."

"What *walls* are you talking about?" I shouted in frustration. "Can someone please tell me what's happening in more than three or four words?"

"You must look below." Something shoved me from the back, prodding me around the side.

I complied and walked around the thick marble structure that held Naomi's unconscious body.

"She feeds it too quickly."

"She is not like other vamps."

"She is strong." The whispers came quickly, jumbled together like they were all talking at the same time.

For some reason the ghosts seemed suddenly nervous.

I spotted a circular hole near the bottom where the tube must have been hooked. My stomach lurched. Naomi's blood had been draining into this thing, filling it up. I inhaled, moving closer to the small opening. There was so much blood. As fast as she could regenerate, it was being siphoned away.

That's how they kept vamps incapacitated. They knocked them out and drained their lifeblood, making them too weak to fight or even wake up.

But what her captors didn't realize was she didn't have ordinary blood running through her veins.

She had mine.

It made her stronger, so she would survive. She had to survive.

"Who did this to her?" I demanded. I addressed the ghosts, because there was no one else around to question. My wolf snarled and snapped her muzzle, urging me to free her. *We just need to feed her and give her more blood. Then she'll be as good as new. We have to believe that.*

I maneuvered myself next to her, leaning over her stark face, whipping my wrist up to her mouth, ready to tear my skin with my teeth.

"No!"

"You must wait."

"Have to stop *it* first."

The voices rushed up against my ears urgently and hands jostled me in place, forcing me to drop my wrist.

"Stop what?" I yelled. "You said two minutes ago I had to feed her. She clearly needs my blood or she's not going to wake up." I glanced down at her arm where the silver had been secured. It wasn't healing. "What do I need to do? Stop giving me one word answers and *tell me*."

"Must release the blood."

"What do you mean *release* the blood? You're not talking about the blood in the bottom of this altar, right? Please tell me you're *not* talking about the blood that has been draining from her all this time and is now sloshing around in this giant marble bathtub."

"If the blood is not freed, she cannot heal."

"It keeps her here."

"The blood binds her to *it*."

They were definitely talking about something I didn't understand.

My arms prickled. Shivering, I stepped back and searched the room again, but I didn't feel any spells. I glanced down at Naomi. The only *it* they could be talking about had to be inside the stone altar. Tentatively, like reaching out to pet a rabid animal, I placed both my palms on top of the white and gray veined marble platform.

Something pulsed beneath them.

Did you feel that? I asked my wolf as I slid my hands to another location trying to sense what was happening. *Her blood is feeding something.* Another small vibration flittered under my palms, like a heartbeat. *Holy shit. Whatever they hooked her up to just got a payday with my blood.*

"What's in there? What's feeding off her?" I called. The marble jumped under my hands again, this time much stronger. It knew I was here and it was angry. But it wasn't formed enough to break free, and I just stopped its food supply. It had been so close. Too close.

"The Strigoi stir."

"The soul wakes."

"It is always hungry."

Oh, dear gods. A Strigoi was the spirit of a dead vampire. In the lore we called them Screamers—vamps whose physical bodies died a true death, but their spirits hung around to wreak havoc on the living. Just like the ones floating around me now, except myth stated that Screamers could still feed on blood. "Can a Screamer really become corporeal if it drinks enough blood?" I urged. I knew only a few stories, but they were legendary. Hideous bloodsuckers with incredible strength that couldn't be killed. "You have to tell me. How dangerous are they?" I gave an inward shudder. When the ghosts didn't answer, I yelled, "*Tell me!*"

At my raised voice, the marble top bounced, jutting to the side. The platform wasn't attached to the bottom of the altar.

No more time.

We have to drain her blood out of this thing, I told my wolf. *I don't think it's full, but I'm not taking any chances. No more blood, no more Screamer.* I crouched down and peered inside the hole, keeping a good distance away. The blood was moving and sloshing around in earnest now. *We have to smash it with something near the bottom so it drains quickly.* I hoped it would be enough.

It had to be enough.

I jumped up and scanned the room. My fist might get through the thick marble in my Lycan form, but now wouldn't be the time to break my hand to pieces. Once the deed was done, I had to get Naomi out as soon as possible. I didn't have time to regenerate. "Is there something to smash the marble with in here?" I asked the ghosts. No one answered. For the first time I noticed everything had gone completely quiet.

One lone whisper came flitting into my ear. "They have gone. We fear the Strigoi. They hurt us."

I made my way around the mausoleum, my hands brushing against the smooth walls searching for something strong enough to bash in the marble. "You stayed. So help me," I told the ghost. The entire room was roughly thirty by thirty. "We have to find something that will withstand me smashing it into the altar. Is there anything hooked to the walls?"

"Look up," the voice whispered.

18

I angled my head toward the ceiling. Right at the very top, secured from the midpoint of the roof, was a marble gargoyle head. "It's not alive, is it?"

"No."

"Thank goodness for small favors," I muttered. It hung about fifteen feet above me. I glanced around. *Okay, we come at it from a run, kick off from the altar and grab it. We have to tear it off in one jump.* My wolf barked her agreement. I jogged back to the corner and took off, springing to the edge of the marble near Naomi's feet and leaping, reaching it easily. My hands closed around its pointy ears and on the way down I cranked like I was twisting the top off a jar and the chunk of marble gargoyle head snapped off in my grip.

I half expected it to yowl at me and come to life, but it didn't.

One small win in this sea of insanity.

I hit the ground on the balls of my feet, landing in a crouch. *Here we go.* I rushed around to the back of the platform where the hole was, because it seemed like the logical place to drain the gunk out.

Naomi hadn't moved at all. Not even so much as a twitch.

It was hard to look at her. She was gaunt and spent, like a real corpse. *We better be able to bring her back. Let's drain this thing and get it over with.* I squatted, angling both my arms back, my wolf fueling me, and swung the marble gargoyle, snout first, into the bottom of the altar.

There was a massive crash as the face hit structure, stone on stone.

The altar cracked—a teensy bit.

Damn, someone had to have heard that. We have to move faster. Several pieces of the gargoyle had broken off on impact, but it had worked to our advantage. Now there was a nice sharp angle protruding from the head. *Smash the pointy part into the fissure.*

Unfortunately, now the Screamer knew exactly what we were trying to do—take his only ride to freedom away. The altar started to rock and jump like a seismic tremor. Blood splashed out of the hole and cracks I'd made. *Yuck. We need to finish this now.* I reared back and smashed the sharp angle into the crack with all my strength. The gargoyle face exploded on impact, sending shards of marble everywhere, but it was enough to split the altar open like a broken dam.

Blood flowed everywhere like a torrential river, gushing all over the mausoleum floor. I sprang too late. Blood saturated my leggings and dripped down my legs. *Okay, that's completely nasty.* I moved farther out of the way, right as a terrible trembling vibration started to build from inside the altar. A low, creepy moan hit the air a second before a shout from outside the crypt filtered through the main door.

We were out of time.

I bent over and scooped Naomi up in my arms and sloshed

through the blood coating the floor, still flowing out of the marble housing at a rapid rate. I bounded for the trapdoor, trying not to slip. If the Screamer became corporeal, whoever was outside would have their hands full.

Better them than us.

"Close the hatch behind me," I yelled to the only ghost left. I had no idea if it had stuck around. "Are you strong enough?"

"Yes."

The opening wasn't big enough to jump through with her in my arms, so I maneuvered her to a vertical position and lowered her down the earthen steps, angling her over to the side as much as I could. Then I jumped down next to her. Once there, I hoisted her carefully over my shoulder and started to move, not pausing to see if the ghost was doing its job.

I flew down the steps. Right after my feet hit the dirty tunnel floor, the wrought-iron door behind me slammed shut and all the ghostly voices returned.

"Must free us now." Fingers grabbed at my arms as I ran.

"Feed the vampire. She is dire."

"The Strigoi is angry."

Ghostly hands prodded me, shoving me off balance. "Hey, back off!" I yelled, still racing through the tunnels. "You didn't stay and help, so I'll get to you when I can. Right now I have other priorities to deal with."

After two more bends, it was time to stop.

I laid Naomi carefully on the ground and brought my wrist up to my mouth. I was in my human form again and ripping through my skin with my dull teeth was going to hurt, but it would save time. *This is going to sting like a mother*, I told my wolf. *Brace yourself.* She sent a jolt of adrenaline through us as I tore through my flesh. "*Gahhh*," I cried as I bobbed my wrist in front of Naomi's mouth, rubbing the flowing blood between her lips.

After a moment she moaned.

"Thank goodness. Naomi," I said, "I need you to feed." In the next breath she clamped on to my arm, sucking furiously.

"You must free us now."

"The earth trembles."

"The battle is coming."

These guys weren't going to leave me alone until I fulfilled my end of the bargain. "I need you to deliver us safely back to the mansion," I said through a clenched jaw. Naomi was pulling hard. "And then I'll try my best to break whatever barrier is holding you in, just like I promised."

Naomi's eyes began to flutter as a loud crash sounded behind us. I wrenched my neck around to investigate the disturbance, but the tunnel was curved and I couldn't see.

"They come."

"You must hurry."

"Come on, Naomi," I urged, infusing power into my words. "You need to wake up. We are short on time and need to vacate the area."

Her eyes blinked open.

She unlatched and sat up quickly, appearing a bit stunned. "*Ma Reine*, what," she stammered, "...what are you doing here?"

"I'm breaking you out of Cryptville. But there's no time to explain right now. Can you run?" I asked, pulling her up before she could answer.

"Of course," she said without hesitation as she stood. She looked composed and ready. "Your blood has fortified me. All aftereffects are gone."

We took off.

So far vamps could go from incapacitated on the brink of true death to moving more easily than any supe I'd ever come in contact with. Naomi had already proven that after the winged devils attack and I was thankful for it.

"Naomi," I called over my shoulder as we ran. "Please forgive me for making you come back here. It was a rash mistake. I put you in danger, caused you harm, and I'm so sorry."

"I do not believe you made an error in judgment sending me here," she answered, her voice firm. It surprised me enough to slow down.

"You can't be serious," I said. "They tortured you and fed your blood to a Screamer. It was a disastrous decision to send you here without a plan or to think Eudoxia would see reason. I made a huge mistake."

"*Non*," she replied, "I believe I am here because fate deemed it to be so. I do not begrudge the outcome. I have waited too long, and been through too much, to question what my future holds."

I thought about that as we continued to run. Fate played a huge role in supernatural lore. Most believed they had a fated path. I knew my father did. He believed his being Alpha had been no accident, and I tended to agree with him. With the Prophecy recently uncovered, finding Rourke, changing Ray, it was likely fate had played a role in everything I'd done so far. But Tally had recently told us Maggie couldn't predict time as an oracle because choices affected outcomes. If the outcomes were set, choices wouldn't matter. That meant there was wiggle room, or more than one path set for each person. Maybe, in the end, no matter which path you chose, you always came back to your fated destiny. Or maybe you didn't. "When I think about the role fate plays, it makes my head hurt," I said. "It's a complicated labyrinth of possibilities, all of them seemingly muddled and unclear."

"Indeed," Naomi answered. "But I believe your path is true, and you will continue to make the right decisions when faced with very difficult choices."

No pressure there. "Your faith in me astounds me, as usual. I have no idea if I'm ever making the right choices. I'm just choosing what makes the most sense." I didn't want to think about making the wrong decisions. They could have life-altering consequences. "Like finding Ray. He's my top priority now. Do you have any idea where they might have taken him?"

"*Non*," she replied. "There are many likely spots, all of them equipped to keep a vampire confined. It is hard to know what they will do to him. Valdov was very unhappy he had become a vampire."

I took the next turn, following my own scent trail. The ghosts weren't objecting to my direction, so I kept going. "Which way now?" I called into the air when I came to another fork. "Going back through the Trows is not an option."

"Here."

"We will lead you."

"You must crawl." Something grabbed my shirt, guiding me to the left.

"I do not know, *Ma Reine*," Naomi answered, clearly not having heard the other voices. "I have never been down here before. It is forbidden. There have only been rumors of what lies beneath the graveyard. The Queen has always kept the tunnels well guarded."

"Can't you hear the ghost voices?" I asked, glancing at her. "They've been guiding us the entire time."

"What?" Naomi said, stumbling as her voice caught for a second. "I hear nothing but your voice."

"Um..." I hesitated, not wanting to upset her. I don't care how strong a supe you were, ghosts were freaky no matter what. "We're surrounded by dozens of trapped spirits. I've agreed to try and break the barrier holding them here, in exchange for finding you."

Naomi was quiet, her face pensive.

"Do you think I should do it?" I prodded. "Break the barrier, I mean? Is it a good idea?"

"The Queen has always stated that she keeps her vampires safe by protecting us *inside* her power shield. If you destroy it, I do not know what will happen," Naomi finally offered. "But I will follow your decision, *Ma Reine*. As always."

"She lies." The ghosts were agitated.

"The Queen keeps us to do her bidding."

"Free us and it shall come true."

"What will come true—" A hunk of dirt exploded from the wall right next to us, exposing a hole no bigger than four feet wide. The shock of it took me by surprise and I eased out of my fighting stance.

"You must enter." Fingers prodded at my legs, unsuccessfully trying to force me to kneel. Next to me, Naomi stilled. "They want us to go through here." I gestured to the new hole the ghosts had blown in the wall. "To be honest, I'm not sure if I should trust them, but there aren't too many other options presenting themselves at the moment."

By her expression Naomi had started to pick up on the energy from the ghosts swirling around us. "As I said, I will follow you, *Ma Reine*. You must honor your word to these spirits and I will help you if I can. It is the correct thing to do."

I knelt down. It was too dark to see much of anything in the new tunnel. Before I started forward, I reached back and grabbed on to Naomi's wrist, pulling her gently down beside me. She lowered herself easily. This close I could see her face flush with my blood. Thank goodness I hadn't been too late. Finding her had been the right decision, any later and it could've been disastrous.

"Listen," I murmured. "I appreciate your willingness to support me no matter what, but I want you to know you always have a choice. If you disagree with me, you can say so. I don't expect you to follow me blindly. In fact, I don't want you to. I value your input way too much. This isn't a monarchy, and it will never be.

Honestly, most of the time I have no idea if I'm making the right choice. The only thing I have to rely on is my gut, which is made up of an extremely bossy she-wolf, and common sense. My wolf is the equivalent of your vampire tutorials, except I don't always understand what she's trying to tell me. It's been a steep learning curve and she's the first one to call me slow on the uptake. I do promise to make the best choices I possibly can, but I can't always guarantee they will be the right ones. Do you understand?"

"I do." She nodded. "But the difference is I have faith that you will make the right choices, where you are still unsure. Your confidence will bloom over time." She smiled. "The Hag was very clear those many years ago when she told me I would have a choice to pledge myself to someone who was worthy. I did so, and I have no regrets. You are worthy of my pledge in every way. I will follow you."

"I appreciate that," I said. "But I want you on my *team*, not as a silent follower. If you believe fate has steered our paths together, and we are in this ridiculous tunnel together for a reason, then I need your help. Vampires, ghost, barriers, magic, politics—I need an intelligent guide by my side to make sense of it all. I have limited knowledge of how the supernatural world works and my only real concern right now is keeping my father alive. He's the entire reason I'm in this place." I gestured around the earthen walls. "We have to make sure he lives, and to do that we need to talk about the barrier and why we should or shouldn't blow it up. I feel like this is a huge decision and it will affect him in some major way." Whether or not to blow up the barrier was beginning to nag at me.

The ghosts whispered around my body, not liking that I'd taken a short break. I hadn't heard anything after us in the tunnels, so we had a minute more to spare.

"You must go."

"The barrier must come down."

"You cannot wait any longer."

I ignored them as Naomi nodded. "Forgive me for not being so vocal," she said. "It is difficult to shed hundreds of years of servitude. The Queen has never asked for our opinions on anything, so it does not come naturally to me."

"I understand," I said gently, "but I'm asking you now."

"We were told the barrier was to keep us safe, that it was dangerous and unthinkable to tamper with it."

"Is the barrier the ward I felt when I first came over the wall? Are we talking about the same thing?" Now that I thought about it, that ward carried the same tartness as the other curious spells.

"*Oui*," she answered. "It is the same. Only, it is not a standard ward. It acts as a shield over the entire Coterie, like a protective dome."

"It has to be extremely powerful if it can keep incorporeal beings trapped inside. But I was able to pass through it no problem this morning. The boys couldn't until the Queen let them in. Why do you think I was able to cross it?"

Naomi shook her head. "It shouldn't be so. It keeps out even the strongest supernaturals. It is very old and has been in place since this mansion has been in our possession. There are rumors it's been crafted from the Queen's own blood."

"But vamps can't wield spells."

"Eudoxia is not . . . ordinary," she said, her voice dropping automatically from years of obedience. One does not gossip about their Queen freely. "She is able to cast spells. Some believe that spell casting is her special gift. Others believe . . . she is more than vampire."

My eyebrows jumped to my hairline.

That was big, gossipy interesting news. More than a vampire meant she had been something supernatural before she'd been turned. "I've seen her power manifest physically," I commented as I thought back to our first meeting when she'd shot her white light straight into my chest, "but I figured it was because she was so old. That her power had grown so much it had manifested itself physically."

"*Non*," she replied. "She has always had the ability to cast spells."

That was extremely valuable information. I sat back on my heels. Naomi and I hadn't had a chance to talk about anything since she had pledged herself to me. I must fix that as soon as I could. Information was power, and I needed more if I wanted to win. "That puts an entirely new spin on all things Eudoxia. A Vampire Queen who can cast spells must be incredibly rare. The vamps must keep that news very close."

"We are required to keep her secrets above all else. If she finds out I have betrayed her, she will kill me." Naomi shrugged her petite shoulders. "But she has already tried to kill me, so it is of no consequence any longer."

I smiled. "Do you have any idea what else she may be?"

"*Non*," she said. "That is a true mystery."

"You linger too long," a whisper hit my ear.

"They are coming now."

"Time wastes."

I batted the ghosts away with my hand in irritation. "The ghosts are telling me we have to move. One last thing—do you think my father can cross the barrier to get to us?"

She shook her head. "No, I do not believe so."

I inclined my head at her. "Then the barrier comes down. Our decision is made."

"*Oui*. We must take it down," she agreed. "For your father's sake."

I started to crawl through the hole. "Naomi, do you still have your cross?" The Lunar Goddess's trinket was very valuable. There was hope in my voice, even though I knew the answer already.

Her voice was dark. "*Non.* It was Valdov's most favored who carried me to the crypt. They wrapped me in silver chains and I could not break free. They took it from me before they bound me to the Strigoi."

I wasn't sure how much Naomi knew or suspected about Valdov. "I think Valdov may be a spy," I told her as I followed the tunnel to the right on my hands and knees. "And he likely had something to do with your brother's relationship with Selene all these years. I also believe that if the Queen confronts him, he will use the cross against her and kill her if he can. He's likely been waiting for such an opportunity for years."

"I know nothing of this. Valdov and I do not interact," she said. "If my brother had told me he was still in contact with Selene, I would've killed him." Her voice turned cold. "But I do not doubt Valdov's prowess or his ability to do such things in the least. He has always been hungry for power. There has always been gossip, of course, but nothing of any substance. If this happens and he kills our Queen, it will be devastating to the Sect. We cannot let him succeed. He will bring ruination to all the vampires, as he is not strong enough to rule."

"I agree," I said. "And I'll do my best to stop it from happening. But in order to do *anything* we have to get out of these god-forsaken tunnels." I was resenting my time spent underground in a big way. I ducked my head as the tunnel narrowed. It was clear no one had used this one in a long time, and anyone who did had been sneaking around. This was not a main artery. "By the way," I added, "was the Strigoi supposed to wake up? Is that what they intended when they siphoned off your blood?"

I couldn't imagine they wanted to unleash a Screamer. It seemed ridiculously extreme.

"Wake up?" Naomi balked. "Of course not! As the Strigoi feeds, we are bound to it fiercely. It is one of only a few ways to keep a strong vampire immobile. It's called a Vassalage, as we are its servants until the binding is broken and the blood is drained."

"Well"—I cleared my throat—"the one bound to you was well on its way to becoming corporeal."

A small gasp came from behind me. "That is very dangerous indeed. I have only seen one Strigoi come to life and it was a truly horrid sight. They eat a living thing from the inside out to gain a new life, but it's only a temporary one. Once it inhabits a vampire's body, it cannot feed properly, so it will eventually die as the host body dries out. But its instinct is to tear others apart in its frenzy to stay alive. It is very strong and almost impossible to defeat."

"That sounds perfect," I muttered as I continued to claw my way through the dirt tube. "I pray it didn't have enough blood to come to life. That would be one too many things to worry about right now."

19

The tunnel turned uphill abruptly. We climbed up the incline to yet another trapdoor. This place was a maze of secret hatches. This had to be the end of my underground road, because I was done. More than finished. It was time to emerge and make contact with Rourke. He would be in a borderline frenzy right now. I hoped all the boys had made progress on the outside. It would be nice to have some good news.

"Okay, we're here. What do I do now?" I asked the ghosts.

"Enter."

"You must go up."

"You will find it there."

"What is *it* exactly?" I grumbled. "The last time you said *it*, *it* was a half-formed Screamer." I glanced down at Naomi. We were in such a small space it was difficult to see her. "Do you have any idea where we are?"

"By the scent and magic, I'd say we are beneath the Reliquary."

"We're under a church?" I lifted my nose and inhaled around

the edges of the door. I caught a trace of candle wax and lots of dust, along with the buzz of magic. "Why do vamps have a chapel on the grounds?"

"Yes, the Reliquary," a ghost voice filtered in my ear.

"It is the key."

"Must break the barrier."

"*Non*," Naomi answered. "Not a chapel, but a shrine. It is where we hold our most scared objects. It is said to be cursed and all vampires stay well away from it. The magic here is old. My bones ache with it even now."

Naomi was right. The magic had begun to filter into my skin, but didn't threaten me directly. The floor above us hummed with it. "Do you think this is where the ward is fueled?" I asked. "It feels strong enough."

"Yes." A ghostly response hit my ear first.

"The barrier begins here."

"I do not know," Naomi confessed. "But it would make some sense. Vampires do not venture to this place. It is said that Vlad's possessions still carry his essence and any who touch them will go insane."

"Vlad, huh?" He had been a powerful Vampire King long ago, but had been dead for centuries. There could be only one great ruler of vampires at a time, and Eudoxia was the supreme Queen now. "If your Queen fueled that rumor, she was smart. Now nobody comes near her ward or her priceless artifacts on threat of possession." From what I knew about strong wards, they were almost always grounded to something solid—the more powerful that something was, the longer it held and the harder it was to break.

I placed one finger tentatively on the underside of the trapdoor. Energy tingled into the tip, but it wasn't anything major. Maybe threats of curses had managed to keep this place untouched. "This door doesn't feel spelled," I told Naomi. "Kind of like the mausoleum you were just in. They must have put up a perimeter spell around the outside but didn't bother to include the inside. I'm going to push it open and see what I can find. If all looks good, follow me."

"Okay," she said. "But be careful. Even if there is no curse, I have heard that some of the relics have . . . a presence. Or it is said."

"I don't know much about your vampire history, but a roomful of Vlad the Impaler's trinkets is a little on the Dracula side, but if he was your King, it makes some sense his things would hold residual power. I'm not planning on touching anything I don't have to, so don't worry."

"Vlad was the most powerful Vampire King of all time—that is, until he was defeated by our Queen. His possessions come from Romania and are said to hold his immortal wrath, and that upon his execution he swore his revenge and his soul was scattered among his treasures."

That was a good story, but I was too shocked to move on. "Did you just say your *Queen* defeated Vlad the Impaler?" I asked. "You've got to be kidding me." Surprise spread over my features as I angled down to look at Naomi. "How could she defeat someone so much stronger? She had to have been newly made judging by her age now."

She nodded solemnly. "*Oui*, she was very young. Vlad turned the tsar's youngest daughter in hopes to rule Russia. But it is said he picked the wrong daughter. He mistook her youthful appearance for innocence and she played him well. She was shrewd in the ways of men long before Vlad found her. Her father had . . . made her life very difficult, and Vlad paid the ultimate price for his actions."

I made a face.

Eudoxia's father was Ivan the Terrible and her maker had been Vlad the Impaler. Another pinch of grudging respect surfaced for Eudoxia that I knew I shouldn't harbor. But she was a true survivor on so many levels. It was hard to quantify that kind of strength and impossible not to respect it.

It was clear she had won her title of Queen of the Vampires.

I pushed the trapdoor upward.

It met with resistance. I repositioned and came at it with my shoulder. I gave it a hard jerk and there was a popping noise as a latch gave way. Once it was free, the door opened slowly like a drawbridge.

Mustiness hit my senses immediately. Old, stale air filled the tunnel.

The ghosts were agitated and excited. They breezed back and forth over my face creating a dusty current. I coughed.

"Must go."

"The time draws near."

"Grab the relic."

"I'm going, I'm going," I muttered. Naomi quirked her head, but nodded, understanding.

I drew my body into the room cautiously. This building had skylights, so it was brighter than the tunnel. But they were weathered and dirty, caked with grime both inside and out. The sun barely shone through, but it was a welcome addition to my dark underground day.

Once I was in, I glanced around in surprise.

Instead of all the prized possessions being laid out lovingly under glass in shrinelike condition, it looked as though everything had all been dumped on the floor haphazardly. It was like one giant junk box.

There were old, dusty cloths draped over things in some areas, and in other places piles of crap had accumulated in no particular order, like someone might sort them later. If they ever got around to it.

"This is it?" I chuckled. "The feared Reliquary? It looks like a church basement garage sale." The trapdoor was situated in the middle of the room. Nothing had zapped me or came to life, which was stellar. I made a slow turn, testing the magic in the room. There were a few pulses from some of the items, but the major power current seemed to flow freely in a circle around me.

"Naomi," I called. "I think it's okay to come in. I'm not getting a read on anything too intense."

Naomi poked her head through the trapdoor. "The power creeps along my skin, but you are right—it is not threatening me either. Still, be careful, *Ma Reine*. It could be a trap."

"Why do you think all these artifacts are piled up like this?" I asked, pacing to the inner edge of the circle. "Wouldn't your most prized possessions be, I don't know, better taken care of? I don't think they're cursed. Nothing in here feels threatening. That must have been an old wives' tale." I reached over to touch what looked to be a jeweled crown of some kind. "Let's find out."

The moment my hand almost connected with it, an arc of static electricity shot into my finger.

"Jeez!" I yanked my hand away. The power had stung me and I hadn't even touched the damn thing. "Did you see that? A mini lightning bolt just shot out of that crown." I turned in a full circle. I hadn't recognized the configuration of all the junk before now.

"What is it?" Naomi asked.

"Your Queen is tricky," I said. "Look at how all these things are laid out. They look haphazard, but they're all connected." The items ran in a full circle around us. The junk was acting like a giant conduit, and we were standing right in the middle of it. "Don't touch anything," I cautioned Naomi. "I'm pretty sure this is what's fueling the barrier."

"Find the saber," a whisper shot by my ear. It was the voice of the only ghost who had stayed with me in the mausoleum.

"What saber?" I asked. Naomi glanced at me. "One of the ghosts is telling me to find some kind of a sword."

We both looked around, but it was hard to see over the heaps of junk.

"The Kilij. The master's sword."

"You must break the circuit."

"It lies on the outside."

"Outside the circle?" I asked. Instead of answering, invisible hands guided me to the right. Lying just in front of the biggest stack of junk was a single curved sword stuck halfway into the floor. It looked as though it was rooted so deeply it ran through the thick marble floor into the earth below. "The sword must be grounding the electricity. That's why we only feel a low hum of power in this room." The massive flow of energy conducted by these relics was being fed into the ground through the saber.

I glanced around the room again.

The Reliquary was circular and the piles of relics were placed in a circle, albeit a haphazard one, and circles held power. I turned to Naomi. "This ward must have been started centuries ago, and to keep it fueled the Queen has tossed powerful things on it. If I can break it, it's going to take everything I have."

"Must hurry."

"The situation grows dire."

"Pull the saber and all will change."

"I believe, now that we are here, it needs to be done, *Ma Reine*," Naomi said. "We have happened upon this place to grant your father entrance, and when this is all over, we must be able to exit. Once this barrier comes down, I believe everything will change. And things must change. This marks the beginning." Her voice was firm.

That sounded a little more ominous than I would've liked. "I know I have to do this, but whatever we do here will set the next events in motion. Are we sure this is the right choice?" That was the big, hairy question. I blew out a breath. It felt right to be here for so many reasons. I needed to talk to my team; my father was in danger; I'd made a deal with the spirits. My wolf growled. *What do you think?* She flashed an image of us pulling the sword out of the ground. *How do you know?* She snapped her jaw.

I had to trust her.

It was the only instinct I had to follow, and so far she'd been right about most things supernatural.

"I believe it is the correct choice, *Ma Reine*," Naomi said.

Ghostly hands prodded me toward the Kilij. "I'm going," I said. Once in front of it, I waved my hands above the pile. "There's no current in the air above this stuff. I'm going to jump over it and try to free the saber from the other side."

"Be careful," Naomi said. "Do not touch anything but the sword."

"Believe me, I won't." I took a small step back and leapt over the artifacts, landing cleanly on the other side. I walked over and lowered myself to the ground next to the Kilij, which was a beautifully curved saber with an exquisitely detailed handle. *Once we grab on, all the juice is going to pump through us. We are going to need to ground ourselves so we don't fry.* She flashed a picture of us standing on the circle of relics right before I grabbed on to the saber. *Perfect. Like a bird on a wire, but even if we do that, the current that rips through us is going to be massive. We have to brace ourselves.* She flashed her teeth. *Excuse me if you were born ready. I wasn't. Some of us are still in the newborn stage and others have to be a bit more patient.*

I tossed a look over my shoulder at Naomi. "If I fry, tell Rourke I'll make my way back. Somehow."

Ready? My wolf barked right as a massive amount of adrenaline raced through me, morphing me into my Lycan form. I lofted myself into the air, landing on the circle, my hands simultaneously clasping the hilt.

When my hands connected, I screamed *"Mother Mary!"* as pure white energy coursed through my body like I'd been hit by the biggest concentration of power in the world. My hands stung with it. The hilt was so hot it felt like my fingers were wrapped around a stove. *We have to stay on the circle or we die.* Electricity sped through me, rocking my brain, but thankfully flowed back into the relics as quickly as it raced through me.

I tried to wiggle the sword, but it was firmly locked into place. *We have to shake it loose, disrupt the current somehow.* I pulled ribbons of power together in my mind and sent them shooting into the saber as fast as I could. *It's too slow. We have to blast it to make it skip.* I yanked my power back with effort and focused it into a bigger mass in my mind until I could see only a golden haze covering my eyes. *Now!* I yelled. My wolf bared her teeth as power exploded down through my arms and into the Kilij. Right as it hit, I pulled backward with everything I had, bracing my feet on the slippery circle. A screeching sound followed as the saber separated a few inches from the floor.

The ground beneath us rumbled and shook.

My arms vibrated like two tuning forks as I tried desperately to keep my grip on the sword. The force of the energy was threatening to disarm me. *We have to hold tight! One more yank.*

I flexed back with incredible force and the Kilij finally sprang free.

A sound bordering on a murderous scream followed as a shock wave hit the Reliquary. The skylights exploded and all the artifacts blasted outward. I lost my footing and flew through the air, the saber still clutched in my burned palms.

I landed flat on my back.

The impact had knocked the wind clean out of me, so I took a few shallow breaths and rubbed my aching head.

I sat up. An eerie silence followed. Nothing moved for a few beats. There were no whispers of energy urging me on, no currents of air moving. The ghosts hadn't stuck around to say goodbye and that was fine with me. "Naomi," I called, tossing the saber to the side. "Are you okay?"

There was a rumble in the corner and one of the tarps moved. "*Oui.* I am alive."

"We have to get—"

Jessica! Rourke roared into my mind with a ferocity I hadn't heard before. The sound was massive, his voice aching with emotion. *Where the fuck are you?*

The barrier was indeed down and the lines of communication were now open.

I'm here, Rourke. I'm in the Reliquary behind the house. I just broke the Queen's ward. I motioned to Naomi and pointed upward. After all that noise, the guards and whoever Eudoxia had protecting her would be on us. It was almost dusk and we needed to move.

Naomi nodded. She shot up and I followed, springing off the wall, my hands grabbing the edge of the open skylight. I swung my body and hoisted myself out onto the roof in one motion.

Tell me you're okay, Rourke continued. *That explosion was huge. It rocked the entire area.*

I'm fine. Just leaving now. Where are you?

I'm standing in a cell, and I've got a withered vampire by the throat, he growled. *He claims he helped you escape. I'm two seconds shy of tearing his heart out.*

He did help me. Don't hurt him. Let them both go. I picked my way along the roof, stepping over the broken skylights.

Fine, they go free. Stay where you are and I'll find you.

"Jessica!" Tyler yelled. "Over here."

I turned and glanced down. My brother and Danny stood by a crypt. Tyler waved his arms. It was clear they'd been trying to tear into it but hadn't had much luck. I rested my hand above my eyes and scanned the yard. There were hundreds of tombs and structures spread out behind the mansion. It was a real New Orleans graveyard.

And I'd just been in the underground network connecting them.

Rourke, I'm heading down into the cemetery. Tyler and Danny are here. I'm going to meet them. I motioned to Naomi. "Let's join the boys down there," I said to her. "Rourke is on his way—"

"*Fool*," the Queen's voice shrilled. My head snapped toward the mansion. Her voice ended on a shriek. "You've ruined *everything*!"

20

My gaze landed on Naomi. Before we could figure out what to do, there was another scream. It came from the house, and it was decisively the Queen's, followed a moment later by Valdov's murderous cackle.

Naomi ran down the slope and took off into the air. "We must get the cross back," she called. "If he kills the Queen, the vampires will be thrown into chaos."

Without thinking, I took off after her.

It was nice not to have to make the decision this time. And Naomi was right—if Valdov took control, it would be very bad indeed. The Queen had honor and played by the rules of supernatural negotiation—they were her rules, and worked in her favor most of the time, but she played them well. If Valdov ruled, there was a chance the vamps would side with the demons, and my Pack, along with many other supernaturals, would be in serious trouble.

The Reliquary sat fifty feet from the mansion, but there was a long portico that jutted from the back of the house. The portico roof looked big enough to hold me. It was a reasonable distance away—"reasonable" being the operative word. My wolf urged me along, agreeing wholeheartedly with getting rid of Valdov. *We have to make this jump in one leap. There's no other way.* I took off running and leapt, soaring into the air. I connected with the roof, my claws digging in, splintering boards and dislodging shingles as my hands slid. I finally stopped my momentum by latching on to the gutters. I hung there precariously for a few beats.

Jess, what the hell are you doing? my brother yelled in my mind. I had to block out the rest of his protests, which were entering my brain rapid-fire, to focus on not falling. Both his and Danny's footfalls raced toward me.

I swung a leg up and hoisted myself onto the small roof. Naomi had already entered through an open window. The mansion was made of big stone slabs, so there were enough footholds and crannies for me to shimmy up easily. I leapt onto the wall, moving at supernatural speed, my claws keeping me steady. I had to answer my brother's protests. *Tyler, I have to stop Valdov. He's with the Queen. I can't let him kill her.*

Fine, but we're coming in right behind you.

That's what I'm hoping.

As I neared the Queen's chambers, her voice rang out. "You will not defeat me!" followed by a strangled scream.

We go straight in, I told my wolf. *No waiting.* There was an open window around the corner of the turret, but we were going to take the closest route.

I hit the casing above a closed window, latching on to the stone siding above me. In the next breath I let go, plunging down, grabbing on to the upper windowsill, my legs bursting feetfirst through the leaded glass.

One second before I crashed through the panes, I heard four words.

"Now you must die."

The glass exploded spectacularly and I landed in a low crouch, fists up, my wolf on high alert.

"You're too late, mongrel." Valdov's precise voice hit my eardrum the instant before I sprang.

My brain took in the scene around me as I lunged, the Queen in her bed, blood everywhere, Naomi crumpled on the floor. My hands came around his neck as I snarled, "We'll see about that, *asshole*." My vocal cords were taut, my words strained. I knocked him to the floor in one motion, my knees pinning him across the chest.

Valdov chuckled beneath me, barely trying to fight back. "She's already dead! You're too late. I can feel the beautiful power transferring to me already." He took a big, satisfied breath and grinned in a way that made him look like the Joker. *"Ahh*, it's taken much too long to gain what was rightfully mine. Once I have the power, I will be the greatest Vampire King the world has ever seen, and I will kill you where you stand. You will be no match for me."

This couldn't be happening. The Queen couldn't be dead.

My eyes found Eudoxia. She was chained to her bed, covered in silver links, her body smoking, Naomi's cross stuck halfway out of her chest.

Her head hung at an odd angle.

She can't regenerate with that thing inside her. We have to pull it out before it's too late for her to recover. My wolf snapped her jaws, throwing up a picture of us ripping Valdov's head cleanly off his body. *We will, but we don't have time to do both. By the time the power transfers completely from her to him, it will be too late.* Valdov would put up too much of a fight right now.

Choosing to save the Queen, I jumped up and ran. But before I could reach her, I flew through the air. My back crashed into a wall, expensive drapes exploding all around me.

Valdov grinned like a fiend. "I am not weak, you filthy little beast! I can catch you. And you will not win, because you cannot save her." He spread his arms and tilted his creepy ivory face toward the ceiling, inhaling, his perfectly sculpted nostrils flaring. "Can you feel it? It's magnificent and so very intoxicating. And it's all mine."

I did feel the power, and unfortunately Valdov was right; it was swirling around the room searching for its next host. When the head of a Sect died, the power itself chose the new ruler, which was usually the strongest and most capable. In our world, the Alpha's power transferred to the next wolf, but that wolf would be immediately challenged for it. An Alpha werewolf still had to prove himself physically.

No vampire would be challenging Valdov.

I had to stop this.

Squatting, I readied myself to lunge toward the Queen, but before I could move, Valdov locked his eyes on me. He was fully vamped out, cheeks waxy, eyes full black, fangs pierced down like swords over his bottom lip. His irises flashed silver, pinning me with their intensity. He knew my next move, but I had to try anyway. I sprang forward in a burst of speed, but I wasn't fast enough. Valdov intercepted me and we tumbled to the ground again.

He hissed in my ear. "Little mongrel, oh, how I would love to drain you right now." His fangs brushed the side of my neck, drawing a line of blood as they scratched along the surface of my skin.

I arched back, out of his grasp, bringing my fist up and slamming it into his trachea. He sputtered, trying to recover, but I held him by the shoulders, my claws digging in.

We rolled twice on the floor.

He was strong.

But I was stronger.

We hit the far wall right as Tyler jumped through the window I'd broken. I'd never been so happy to see anyone in my life. "Get to the Queen!" I yelled. "Yank the cross out of her chest."

Tyler didn't hesitate. He ran to the Queen's bedside as Danny tumbled into the room behind him.

Valdov hissed, "I doesn't matter. It's too late. I will be King." Power swirled in a heavy cloud around Valdov, his body vibrating as it absorbed the magic.

"Tyler, hurry!"

Valdov reared up beneath me, snapping at my neck, his face awful this close. His eye sockets were sunken and the bones in his face were stretched outward. His white, chalky, paper-thin skin didn't look like they could contain them any longer.

"I did it," Tyler said. "I pulled the damn cross out, but nothing's happening. She's not healing! Her neck is completely severed."

Valdov cackled. "I told you. It is done."

"It's not over yet," I snarled. "My guess is if the magic has a choice, it would still choose Eudoxia." I yelled, "Vamps aren't like us. They're already dead. They don't need communication to the brain. Put her neck back together and give her your blood." I was banking on the fact she could regenerate with his blood. I'd learned the hard way with Eamon. I thought I'd killed him by breaking his neck, but he had healed after drinking from Ray.

Tyler's face hardened.

I nodded, urging him on. "Tyler, you have to do this or Valdov will be the new King. We can't risk it. I'd feed her myself, but I can't give her my blood."

Valdov struggled in earnest beneath me and my claws dug deeper into his shoulders. He hadn't expected us to feed his former Queen. "That's right," I growled. "You underestimated what we would be willing to do. And for that, you lose."

Tyler ripped his sleeve open and bit into his wrist.

Valdov's cruel nails found my face. He raked them over my cheek, and blood poured down my face. I batted his hands away and bared my teeth. "Do you see this? This is me ending you." I switched control to my wolf and our hands locked around his neck, our power pressing him tightly to the floor.

"Little...mongrel...you cannot..." Valdov hissed as he thrashed.

From the bed, the Queen gasped, her chest bowing upward. There was a tremor below me as the magic began to leave Valdov, his body weakening as I held on.

The Queen's arms flung to the side as the magic shot back into her.

Tyler stepped back, running a hand over his face. It was the second time in his life he'd been required to feed a vampire. And he had my undying admiration and love for it. It was no small thing for a wolf to aid a vamp.

"No," Valdov insisted. "I will be *King*—" His body convulsed as the last of the magic left him, transferring back to its *true* sovereign.

"Looks like you won't be after all," I said, my hands tightening around his throat. "You shouldn't feel bad, though, because if you were indeed more powerful than Eudoxia, the magic would've stayed inside you. You were never meant to rule, Valdov, and I'm happy to make sure it stays that way."

My wolf snapped her jaws and twisted. Valdov's scream was lost as the door to Eudoxia's bedroom burst off its hinges.

Rourke roared as he lunged into the room, his eyes blazing, his body primed for a fight.

But the deed was already done.

I sat back on my haunches and tossed Valdov's head away in disgust, taking a few deep breaths. The gruesome killing requirement of this job sucked, but there was no other way around it. "There has to be an easier way to do this," I said.

Rourke was to me in three steps.

He yanked Valdov's body by the arm and sent it flying across the room, well away from me. Then he drew me up off the floor. "I'm sorry I couldn't get here sooner, but I was on my way to the Reliquary." He tipped my head back gently with his fingertip, searching my eyes. "Downstairs, the house is in an uproar. Whatever you did by blowing up the ward opened a Pandora's box of shit and everyone is in a panic. The vamps are all freaked because they think Eudoxia is dead. We have to get out of here."

I nodded over his shoulder. "We can't leave until we finish this."

Rourke followed my gaze.

The Queen was still bound to her bed with silver cuffs and she was furious. Tyler stood back with his arms crossed. Danny and Naomi stood off to the side. I was happy to see Naomi was up. Valdov must have hit her hard.

Rourke gave me a small kiss and let me go. I moved around him and walked toward the Queen.

"This is your fault," she spat as I came closer, her eyes a dead black, her fangs inching their way down slowly. "You've brought chaos down on the House of Vampires, as predicted, and I will enjoy tearing out your spine for it." She ended on a hateful hiss and shook her chains, blood oozing out of her wrists.

I didn't kill her arch nemesis so she could pour on more of the same bullshit.

"I just *saved* you," I ground out, my hands balled. "I killed Valdov by ripping his head off. You remember him, don't you? Your faithful advisor who almost succeeded in killing you not five minutes ago? In our world that means you *owe* me. A life for a life." I walked up to the bedside. "I get anything I ask for. Swear it, or I'll kill you where you lie."

Loathing consumed her features, her eyes oscillated between

silver and black, and her cheekbones slid as she fought for control. Her power was not back at one hundred percent and I could end her life easily. She was one pissed-off Vampire Queen and I didn't give a shit. "Fine," she raged, her fangs snapping down completely, needle sharp. "I swear to you *one* favor, but only because my honor demands it. But once the debt is settled, we are mortal enemies, you and I. Do not forget it."

"I wouldn't dare." I grinned, putting my face next to hers. "You will be required to fulfill the favor immediately, Eudoxia, so settling the debt won't be a problem. Guess what's on the way to your doorstep?" I didn't wait for her to answer. "Demons. That's right, the demons will be here at nightfall, which by the looks of it will be shortly. And the favor I want from you is protection." Before she could form a retort, I held my hand up. "For one night only. When day breaks, I walk away. That's it. It's a small favor in return for avenging your death and killing a traitor."

"You are out of your mind." She hissed. "I will not fight demons on your behalf!"

"You will," I said. "Or you die. Swear it."

Before she could answer, the door banged open and Conan the Enforcer came flying through the room yelling, "Get away from my Queen!"

Rourke took one step into his path and leveled him with a clothesline to the throat. The look of surprise on Conan's face was priceless. If the situation hadn't been so tense, I might have chuckled. Conan's trachea exploded as he soared back into the wall. He landed hard and crumpled to the ground, his body limp. Rourke moved toward him to make sure he stayed down.

I motioned for Tyler and Danny to move out into the hallway to keep watch. We didn't want any more vampires barging in. They moved soundlessly; Tyler's anxiety bubbled in my blood while Danny's jumped with excitement. I shook my head.

I focused my attention back to the Queen. "Why don't you have hundreds of vampires guarding you?"

"My rooms are warded. They cannot find me here."

"You mean, before I broke your ward?"

"Yes, you *fool*," she shrilled as she tried to sit up, her chains rattling. Her elegant clothes were tattered and torn, the silver still burning her skin, leaking blood all over her gold satin sheets. "You have no idea what you've done. You've unleashed things kept from humans for centuries. I will not be able to undo all your recklessness. It will be impossible." Her eyes narrowed. "And if the demons ascend as you are saying, there is nothing I can do to keep them out. You have destroyed the only thing that would've kept us safe."

I inclined my head. "You said a minute ago that I brought chaos down on the House of Vampires, as predicted. Predicted by whom?"

Her mouth snapped closed in a thin line, making her incisors look like they were sealed between her lips. "Get me out of these chains."

I crossed my arms. "You're not really in a position to demand anything. Agree to my favor and I'll let you go. I'm assuming the key is in Valdov's pocket?"

"I will not fight demons. What you ask will risk many lives, not just *mine*. I will not bargain away the lives of my flock for your protection. Demons are not sorcerers—they are a wicked breed. They will come to destroy everything in their path, nothing less."

"If they come to destroy, you and your flock will be in the middle of it anyway. You harbored me of your own free will," I pointed out, dropping my voice. "Eudoxia, I know you can craft spells. I don't know why, or what you are, but I know you have the power to protect us. We came here seeking that same protection for a reason. That's what we bartered for when I arrived. That hasn't changed."

"Everything has changed!" She yanked on her chains, causing plaster to fly from the walls as an evil snarl came out of her mouth. "I offered you protection and instead you wreaked havoc on my Coterie. I will not be subjected to—"

"I don't believe that."

She had the gall to look taken aback.

"You ordered me into a cell with your uncle for a reason," I challenged. "You gave me a lone guard I could've killed. The mighty chains you had me shackled to snapped off the wall at my merest tug. Yuri had a way out and he ominously told me he'd been *waiting* for me. My escape was no mistake." I peered down at her, my eyes shrewd. "You knew Valdov was a spy, didn't you? You also knew he would attack. You made yourself vulnerable at the right time and used me to kill him so you didn't have to."

"I did no such thing," she retorted. "My head was severed from my body. I would never allow it. He was my most trusted advisor and he turned on me, but only once you broke the ward. You did this!"

"Eudoxia," I said, shaking my head. "I'm tired of the mind games." I was so, so tired. "I don't know what's really going on here, but by my calculations my brother and I just saved your life. The truth behind it doesn't concern me. If we hadn't been here, Valdov would've taken your power and finished you off completely. By all rights you owe us. And I want protection from the demons. For one night. After that, we go our separate ways. If not, I leave you chained here to your fate. The demons will ascend and you will be destroyed alongside all of us."

Her eyes flickered. She knew I'd reached the end of negotiations. "Your *favor* will be a ward of protection," she said, her voice full of hate, "but no matter what I do, it will not be as strong as the last. That's all I will do. I will not fight the demons once they arrive, nor will I put any of my vampires at risk. If the demons ask me for you, I will gladly hand you over."

I glanced at Rourke, who stood by the foot of her bed. "What do you think?"

"I think it will be full dark in twenty minutes. We aren't leaving, so another ward may be the only thing we can do. The vamps won't be much help against the demons anyway." He growled at Eudoxia, "They can't fight. They're courtiers in every sense. More concerned their frocks will get rumpled and soiled if they lift a finger. They prefer to feast on innocent humans who pose no threat, and when the real danger sets in, they simply fly away."

"We are a refined race," Eudoxia snapped. "Unlike you filthy animals. But that does not mean we are weak." Her power sparked, white forming at the tips of her fingers for the first time. It was building fast, repairing her to full strength. She grinned, her fangs still sharp. "We enjoy a good fight, and tearing you apart limb by limb would be an especially welcome treat."

I waved my hand, dismissing her threats. "Here's the deal. I let you go, but you cast the ward when I say so, not a moment before."

She balked. "As your feline just pointed out, it will be full dark momentarily. I will not wait."

"You will."

"And why should I acquiesce to such a demand?"

"Because I'm waiting for my *Pack* to arrive." My father needed every opportunity to arrive, and I was going to make sure I gave it to him. "It's the main reason I took out your barrier. Once they reach us, we will have enough backup to fight the demons, with or without your help."

Her lips pursed. "Fine. I will wait until the last ray of sunlight filters out of the sky, but not a moment later. I care not if your precious Pack arrives."

I turned to Naomi. "Check Valdov's pockets for a key to these."

"There is no key, fool," Eudoxia retorted. "They were spelled to my signature and mine alone. You can break them."

"Valdov pulled out all the stops," I said, reaching for the chains. "How did he get you into these willingly?"

Her eyes slid to full black.

I wasn't going to get an answer, but they had obviously laid some elaborate plan and, in the end, something that had gone very wrong for Valdov. He would never have chosen to die. "Let's not forget, Eudoxia," I said as I pried open a silver cuff, "I still have something you want. Keeping me alive is still in your best interest." I ignored the burn and crushed the manacle. It popped off her wrist. Then I reached over and did the next one.

She stood immediately.

Her hair had fallen from the elaborate coif of curls she wore tightly pinned to her head. She was several inches shorter than I was, and her long pale ringlets made her appear very young, possibly in her teens as I had originally guessed. The only thing marking her true age were her shrewd eyes, which were latched on mine. "I have not forgotten. It is the only reason you still live."

In the next blink she was gone.

21

The Queen had disappeared out the window so quickly that it appeared she had vanished.

The moment she left, my entire body relaxed. I walked over to an empty chair and sat down with a thump. Tyler and Danny paced back into the room. "Danny, take the muscle vamp and toss him somewhere, will you?" I asked.

Without hesitation, Danny picked up the vamp and slung him over his shoulder and headed straight for the windows. I was too tired to argue, and Conan likely wouldn't die from the fall.

Plus, he kind of deserved being tossed out a window for being a stone-cold asshole.

"We need to regroup. Tyler, can you fix the door or at least shut it?" I glanced over at Valdov's dead body. Without its head, it had withered to bones. I met Naomi's gaze. "There must be a time limit to the severed-neck rule?"

"*Oui,*" she responded. "If the head is completely severed from the body with no connecting tissue, it is only a matter of moments. If the vampire is very strong, they can last longer, but the head must be replaced."

"Ugh," I said. "What did Valdov do to you? You were down by the time I broke through the windows."

"It was not Valdov," she said. "It was the Queen."

I sat up in my chair. "The Queen?"

"I came into the room and she said only three words—*do not interfere*. And then I remember nothing. Her power still aches in my chest." She rubbed her sternum absentmindedly.

"That solidifies my theory," I said. "This was something they had cooked up together." I ran both hands through my hair and exhaled. "These games make my brain hurt. She risked death, and for what? What does she want from me?"

Rourke stood next to me. "Vampires are not skilled fighters, but they are known for their conniving ways. There's no doubt she had plans in place from the moment you left her weeks ago. All she needed to do was pick which one to implement once you were here."

"Her manipulation agitates me," I said. "We all know she wants my blood or my life force or whatever, and she's going to scheme until she gets it. But in this particular scenario she didn't have a chance to get what she wanted. Something went very wrong here, but hell if I know what. I hate being her pawn."

Rourke growled. "The Queen isn't the only one around here with power or plans. She can connive all she wants, but it was clear her second-in-command was equally as scheming. Valdov used the plan to a perceived advantage, but neither of them got what they wanted and Valdov died for it."

I sized up my mate. Just being this close brought me some much-needed calm. His warmth radiated into my body. I was happy to see him again. I hadn't realized how much I missed being near him until right this minute. "How did you get into the crypt with Yuri, by the way?" I asked.

"I dug my way in."

"From the outside? Like"—I blanched—"with your bare hands?"

His eyelids went to half-mast and a sexy growl sent the hairs on my arms jumping to attention. "Yes. Did you expect me to do any less?"

Danny exaggerated a cough. "Okay, let's stay on track, shall we? Or your combined pheromones may choke us all before we can defeat anyone properly."

"That's poetic justice coming from you," I chuckled, turning toward Danny, "since I'm the one usually telling you the very same thing." I stood from the chair and maneuvered myself against Rourke's chest. I needed to touch him. Pheromones be damned.

Are you purring?

Yes, Rourke answered.

I like it.

Time to get back to business. Now wasn't the time to dwell on wonderfully purring mates. With effort I directed a question at my brother. "Did you find Ray?" I asked. Ray wasn't here with us, so it was a good guess they hadn't. "Or do you at least know where they're holding him?"

"We think they're keeping him in one of the crypts," Tyler said. "There was no trace of his scent out there, but that was before the ward came down. We should be able to scent him now."

"Okay, our first priority is to find him," I said. "Since we don't know exactly where he is, we split up. Once we have him, we regroup. Rourke and I will take the interior. Tyler, I want you, Danny, and Naomi to take the grounds outside. Search until dark; after that I want you to shift. If Dad is in New Orleans, like we hope, keeping the lines of communication open becomes the top priority."

Tyler nodded. "It's going to be dark very soon. That doesn't give us a lot of time, but if we find Ray, I'll alert you. After Danny and I shift, we meet up with you guys no matter what. The only thing we'll have once the demons arrive is strength in numbers."

Rourke voiced his agreement. "He's right. We need to stand together. If the Queen's ward works, we will have an advantage, but it will only be a slight one and won't mean anything if we're not united."

"Okay," I said. "We meet on the east side of the mansion in twenty minutes. Doesn't give us a lot of time, but we can still cover ground. Has anyone seen Nick?"

"Once we all left, he went over the wall like you asked him to. Haven't seen him since," Danny answered.

"Good," I said. "That means he's found something. I can only hope it means James and Marcy are here somewhere and they're rallying the wolves. If there's enough time, circle around to the front and see if you can find him, but don't leave the grounds."

"Aye, aye, Captain." Danny saluted me with a grin.

"Very funny. The salute was a nice touch." I chuckled. "You're the embodiment of the word 'cheeky,' Daniel Walker."

"The cheekiest," he said with a straight face. "But that's why you adore me."

It was true. I did adore him. He was proving to be the perfect underling to my temporary Alpha. I was going to miss my connection to him when he swore his oath back to my father. "Danny, you always provide a bright, shiny spot in my day. Though I'm not surprised my father had you stationed two hours away."

He gave me a sardonic grin. "Yes, my humor is lost on the old dog. It's a shame really, because most of the time he could use a good laugh."

Talk of my dad brought me back quickly. "Let's get moving. Instead of roaming through the cemetery, there's a trapdoor in the

Reliquary that leads into the tunnel system below the graveyard. You may have an easier time locating Ray's scent down there. The ghosts said something about a bad man. I don't think they were talking about Ray, but it wouldn't hurt to investigate."

"*Ghosts?*" Danny balked. "Don't tell me you've been communicating with the undead now? You can't be serious."

Tyler appeared uneasy as well. "You want us to go down in a tunnel and try to talk to ghosts?"

Their faces were comical. "You're both badass werewolves. I had no idea you were scared of ghosts."

"I'm not scared of spirits." Tyler cleared his throat. " 'Wary' is a better term. I've never actually seen one, but it seems like it would be impossible to defeat something without substance. Badass werewolf or not."

Danny added, "Exactly. It gives them a bloody unfair advantage."

"You tough guys don't have to worry, because once I broke the ward, they all left. Plus, they can't really fight," I said. "They just sort of poke and prod you with their ghostly fingers." I couldn't help smiling. "They're completely insubstantial with no magic, but if the Screamer had come to life, that would've been a different story."

"Screamer?" Tyler asked incredulously. "You left a *Screamer* down there?"

"I've only heard of those as legend." Danny whistled as he turned to Naomi. "Do they really exist, then? Ghost vampires who dine on your blood?"

She nodded. "I have only seen one in my lifetime. It was very long ago, but yes, it was horrible. They don't just eat you—they devour your soul from the inside out. They do not become corporeal often, because our blood purity has been diluted. They

need incredible power to regenerate. But we pacify them with...
offerings. If we do not do this, they get disruptive, like angry pol-
tergeists."

"Unfortunately," I added, "this thing got a taste of my blood
from Naomi. If I hadn't put a stop to it, it may have had enough
to come to life."

Danny glanced from Naomi to me and then back. "The vampires who took you prisoner drained your blood to feed this
thing?" He half snarled, which was a lot of emotion for Danny.
"And if you had been drained completely, this creature could've
risen? And you would've died?"

His anger jumped in my blood, surprising me.

My eyebrows went up. He made a move to touch Naomi but
drew his hand away as she stepped back out of his reach. I glanced
at my brother, who, in turn, shrugged.

"What happened to me is of no consequence. The crisis was
averted," Naomi murmured, turning her gaze toward me. "Jessica
was able to drain the altar before it could arise."

Hearing her call me Jessica was odd, but nice. "But keep your
eyes and ears open when you're in the tunnels," I said. "If you
see or hear anything out of the ordinary, get out of there as fast
as you can. Once you find Ray, let me know here." I pointed to
my head. "I'm hoping one of us can find Ray before the fighting
begins." I still had no idea why Ray was key to saving my father,
but I wasn't going to begin to doubt Maggie now. We needed to
find him.

"We can leave out the window," Tyler said. "It's the easiest way
to get to the Reliquary." He started walking and glanced over his
shoulder. "Stay safe, Jess."

"I will," I said. "You too. I'll see you in twenty."

He nodded once and leapt, followed by Danny. Naomi turned

right before she flew out. "*Ma Reine*, remember no matter what happens tonight there is a reason, even if it is difficult. I am certain we will be victorious."

"Thank you, Naomi," I said. "I hope you're right and we get a chance to take down some demons."

"*Oui*," she agreed, smiling like a shrew, her eyes narrowing. "I am looking forward to it."

Then she was gone.

Flying was so damn handy. And who said vamps couldn't fight? Naomi had a definite lethal side.

Before I could move an inch, Rourke had me around the waist. He twisted me to him while guiding me steadily backward toward the broken door. Once my back hit the wall next to it, he growled as he pressed himself against me. Every inch of us sealed tightly together. "You're a handful, you know that?" Before I could protest, his lips were on mine.

I opened them immediately, drinking him in. The scent of cloves ran up my nose and currents of sensations wound up my spine in a delicious tingle. My fingers flexed against his taut shoulders, itching to explore his beautiful body. After a long kiss, I pulled back. "But I'm so very worth it."

He licked his lips. "Yes, I'm well aware."

His eyes were so heated it was hard to gather my thoughts. *We have to go*, I told him internally. I eyed the Queen's bed. I couldn't help it. My mate was incredible and all the built-up adrenaline was pounding for a release. My wolf gave a long howl.

But it so wasn't happening right now.

Instead, my hands slid down his chest, my nails digging in with just enough pressure to convey exactly how I felt about breaking things up. "Rourke, we have to find Ray—"

Jessica ... static ... can you hear me ...

I jumped out of Rourke's grasp like I'd been stuck with a cattle prod. My hands flew to my head and I turned in a circle. *Dad? Is that you?* Hope ran through me. *I can barely hear you.*

I'm coming… buzzing…*I'm injured…in the lead…rogue wolves…right behind us…*

Are you in New Orleans? I held my breath.

Yes…soon…

Then the signal went dead.

Dad! Dad, can you hear me? I shouted in my mind.

No response.

We'll be ready for you!

Emotion welled in my throat. I hadn't seen my father since before I'd left to find Rourke. He'd clearly been running in his wolf form. He was alive, but he was injured.

Rourke's face was grim. "Your father?"

"Yes," I said. "He's injured and the fracture pack is close behind. If he's hurt, there must've been a battle already. He also said he's in the lead, ahead of his Pack. That means they think he's weak. If he stops running, one of them could challenge him for status. He's leading everyone here. If Nick was able to reach James, that could be the reason why. If either of them shifted, they may have been able to get him the message."

"Did he say how close he was?"

"No, but he said soon. The signal was buzzing and cracking. Do you understand how internal communication works? It's a mystery to me."

Rourke shook his head. "It's been a long time since I could talk to another internally," he said, switching to my mind. *But if I had to guess, your brain is connected to your Pack, or mate, as we've just found, and it sends out waves of some kind. It makes sense that when you're fighting or hurt or distracted, those waves get interrupted. We'll have to prove it sometime.* He smiled. *See if we can talk while we…get distracted.*

He'd come close and I leaned my forehead against his chest. "He just has to be okay."

Rourke's hand slid around to the back of my neck and his fingers caressed me lightly. "He's one of the strongest Alphas on the planet. He's alive and that's the most important thing. You did the right thing by blowing up the barrier. He'll get here, and when he does, he will have access to finding us. Access he wouldn't of had otherwise."

What Rourke said was true, but it didn't lessen my angst. "We need to move. It's time to go find Ray," I said. As I stepped back and turned, Rourke caught my arm.

"Wait for a second," he said, his voice earnest. "Jessica, you have to know you're not alone in this. I'm not going anywhere. Ever. I'll stand by your side and we'll take care of this threat together, just like the last one—and just like the *next* one. We're stronger than the opposition." A low growl escaped his throat. "What you did to Valdov was nothing short of spectacular. You're incredibly strong and capable, and as a team, we can be invincible. The demons and sorcerers don't have a real chance against us."

I wanted to believe him, but I still had the habit of thinking like a human. Rourke sensed my trepidation and brought his arms up and flexed, his T-shirt bunching ridiculously over his well-defined muscles. The flowing lines of his tattoos wound their way up to his biceps like beautiful vines.

"Very funny," I said, pushing at his chest. "No need to grandstand. I know you're strong."

"No, I'm serious. I want you to feel them." He leaned into me and I acquiesced. The pads of my fingers prodded the muscle. They were like steel. No give. I let the palm of my hand flow over his smooth skin and I tried not to sigh.

"It feels like armor," I contended. "Very strong."

"Exactly. This is to show you not all supernaturals are created equal. If we were, it would be chaos all the time." He put his arms down and wound his warm hands around my middle, pulling me toward him one last time. "Equality would mean constant status fights against every Sect. We have hierarchies in place for a reason. The most dangerous supernaturals are those who try to advance their station. Selene, who wanted ultimate immortality. Valdov, who wanted to be the Vampire King. Those are the supes who will fight to the death. But Tally, who is arguably one of the strongest witches in the world, is not a threat to us unless we attack. Why do you think that is?"

That was a good question. "I don't know. Why?" Rourke let go of me and grabbed my hand, leading me out of the room.

"Because power respects power. For eons supernaturals have coexisted in this world *together*. If there was truly only one who was the strongest of them all, we would have a King or a Queen of all supernaturals. But we don't."

"But isn't that exactly why everyone is so upset about me? They think I could finally be *that* Queen. The supernatural who is finally strong enough to rule everyone."

"But the Prophecy states you are a *reincarnate*," he pointed out. "One who walks *again*."

I nodded. "That's true." It was weird to think of my wolf as a reincarnate, but she definitely had the knowledge and diva attitude to back it up.

"Then we would have had several Queens over the last millennia, correct?"

"But it doesn't really matter if I wasn't put here to rule"—which I could've told anyone who bothered to ask—"because unless we convince each Sect, they'll interpret the Prophecy any way they wish. I'm a threat to their power. End of story."

"Then we convince them all," he growled. "If the supernatural race had a King or a Queen, we would know it by now. But make no mistake: I will bloody anyone who chooses not to listen, and we will fight to *win*."

"That's exactly what my father said. We have to fight until they fear our power, and when they stop fearing us, we fight again to prove we are the strongest." We turned down a long hallway decorated in deep blues. It was weird no vamps were around. We must still be in the old warded part of the Queen's wing.

"Your father's right. You're incredibly strong, Jessica, and it's clear you don't realize it. Power leaks out of you. Some will covet that strength, but most will seek to destroy it. Valdov died because he chose to fight you for power, but defeating him equalized us with the vampires. You made the right choice to end his life."

We arrived at the top of a back stairway. The old treads looked well used. Rourke moved aside to let me go first, grabbing a handful of my ass as I went down.

I had to admit, no matter how shitty my future was as an equalizer of the supernatural race, I loved this man.

22

"Are you sure we're heading in the right direction?" I asked. My fingertips brushed against cool stone. Feeling the rough texture of the wall was the only thing rooting me in place. We were trying to reach the area where I was held the first time, thinking Ray may be in a similar room. "I can't see a single thing."

"I smell something," Rourke answered. "But it's not Ray. It's the old vamp I had by the neck." Rourke was directly in front of me, his scent making him easy to follow. "I left the door of the cell open, but they must have stayed in the area. If the underground tunnels you told me about were a maze, this place is one too."

All my senses were muted. "I can't smell anything. How are you able to get through the mask?" Whatever spell this was, it was strong enough to blanket my senses. "This feels nothing like it did with Conan. Before, I could see everything, except for the fact I thought we were in a dungeon the entire time."

"I think this is a new ward," Rourke answered. "It has a taste, but it's fresh."

I inhaled, but I couldn't taste anything. "The other spell had a flavor too. Is it tart?"

"Yes." Rourke stopped abruptly.

I pulled up just short of running into him. "I wonder why I can't sense it."

Rourke's body tensed, suddenly alert. "There's something else here. Can you feel it?"

"No," I said, frustrated. "I'm going to throw my magic out again and see what I can find." I gathered my power and extended it into the area.

This time I did detect something. It was very faint and heavily masked. "Whatever it is, it has the same crab-apple taste I told you about. I'm thinking—"

"Come." A broken Russian accent cut through the darkness. "We are here."

Rourke's blood jumped. He was a hairsbreadth away from reacting, which wouldn't end well for the old vampire.

We both knew it was Yuri's voice, but we couldn't tell where it was coming from, or if there was another threat attached to it.

"Yuri," I called. "Are you and Alana alone?"

"For the time being," he replied. "But you must hurry. The Queen is angry with us." His voice sounded strong and sure, nothing like before.

And he seemed to be waiting for us.

Rourke and I edged farther into the darkness, moving carefully, trying to sense if this was a trap. "The spell breaks here," Rourke said, reaching out to grab my wrist and guide me around a corner.

Once my hand skimmed over a doorjamb, the haze immediately lifted.

We were in some sort of storage room. It was covered in cobwebs and dust, more than a few inches thick in some places. A single lightbulb illuminated the far corner, shedding some weak light, but everything else was etched in shadows.

Alana hissed.

I glanced around Rourke's shoulder. She sat in the middle of the room. Her head wound was more or less healed, if you called a gaping scar with a partial indent *healed*, but at least she was awake and it wasn't oozing. The most alarming thing, however, were her eyes. They were pulsing a pewter color and she seemed to be leaking bloody tears.

"What the hell is this?" Rourke said. "What is she doing?" He'd come to a full stop ten feet from where she was bound and hadn't moved.

Alana rocked in place, and was mumble-hissing over and over again in what was likely Russian, but it was too garbled to tell.

"Yuri," I asked. "Did you bind her to that crate?" I pointed to the chains he'd obviously brought with him from the cell, which were strung around her body and hooked to some kind of wooden storage box to keep her in place.

Instead of stating the obvious, he said, "We could've stayed well hidden from you, but Alana knew you were coming and bid me to find you. Tying her was the safest thing, as she is . . . unpredictable."

My eyes flicked back to Alana, who appeared to be out of her ever-loving mind. "Unpredictable" was a quaint way to say she would rip our faces off if she had the chance.

I found it hard to believe she could form a coherent thought and speak to Yuri. She caught my eye and started waving a yellowed fingernail around in a circle, chanting something while sniffing the air in front of her like a dog.

Jesus.

"Yuri." I slid out from behind Rourke and moved into the room. "What's going on here? How did Alana know we would be coming? And was that your spell out there? The one that tastes like crab apple?"

"Alana grows stronger out of the cell," he responded. "But we must vacate this place soon. Danger is coming quickly and they must not find her here. If they do, things will not be as they should. We have waited too long for our freedom and we grow impatient."

Okay, *what*?

"Why have you been kept prisoner here?" Rourke demanded. "If you are indeed the Queen's blood-kin, she has broken a law by jailing you. It's a high crime to harm your relatives according to vamp laws. That I do know."

Yuri appraised Rourke, a reserved expression on his face. "It was necessary. She had no choice in the matter. Alana could not be contained . . . any other way."

"What do you mean *necessary*?" I asked. "You willingly chose that lifestyle? Starved and rotting in a dirty cell? You can't make us believe that was your only option. There had to be another way."

Yuri sighed. "Alana is a seer. Eudoxia had no knowledge of us for many years. Our existence was kept from her on purpose. Once she found us, the damage was already too great. We had no other choice."

"*Seer?*" My mouth fell open. I glanced over at Alana, who was still chanting and drawing circles in the air. Oracles and seers were of the same ilk. My first thought was poor little Maggie. Her future was looking bleaker by the second. My second thought was *holy shit*. "It was Valdov, wasn't it? He turned you for some kind of gain of his own. Maybe for the throne?"

"Yes," Yuri answered. "He turned me into a vampire because he wanted the throne. He saw that Vlad would not succeed and was determined to gain his own power." He glanced lovingly at his wife. "But he did not turn Alana."

Rourke's face was stoic. "You turned her."

"Of course." Yuri sighed as he sat on the edge of the crate next to his wife. "I kept her turning a secret as long as I could, but I was a fledgling and we were both very weak. I should not have been able to turn her so young and I blame myself for her insanity. We had no guidance and craved the teachings of a true Master. Valdov punished us soundly for my interference. He took away all our wealth, our status, and closeted us away. Until..."

"He found out what your wife was truly capable of," Rourke finished. "Seers are very rare in any Sect, but vampires especially. I've never even heard a whisper of one."

A pained expression crossed the old vampire's face. "Yes." He bowed his head. "Turning my wife was the biggest mistake I ever made. She deserved a happy life and I made it a horror instead." Misery etched his features. I glanced at Rourke. His face didn't need to tell me what I already knew.

We would've each made the same choice, given the same circumstances. Living without the other now was unthinkable. We couldn't blame Yuri at all.

"How long did Valdov keep your existence quiet from the Queen?" I asked.

"Four hundred years."

I sucked in a breath. "How could he do such a thing? It should've been an impossible task. If the Queen was the ruler—"

"At the time of our making, she was not our Queen," Yuri said firmly. There was respect in his voice for her. It surprised me. Why would he have love for a Queen who had forced them to live like rats? "Eudoxia had been turned by Vlad only a single year before, in the hopes he could gain power through the family. My brother, Ivan, was terrible indeed and had committed many atrocities by that time. Vlad had hoped to marry Eudoxia to put himself in power, but she... resisted... and things fell apart. They were forced to flee the country—"

"Life force...she craves it..." Alana's voice sounded shrill and a lot more precise than anything she should be capable of uttering. "But...she will not get it," she continued. "They will come... those who wake...from those below...they take much..." As she spoke nonsense, blood tears coursed from the corners of her pewter eyes, etching trails of red down her white face. Her hair was wiry and askew, her features sunken and bleak.

I took an unconscious step backward. Rourke reached out to comfort me, sensing my distress. "I don't think weres and oracles mix very well," I said, turning my head slightly toward Yuri. "We need to get her some help—"

"*Silence!*" she screeched, a curved nail pointed straight at my chest.

My mouth snapped shut.

She began to rattle her chains, her arms and legs twisting erratically. Yuri stood and tried to calm her. "My love, you must relax. We will leave here soon, as promised." His voice was tender. "You wanted to talk to the girl. She is here. Say your piece and we will leave."

All at once, a power surge shot around the room. It was so strong it slammed both Rourke and me against the wall. The only words Alana uttered before Yuri screamed were garbled.

But I understood them just fine.

"She is mine."

The power signature Alana had emitted reeked of alcohol, of all things. I righted myself quickly, but Rourke was one step ahead of me. Yuri was down and Rourke was already by his side, kneeling at his chest.

There was only one problem.

Houdini had escaped her chains and she wasn't anywhere to be seen.

The room wasn't that big.

There were various shelving units and darkened areas stacked with goods, but I should be able to get a bead on her. "Um, Rourke?" I said as I inched forward cautiously. "Where's Alana?" I glanced toward the door of the storage room, but it was closed and had no sign of a forced exit. She wouldn't have had enough time to go through without us seeing her. "I can still smell her all over. It would be impossible for her to become invisible right—"

With a wicked shriek, she dropped from the ceiling onto my shoulders.

We tumbled to the floor as my mate yelled, and pandemonium hit the storage room.

Goddammit. I hadn't looked up. That was the oldest trick in the book. But now that I was on my back, I could see the old rafters cut deeply into the weathered ceiling. Perfect place for a crazy lady to hide.

My wolf snarled fiendishly, trying to roll her off of us. Adrenaline raced through my system as my body morphed. "What are you *doing?*" I yelled at Alana as we tumbled. "*Ow!*" She'd locked her skinny arms around my neck and plunged her fangs deeply in my neck.

I gave a strangled howl.

"I can't tear her loose," Rourke shouted from above us. "There's no space between you." He clutched her around the waist, but her legs were locked like a vise around me, and we both rose in the air as he lifted, her fangs tearing deeper into my flesh.

"Gag, *stop*," I gurgled. He set us back down carefully. "You can't get her off me," I gasped, trying to force her head backward, my claws digging deeply into her back, "because she's not trying to fight me. She's trying to eat me!"

Alana had clamped herself onto me like a vampire second skin and she was a lot stronger than she looked. Her power needled into my skin as she drank, her head buried so far in the crook of my neck her face wasn't showing. I rolled again, trying to shake her loose. We knocked into crates and boxes, but she held on. Rourke swung his fist down on her head and then on her back. I heard bones break, but she didn't move. Not even an inch.

"She's not reacting," Rourke yelled. "I don't know how to get her off without ripping open your neck." Her fangs were embedded so far into me, tearing her off would cause major trauma and take me too long to heal. Plus, it would hurt like a mother.

"Let me...try something." I raked Alana's back with my claws, using all my strength, tearing what little clothing she had. She gasped and writhed but wouldn't unlatch. I turned her on her back, managing to make my way to my knees. Once up, I slammed her down. "Get *off* me!" I shouted.

Rourke was behind with something in his hand. "Look out, Jessica. I'm going to smash this—"

And just like that, she unlatched.

Once free, I jumped off the floor, my hand covering my dripping neck as I backed away.

Alana staggered like a drunk and laughed like a possessed cartoon character. She sounded like Woody Woodpecker on acid.

My gaping wound healed quickly, but for some reason I felt dizzy. She must have taken a gallon. Rourke was in front of me, throwing what appeared to be an ice pick into the corner. That would've been gruesome. "Are you okay? Did she take too much?" he asked. When I didn't answer right away, he put his hands on my shoulders and urged, "Jessica, answer me. Are you hurt?"

I shook my head.

He didn't need any more than that. He let go of me and turned, bearing down on Alana fast. "I don't care what you are." She didn't make a move to dodge him. He took her by the throat, lifting her off the ground, shaking her thin body. "You do not get to do whatever you want."

"You are too late," Alana gasped, her teeth stained red with my blood. She ran her tongue over her pointed canines to prove her point. "I already took my fill."

Those were coherent sentences.

Spoken from someone who had been mostly nonverbal a few short moments ago. I angled my head toward Alana, wiping the blood off my neck with the collar of my shirt. My eyes were semi-unfocused, but I was regaining my strength by the moment. I narrowed my line of sight with effort so I could take in her appearance. Her head was almost fully back to normal. She was changing, morphing into what must have been her old self as I watched. My blood was healing her too quickly.

I inhaled, and her real scent hit me.

It was crab apple.

"Wait!" I shouted at Rourke. He had backed her up against a wall. Her eyes were beginning to roll back in her head. "Put her down. It was her ward we just felt in the hallway. She can cast spells, and she's a vampire! Just like the Queen."

"Are you sure?" Rourke replied through clenched teeth. "I'm having trouble... wanting to let her go. She's a menace and needs to be stopped. What if she goes after you again?"

I placed a hand on his outstretched arm, his muscles corded like steel, just like he'd proven to me a few minutes ago. Alana was no match for his strength, which is why she hadn't struggled. The hierarchy was certainly in place here. "I'm sure. Let her go. We need information more than we need to take her life. If she can cast spells like the Queen, I want to know why. There's a link we're missing. Let's fill it in and then we can decide what to do after we hear it."

Yuri staggered to stand, finally recovering. His face was bloodied, but he was rallying. "Yes," he urged. "Please let her go."

Rourke released her and took a step back. She dropped to the ground.

Alana stood for a second, a lopsided grin on her face, and then she began to clap like a little girl. She gazed at me. "Bravo! It is exactly as I had hoped it would be. Your blood is like an ocean of power coursing through my veins. I've waited so long for this. Oh, how I can *see* again! It's like a miracle, only not really, because, of course, I knew this was going to happen."

I tried not to show my surprise by her complete 180, or her predictions. "How is it that you can cast spells?" I asked, ignoring the comments about my blood. Having it running through her veins was not at all optimal. I had no idea what she would be capable of now, or if we'd be linked, and I really didn't want to think about killing her. One thing at a time. "Are you related to the Queen by blood?"

"Of course I am," she replied. "Why wouldn't I be?"

"That's not really an answer," I pointed out. "If you're both related to the Queen by blood, that means"—I turned my head toward Yuri, who looked agitated—"you married your cousin." I glanced back at Alana. "I'm right, aren't I?"

"Yes," Yuri said quietly. "We are distant cousins."

I turned back to Alana. "What are you? You were turned into a vampire, but you were supernatural already. If Eudoxia could defeat Vlad as a fledgling, and she can cast spells, you both have to be something more."

Alana sized me up, still grinning. "We are fae."

23

My mouth hung open. Fae had not been the answer I expected. I don't know what I'd been expecting, but possibly something along the lines of nymph or pixie. "Fae have been rumored to be extinct for centuries. There hasn't been a single sighting of one since before the birth of my father," I said, still feeling slightly astonished. "How can this be?"

Alana strode from the wall and Rourke shot his hand out in warning. She stopped. "We are half fae, if you must know," she said, "which you do, so I will tell you. Long ago our race was in threat of dying out and we were forced to breed with humans or become extinct. We chose humans with wealth and power, naturally, and kept our existence well cloaked." Her hair had darkened considerably, and her cheeks had become a more palatable color than dead, bleached bone. Her eyes were now a luminous brown, not glowing pewter.

She appeared...strangely normal.

Not someone who'd spent eons as a spooky ghoul locked in a

cell. She continued. "I am telling you this because it will aid you later. Much later. But we are running out of time and you must go or things will shift once again."

Shift? "I'm sorry, but I'm not going anywhere until I understand what you're talking about," I said firmly. "You're a seer and blood-kin to the Queen, but she kept you locked up. Why did you continue to aid her?"

"It was necessary," Alana replied. "After hundreds of years of cruelty at the hands of Valdov, my mind had shattered. A newly made vampire starved for blood becomes damaged beyond repair, but a fledgling vampire who is also a seer who is also half fae is irrevocably lost. Because the Queen is powerful, and my kin; she alone could coax me into intermittent sanity. But she could not stay with me twenty-four hours a day."

I nodded, not because I understood, but because it was all so insane. "So the Queen knew Valdov was a spy."

"Of course," she said. "She knew his true nature when she found out about us. But she needed to keep him for this very day. So he lived."

"The Queen orchestrated the events today. Why?"

"Valdov and Eudoxia would've ended you together if you had come when your oath demanded. When you showed up early and unannounced, it put their plans askew. She came down to consult with me once you were granted entrance into the mansion. I told her what must be done."

"She wants my blood."

"She *needs* your blood," Alana said, holding up a single finger. "There is a distinction."

My eyebrows arched. "She needs it like you needed it?"

"No," she answered. "Your blood has cured my madness. It was necessary and the only thing that could bring me salvation, but your blood will bring her to *godhood*."

I was stricken to silence.

"Vampires can't attain godhood," Rourke growled. "You're lying. A god must be born, not made." Vampires were "made" into supernaturals by powerfully magical blood, while shifters, witches, and most of the others were born.

Alana smiled. "Ah, but she was born a supernatural, was she not? Eudoxia's destiny is vast. But what she does not know is… I have lied to her. Repeatedly. It was a shame, but necessary. If I had not, her path would have turned very dark, and even in my madness I still loved my niece."

"Godhood?" I said. "No wonder she's on a rampage. A vampire in line for true immortality is very rare." Once a supe reached godhood, which only very few could, it meant the coupling of vast power and true immortality. A regular supernatural could live for thousands of years but could be killed a number of ways.

It was almost impossible to kill a god.

"Fate weaves a path for you at your birth, as it does for us all, and thus far you have stayed true to yours." She stepped closer and I nodded to Rourke that it was okay. "If you continue to choose the right course, it will lead you to greatness. If you do not, it could be detrimental to us all." She peered at me, her eyes hooded, like she was trying to see into my soul. "It is unclear how this will end, which is puzzling."

That wasn't exactly comforting. "How am I supposed to know which one is the right path?" I asked, frustrated. "That's a lot of pressure, especially since making the wrong choice *could be detrimental to all.*"

"There is one path for each of us." She held up a finger. It was free of wrinkles, but the nails were still yellowed. "But it comes with many detours. Some will circle back and some will not. It is fluid, yet set. The true mystery lies in all of us and what our hearts desire."

"You mentioned salvation," I said. "I need to know if my father will survive."

She cocked her head. "His salvation depends on another. But it is ultimately up to you."

"That wasn't exactly helpful—"

Something rocked the mansion from the outside and the storage shelves clattered and dust fell from the rafters.

"It begins now," she said, shuffling away from me. "We must part."

"But you haven't answered my question yet," I complained.

"I can say no more." Alana moved toward the far wall. "Just know that everything is up to you. And you must make choices true to your heart; if you do not, you will suffer the consequences." Another explosion hit the ground. "Quickly, you must exit through here."

I strode toward the grate she had just pulled open. "You want us to crawl through the venting?" I asked.

"It is necessary," she said, her voice firm. Yuri had come to stand by her side. It was hard to disagree with a seer when my father's life was on the line.

I turned to Rourke, who was already leaning in to take a look. "This must be a shortcut to the main part of the mansion." The house shook again. We could feel the vibrations, but they weren't direct hits. If they were, the walls would be coming down around us. That meant the Queen had put up her ward. I hoped my father made it in. It was time to get out of here. "We may as well take it. It looks maneuverable."

"Okay," I said. "Let's do it."

He eased his large frame into the small opening.

I turned to follow, right as Alana laid a hand on my arm. "Eudoxia will be resistant at first, but she must perform one last task before she is worthy of the power required. Make sure she agrees to it."

"I'm tired of crawling through tunnels in this place," I growled, because I could. "There has to be an easier way back to the main rooms than taking old venting units."

Rourke was ahead of me, his massive body barely fitting through the narrow passageway.

"The moment the demons spot you, this battle will start in earnest," Rourke said. "We have to be methodical about this." He'd been going over strategy since we started our crawl. The sun had set. We'd spent too much time with Alana and Yuri and now it was time to start planning. "We regroup with everyone and hope they have Ray." He stopped moving. "I see something with a knob ahead. Let's try it."

A whispery voice hit my eardrum. "No, not that way."

"Hey, where did you come from?" My head hit the top of the tunnel in surprise. "Ow." It was the same ghost who had stayed with me in the mausoleum. I rubbed my head. "I thought you left with the rest of them."

"What?" Rourke said. "I'm not leaving."

"You must stop him," it said. "That is a gate, not a door. It will lead to agony."

Rourke started shouldering the small doorway. "Rourke, wait! Don't open that."

"Why?" He craned his head toward me. "Let's see where it leads. If it's not the right one, then we can keep crawling."

"It's not a door. Apparently it's one of those gates. It could open us up to something shitty, like more Trows."

"How do you know? I can't smell anything dangerous." He leaned his head toward the portal, inhaling.

"Um . . . a ghost just told me."

Rourke snapped his head back at me. "What ghost? I thought you said they all left."

"I have stayed," it whispered, "because you are still in danger."

"It says I'm still in danger, so it stayed," I relayed. "Tell me something I don't know, Mr. Ghost. So where do we go?"

It brushed by my ear. "You must climb."

"Climb? You mean up? We're in a four-foot-square tunnel that happens to be running horizontally."

"How do we go up?" Rourke maneuvered himself to his back and examined the top of the tunnel. He grabbed on to the flimsy sheet metal of the venting and tore. It opened to expose red brick. "It's solid above us."

"The passageway is above you." The voice was soft and muffled, like it had drifted through the stone as it talked to me.

"The ghost says we have to go up," I said. "Honestly, I don't know if we should trust it. But this is the same ghost who aided me with Naomi, and we're kind of out of options. And this vent is making me edgy. Why did we agree to crawl in here again? I think Alana slipped us some of her Kool-Aid. There's no other explanation."

"Fine, we go up," Rourke grunted. "The reason we're in here is we believe she's right." Without any more discussion, he rammed a powerful fist into the ceiling above our heads. "And she had better be right."

The old bricks cracked immediately, crumbling down around us.

The top of the tunnel sounded hollow. I covered my mouth and nose as dust flew around the small confines of our space. "If she's not right, I say we track her down and string her up by her skinny ankles."

"One more time should be the charm." Rourke smashed

through the stone in another stellar hit and more chunks and debris came crashing down around us.

Once everything settled, there was a hole, but it wasn't big enough for us to climb through. "Here, let me help. I can use my legs to open it up," I said. "You're too big. I can angle myself in a better position than you can." He slid forward and I rolled once, scooting myself into place. I brought my legs up. They almost touched the top of the tunnel. *Give me some juice*, I told my wolf. My legs bunched under my skin and I shot them upward. They busted straight through the rest of the loose stones, making the hole big enough for us to fit through in one go. I coughed, twisting my body to kneel, ducking my head through the hole to take a look. "It's an old elevator shaft." That was a surprise. "And it smells stale. Nobody's been in here for a long time."

Beneath me I kicked away errant bricks and rose, lifting my head and shoulders through the small space. There were wooden beams directly above me, and I dug my nails into one to get some leverage. As I continued to pull myself through the hole, I felt Rourke's hands begin to slide down the length of my body, ending at my hips, where he grabbed on and hoisted me through. "Resorting to cheap feels?" I chuckled.

"At this point, I'll take what I can get," he growled. Once I was up, I splayed my feet across one side and made room for him to join me in the small shaft. He started through the hole, knocking away more stone so he could fit. "All these adrenaline jumps are making me nuts. My cat wants a release yesterday."

"I couldn't agree more." I started to climb. I'd gone only a few feet when Tyler's voice shot into my brain.

Jess, where are you? His tone was frantic.

How could I explain where I was? *We're inside the mansion, trying to find a way out. Did you find Ray? Please tell me you found him.*

Yes, we found him. Relief swept through my body so clearly I almost lost my grip. *He was locked in a crypt and is pissed as hell, but there's more trouble. The sorcerers have set up summoning rings around the perimeter. But that's not the worst part. The Screamer is loose.*

What do you mean it's loose? It's fully corporeal?

Yes, and Ray has already fought it once. I've been trying to reach you for a half hour. Where have you been? I was about to go balls out ripping down walls in this place.

We ran into an important... complication. Too much to explain. Tell me about the Screamer. I don't get why Ray is involved.

It's after you, Jess.

What do you mean, after me?

It's linked to your blood somehow and it's trying to find you. Naomi says it craves your power and it needs more. It's like a possessed banshee. Everyone is running.

Stay away from it. Once we get out of here, we'll find you outside.

Jess, it's in the house.

In the house?

Tyler, don't worry about me. I'm concealed right now. If the Queen has fueled the new ward and it's protecting us from the demons, our priority is still finding Dad. I'll get out of the house as soon as I can. Start searching the grounds—

"It comes too soon," the ghost cried. "Climb!"

Before I could react, a hand shot through the wall and grabbed me by the neck like a homing pigeon.

"*Jessica!*" Rourke bellowed as my skull crashed into the wall.

At the thing's touch, a current of pure electricity shot through me, so strong I couldn't breathe.

In the next instant I was in my Lycan form.

I thrashed, but it wouldn't let go. Its hand was generating more electricity and it held on like a clamp. I lost my footing and dangled in the air as the Screamer continued to bash me into the wall.

A fierce screech hit my eardrums.

I took hold of its forearm, painful currents washing over me, and tried bracing my legs against the shaft so I could rear back, but its hold was unyielding. It bellowed at me and gave one more huge thrust. My body crashed through the rest of the wall, splinters and broken wood raking my body.

Once it had me on the other side, it tossed me onto the rug.

We were in some kind of parlor.

Then it turned and picked up an armoire like it was nothing and smashed it into the opening, dropping it right over my howling mate.

"Well, hello, Conan," I said from the floor. "It's so nice to see you again."

24

This wasn't the adorable Conan I knew and loved. This was Conan meets *Hellboy*. "I will drink you dry," it moaned as it advanced on me. I scuttled backward on my arms and legs. "And feast on your entrails."

"It cannot be stopped," came a panicked whisper in my ear. "It has manifested itself."

"I can see that," I muttered. "It's kind of hard to miss."

"You must leave here," the ghost urged.

"I'm working on it." My back hit a wall and I immediately shimmied to the right. There were windows directly on the other side of the room. It was the only viable option. Conan had shoved furniture in front of the only door. It would take too long to dismantle it.

The Screamer had gobbled up so much of Conan there was only a shell left. Its eyelids drooped, its fangs bit into its lower lip, blood leaked down its chin, and its hair was falling out. It resembled a zombie vampire as it shuffled at me.

It was dead, but in a whole different way.

It was double dead.

"It seeks more power." The ghost pushed against my body, trying to move me.

"I know that. Listen, if you don't have any helpful advice to give," I told the ghost, "then do me a favor and keep your breathy comments to yourself."

Before the Screamer could reach me, I snatched up an end table and hurled it.

It batted it away like a mild irritant.

"What makes them so strong?" I asked. "It's like the Hercules of the Undead."

"They are fueled by raw energy," it whispered in my ear. "It cannot be defeated."

"Bullshit," I retorted. "If that were true, Screamers would be running around all over the world eating people's souls. This thing is going down. We just have to figure how."

It kept hobbling at me with single-minded intention as I inched my way along the wall. It was a good thing it was slow. *Let's try and knock its head off and see if that works*, I told my growling wolf.

"That won't work."

"Hey," I accused. "Stay out of my brain. How do you do that anyway?"

"I can hear your thoughts," the ghost said. "They are the same as speaking them."

The Screamer lunged and I dove out of the way.

Its arms went through the wall where my head had just been and a horrible keening erupted. Unfortunately I'd had to dive away from freedom.

The Screamer still stood between me and the windows.

"If you want my blood, you have to be faster than that, big guy." It spun around. "And you're not moving too quickly with your two...broken kneecaps." For the first time I noticed its legs weren't working properly. Conan must have broken bones when Danny tossed him out the window and they hadn't had time to heal before the Screamer had possessed him.

Ick.

It came at me again, faster this time.

I rolled twice and brought my legs up in a scissor kick behind its head. But instead of sending it flying, a jolt of high-voltage electricity tossed me backward. "*Dammit,*" I yelled as I smashed into an antique desk, shattering it. My leg gave out beneath me. "What just happened?" I panted.

"I told you it is made up of pure energy," said a whisper. "It cannot feel pain."

"What, is it made up of lightning bolts? That was a gigantic electrical charge. That amount of energy shouldn't be possible. "

The ghost gave a hollow chuckle.

"Did you just laugh?"

"Jessica!" Rourke yelled. My head whipped to the hole in the wall. His fury was palpable. He had begun to tear through the rest of the armoire trying to get me.

"Rourke," I called. "We can't beat this thing in here. I'm going out the window. Meet me outside."

The Screamer understood my words and roared its displeasure. "You cannot escape," its garbled voice cawed at me. It sounded nothing like Conan.

"The only way you can devour me is if you can catch me, ass-hole. And I'm much faster than you are." I was close enough to the back windows to act. I sprang, the glass shattered easily. I soared out the window in a semi-graceful dive. But it was dark and I couldn't fly. *Get ready for a hard landing*, I yelled to my wolf. I was already in my Lycan form, but more power coursed through me courtesy of my wolf.

"You will not die," the voice sounded in my ear right as I hit the ground feetfirst.

I tucked and rolled and rolled and rolled, finally smashing up against the bushes at the edge of the stone gate that ran around the property.

"I told you," the ghost whispered.

I groaned. Several bones were broken, including a couple ribs, which made it painful to breathe. They were healing, but I hurt a ridiculous amount while each of them knit back together. They had to heal fast, because I knew the Screamer would be right behind me. I inhaled sharply as my body gave a few jumps as bones shifted. "Who are you anyway?" I asked the ghost through gritted teeth.

"My name is Benjamin."

"Why are you helping me?"

"I want my property back."

"So you're tied to this place? You're its rightful owner?"

"No."

"Well, you're certainly good at answering all my burning questions, Ben." I lay there for a second, trying not to breathe as my ribs mended. "Please don't tell me you're my ghost pal for life. My heart can't take it—"

Jessica.

My head shot up, the pain forgotten.

I was on my feet in the next moment. "Dad? Dad! Where are you? Are you hurt?" His voice had been shallow. *Dad! Tell me where you are!*

"Here," he said weakly.

I ran toward the next hedge and ripped through a screen of branches, breaking them off without thought. We were in a small patch of side yard, away from anything. This is why Alana sent me through the house. I had to exit these windows in order to find him. Now that I was outside, I could hear all the commotion on the other side of the wall, just as Tyler had said.

Once I saw him, my knees gave way and I dropped to the ground.

He was naked, lying on his side. He'd just shifted back from his wolf form, which meant he'd arrived right before Eudoxia set the ward. He must have jumped the wall.

His body was covered in festering angry welts.

Those weren't normal welts.

"What are these? What's going on?" My voice was rushed. When he didn't answer, I panicked. "Dad, you have to tell me! I need to know what's going on."

He tried to lift his head, but succeeded only in raising it a few inches. "The rest of my wolves are behind me. I had to pull ahead. But the fracture pack is right behind them, Redman in the lead. He crossed over to their side at the last moment. There were too many wolves to fight. I should've brought an army with me. It was a bad decision, and now I'm paying the price."

"You weren't going down to fight," I cried. "You were going down to cement alliances. How would you have known? But I need to help you now. What are these welts?"

His breath was shallow. "I was cursed."

"Cursed?" I repeated, stunned.

"Not by a witch." He reached out and grabbed my wrist. A trickle of power tingled up my arm. Whatever was harming him was sucking away his magic.

"Then by what?"

"Jessica," he said quietly. "It's already ravaged me from the inside out. What you're seeing is the latent damage. The only thing that's kept me alive was shifting into my wolf and knowing I had to get here to you. Now that I'm human, I have very little time left, so you need to listen—"

"*No!*" I said, balling my fists. "We can fix this. You're not going to die! Maggie said you'd be fine if—" I needed Ray. "I need to find Tyler." *Tyler! Where are you?* I yelled in my mind.

We're in the front yard. Where are you? In good news, the witches are outside the gate with Nick. It seems he's been coordinating the Pack and the witches. There's a solid defense going on, but we can't get in or out because of the ward.

Never mind all that; I found Dad and I need you right now! Bring Ray. I'm on the north side of the house in the bushes. Dad's been cursed. I can't figure it out. But, Tyler, he's dying.

We are on our way. I heard him yell something to someone.

"It comes again," a whisper floated against my ear. "You must get away."

I waved my hand, trying to shoo away the ghost. I didn't have time to deal with it.

A crash, followed a second later by a big thud, sounded right behind us.

My father snarled. He tried to get up. I put my hand on his shoulder. "I'll take care of this." I stood and turned to see the Screamer stumbling toward us, even more disfigured from its fall. Behind me, my father began to shift into his wolf form. I hoped he had enough strength to finish the change. He would be better protected in wolf form.

"I don't have time for this, Conan. Do you hear me?" I walked toward it, determined to keep it away from my injured father.

The Screamer almost smiled.

But instead of engaging me, its horrid nostrils flared. It scented death in the air.

"Oh no, that's so not going to happen," I said, waving my arms to center its attention on me. "You want me, remember? I have all the kickass blood you need right here."

There was noise above us. I glanced up right as my mate burst out one of the windows, jumping through the air cleanly with his powerful arms splayed. He came down hard, landing and rolling twice, twisting at the last moment, his feline abilities at the forefront. Both of his feet crashed into the Screamer's knees from behind.

The Screamer flew to the side and struck the wall. I knew it wasn't enough to keep it down for long, but Rourke had bought us some much-needed time.

"Go to your father and I'll keep this thing occupied," he urged. "I can smell him from here. I will make sure this thing stays away from you." Fur sprouted along his powerful forearms. He'd have his work cut out for him.

I nodded once and ran back to my father, calling over my shoulder, "Tyler and Ray are on their way."

Rourke was right—the smell was awful. The scent of rotted flesh wound its way up my nose, making me gag. It was stronger now that he was in his wolf form. Without thinking, I dropped to my knees and dug my hands into his fur and grabbed tightly, pouring as much power as I could into his body. *More*, I urged my wolf. *Can you see anything?* Images of mustard-colored masses emerged in my senses. *Ohmygods, they're everywhere. We have to try and get rid of them.* I aimed my power at the masses, trying to encapsulate them. Once my essence touched the putridity, it scorched me. The curse fought back, burning along my senses, trying to keep me out.

The festering sores didn't give at all.

Instead, they seemed to feed off my power. But my father's relief was palpable. I was insulating him from the pain by wrapping my power around the globs.

I shoved more power into his body. *Dad*, I said. *Is this better?*

Yes. His voice was hollow. *It's helping, but I don't want to hurt you. Be careful.*

Don't worry about me. Tell me what happened to you. Who's behind this? I left out *because I will kill them*, as we both knew they would die for this, whether it was at my hand or his.

We were tracking the fracture group in the Everglades, but it turned out they weren't working alone. The magic they were using was strong, but I couldn't place it. They attacked. When we fought, several of the humans shifted into wolves... but they were not... true wolves.

I don't understand. What do you mean?

Jessica, these wolves were made with some kind of black magic. They were not born.

Made? That's impossible. How can anyone make *a wolf? Our gift is genetic, passed on by birth.* Saliva wasn't enough to change anyone into a wolf. You had to be born or nothing.

I witnessed it with my own eyes. They were wolves, but changed. They were rabid and feral. Someone must have taken our DNA and cursed it somehow. There is no other explanation.

If that were true, it was incredible. And horrific.

So we eradicate them, take out the culprit who is crafting the curses, and we win.

My father chuckled and sucked in his breath. My power had begun to leak out of his body. I readjusted, trying to keep it better contained. It took everything I had not to show my emotion to him and start weeping like a child.

It won't be an easy task, he managed. *They are making war machines. They don't care if it goes against nature. They want to win at all costs.*

How many were there?

There were at least three in the first group that followed us out. If they bite you, they spread their vile curse. Their bite will change a human to wolf, but for us it means death.

There was a deafening boom behind us.

I jumped, shielding my father's body with my own.

Rourke was down and the Screamer was ambling toward us. Anger and fury fueled me as I leapt forward. "You want me? Is that what you want?"

"No." Ben's voice hit my eardrum a second before I sprang. "You must not engage it."

Too late. Better me than my father. I lunged, my arms wrapping around its chest. The force of the electricity blinded me, trying to buck me back, but I held on, digging my claws into its decaying flesh.

It roared.

"I will not let you kill us," I groaned. The voltage was agonizing. My face contorted in pain. I tried to funnel the energy out of me as fast as I could, but I couldn't do it quickly enough. Once it filled me up completely, I would either pass out or my heart would explode. "I don't care if I die," I yelled, "but I'm taking you with me."

"Your death won't be necessary, Hannon." A familiar and the most welcome voice I'd ever heard sounded next to me as the Screamer was efficiently ripped off me.

I collapsed onto the ground, my body ringing with nasty aftershocks. I struggled to catch my breath. Tyler and Danny hovered over me with worried expressions. "I'm...fine." I coughed, rolling over onto my knees. "Go...protect Dad. He needs...Ray."

"Sorry it took so long," Tyler said, stepping back. "We ran into a group of mouthy vamps who tried to stop us." A look of horror flashed over his face as he spotted our father in the bushes.

"Ray is a wee bit occupied at the moment." Danny crouched next to me. "But it looks like he may be freed up in a second or two."

Ray had the Screamer by the throat.

But that wasn't even the most unbelievable part. He appeared to be pulsing with the same kind of energy as the Screamer.

"What is *he* doing?" I said, staggering to stand. "Why is he lit up like that?"

"I have no idea," Danny said. "But it's a fairly incredible thing to witness if you ask me."

Rourke paced back and forth on the other side of the fight, ready to spring if Ray collapsed. I was glad to see him back on his feet. The look on his face was pure determination. No doubt he was pissed the Screamer had gotten the best of him.

"You're not gonna mess with me again," Ray yelled. "This time I'm making it permanent." He maneuvered the Screamer to a kneeling position. "You don't get to eat me or any of my goddamn friends."

It was nice to hear we'd graduated to friends, but the entire ordeal between them was so strange I stood there unmoving, the aftereffects of the energy still ringing in my ears.

"Jessica," my brother yelled. "What do we do now?"

My brother's voice shook me out of my stupor. I ran over to where he sat with our father. "I don't know." I knelt again, plunging my hands back into my father's fur. "We need Ray. But even if he can kill the Screamer, that isn't going to save Dad's life. I don't understand what Ray needs to do."

Jessica . . . my father's voice trickled weakly in my mind. *Don't worry about me. Defeat . . . that thing . . . before it kills you . . .*

Dad, we're not leaving you. They have this handled. Please don't give up on us. I talked to a seer and she said Ray would help us. You need to stay alive—

"Jessica! Move!" Rourke yelled.

"Argh!" I spasmed and fell forward as white-hot energy raced through my body once again.

The Screamer had me in a choke hold.

It had escaped Ray's grasp. My back arched as my hands clawed at its forearm. Its mouth was right by my ear, its dirty fangs an inch from my neck. "I will have you."

I shot my elbow into its ribs and tried to force it backward. *We have to try and absorb the energy.* But my brain was too fuzzy and I couldn't catch my breath.

Ray yelled behind me, but I couldn't make out what he was saying.

In front of me, my father rose on unstable legs, Tyler springing up next to him. My father growled and bit the air, wanting to help me. I pushed back into the Screamer with everything I had, trying to put space between us and my family. If my father got his teeth onto the Screamer, it might be enough to finish him off.

Dad, get back!

"Jessica," Rourke yelled from above me somewhere. "Hold on!" There was movement all around me. I was spinning out from the Screamer's hold.

Right into someone's waiting arms.

"It is okay, *Ma Reine*." Something smoothed my hair. "We have everything under control now."

25

"If this is *under* control"—my throat rattled as I brought a hand up to my head—"I don't want to see out of control. My brain feels like two fried eggs in a hot pan."

"*Oui*," Naomi said. "Screamers, as you call them, are hard to defeat and often ravage for weeks. But it looks as if we will be lucky with this one."

Ray had the Screamer again and they were struggling on the lawn. Rourke was rooted firmly in front of us, standing sentinel between us and it.

Tyler yelled, "Jess, we're going to shift. We can help better in our true forms."

I nodded. "Naomi, we have to help my father," I said, anguish in my voice as I stood, stumbling to get my footing. "It may take Ray too long to finish the Screamer off. We have to find a way to help him."

On cue Ray yelled, "This is it. I'm new to all this supernatural bullshit, but you must die now."

I turned to watch Ray radiate power into it. The Screamer was strong, but Ray held his own. "I don't understand, how's he able to do that? That's not a normal vampire thing, is it?"

"*Non.*" Naomi shook her head. "I do not know. It may be that his special gift is to handle the Strigoi? It is a unique gift, but he is...unique."

"No," a thin breath whispered in my ear. "*Reaper.*"

"What?" I asked absentmindedly, moving toward my father, who had lain down again after his brave attempt to help me. I sat, placing my hands into his fur one more time. My body was still recovering from the blast, but I forced as much power as I could into him. Upon feeling our connection, he whined.

The welts had grown in the short time I'd been gone.

"A reaper," Ben persisted. "Those who claim souls."

"How can Ray possibly be a reaper?" I asked. I'd heard of reapers from legend only. My brain was still focused on my father. "Ben, can you do something useful and tell me how to help my father and reverse this curse?"

"I know nothing of curses."

Barking erupted behind me. I brought my head around to investigate and something near the roof of the house caught my attention. Eudoxia stood high atop the house on a widow's peak I hadn't noticed before. Her hands were held up to the sky, her dress billowing in the air.

"She's keeping the ward going," I commented.

"*Oui.*" Naomi nodded. "She has stayed the Underworld. For now. But there is much sulfur in the air. I flew up to the sky before we found you. There are rings around the entire perimeter of the Coterie, except for the front. The witches have amassed with your wolves. It is unclear why they have come, but your partner is with them."

I could always count on Nick. He'd been busy. If Tally had

shown, it likely meant Maggie had seen something else, or she'd decided to come find Marcy herself. Either way, it was a bonus. The fact that the wolves were here meant Nick had made contact and had enough time to get reinforcements here. That boy deserved a medal.

"Now you finally die, asshat," Ray yelled. He was on his knees, hovering over the Screamer, his entire arm inside its back. I watched in fascination as he slowly pulled something out of Conan's abused body.

It was a shimmery half-formed mass.

Once it was out of the body, Ray struggled to hold on to it. Tyler and Danny barked like mad, clearly uneasy. It was quite a sight.

Rourke stood near me now, a snarl ripping from his chest. "If that thing gets near Jessica, I will kill you, vampire."

"Hold on to your pants," Ray grumbled. "This thing is like glue in my hands. I just don't know exactly what to do with it now." His eyebrows quirked in concentration. "There isn't a mind manual for this shit."

"He must consume the energy," a breathy voice filtered in my ear. "The reaper must eat it."

"Ben says you have to consume the energy," I called to Ray, my hands still deeply buried in my father's fur. "It sounds fairly revolting, but I'd trust him on this."

"Who's Ben?" Tyler asked, running up to us. He and Danny had both changed back once they saw Ray had harnessed the Screamer.

"He's the resident ghost," I answered. "He says Ray has to eat the energy to get rid of it."

Ray said, "I heard him."

I was beyond being surprised by anything. "I guess if you're a reaper that would make sense." My father stirred beneath me.

"Ray, you need to get a move on, because my father needs you much more than the Screamer."

Ray seemed to notice what was going on with my dad for the first time. "What's wrong with him? He smells like death." He paced closer, still holding the squirming mass.

Rourke stepped in his way. "Don't come any closer. That thing is unpredictable."

"My father's been cursed," I answered. "You're supposed to be able to help, but I don't see how." My voice was beginning to edge toward panic. "Ray, please, you have to do something."

Ray's voice was somber. "I'll give it my best shot once I'm done with this." He turned his head to address the ghost. "How do I get rid of this?"

"You must consume it." Ben's voice came out a little stronger. "The Strigoi's soul must be ripped from its power source. You hold the power source in your hand."

"How?"

"You must drink it."

Ray eyed the thing squirming in his hands with distaste as his incisors snapped down and his face started to shift. "They don't pay me enough for this job," he muttered as he reared up and sank his fangs into the wiggling mass and sucked.

"That can't be good," I said as my lips curled.

"He is dislodging the soul from its shell," Ben said next to my ear. "Without a host, its energy will crumble and it will be gone."

"I thought you said there was no way to defeat it before?"

"You never told me you had a reaper in your midst. They are very rare."

I had no idea I had a reaper in my midst either. Seeing Ray in action was totally surreal. Salvation indeed. He was a maniac.

After a minute Ray unlatched and threw his head back, gasping. He opened his mouth toward the sky and a shimmering mist erupted like hot breath on an icy day and shot skyward. "Hannon," Ray gasped, still emptying his lungs. "It won't—"

"It seeks." Ben's thin, breathy voice shook with fear. "It still holds too much power."

"What's wrong?" I asked urgently. "What are we supposed—"

Before I knew what was happening, Ray dove for my father right as the shimmering mist plunged into his body.

My father convulsed once on the ground and his legs began to kick.

Tyler collided with Ray before I could stop him.

He grabbed him around the throat and dragged him away from our father, moving quickly.

"Tyler!" I shouted, running after them. "What are you doing?"

"He's going to bite him," Tyler yelled, his voice full of emotion and panic. It swirled in my veins, his instincts coming to the forefront, more wolf than human. "I can't let a vamp bite him. My wolf won't allow it to happen. He's our *Alpha*."

"Tyler, listen to me. You're not thinking straight. If you don't let him do this, Dad will die," I said as calmly as I could. Tyler snarled and gnashed his teeth and I held my hands up. If Tyler broke Ray's neck, it would take too much time for him to heal. "You have to let him go. That thing is *in* Dad. Ray is the only one who can help him. And if we don't hurry, he dies."

"I can fly, you meathead," Ray grunted. "Do you want to go for a ride?"

"Shut up," Tyler spat. "I don't trust you. You just let that thing go and because of it, it landed in my father. Why should I trust you?"

"Tyler, you need to be reasonable. I know you're freaked out and I am too." I injected as much reassurance into our bond as I could. Tyler's wolf was fighting him for control, rearing up to save his Alpha. "But we have to do whatever we can to save Dad."

"She's right," Danny added, treading cautiously. "You have to let him go, mate. He's not just a vampire—he's a bloody reaper. He sucked that thing clean. This is what the child oracle was talking about. This is why Ray is here. He can help us. He's the only one who can help us. You must release him."

Rourke eased in behind Tyler.

I nodded once. My brother's irises swirled in anger and confusion as Rourke took him by the shoulders.

"Get off me, cat," Tyler snarled.

Let go of Ray.

"The reaper must do his job. The wolf will not last." Ben's voice was in my ear. "The Strigoi is too strong, and it's gaining more power by the second."

Tyler, let him GO! I hurled power into the words like never before.

Tyler dropped his arms and Rourke walked him backward. Ray lunged at my father, taking him around the neck, sinking his fangs in deeply.

I closed my eyes.

Rourke was next to me before I opened them. "I get it now," I whispered as I watched Ray, wrapping my fist into Rourke's shirt. "He's a reaper, but not a vamp reaper. He's a reaper *and* a vamp."

"You have to be born a reaper," Rourke said, pulling me closer. "I've never heard of one being made. It's an ancient race."

"My blood must have triggered something he already had inside. By all rights he should've died many times over on that journey. Eamon ripped his neck out and he still had a pulse. And he's always been immune to persuasion. I thought I'd seen something in him once, but he never smelled like a supe, so I dismissed it."

"A vampire mixed with a reaper is a deadly combo if you ask me," Rourke murmured close to my ear. "We're going to have to watch him carefully."

Tyler paced ten feet away, his head in his hands. There was nothing I could do to comfort him. We both had to endure Ray as he tried to save our father.

I glanced up at my mate, shivering. I was bone weary and the fight hadn't even started. I could hear the sorcerers arming themselves outside the walls, and the Queen still stood on the roof, arms raised. We were running out of time. "Do you know what a reaper is exactly?" I asked while we waited. Ray was still hunched over my father. I tried to block out the noises.

"I've never known of one," he answered. "But from history, they are said to have control over souls, sending them to their next resting place when they die. It's pretty clear he can catch them. Other than that, I don't know."

"They can also pull a living soul from a body," Naomi replied quietly as she neared. "Selene had one in her employ, before she got wary and killed her. They are an asset, but they can also be deadly. A reaper can kill by taking a healthy soul from its host. The stronger the reaper, the bigger the supernatural soul they can snatch."

That was a lot to take in.

Ray made a gargling noise and finally staggered backward.

Then he doubled over and vomited.

26

The stuff pouring out of him was putrid. Globs of yellow mixed with blood.

"*Jesus*, Ray!" I shouted. I broke away from Rourke and took a step toward him and then one back. I didn't want to get close to whatever was ejecting out of him.

My father twitched and raised his shaggy head slowly. I rushed to him, my hands grazing lightly over his fur. *Are you okay? Is that you?*

Did you let a vampire drink me? His voice was sardonic and I almost cried out in joy.

He sounded like himself, or at least on his way.

I tentatively pushed some power into him, searching, but I didn't feel the Screamer or the masses anywhere. *That vampire just saved your life.*

Ray was still churning out the mess a few feet away. He'd managed to suck out the curse, but he was paying for it.

"Good grief, man. That's a nasty business," Danny commented.

"Glad I'm not in your shoes, then. I'd likely choke to death on the first go."

"Danny," I called. "Run into the house and find my father some clothes. Take whatever you can get your hands on."

"I'm on it." He saluted as he turned to leave.

"Naomi." I flicked my head. "Go with him, in case he runs into trouble." Eudoxia was still on the roof; who knew what the vamps were doing.

"Of course," she answered.

"Try Conan's room. He's about the right size and he won't be needing them any longer." A shot of pity ran through my body. I disliked Conan, but seeing him die so violently had been awful.

"Conan?" Naomi cocked her head at me.

I pointed to the bones in the yard. Once the Screamer had exited, the vamp had decayed immediately.

"*Oui*," she said. "That was Francis. He will not be greatly missed. Eudoxia had him changed on a whim. She was curious about his body, but he was not...an intelligent being. I know where his rooms are."

Tyler paced tentatively to us, running a hand over his face. "Is he okay?"

"It looks like it," I said. My father was still in his wolf form. "I don't want to be overly excited until we know for sure."

My father's body began to vibrate, and I stepped back as he started shifting into his human form. That was a good sign.

"Listen, Jess," Tyler said. "I didn't mean—"

"Tyler," I cut him off, "it's absolutely fine. You were protecting your father. Totally understandable and I wouldn't expect any less. It's all finished. He survived."

It took my father no time to shift.

He appeared haggard in his human form but was regaining his

color quickly. "What did that vampire do to me?" He rubbed his neck.

"I'm not sure." I glanced over at Ray, who was still bent over, hands braced on his knees. For the moment it appeared he was done regurgitating the nastiness. "I think he sucked the curse out of you along with the Screamer. It was incredibly lucky he was here." There was no time to explain everything that had happened over the past few days. My father would get a full report once we were out of danger.

My father nodded once. "I am indebted to him, then." He sat up, looking more aware by the second. "But that will have to wait. We need to prepare for battle immediately. My wolves have told me internally the fracture pack is aligning just outside the city limits. We need to amass the Pack in here and ready ourselves for war."

"The Queen has the perimeter warded," Rourke said, coming up next to us. "No entry is possible at the moment. The fracture pack is a problem, but that's not the only thing we have to fight. The sorcerers have been summoning demons, and as of right now, they line the perimeter three-fourths around the mansion. We have staked out a fourth, outside the front entrance."

"Eudoxia will have to open the ward, then. I want my Pack in here." My father's voice was firm. "We can't defeat any opposition without any fighters."

"That won't be an easy task." Rourke pointed to the roof. "It's taking everything she has to fuel the ward. The magic from the outside is pushing back against it already. She has to keep a constant stream going or it will fall. It's the only reason why the sorcerers and demons are not inside yet."

I felt the magic building, the two sides pushing against each other, fighting for power. One had to give eventually. I just hoped it wasn't hers. "Dad," I said. "Nick is on the outside with the rest of the Pack and has been joined by the witches. I hope Tally's presence means they will stand and fight with us. We have a better chance of winning by aligning with them on the outside. I say we go over the wall if the ward fails and regroup there."

Danny loped over, waving a pair of jeans and a shirt. "Just in time, I see," he said, nodding to my father. He tossed them with a chuckle. My father caught them and without pausing ordered, "Daniel Walker, get to the highest point on that house. I want a full report of what's happening around us."

"On my way," Danny said immediately.

"Go with him," I told Naomi, who had come up behind him. "If he'll let you, fly him up." I had a twinkle in my eye when I added, "He'd do almost anything to get himself into a woman's embrace, so this should be a no-brainer."

"Well"—Danny turned, glancing back at Naomi—"why not, then? I've always had a hankering to fly."

Naomi put her head down for a moment. I couldn't tell if she was blushing—if vampires even could blush. "I will take you," she finally said, lifting her face toward his. "But...because of your size, I cannot guarantee I will not drop you."

"That's all right by me," Danny replied jovially. "Won't be the first time my massive frame has been hard for the ladies to handle—"

Naomi had him around the waist and up before he could finish his sentence.

My father cleared his throat.

"That was Naomi," I told my father. I couldn't read his expression, but he wasn't overly excited that a vamp had taken his head of security for a ride. "She's the vamp tracker I told you about briefly on the phone when we left Selene's lair. I have so much to share with you, but she and I are now bonded by blood and she has proven herself loyal again and again. I trust her with my life and with his."

"This is indeed a new world," my father said, shaking his head as he pulled on a black shirt. "Vampires have never been our allies. This is unprecedented. It's going to take me some time to figure out a new way to handle things." He met my eyes. "And I will agree to examine all the new developments on a case-by-case basis, but that's all I will promise at this time."

That was enough for me.

My father was a savvy leader. You don't stay in charge if you don't learn to adapt. I was confident we would figure out a new way to move forward that included all of us. And I was content to wait until the right time to fight for what I wanted.

"Jessica," Rourke said. "I think your father, Tyler, and I should scout around the gate to see if there's a way to get in or out. Once the wards come down, we have to find a way to stand united, whether it's in here or out there. If we split up we can cover more ground."

"Sounds good," I said. "I'll wait here with Ray and see what Danny and Naomi have to report once they come down."

My father nodded once at my mate, appraising him. There was a glimmer of respect growing there, but I knew it would take time for them to get to know each other. I was exceptionally proud of my man for being respectful of my father and not fighting him for control. I would see that he got an extra special gift as soon as I could. My wolf yipped her agreement.

As they trotted around the house, I walked over to where Ray stood. "I can't thank you enough, Ray. That was heroic and... bizarre, but you saved my dad's life. If you hadn't been a reaper all along, this wouldn't have been possible."

"Honestly, Hannon, I have no idea what a reaper is," Ray retorted, spitting on the ground and easing himself upright. "All I know is that I'm attracted to dead stuff and my mind is telling me I can fix it. But with all the other vamp info clogging my brain up, it's confusing as hell—a swirl of shit all getting stuck in the drain at the same time."

"You've only been a supernatural for a few days," I said. "It's a lot to take in. It will likely all sort itself out soon." I hoped. "And I think that's exactly what a reaper is. I don't know much about them, but they do fix dead stuff. And if you ask me, it kind of suits you. Did you ever talk to dead people as a kid?" I chuckled. "Or see your grandma floating around the house?"

"No," he said gruffly. "I never paid attention to any of that kind of crap."

"It all means you're a very powerful supe—"

Simultaneous Orbs crashed into the walls all around us. There must have been ten. We hit the ground.

The sound was deafening. It was a concentrated effort. I was actually surprised it had taken them this long to ramp up an attack.

Ray and I stood from our crouched positions as wolf howls echoed in the night and a cloud of sulfur surrounded us. More Orbs crashed into the ward, but before I could react in any way, the Vampire Queen landed in front of me.

"See what you've done! My wards will not hold with this continued onslaught," she snapped. "You have a lot to answer for—bringing war to my doorstep." She stalked closer, challenging me. "There is no reason for me to protect you any longer."

The next assault shook the foundation of the entire Coterie. The wards were indeed cracking. I faced her. This was between Eudoxia and me and no one else. "Bringing war to your doorstep was not my intention," I said. "I came here for protection only."

"I should break your neck and drink the spoils of your blood right now for putting my entire Coterie in danger," she hissed.

"You can try," I growled, taking a step toward her.

Her eyes glittered with a threat. "You come here with your

newfound power and think you are stronger than I am." A strange laugh, bordering on manic, escaped her throat. "You have no idea what I am, or what I'm capable of. Once again you tarry where you do not belong—a *very* dangerous place for a lone wolf to be. You are no match for me, Little Wolf Girl. It's time for you to cut your losses and move on from here, and take your trouble with you."

"Oh, but I do know what you're capable of, Eudoxia," I said, closing the gap between us. She stood a foot shorter than I, but she held her stature high. She was impressive, but I was stronger. "Alana and I had a nice little conversation a few minutes ago." Her face stayed stony, but I saw a hint of surprise. "But none of that matters, because I know you won't kill me. You can threaten me all you want, but in the end I live. So let's end this charade. I think we're both tired of it. You need what I have"—I pointed my finger at her chest—"and without it you *lose*."

Her eyes narrowed, her power swirling around us. "Ah, but you need not be alive for me to take it," she said. "I can just as easily drink my fill from your cold, dead body."

"That's not how this is going to work," I answered, fisting my hands, my own power at the forefront, challenging hers equally. "You can fight me here and lose"—I bared my teeth—"because, make no mistake, you will not win. Or you can make one last deal with me and get what you so desire."

She lunged at the same moment I lashed out.

We clashed in the middle, my hand landing around the throat, hard and fast. I was in my full Lycan form, my grip sure. I dragged her face within an inch of mine. "Do you feel that?" I snarled while she tried to throw more power at me, her fangs down, a savage sound issuing from her throat. But my shields were already in place, my magic kept her out. "That's my power telling yours to fuck off. I'm not the newborn I was when we first met. It's a funny thing harnessing power. It was in me all along. I just had to listen to my wolf and learn how to mold it." My voice dropped so only she could hear me. I pulled her even closer. "Now, do you want to live, Eudoxia? Because I'm done playing these games with you. We make a deal here for the last time. My blood for your cooperation."

Hate radiated from her. Both her hands tore at my grip and I let her go, tossing her back as I released her. She recovered instantly, her fangs down, eyes blazing. "You would give up your blood to me so easily," she sneered, "for a mere favor?"

"No," I retorted. "For an army." Another large boom shook the walls. Stone crumbled inward, chunks of rock falling to the ground. She was no longer fueling the ward so it had only moments before it gave way. "The vampires align with the wolves indefinitely until this war runs its course. Our fights are your fights. Take it or leave it."

"Never," she raged, her hands fisted. "Nothing is worth aligning myself with you."

I shrugged as more howls outside the walls rent the air. "Suit yourself, Eudoxia. But if you're not willing to help me, stay out of my way." Another shock wave hit just outside the yard and holes formed in the wall big enough for a human to crawl through. "No more games or I'll kill you. I swear it."

A sly smile crossed her lips and she took off into the sky without another word.

Well, that had gone well.

Rourke jogged toward me. "The ward is coming down. We need to gather everyone—"

My father flew around him, coming toward me in his wolf form incredibly fast. His eyes flashed a deep amethyst as his howl filled the air. He charged me without stopping and at the last moment leapt, sailing straight overhead, colliding with something coming through the wall behind me.

I scrambled to the side and saw an unfamiliar wolf, feral and dangerous, emerging from the outside. Half his fur was gone and he appeared crazed. He wasn't nearly as big as my father, but his muzzle was foaming and his eyes were opaque, coated in a thick film of white.

More commotion erupted from behind the wall. Wolves were baying. They had tried to corner this abomination, but he had gotten through. They must have alerted my father internally. There's no other way he knew it was coming.

My father had it pinned against the wall, his teeth in its neck. I had no idea if the blood alone would curse my father again, but there was nothing I could do.

The feral wolf flipped in his grasp, contorting its bones as it sprang free.

That wasn't normal.

The wolf turned before my father could grasp it again and lunged for me. I crouched as it barreled toward me. But before it reached me, a fist shot out, connecting with its skull. It crashed into the wall, and with supernatural speed Rourke caught it by the neck before it could stand.

"Don't let it bite you!" I shouted. The beast didn't even seem fazed. Rourke twisted its neck and bones popped, but it kept moving, struggling to free itself.

It wasn't going to die the normal way.

We needed something stronger.

"Looks like you could use some help," a voice sounded from atop the wall behind me. "Those things are truly dreadful."

Tally stood alongside six other witches, each armed for battle. She'd lost her black skullcap but had switched it to one of those badass green army hats pulled down low over her eyes, her long white hair pulled back in a tight ponytail.

She looked eons younger and tough as hell.

Relief flooded through me.

You knew things were at a breaking point when witches broke into a Vampire Coterie with spelled AK-47s strapped across their chests.

"That thing is cursed," I yelled, pointing to Rourke and the struggling wolf, "and if it gets loose and bites one of your witches, they die. We need to take it out. Magic may be our only chance."

Rourke had one hand around its middle and one around its neck. Its head was at a funny angle, but it was still struggling. Rourke was stronger, thank goodness. My father circled, waiting for a chance to help.

"This thing won't die. I broke its neck twice," Rourke ground.

"Toss it into the yard and we'll take it from there," Tally called.

In an instant her flock spread out along the top of the wall, legs splayed as they cocked their guns at their shoulders. "Don't be shy," she said. "The ammo in these guns is spelled. We will either kill it or maim it, but it will be down long enough to find a way to take it out permanently. I don't care if the most powerful priestess in the world cursed that thing. My magic is stronger."

Rourke nodded once. He twisted at the waist, and with a huge roar sent the abomination flying into the yard.

It hit the ground once and the witches let loose.

27

They all fired at once and bullets poured into the beast. "Cease-fire." Tally raised her hand and they stopped like clockwork. We all waited a few seconds. The thing was riddled with holes as big as softballs.

It convulsed once.

"Stand back," Tally ordered. "Things are about to get messy." It started to quiver, and foam began leaking out of the holes. "I take that back—run!"

"What's happening?" I shouted as I took off.

"It's going to blow that curse all over the yard. I never know how a supe is going to react to my spells until I see it. My 'kill' spell is killing the wolf, but the only way to truly kill it is to rid it of the curse, so that's what it's doing."

Her witches had no need of a second warning. They were already gone. I glanced around me as I raced along the wall. Rourke was too far the other way. "I'm going through a hole in the stone," I called.

"I'll follow you when I can. Go now before that thing explodes," he yelled.

The thing started to gurgle.

"Go!" he shouted.

I dove through a small opening right as the beast exploded, raining a curse around the yard. It sounded juicy, like a gigantic water balloon splattering. I rolled twice without looking and crashed into something solid.

My head smacked it cleanly.

I sprawled on the ground, my arms at my sides. My wolf yipped at me to get up. *I'm going, I'm going. I think I just cracked my skull open. Give me a second.* Adrenaline coursed through me, trying to heal me quickly, but I was still fuzzy. I brought a hand up to my forehead.

"Hiya," the most welcome voice ever said from above me. "Whatcha doing on the ground? Don't you know there are demons running around all over the place? Didn't you learn a single thing while I was gone? Safety first."

I rolled over and stumbled to my feet, crushing her in a big hug. "Marcy! You're here and you're alive! I knew you would be, but I'm so incredibly happy to see you."

"I can see that, because you're squeezing the ever-loving life out of me. Time to ease up before your superstrong wolf power breaks me in half." She chuckled and I let her go reluctantly. "Seriously, though, what are you doing out here? You were much safer back in there." She gestured over the wall. "Once they find you're out here, they'll swarm us."

"I had to come out so I didn't get cursed. It was either hightail it through the wall or die a horrid, painful death. And the ward just crumbled anyway, so I imagine the demons will be everywhere soon."

"Come on, then." She waved me to follow. "James has all the

wolves worked up into a frenzy back here. They're barking and jumping all over the place. No demons or sorcerers have messed with us yet, but that's because Nick—"

"Nick!" I yelled as I ran ahead and embraced him. After a big hug, I brought him back at arm's length. I had so many questions. "Great work out here. When did the wolves arrive? And how in the world did you coax the witches here?"

"They came on their own," he said. "I had nothing to do with that. But Marcy and James are the ones to be thanked. They arrived shortly after I jumped the wall. James shifted and finally contacted Callum. He's been rallying the Pack out here since they started showing up. We have a good contingency assembled now."

I turned to Marcy. "How did you guys find us?"

"We were trailing the sorcerers who kidnapped me. We knew they were going after you, because I'd overhead them scheming, so when they abruptly headed south, we followed. We ended up here, and once we saw Nick, we knew there was big trouble— which was no surprise, since trouble follows you like a horde of angry bees to honey." She grinned. "So we adopted a new, sparkly agenda that included saving you from the bad sorcerers and the evil demons."

I glanced around me for the first time. "What is this place?" We stood in the middle of a large barricade made up of what appeared to be car parts. "Marcy, did you make a fort?"

"Yes, and it's spelled," Marcy said proudly. "James ripped the cars apart to protect me and I spelled it. That's why it hurt your head. It's meant to stun anyone who touches it. But when I saw it was you, I snapped my fingers and, voilà, you were cured. No more massive head injury."

"We've secured the perimeter around this entire area," Nick said, gesturing to a wider arc. I didn't see any Pack wolves. I could only hear them, so the contained area had to be a lot bigger. "The

Pack has managed to keep the fracture wolves back, except the one who just snuck through. I also found I can use my persuasion to some degree on the younger sorcerers and the low-level imps. I've managed to convince a few to abandon their plans, but it won't hold for long. The High Priests are starting to show up and that means they will call up Demon Lords. Things are about to get heavy."

We heard some commotion to the left and James came into view. He strode up. "Hello, Jessica, it's good to see you are well."

I reached out to give him a hug.

"Don't even think about it, missy." Marcy's voice held an order. "He's mine. A simple handshake will do. No touching anymore. Like ever."

I stifled a laugh and reached out to shake his hand. "James, it's such a relief to see you here. My father will be happy to hear you've coordinated things on this side."

"I don't know if 'happy' is the correct word," James said. "But we have spoken and he has been...amiable. It was by chance I shifted when I did and called out to him. He wouldn't tell me what was wrong, but I told him you were here and he changed his course."

"If you hadn't done that, he would've died," I said firmly. "We owe you and I'm certain he will welcome you back when he understands the scope of what went on. And I can see I was right in thinking you'd gone after your mate." I addressed Marcy. "Congrats, by the way. He's quite a catch."

"Thank you. I'm keeping him." She preened as she glanced at him with adoration and genuine happiness.

James nodded once.

As always, he was a man of few words.

For the first time I noted their appearances. They were both dirty, clothes ripped. Marcy's stellar red hair, which always looked impeccably styled, hung loosely around her shoulders. It was clear whatever they'd been through had been rough.

"The feral wolves in the fracture pack are cursed. We need to warn the Pack to stay away from them. One bite and they're deadly to us," I said. "My father said they'd been made."

"What?" Nick exclaimed. "That can't be right. Shifters can't be *made.*"

"That's what he believes," I cautioned. "And now that I've seen one, I have to agree. They're not normal wolves and if we engage them, it could be fatal."

"Then it's time for me to shift," James said. "We'll have to change our focus from the demons to the wolves if that's the case. The demons want you, but the wolves will fight us to the death no matter what."

I peered out into the night. "Speaking of shifting, Rourke should've been here by now," I said. "I wonder what happened?" A shiver ran through me at the thought the curse had touched him. But I would've known, or felt something, so I tried to relax.

"I haven't seen anyone else come over the wall," Marcy said. "But if he's anything like mine, they growl a lot when you're not around."

I made a move to leave the junkyard fort, but Nick caught my arm. "Jess, you can't go back out there. It's better if you stay in here. Once the demons know you're here, they'll come soon enough." He shook his head. "What's happening here shouldn't even be possible. Sorcerers don't have the power to summon Lords. No one can. So it's clear they've made a prior agreement with each other, which makes the entire thing unprecedented on the biggest level."

I shivered, remembering the Demon Lord in the cave.

"The sorcerers want my life force," I said, "but the demons think I'm an outlaw, powerful enough to rule their race if I were given the opportunity. They want to stop me at all costs. I have a court date in the Underworld already, and once the date arrives, the Lord said I would pop to that plane automatically. But if that's the case, why are they here now?" None of it made much sense.

"I have no idea, Jess," Nick said. "All the information I have about the Underworld is strictly from books. They are intensely powerful and their magic feels strange and foreign."

He was right. "Foreign" was a good word. It tasted strange, more than just sulfur. It had an odd undertone.

Something flew over the wall in front of us.

It howled on the way down, crashing into a nearby Dumpster. It was an imp. There was a ferocious roar and another one flew over, greasy hair flying. Then Rourke's entire body smashed through a hole in the wall.

He was livid, his arms braced.

I crossed my arms. "There's my guy now." I smiled at Marcy. "He must've come across some more trouble. The ward has completely fallen, because the imps must be coming in from the other side. Can he see us?"

"Holy caveman. He can see us, but we look like human bag ladies watching the show from behind a heap of scrap metal." Marcy chuckled.

I glanced at her sideways. "You know, you never cease to amaze me." Marcy had definitely found her groove. There was a time when she'd suffered from a lack of confidence, which had kept her out of her aunt's Coven, but the world wasn't dealing with the same girl any longer. Her recent adventures had changed her in a big way. "Did I mention I'm glad you're alive? Not only do I love seeing your smiling face but if you'd have turned up dead, I would've followed you shortly if Tally had anything to say about it."

"Yeah, she's a cranky old bitty. She would zap you into

never-never land just because she can. But can you believe she showed up here?" she exclaimed. "She never does anything for anyone. So consider yourself part of the elite. But, honestly, do you know how much this is going to cost you? Witches never do anything for free. You'll never make another dime. All your future paychecks are going straight to the Coven."

"Not this time," I said, shaking my head. "She's fighting for you, not me. I'm pretty sure she's here because Maggie told her to come. That child probably had another vision and said, 'If the wolf lady gets killed, Auntie Marcy will die.' So Tally felt compelled to come to save her favorite niece."

"Isn't Maggie a little charmer? Spooky as hell, but you can't help wanting to give those cheeks a squeeze. I love her up every time I see her. But I also plug my ears whenever she starts chanting. Some things are better left unknown."

"You got that right," I said.

"Jessica, where are you?" Rourke's bellow was just short of manic. "The low-level demons have broken through the wall. If they have you, I'm going to tear this place apart."

"I'm right in front of you," I called, waving. "But you have to come inside the barricade to see it's me."

He paced closer, growling fiercely. "The vamps have disappeared. They were there one second and gone the next. The witches seem to know what's going on, however, and are prepared to fight. Whatever's stocked in their ammo is working on the imps." He lifted his nose to scent the area. "I can smell you, but I can't see you."

"Keep walking. Marcy has spelled a small area. Once you get closer, you should see a couple of old ladies. Did the curse get on anyone?"

"Yes, one of the witches who was coming around the yard got sprayed, but Ray is on it." He made his way over to us. "Tally has him by the neck, even though he's cooperating. She doesn't trust him not to drink her witch dry."

"What about my dad?" He had taken off like the rest of us.

"I haven't seen him," he said, coming closer. "I see three old ladies, one who smells like you."

"Three?" Nick said. "He thinks I'm an old lady?" He turned to Marcy with a questioning glance.

Marcy pressed her lips together and replied, "Gender bending is hard, so you get lumped in, my friend. My spell reads lady, so lady it is."

Just before Rourke reached us, flames erupted in a single circle around Marcy's blockade, separating us.

"Jess!" Nick yelled, grabbing my arm. "We have to get out. This is a demon circle!" He leapt around a car door, pulling me along.

I didn't need any urging. I was right behind him. "Go, go! I'm following you."

"Jessica," Rourke yelled. "The flames won't kill you. Get the hell out!"

"I'm going as fast as I can—" There was a popping noise and something grabbed me by the neck.

"Going someplace?" it hissed in my ear.

"In fact she is, asshole demon guy," Marcy said. "Let go of her."

I twisted in its grasp right as Marcy hit him with a spell. I'd never seen her spells manifest physically. This information was new and very welcome. Her signature was pink.

So very Marcy.

The demon let go and howled in pain. He wasn't a Lord, so his power signature was much lower. We were lucky. But that meant the sorcerers were hiding somewhere close and they'd discovered our location and cover.

Things were about to get even uglier.

"Come on, Jess," Nick urged from the other side. "You have to get out before the wall of flames grows."

"I've got this demon businessman. Go while you can," Marcy ordered. She glanced down at the demon that was sprawled on the ground. "Where's your briefcase? Huh? Who comes to a fight in a three-piece suit? Take that for being such a dumbass." She shot him with another spell and he went limp.

I took a running leap through the flames.

They weren't hot like normal fire, but they still licked along my skin, stinging me like burning sandpaper scraping along every nerve ending.

I landed in a crouch next to Nick. His hair was singed, but other than that he appeared to be fine. "We need to find your father," he said. "I may be able to use my persuasion and I want to find the source. The imps fell easily, but I've never met a Demon Lord. It's worth a try."

"How do you find the source?" I asked, glancing to the right, noting that Rourke was engaged with what looked to be a group of sorcerers. They were all wearing robes, but he had it handled.

"From what I understand, there are six Lords, but there is only one Prince of Hell. If he's here, he's in charge. If I can convince him to leave, maybe they'll all leave."

"I've met a Demon Lord and it was incredibly powerful, but I'm willing to try anything," I said. "But we don't need my father—we need Naomi. She can fly you closer. Scale the wall in front of us and we'll go from there."

I made a move to help Rourke. Most of the sorcerers were already down. "Go!" he yelled. "I'll be right behind you. These guys are useless."

Nick leapt easily to the top of the wall and I followed. The scene below was ridiculous. Wolves were fighting wolves, witches were shooting demons, and the vamps had formed a ring around Eudoxia in the corner.

"What are the vamps doing?" I asked.

"It's a circle of some kind. I think she's generating power. See her hair billowing out?" he said. Orbs crashed into the wall below us and footfalls were coming fast. We'd been spotted. Nick sprang off the ledge.

Right before I joined him down in the melee, something caught my eye.

I landed next to Nick and grabbed on to his shirtsleeve. Without talking, I directed his gaze to where I was looking. As we watched, one by one, they popped into existence in the ruins of the far wall, just outside the grounds.

Five Demon Lords.

There were all dressed impeccably, each one more precise than the next.

"Eudoxia knows what's coming," I whispered. "She's trying to block it from happening." As much as she hated me and wanted me dead, she still had to protect herself and her flock. "See how these Lords are all just outside the wall? It's working so far. We have to help her keep the ward up." I took off. "If the Lords get in, the chance of me dying increases exponentially."

"Go," Nick urged. "I'll take care of this." Several imps had converged on us.

I raced over the lawn, outrunning them easily.

But before I could reach her, one of the fracture wolves, this one luckily not cursed, came barreling at me. I shifted power to my wolf and we collided. I grabbed its neck, and as I rolled I yanked.

It stayed on the ground and I kept going.

"Jess, look out," Nick called from behind me. On instinct, I flipped, bringing my feet around, fingernails digging into the grass to propel me. This time it was one of the possessed wolf-hybrids. It was mangy and awful. My body was already in motion, my feet hitting its flank soundly. It flew backward, but before it crashed into the wall, Ray snatched it out of the air, his fangs at the ready.

"This is the last one, Hannon," he yelled. "After that it's all regular wolves. Your father took down the Southern leader, so they should be running home to lick their wounds shortly." The cursed wolf tried to break out of Ray's grasp, but he reared up and bit deeply into its neck.

That meant my father had killed Redman Martin.

It was going to cause huge ripples in our world. Redman's wolves would have to join our Pack, the fracture pack, or go rogue.

Too much to think about now. I had to get to the Queen.

I nodded at Ray and turned to run. The vamps were still linked in a tight circle. Two deep, no spaces. I had to add my power to hers to keep the ward strong, but before I could reach her, the ground started to quake.

I slid to a stop.

A huge vibration spread through the yard, followed by a gigantic sucking sound, like a cork being yanked out of a bottle of champagne the size of a building.

But this was no celebration.

The Prince of Hell had arrived.

28

"You cannot stop me no matter how hard you try, so I advise against trying to do so." Its voice was exact.

It was the same Lord who had come to pick up Selene.

This demon was the Prince of Hell.

It had called itself a Prince of Thrones, but I had no idea it was *the* Prince. I'd pissed it off once already, and there was no way it was going to turn tail and leave without something in return this time.

There was only one thing I could think of that could help me. "Ben?" I called. "Are you out there?" I hadn't heard from the ghost in a while, so I figured he'd split. If I were him, I'd escape the anarchy if given a chance.

"I'm still here."

"Know anything about demons?"

"I have never seen one before, but I can feel its power and it has a strange color."

"Color?" I asked. "Like an aura?" Ghosts could see auras?

"I don't know. Humans have no pigment, but supernaturals glow."

"What color is it?"

"It is black. Like a void."

"What color is the Queen?"

"She is white."

"And me?"

"You are gold."

"I think you're picking up our power signatures. Gold is the color that manifests in my mind and would come out in my fingers if I could cast a spell," I said. "Ben, more importantly, can you get into this thing's mind like you can mine?"

"It is not the same, but there are scattered pieces I can read."

The Prince of Hell stood very still as its serpentine gaze scanned the grounds. I knew what was behind that glamour and it wasn't pretty. Everyone had stopped fighting. It was hard to fight each other when you were all facing the biggest threat in the room.

Ben whispered, "It wishes to blow up this entire place. It seeks to destroy you at all costs. It is not thinking clearly. You make it nervous."

Pay dirt.

Having a ghost was handy.

"Why are the other Lords outside the boundary?"

"They do not seem stronger than the Queen. She is warding us. But the Prince can enter. All will be lost soon. He will kill her first."

"Not if I can help it." As the Prince lifted his hand, I ran, leaping over the screen of vamps who stood in front of their Queen.

The Prince intoned, "You will die now, Queen of Vampires."

Power sizzled through the air.

I collided with the Queen right as a shock of demon power hit me squarely in the back. It plowed us both to the ground, me on top.

The vamps went crazy, tightening the circle around us.

All my limbs were locked together. The same black mist Selene had shot into my psyche before, infiltrated my senses now, but this time it was a million times stronger. I could barely see through the thick cloud of darkness that was quickly engulfing me.

My wolf fed power in a constant stream, but it wasn't enough to clear it out.

"You don't seem so powerful now, Little Wolf Girl," the Queen said, her voice slick and devious. "Looks like I will win after all."

She made a move, but I grabbed her wrist, forcing my muscles to react. I focused on her through the darkness. "Give me your power," I ground out. "Help me fight this and I will give you mine. We will fortify the ward and send these assholes back to the Underworld."

Her irises shot silver. This was her chance to kill me. "Why would I possibly do that now?" she spat. "Feeding you to the demons works perfectly for me."

"Because I just saved you," I said, still fighting the power, "*again*. And you have honor. You chose this path over another. And no"—I grit my teeth—"god is without honor."

She sucked in a breath.

"Yes, I said god," I gasped. "I know what you want and there's only one way to get it. We could've solved this twenty minutes ago, but you"—I struggled to get another breath in—"chose to be difficult."

"Fine." She hissed, placing her palms on either side of my head, "But if you do not survive this, it is your fault, not mine."

"Deal," I managed.

The shock was instantaneous.

Her power entered my system like a white-hot light, infusing every cell in my body. But instead of coupling with my own power, it reverberated around my mind like a giant pinball of energy on steroids, threatening to short-circuit me as the black continued to fill in around it. *We have to merge our power together. Neither of our magic is strong enough to defeat this on its own.*

It took everything I had. Eudoxia's magic was heady, but I managed to grab hold of it, but only for a moment. It was enough. As I forced my gold to meld with her white, I rolled off her onto the ground. Starburst lit behind my eyes and I convulsed. Once they were connected I shot the magic forward, obliterating the black mist in one explosion of power.

I blinked.

I could see again.

Gunfire blasted around us.

The witches were firing on the Prince of Hell.

Eudoxia was already up. The vampires had moved back. Seeing their Queen alive and well had improved their attitudes greatly.

"I will take my prize or I destroy this place," the Prince of Hell intoned.

"You're not taking anything," Tally called. "You're not welcome on this plane and we're prepared to send you back."

"That's interesting indeed," it said. "And how exactly are you planning on *sending me back*, lowly witch?"

I stood. The vamps were in front of me, but I could see the Prince of Hell from my vantage point.

"We know your rules." Tally's voice was confident. "And I came prepared." There was some clanging and shuffling, and then as one, the witches lobbed spelled grenades at all the Demon Lords.

As the devices exploded, the Demon Lords disappeared one by one, popping out of existence like firecrackers, leaving behind a trail of smoke.

Tally was right.

She'd come prepared. Whatever was contained in those explosives had been enough to send the Lords back to the Underworld.

Except for one.

"You may have temporarily sent my comrades back to our home, but your spells do not affect me, witch." Everything quieted as the Prince of Hell strode forward for the first time. He wasn't confined to a circle, and that was enough to make everyone take notice. A deep feeling of unease hit the yard. "I will take what I came for, and only then will I leave this plane."

Its eyes scanned the grounds and landed on me.

One of the witches lobbed another hand grenade. It flew directly at the Prince, who reached out and plucked it from the air and crushed it into dust.

"Well, crap," the witch said. "That was my last one too."

"I'm not going anywhere with you." I stepped forward, the vamps parting for me.

It knew I'd been struck down by its power and it sized me up, its eyes narrowing. "You will come of your own volition, or I will destroy this place." It crossed its arms. "And everyone in it."

Rourke moved to meet me in the middle, his face set, his energy palpable. Instead of forming a rebuttal, I asked, still moving forward, "Why are you here? You said I had a court date, and my trip to the Underworld would be nonnegotiable. If that is true, why come here at all?"

"I needn't explain myself to you or anyone else," it said. "You are a criminal. An outlaw in our world. We apprehend those who act against us. It is our way."

My father, still in his wolf form, paced up behind me as I stopped, growling and snapping his jaw. He was ferocious, and it was nice to see him back to his full power.

I took a decided step toward the Prince of Hell to let my father know I had this. I couldn't risk him attacking the most powerful Demon Lord in the Underworld, unless absolutely necessary.

As I moved forward, I said, "I'm no criminal, and I've told you already I want nothing to do with your race. That still stands, but things on this plane have changed considerably. From now on, any imp or demon that crosses my path, or any of my Pack members, will be killed on sight." I snarled as I moved closer. "Do you hear me? By coming here, you've started a war with all of us— the wolves, the vampires, and the witches. We will not be cowed by you. You cannot defeat us all." To help accentuate my point, my father and all his wolves, including my brother and Danny, fanned behind me. My father gnashed his teeth, snapping his muzzle down hard to show his intent. It was a show of strength and I hope it made the Prince of Hell think twice.

Instead it snickered.

"You only prove my point by challenging me," it declared. "You are a nuisance and must be stopped at all costs."

"I'm hardly a nuisance," I retorted. "You came here seeking a fight, not the other way around. I wasn't lying when I told you I wanted nothing to do with you or yours. If you had stayed away, our paths would never have crossed again. The Underworld is no place I wish to visit."

"I could hardly stay away when our *sidekicks*, as you referred to them when we first met, alerted us to your recent misdeeds. We reacted in kind." He was talking about imps, who were technically only half demons.

"What are you talking about?" I asked. "What misdeeds?"

"Your alliance with the witches, our natural enemies, of course."

"Are you kidding? The only reason the witches are involved at all is because the sorcerers, your new buddies, took a witch hostage," I stated. "As far as I can see, they lured you into an agreement under false pretenses. They had already started a war with the wolves and the witches."

"It does not matter." Its voice shook with anger. "Whatever their actions, it is abundantly clear you have allied yourself with the witches. And in the light of your court date, and your crimes against the Underworld, it's in strict violation of our laws. It is unacceptable. You will accompany me now, or I will kill everyone where they stand."

The demons had accused me of killing two imps, their precious pets, the winged devils, and harming Selene by killing her immortality, since she had sold her soul to them already. None of it would hold up in a regular supernatural court, but in the Underworld I wouldn't stand a chance. I had no idea what my penance would be, but the Prince of Hell had already indicated it would be a long and lengthy servitude in the Underworld.

From what I gathered, demons enjoyed playing with their prey instead of killing them outright.

"You can't take her anywhere without her consent, demon." Rourke moved next to me. His clothes were ripped, his face muddied, but he was still formidable. His power was coiled, ready to spring. "You came here hoping she'd die in battle so you wouldn't have to dirty your hands, but you hadn't expected more alliances. You made a mistake by tying the sorcerers' hands. If they hadn't had to use all their combined power to maintain these circles for you, you may have had a chance. That was poor tactical planning on your part. You were too eager to get your prize and it shows."

"She will come with me one way or another, beast cat," it said, its eyes flickering. "Her guilt is absolute in our world. Her crimes are indisputable. She seeks council from witches. I will not let my race be torn apart by a *female werewolf.*"

Before Rourke could engage it further, I stepped forward, putting myself in front.

"If you could kill me outright, you would've done so already," I said. "And if you could've taken me by force, I'd be in the Underworld already. But instead you stand here bantering with us. Why?"

"It shakes with anger," Ben whispered in my ear. "You are right—there is a complication."

"I think the court date is bogus," I challenged, bolstered by my ghostly informant. When it didn't answer, I continued. "And you can't kill any of us because we've committed no real crimes against you."

"You indeed have a court date with the High Court of Mephistopheles. It is written in our Book."

"What's the date?" I tilted my head, measuring it.

Its irises flashed serpentine, and a lock of its perfectly shellacked hair fell by its ear.

"Its anger boils," Ben said. "You puzzle it."

"When the date arrives, it won't force me to the Underworld, will it?" I said. "I'm too strong, or the infractions are too petty. So now you're stuck trying to take me hostage or hope that your new teammates take me out for you."

"It can't take you hostage," Rourke murmured. "You have to verbally agree to its terms."

"Demon, I'm not agreeing to anything," I said. "So you're wasting your time here, causing all this uproar for no reason."

Rather than speak, the Prince of Hell took a bold step forward. We were only twenty feet away from each other, both of us glaring.

Growls and teeth gnashing rent the air.

I glanced sideways at the Queen. Her arms were folded. She was done fighting or aiding me and I knew the only way she would engage the Prince directly was if her vampires were in direct danger.

"Take a single step closer and I'll blow you up," Tally said, cocking her gun and locking her sights.

Its gaze flicked to the right. "You have proven inferior to me, witch," it said. "Why waste your time?"

"Because I saved the best for last," she countered. "And because you don't get to take my friend just because you feel like it."

That was the best news I'd heard all day.

"If the gun doesn't stop you, we have other means." Marcy's voice cut through the group like a caustic bullet. I hadn't known she followed me in. "I happen to know how to incapacitate a Demon Lord, because your sorcerer friends are careless and have big, flapping mouths when they think crafty witches are unconscious. When you were forced to make your deal with them, you gave away some very valuable information."

"There is no way to incapacitate me. They were lying."

"Seriously? You just have to—"

Power shot out of the Prince, hitting Marcy fully in the chest. She soared backward and crumpled to the ground like her strings had been cut.

James roared and I started to run.

"What do you think you're doing?" I screamed, barreling toward it. "You can't hurt innocent people like that."

The Prince looked insanely happy I was coming at him, his mouth quirking up at the sides. It looked all wrong and a moment of doubt crept into my psyche, but I couldn't stop now. I was almost to it.

"She attacked me verbally," it said in a singsong voice. "Revealing a sworn secret is an act of aggression."

I lunged, but something collided with me at the last moment, knocking me off balance. I tumbled, spinning, landing back on my feet in time to see Tyler change directions and sprint for the Prince of Hell.

He was beautiful in his wolf form, fangs bared, howl ferocious.

He leapt and the Prince caught him around the middle easily, like netting a fish, but not before Tyler's teeth caught its neck.

Dark black liquid dribbled out of a gash, marring its perfect, shiny, unnatural skin.

The exertion from catching a werewolf didn't even seem to compute. It didn't even look flustered as it held Tyler's massive form.

"No!" I shouted, agony ringing in my voice. "Put him down!"

The Prince's head snapped to me.

Something new crossed its features. "Ah, you love this one, do you?" it said. "How perfectly wonderful."

"I said put him down," I snarled, stalking forward, hands fisted. If it wanted a fight, it would have one.

"I plan to do just that," it said. "But your version of *down* and mine are likely not one and the same."

Tyler squirmed, whining.

Then suddenly he went limp.

I knew what the Prince of Hell was going to do and I switched control to my wolf and sprang. My father and Rourke both lunged forward at the same time, all of us howling our rage.

"Too late," it cackled. "If you want this one back, you must claim him in the Underworld."

They both popped out of existence.

29

I cradled my head in my hands. Rourke sat beside me. We had all gathered in the main living room of the Coterie. The Queen hadn't wanted us here, but my father had forcefully convinced her to acquiesce.

At the heart of it, she still wanted my blood, so she abided having us in her space for the time being.

"Jessica," my father said. "You couldn't have known. None of us knew."

"He's right." Tally paced in front of the ornate fireplace still dressed in her battle gear. Her witches fidgeted against one wall, vamps and wolves spread out along the others. The entire room was amped up on adrenaline from the fight, and even though the room was huge, and each Sect had its own space, tension still ran high. "It's a little known fact that if you draw blood on a demon, it's free to defend itself any way it wishes," she told the room. "Marring their skin is considered a high crime against them. I don't know if I'd call that stuff blood, but it still counts."

"I don't care if we didn't know ahead of time. The question is how are we going to get him back?" I lifted my head. "I'm not leaving my brother there for a moment longer than necessary. They want me. He's the bait, so I go. Just tell me how to get there." My Pack knew nothing about demon circles or the Underworld. If the witches didn't choose to help, I was screwed.

"Getting you to the Underworld is no small task," Tally said. "It's a huge ordeal that will take time and planning. We can't send you unarmed, but only organic compounds can travel across the boundaries. There will be training involved."

I couldn't think straight. Grief pounded behind my temples.

As soon as Tyler had blipped out of existence on this plane, his connection to me had vanished. I hadn't realized having him bound to me had become like second nature, like the best security blanket in the world. Without being aware, I'd known he was alive and functioning at every moment. It was a bond we should've forged a long time ago and I desperately missed it.

"I will go with you," Naomi said, her voice thoughtful. "You need not battle the Underworld alone."

"Me too," Danny added. "I'm not going to let my best mate die down there without a fight. I'm in for whatever it takes to bring him back."

"Count me in too," Marcy said from across the room. "You just saved my life. I owe you. But more than that, I can help because I'm a witch." After the Prince of Hell had struck her down, I had poured my power into her and eradicated the last of the blackness. But Tally had already been on it, spelling the mist out with her magic.

It was debatable who had saved whom.

"If she goes, I go," James said. "There is no reason we can't all accompany you, Jessica."

"Okay, that's enough," Tally said, marching forward with her hand in the air, turning to address the entire group. "It's all well and good everyone here is dying to jump on board. And by dying, I mean that literally. But none of you are going. Not one of you is powerful enough to survive the journey by circle, much less what you'll find when you get there. They have pet beasts, demons in every size and color, and all of them can kill you with a small flick of their wrists. The Underworld has the home-court advantage and we have to play this smart if we actually want to bring the wolf back."

Rourke stood, growling, his eyes blazing, arms folded.

Tally sized him up. "Well, except you. You'd survive the transition, but you still can't go."

"My daughter isn't going alone," my father interrupted, standing in front of his seat, before Rourke could tell Tally what he thought of her fantastic plan. "I will fight with everything I have to get my son back."

"Sorry, but you can't go either," Tally said, dismissing him. "It's a noble undertaking, but not advisable."

"*What?*" My father's voice jumped and power whipped around the room. Several of the wolves growled. "Are you saying I wouldn't survive the transition?"

"No, Callum, you'd survive just fine. You're a Pack Alpha," Tally said in a patient tone. "Arguably the most powerful one in the world. But you know as well as I do that because of that, your signature is well documented. If you land in the Underworld, dinner bells will ring. The demons would have something delicious planned just for you. If we do this, and give Jessica the best shot at saving your son, she has to go in the back way. One with no alarms."

My father nodded his head in agreement. "I hadn't thought of that. But you can't tell me my daughter isn't documented as well," he said. "And if that's the case, she'll be tossed into the same trap I would."

"I believe it may be different in her case, which is a lucky break," Tally answered. "The demons want her, and obviously have information about her signature, but from what I've seen firsthand, her powers are somewhat malleable. That gives her an edge the rest of us don't have. With our help, she can learn to muddle her signature enough. And, no, she's not documented in the Book...yet." Tally glanced at me. "But I suspect she will be shortly. Power like that is not ignored by the Coalition for long."

"How do you know she's not in the Book?" my father asked. "It can take centuries to find out what's in the Book of Records."

"My daughter is an oracle," Tally said patiently. "Every time there's a new entry, she draws me a picture. There's only been one in the last year. And it wasn't female."

Tally's voice dared my father to disbelieve.

Instead, he nodded, satisfied.

I had no idea what the Book of Records was, but it was clear it noted powerful supes. "It doesn't matter if I trigger their alarms. I'm going regardless," I said. "And the demons already know I will go after Tyler, so surprising them may never be possible."

"Jessica," my father said, turning toward me. "You're not going alone. It's too dangerous. Tally's right—my signature will be a disadvantage...one I'm not willing to risk. The element of surprise is all you'll have. But I'll be damned if I let you go without backup. And if my signature is documented, so is your mate's." He addressed Rourke. "There's no way you've gone unnoticed all these years. Even if you were not the Alpha of your kind, you are the last and have been for some time."

"I am Alpha," Rourke ground out. "And I've never had reason to look in the Book, so I do not know what is written there. But I agree with you, there's no way Jessica's going without adequate protection, so it doesn't matter. We will find another way in."

"If you insist on going," my father replied, "you put her in the same peril I would. If she has to go in through the back door—if there is such a thing—she has to take someone powerful enough who *won't* be noticed."

"She can only take two others," Tally said. "The circle holds three. When they come back, we'll have to summon them in twos, but it adds risk. Calling someone back from the Underworld takes time and energy, but my recommendation is she still take two others. That gives them the best chance of survival."

Before Rourke and my father volleyed again, I stated evenly, "I don't understand why there's so much importance placed on the Book. I told you, I'm going even if they know about me and have a welcome squad waiting."

The Queen rose from the high-backed chair she'd been sitting in. She was edgy and reserved. All eyes in the room landed on her as she moved forward. "I find it amusing you are so very uneducated about our world. And that our well-being must lie cupped in the hands of your vast ignorance." She swept past me in a new gown, this one black with silver accents. "When a supernatural is the strongest of its kind, there is a record of it. You can access the Book of Records by appealing to the Coalition directly. I did it on occasion long ago. The Prince of Hell also has access. We, in this room"—she nodded grudgingly to Tally, my father, and Rourke—"are the strongest of our kind. Our power is noted in detail. The demons live for information. They likely have thick files on all of us and will have our signatures monitored at all times. Our presence will alert them to our arrival like shooting off a flare gun in a library. Sending one of us would be asking the demons to end our lives."

"Well, there's no way I'm in the goddamn Book, since I was just made. And the demons can't have anything on me yet," Ray interrupted, pushing himself off the wall where he'd been standing. "So I'll go."

I shot him a look of surprise.

Tally sized him up with a skeptical eye.

"Ray," I said. "I appreciate your willingness to fight demons on my behalf, but there's no way you're strong enough—"

"He's in," Tally said, her voice resigned. "It's perfect, really. He's a reaper and a vampire. A supernatural who technically should never have been created. He will muddle their monitors naturally, and the fact that he's a reaper can only help you. His signature also feels strong enough—in fact, it feels a lot like yours." Her eyes were shrewd. "But we won't know until we test him fully." She addressed Ray. "Vampire, can you suck the absence of a soul from a demon?"

His eyebrows shot up. "How the hell should I know?" he answered. "I just figured out I was a reaper two hours ago."

Tally tapped her foot patiently. "Not all reapers are created the same. Some are tailored especially for certain jobs. It depends on your genetic line. What did the Demon Lord look like to you?"

"Its skin was made of smooth shiny scales and it had an ugly face, like some kind of serpent man," Ray said.

My eyebrows shot to my forehead. The demon's glamour hadn't worked on Ray. I'd seen a few snippets of its reptilian side, too, so I knew he was telling the truth.

"Good." Tally nodded. "You saw its true nature. That's promising. Very few are able to do such a thing."

I shook my head. "If Ray is willing to come on his own free will, that's fine." My eyes found Rourke. "But I'm not willing to risk anyone else I love accompanying me. Tyler being taken overwhelms me on all levels and I refuse to let someone else I care about be lost to the demons."

"Jessica," Rourke said, turning toward me. "You have to be reasonable. Letting you go alone, with only a new vampire to aid you, is insanity."

"We won't be alone," I assured him. "And Tally will prepare us the best she can. If we have a chance to take the best tactical attack, we need to use it—I agree with that." My voice was strong. "Please don't ask me to abandon my brother."

"Of course I'm not asking you to do that," he reasoned. "But there have to be other ways around this we can discuss."

His fear and uncertainty rang inside me. Letting me go to the Underworld without him would be the hardest thing he'd have to do in our short time together.

But I had something that would help.

"How about I make you a promise I won't go unless I can fortify the odds in our favor?" I told him.

"How are you possibly going to do that?" Rourke asked. "A brand-new vamp who has no idea how to work his powers and who else? Who is strong enough to aid you?"

I paused, taking my time with the announcement.

It had to have the desired effect.

"Eudoxia."

There was an audible gasp from everyone in the room.

Rourke's face flashed surprise, my father blew out a long breath, and the Queen's voice tinkled with laughter. "You are delusional, as usual," she almost purred. "I just finished explaining why it would never work, Little Wolf Girl. But let me try again because it's clear your brain has been jarred from all the heavy lifting: If I go to the Underworld, the demons will swarm us the minute we arrive." Her face elongated and her fangs snapped down. "But, even if they didn't"—her eyes went dead black—"there is no way I would go to hell for *you*."

"I saved your life out there," I said, pacing forward, "again. That makes it twice in one day."

She hissed, her face still cruel.

"This is it, Eudoxia. It's your chance. Once we come back, all debts are wiped clean. You are the only one strong enough to give us the best odds of getting Tyler back, and your power combined with mine is lethal. It managed to wipe out even the Prince of Hell's magic. Together we can defeat anything down there."

Her power jumped out before her, pressing against me. It licked at my face and pushed at my chest. But I was ready, my power wrapped up inside me like a coat of armor.

Molding my power had become second nature and it felt good to master it.

"You're as foolish as you look," she snapped. "Even if I owed you another favor, which I do not, I would never agree to accompany you to the Underworld." Her face slid even farther, her control slipping. "My debt to you has been paid. The ward went up and, as an extra token, one for you taking the demon magic— which would not have *killed* me—I gave you my power freely. It was not my fault the opposition was too strong."

My father walked toward me. "Jessica, I don't know what you're getting at, but taking the Queen won't work because of everything we've outlined so far. If she's the one you pick, you can take your mate or me just as easily." His voice was wary. "We need to think of someone else."

"He's right," Tally agreed. "I'm not sure why you picked her, but the Vamp Queen will sound the alarms. She'll be like a lighthouse flashing a signal in the darkness."

"No, she won't," I said confidently.

Tally inclined her head at me in question, clearly thinking I was presumptuous, but smart enough to hear me out.

"Are you calling me a liar?" The Queen's fury radiated outward. "I should've ended you when I had the chance! You are nothing but a nuisance." Her hands fisted at her sides. "Just like the Prince of Hell stated in front of us all. You are a blister on the heel of every supernatural ever created."

"But you didn't kill me, did you?" I said as I took a bold step toward her. "You could've killed me when the Prince threw his power at me, but there was a reason you aided me." I leaned forward and whispered, "It's because I have something you desperately want and without it you will be stuck here to rot for a thousand more years."

"You're wrong. I want nothing from you," the Queen spat, her face barely contained.

"You're not fooling anyone. You *need* my blood. And I want my brother. Sounds like a fair trade to me."

She hissed. "Your blood will never be worth what you ask of me!"

"It's worth it and you know it." My irises jumped to violet. "You're just hoping you can acquire it for free, sometime down the road. But your seer has left for good. There won't be any other opportunities, because once I leave here I will make sure our paths don't cross."

The Queen was one outburst away from losing her mind.

I had a strong feeling this was what Alana had alluded to in the storage room.

I was in a position to force the Queen to act—to do one last task to prove her worth. It had to be this. And I had to think that meant we would be successful getting my brother back. The two had to be tied.

The Queen's power continued to rocket around the room and the witches started fiddling with their guns and the wolves started to pace.

"Why would I ever risk the Underworld for you?" the Queen countered. "Even for a precious drink of your blood?"

Tally had lost her patience with our pissing match. "I hate to break it to you both, but we need to get moving. I want my witches in a safe place before nightfall. The sorcerers were patsies this time around, bound by their agreement with the demons, but when they come again, they will bring their artillery. They are inferior in strength to us, but they will pack a punch in numbers, and I don't have time to summon witches from all over the U.S."

I faced Tally, essentially turning my back on the Queen. The timing had to be right if I was going to make this work. I waited a few beats and then I played my ace in the hole. "If the Vampire Queen drinks my blood, her signature will change. She'll be under the demon radar, and she's an asset because . . . she'll be infinitely more powerful."

Everyone in the room went crazy, talking at once.

"Leave us!" the Queen yelled. The vamps froze at her words, but hesitated. "I said *go.*"

"Meet me outside, everyone, but keep up the vigil," Tally told her witches.

"Escort them out," my father told his wolves, including Danny and Nick. "Find any others who were left on the outside. Daniel Walker, coordinate the move north." James and Marcy walked over. My father nodded curtly once to his second. "We will speak. I will be out shortly."

James nodded, putting his arm around Marcy's waist as he led her out.

When everyone except Rourke, Tally, and my father left the room, my father turned to me and said, "What are you talking about, Jessica? How do you know what your blood will do to a vampire?" He knew no real details about Naomi or Ray. He also had no idea my blood had changed Danny's connection to him so fully I feared it might be permanent.

The Queen stalked to the massive double doors and slammed them shut. Then she turned to Tally. "Spell the room, witch. No word spoken here leaves."

Tally was about to give her grief but thought better of it. She knew whatever was coming was big. Her fingers moved as she incanted a spell.

I wished for a moment it were only my father and me in this room. It would be so much easier to do this alone. Revealing your secrets to other Sects made you weak. But I had no choice. Tyler's life was worth it and I was willing to do anything it took.

"My blood breaks bonds." I cleared my throat. "It severed Naomi's bond between her and her Queen, which Eudoxia figured out fairly quickly. My blood also changed Danny's connection to you." I nodded toward my father. "But what you don't know is he smelled like me after we had exchanged a very small amount. My blood also connected Tyler and me on a different level. He said it had something to do with our close genetic bond." I wished my brother were here to explain it. He did it so much better. My heart clenched. "If the Queen drinks from me, I believe it will alter her signature enough, and significantly change any samples they may have on record, so she won't set off their alarms."

My father was silent.

I hoped it was a good sign.

"If that's true, it's huge." Tally ran her gaze over me. "I don't know of another supe who can change genetic markers permanently. If what you're saying is even slightly true, you could change anyone's markers, including a human with latent supernatural genes."

"I believe that's what happened to Ray. My blood brought out a recessive gene he already had and made it pronounced," I said. "It's only a guess, but it makes the most sense given what my blood has already done to others."

The Queen had seen Naomi for herself, but she didn't know how potent my blood actually was.

The only unknown was Alana. I had no idea what my blood had done to her other than clear her insanity. I didn't feel a connection to her and I was hopeful it would stay that way.

All the supes seemed to be connected to me in different ways.

There wasn't one pat answer and I was relieved. If the Queen drank my blood, I had no idea what would happen. I just knew she would be different. And more powerful. That wasn't ideal, but I would gladly take my chances if it meant getting my brother back in one piece. Alana had said Eudoxia's future was vast. To me that meant she would live a long powerful life, whether I interfered or not. Why not give her what she wanted and do it on my own terms? If I did, there would be a greater chance she would ally with us in the future. And the way my future was going, that wasn't such a bad idea.

"Jessica," my father said finally, running a hand over his chin. "This news is staggering."

"That's why the sorcerers want you." Tally nodded, like everything had clicked into place for her. "But this is something they can't take out, because it's tied up in every fiber of your entire being. It's what makes your blood so potent. You are a fascinating supernatural, I'll give you that."

"By my estimation," I said. "If Eudoxia drinks from me, she becomes exponentially stronger. And she also becomes something more—something different," I half taunted, glancing directly at the Queen. This was my bait and I desperately wanted her to take it. "If my life force is contained in my blood, she gets it by proxy, just like everyone else who's ingested it. There's also a chance her latent genes will be more pronounced, like Ray's, *if* she has any."

I didn't have to spell out the possibilities. Eudoxia knew what they were. She also knew I was giving her a gift. One she hadn't bargained for. Godhood was one thing, but having her fae powers come to the forefront was quite another.

"Yes," Tally answered. "I would assume so. A vamp's vitality is through blood—it's what fuels them—so they would be the most sensitive to any changes, though I'm no expert. But I agree; what your blood gives can only enhance, not take away. My feeling is she will become very powerful indeed." Tally's voice held a note of hesitation.

Rourke's unease hit me as he grabbed my hand and gave it a gentle squeeze, our bond pulsing between us. It was his way of asking if I was sure I knew what I was doing.

I was. I was willing to go all in. If my brother was faced with these circumstances, he would not hesitate to do the same for me.

"So what's it going to be?" I directed my gaze to the Vampire Queen. "Are you in or out?"

She hissed once. "In."

Acknowledgments

This has been such an amazing ride. There are so many people to thank. First and foremost, I want to thank all the readers and fans, new and old, who have supported this series. It astounds me each and every day that so many of you have fallen in love with Jessica and her entire team. I love getting your e-mails, tweets, comments, and messages. It puts a smile on my face each and every time. Thank you.

As always, thank you to my wonderful husband, Billy. My life is so much brighter with you in it. I have no idea how I got so lucky. Your editing prowess knows no bounds and you make me laugh. I love you.

To my three kids, Paige, Nat, and Jane, you guys continue to amaze me and make me proud every single day. Thank you for enduring my deadlines, doing the dishes, taking out the trash, and folding the laundry. I love you with all my heart. You are the reason I do this.

Once again, a big thank-you to Amanda Bonilla for a wonderful friendship. Our daily e-mails, texts, and laughs fuel me. I thank my lucky stars we found each other. You are my supreme partner in goat crime and you always will be. Love you, Scooby!

To Julie Ann Walker, thank you for always being there. You're such a great friend and an amazing supporter. When we get together and laugh, it's the very best. I can't wait for more trips together. Being under the covers giggling with you is the very best way to end the day. I lovers you.

To Kristen Painter, my Boo. You get me, you make me giggle, you hold my hand and roll up the newspaper when it's necessary. I can't possibly thank you enough. Without your guidance and advice I'd still be making puppy paws. I love our friendship. It means the world to me.

To my awesome writing (i.e., emotional) support group: Kristen Callihan, Mira Lynn Kelly, Lea Nolan, and Chelsea Mueller (my little bear cub), and my pals at Magic & Mayhem— Shawntelle Madison, Sandy Williams, and Nadia Lee. Thank you all for always being available with a shoulder, advice, laugher, jokes or just a :) You make this road such a happy place to be.

To my beta readers, DeLane and Kathy, as always, your support means the world to me. Early cheerleading is the very best kind.

To my KICKASS #JessicaMcClainStreetTeam: Angela, Annie, Ash, Brandy, Carmel, Chelsea, Delhia, Jenese, Jennifer, Jo, Julie, Kat, Kathy, Kristin, Marcela, Melanie, Melissa, Lesley, Sally, and Stacy! You guys rock so hard. I am so lucky to have you guys in my corner. I have an immense amount of gratitude for all you do to support the series and me. I couldn't possibly do this without all of you.

To my awesome parents, Daryl and Koppy, thanks for being so involved in the process, early reading, raving about the books, giving me confidence, and all the shuttling of children, cooking, and the love you give so freely. We appreciate everything you do. I love you both.

To Cindi, thanks for prying me out of my writing cave on a regular basis. I can always count on you for a sushi lunch date and some good shopping therapy. Without it I would surely go insane.

To Anna, thanks for your undying support in all facets of

my life. I'm so lucky to have you. Our Rudy time is my absolute favorite and your narcolepsy is endearing. I love you and your entire family. Hi, Cory!

To the entire Meneely crew, I owe you all a beer and a Crave Case of White Castles. Thanks for enduring my e-mails and supporting my career. Molly Winkels, you are a shining star. Your full support of me and my career is incredible. Everyone should have an aunt like you in their corner. I feel lucky to have you every day. Your texts make me laugh and they are always filled with love. Can't wait to have another Phil's Tara night with you and Brad! To Shannon, I love you, my Scrabble Baby. Thanks for making my day go by a little quicker and for all your support.

To my agents Alexandra Machinist and Stefanie Lieberman, thank you for championing this series with such dedication. I'm so excited to enter a new chapter with you both. May our future be filled with tiny cupcakes, Nashville, and a whole lot of books.

To Carrie Andrews, thank you for copyediting this book and making it shine, and for correcting all my "spring" and "sprang" errors, as well as catching on to the fact that my supernaturals might have had some serious "Collation" issues.

To my editors, Devi, Susan, and Anna, thanks for all you do to make the books the best they can be. I appreciate all of your time and energy. And to everyone at Orbit, thanks for a really great ride.

extras

orbit

meet the author

Paige Carlson

A Minnesota girl born and bred, AMANDA CARLSON graduated from the University of Minnesota with a double major in speech and hearing science and child development. After enjoying her time as a sign language interpreter, she decided to stay at home and write in earnest once her second child was born. She loves playing Scrabble, visiting tropical beaches, and shopping trips to IKEA. She lives in Minneapolis with her husband and three kids.

To find out more about the author,
visit www.amandacarlson.com
or find her on Twitter @AmandaCCarlson.

introducing

**If you enjoyed
COLD BLOODED,
look out for**

CHARMING

by Elliott James

John Charming isn't your average Prince...

*He comes from a line of Charmings—an illustrious family of
dragon slayers, witch-finders, and killers dating back to before the
fall of Rome. Trained by a modern-day version of the Knights
Templar, monster hunters who have updated their methods
from chain mail and crossbows to Kevlar and shotguns, he was
one of the best. That is—until he became the abomination
the Knights were sworn to hunt.*

*That was a lifetime ago. Now he tends bar under an assumed
name in rural Virginia and leads a peaceful, quiet life. One that
shouldn't change just because a vampire and a blonde
walked into his bar... Right?*

extras

Once upon a time, she smelled wrong. Well, no, that's not exactly true. She smelled clean, like fresh snow and air after a lightning storm and something hard to identify, something like sex and butter pecan ice cream. Honestly, I think she was the best thing I'd ever smelled. I was inferring "wrongness" from the fact that she wasn't entirely human.

I later found out that her name was Sig.

Sig stood there in the doorway of the bar with the wind behind her, and there was something both earthy and unearthly about her. Standing at least six feet tall in running shoes, she had shoulders as broad as a professional swimmer's, sinewy arms, and well-rounded hips that were curvy and compact. All in all, she was as buxom, blonde, blue-eyed, and clear-skinned as any woman who had ever posed for a Swedish tourism ad.

And I wanted her out of the bar, fast.

You have to understand, Rigby's is not the kind of place where goddesses were meant to walk among mortals. It is a small, modest establishment eking out a fragile existence at the tail end of Clayburg's main street. The owner, David Suggs, had wanted a quaint pub, but instead of decorating the place with dartboards or Scottish coats of arms or ceramic mugs, he had decided to celebrate southwest Virginia culture and covered the walls with rusty old railroad equipment and farming tools.

When I asked why a bar—excuse me, I mean *pub*—with a Celtic name didn't have a Celtic atmosphere, Dave said that he had named Rigby's after a Beatles song about lonely people needing a place to belong.

"Names have power," Dave had gone on to inform me, and I had listened gravely as if this were a revelation.

Speaking of names, "John Charming" is not what it reads on my current driver's license. In fact, about the only thing accurate on my current license is the part where it says that I'm black-haired and blue-eyed. I'm six foot one instead of six foot two and about seventy-five pounds lighter than the 250 pounds indicated on my identification. But I do kind of look the way the man pictured on my license might look if Trevor A. Barnes had lost that much weight and cut his hair short and shaved off his beard. Oh, and if he were still alive.

And no, I didn't kill the man whose identity I had assumed, in case you're wondering. Well, not the first time anyway.

Anyhow, I had recently been forced to leave Alaska and start a new life of my own, and in David Suggs I had found an employer who wasn't going to be too thorough with his background checks. My current goal was to work for Dave for at least one fiscal year and not draw any attention to myself.

Which was why I was not happy to see the blonde.

For her part, the blonde didn't seem too happy to see me either. Sig focused on me immediately. People always gave me a quick flickering glance when they walked into the bar—excuse me, the pub—but the first thing they really checked out was the clientele. Their eyes were sometimes predatory, sometimes cautious, sometimes hopeful, often tired, but they only returned to me after being disappointed. Sig's gaze, however, centered on me like the oncoming lights of a train—assuming train lights have slight bags underneath them and make you want to flex surreptitiously. Those same startlingly blue eyes widened, and her body went still for a moment.

Whatever had triggered her alarms, Sig hesitated, visibly debating whether to approach and talk to me. She didn't hesitate for long, though—I got the impression that she rarely hesitated for long—and chose to go find herself a table.

Now, it was a Thursday night in April, and Rigby's was not empty. Clayburg is host to a small private college named

Stillwaters University, one of those places where parents pay more money than they should to get an education for children with mediocre high school records. This sort of target student—an underachiever with upper-middle-class parents—not surprisingly does a lot of heavy drinking, which is why Rigby's manages to stay in business. Small bars with farming implements on the walls don't really draw huge college crowds, but the more popular bars tend to stay packed, and Rigby's does attract an odd combination of local rednecks and students with a sense of irony. So when a striking six-foot blonde who wasn't an obvious transvestite sat down in the middle of the bar, there were people around to notice.

Even Sandra, a nineteen-year-old waitress who considers customers an unwelcome distraction from covert texting, noticed the newcomer. She walked up to Sig promptly instead of making Renee, an older waitress and Rigby's de facto manager, chide her into action.

For the next hour I pretended to ignore the new arrival while focusing on her intently. I listened in—my hearing is as well developed as my sense of smell—while several patrons tried to introduce themselves. Sig seemed to have a knack for knowing how to discourage each would-be player as fast as possible.

She told suitors that she wanted to be up front about her sex change operation because she was tired of having it cause problems when her lovers found out later, or she told them that she liked only black men, or young men, or older men who made more than seventy thousand dollars a year. She told them that what really turned her on was men who were willing to have sex with other men while she watched. She mentioned one man's wife by name, and when the weedy-looking grad student doing a John Lennon impersonation tried the sensitive-poet approach, she challenged him to an arm-wrestling contest. He stared at her, sitting there exuding athleticism, confidence, and health—three things he was noticeably lacking—and chose to be offended rather than take her up on it.

There was at least one woman who seemed interested in Sig as well, a cute sandy-haired college student who was tall and willowy, but when it comes to picking up strangers, women are generally less likely to go on a kamikaze mission than men. The young woman kept looking over at Sig's table, hoping to establish some kind of meaningful eye contact, but Sig wasn't making any.

Sig wasn't looking at me either, but she held herself at an angle that kept me in her peripheral vision at all times.

For my part, I spent the time between drink orders trying to figure out exactly what Sig was. She definitely wasn't undead. She wasn't a half-blood Fae either, though her scent wasn't entirely dissimilar. Elf smell isn't something you forget, sweet and decadent, with a hint of honey blossom and distant ocean. There aren't any full-blooded Fae left, of course—they packed their bags and went back to Fairyland a long time ago—but don't mention that to any of the mixed human descendants that the elves left behind. Elvish half-breeds tend to be some-what sensitive on that particular subject. They can be real bas-tards about being bastards.

I would have been tempted to think that Sig was an angel, except that I've never heard of anyone I'd trust ever actually seeing a real angel. God is as much an article of faith in my world as he, she, we, they, or it is in yours.

Stumped, I tried to approach the problem by figuring out what Sig was doing there. She didn't seem to enjoy the ginger ale she had ordered—didn't seem to notice it at all, just sipped from it perfunctorily. There was something wary and expec-tant about her body language, and she had positioned herself so that she was in full view of the front door. She could have just been meeting someone, but I had a feeling that she was looking for someone or something specific by using herself as bait... but what and why and to what end, I had no idea. Sex, food, or revenge seemed the most likely choices.

I was still mulling that over when the vampire walked in.